OXFORD WORLD'S CLASSICS

GREEN MANSIONS

WILLIAM HENRY HUDSON was born on a ranch near Buenos Aires, Argentina, on 4 August 1841, to North American emigrant parents. In a memoir written late in life, *Far Away and Long Ago* (1918), Hudson vividly evoked the romantic freedom of his childhood on the pampas. At 15 an attack of typhus followed by rheumatic fever permanently impaired his health. Over the next few years he read Gilbert White's *Natural History of Selborne*, which fixed his determination to become a naturalist, and Darwin's *Origin of Species*. During the 1860s Hudson travelled extensively in South America, collecting ornithological specimens for the Smithsonian Institution in Washington, DC, and the Zoological Society of London. In 1874, following the death of his parents, he sailed to England, where he spent the rest of his life. He married Emily Wingrave, a singer and boarding-house keeper, in 1876. For the next twenty-five years Hudson struggled to make a living by writing, often in circumstances of dire poverty. His first novel, *The Purple Land that England Lost* (1885), was a critical and commercial failure. Hudson devoted himself to nature conservation and helped found the Society for the Protection of Birds in 1891. During the 1890s he began to acquire a reputation through his natural history writings, including *The Naturalist in La Plata* (1892) and *Idle Days in Patagonia* (1893), and in 1901 he was awarded a Civil List pension. His later writings, such as *A Shepherd's Life* (1910) and *The Book of a Naturalist* (1919), celebrate the English countryside and wildlife. The success of the 1916 American edition of *Green Mansions*, first published in 1904, brought Hudson a measure of fame and financial comfort late in life. He died on 18 August 1922, one year after his wife.

IAN DUNCAN is Barbara and Carlisle Moore Professor of English at the University of Oregon. He is the author of *Modern Romance and Transformations of the Novel* (1992) and has edited Scott's *Ivanhoe* and *Rob Roy*, John Buchan's *The Island of Sheep*, and Conan Doyle's *The Lost World* for Oxford World's Classics.

OXFORD WORLD'S CLASSICS

For almost 100 years Oxford World's Classics have brought readers closer to the world's great literature. Now with over 700 titles—from the 4,000-year-old myths of Mesopotamia to the twentieth century's greatest novels—the series makes available lesser-known as well as celebrated writing.

The pocket-sized hardbacks of the early years contained introductions by Virginia Woolf, T. S. Eliot, Graham Greene, and other literary figures which enriched the experience of reading. Today the series is recognized for its fine scholarship and reliability in texts that span world literature, drama and poetry, religion, philosophy and politics. Each edition includes perceptive commentary and essential background information to meet the changing needs of readers.

OXFORD WORLD'S CLASSICS

W. H. HUDSON

Green Mansions

Edited with an Introduction and Notes by
IAN DUNCAN

OXFORD
UNIVERSITY PRESS

OXFORD
UNIVERSITY PRESS

Great Clarendon Street, Oxford OX2 6DP

Oxford University Press is a department of the University of Oxford.
It furthers the University's objective of excellence in research, scholarship,
and education by publishing worldwide in

Oxford New York

Athens Auckland Bangkok Bogotá Buenos Aires Calcutta
Cape Town Chennai Dar es Salaam Delhi Florence Hong Kong Istanbul
Karachi Kuala Lumpur Madrid Melbourne Mexico City Mumbai
Nairobi Paris São Paulo Shanghai Singapore Taipei Tokyo Toronto Warsaw

with associated companies in Berlin Ibadan

Oxford is a registered trade mark of Oxford University Press
in the UK and in certain other countries

Published in the United States
by Oxford University Press Inc., New York

British Library Cataloguing in Publication Data

Data available

Library of Congress Cataloging in Publication Data
Hudson, W. H. (William Henry), 1841–1922.
Green mansions / W. H. Hudson ; edited with an introduction and
notes by Ian Duncan.
(Oxford world's classics)
Includes bibliographical references.
1. Man–woman relationships—South America—Fiction.   2. Rain forests—
South America—Fiction.   3. Wild women—South America—Fiction.
I. Duncan, Ian.   II. Title.   III. Series: Oxford world's
classics (Oxford University Press)
PR6015.U23G7 1998   823'.8—dc21   98–10538

ISBN 0–19–283288–3

3 5 7 9 10 8 6 4 2

Typeset by Jarvee, Trivandrum, India
Printed in Great Britain by
Cox & Wyman Ltd.
Reading, Berkshire

CONTENTS

ACKNOWLEDGEMENTS

I AM grateful to Roland Greene, Nina Prytula, and Julian Weiss for their assistance with the notes, Penny Fielding for information on Enlightenment linguistic theories, Bill Rossi and Molly Westling for suggestions about natural history writing, and Lewis Klausner for his comments on the Introduction; and I thank Judith Luna for her encouragement, advice, and good humour throughout the series of novels I have edited for Oxford World's Classics.

INTRODUCTION

WHEN it first appeared in 1904 *Green Mansions* was a cult book and its author a cult figure, favoured by literary coteries rather than by the general reading public. Hudson's 'Romance of the Tropical Forest' became a best-seller after its republication in the USA by Alfred A. Knopf in 1916. The new edition carried a foreword by John Galsworthy, praising Hudson as 'a very great writer'—since the death of Tolstoy, 'the most valuable our Age possesses'. The encomium took: *Green Mansions* was reprinted more than twenty times over the next decade, and the standard Hudson bibliography lists some seventy different editions through the early 1970s, in formats ranging from cheap paperback to illustrated limited edition, along with translations into at least sixteen languages.[1] After his death a memorial to Hudson, graced with a relief by Jacob Epstein depicting Rima, the heroine of *Green Mansions*, was put up in Hyde Park. The vogue for *Green Mansions* culminated in a 1959 film version starring Anthony Perkins and Audrey Hepburn, which may well have finished it for a popular audience: the evanescent figure of Rima could scarcely survive embodiment on the big screen, even when the body was Hepburn's. (Disembodied, Rima lives on in such ecologically correct forest nymphs as Disney's Pocahontas.) In the 1960s *Green Mansions* sank back towards its cult-book status. Perhaps few books are more unreadable than an expired best-seller; but *Green Mansions* was never simply a best-seller. Adapting the formula of late-Victorian imperial adventure (white man has mythic encounter beyond the colonial frontier), Hudson invented a new sub-genre, of which *Green Mansions* remains the outstanding example: David Trotter calls it an 'eco-romance'.[2] At the end of the millennium, it still has much to say to us.

The author of *Green Mansions* remained a legendary figure, a romantic exile from a vanished wilderness, until his death in 1922—the year of *Ulysses* and *The Waste Land*. Hudson was 63 years old when *Green Mansions* appeared, 75 when it achieved popular success. Until

---

[1] For details see John R. Payne, *W. H. Hudson: A Bibliography* (Folkestone, 1977), 79–94, 214–22.

[2] David Trotter, *The English Novel in History, 1895–1920* (London, 1993), 89.

then he was best known for a series of luminous essays in natural history—*The Naturalist in La Plata, Idle Days in Patagonia*, some books on British birds. He had begun his literary career as a correspondent of the London Zoological Society on the ornithology of the South American pampas, and came to England in 1874, hoping to make a living as a naturalist. But Hudson found the doors of a professionalizing scientific guild closed against him, and had to weather two decades of poverty and obscurity in London. He married his landlady, Emily Wingrave, and in a mutually supportive if (it appears) asexual union they carried on the struggle together—subsisting for a week, according to one anecdote, on some biscuits and a tin of cocoa. In the 1890s Hudson's nature writings won him esteem in literary circles, with R. B. Cunninghame Graham, Edward Garnett, Edward Thomas, Ford Madox Ford, and Joseph Conrad enrolled among his admirers. These acquaintances tended to view Hudson as though he were himself one of the wild beings he wrote about: noble, austere, touched with an unappeasable grief. 'One might figure him some bird pressing forward against a gale,' wrote Violet Hunt; 'a lonely man, with something of the animal about him,' wrote the painter William Rothenstein.[3]

Hudson had spent the first three decades of his life on the Argentine pampas, before they were broken up by large-scale settlement and agricultural development. The Homeric ways of the gauchos were still current, Rosas' genocidal campaigns against the Indians fresh in memory, civil war a perennial hazard. Hudson grew up surrounded by an immense splendour of natural life, most vivid in the birds of the country. He would recall this boyhood Eden in a memoir written late in life, *Far Away and Long Ago* (1918). Hudson's sense of loss bore a heavier burden than nostalgia. Its gravity was mythic, for he could understand his life as having traced a universal disaster—the fall of nature itself under the onslaught of human civilization. Already in his last years in South America Hudson had sensed the destruction of the wild horizons by drain and fence and plough, the end of the barbaric freedom of the gaucho, the extinction of the brilliant flocks of birds. To that world there could be no going back:

And when I recall these vanished scenes, those rushy and flowery meres, with their varied and multitudinous wild-bird life—the cloud of shining wings,

---

[3] Quoted in Ruth Tomalin, *W. H. Hudson: A Biography* (London, 1982), 211–12.

the heart-enlivening wild cries, the joy unspeakable it was to me in those early years—I am glad to think I shall never revisit them, that I shall finish my life thousands of miles removed from them, cherishing to the end in my heart the image of a beauty which has vanished from earth.[4]

Victorian London allowed Hudson, or perhaps it forced him, to imagine this vanishing as a world-wide catastrophe. He was dismayed not only by the extent of pollution, habitat loss, and slaughter of wildlife within Britain; indeed, his books would celebrate the stubborn persistence of wilderness in industrial England's nooks and crannies. More offensive were the spoils of a global imperial commerce in natural beauty. Devoting himself to a series of conservation campaigns on behalf of the Society for the Protection of Birds, which he helped found in 1891, Hudson turned his fiercest indignation against the fashion for decorating women's costumes with the plumage, wings, and even entire stuffed corpses of mass-murdered avifauna. 'Feathered Women', as he called them, were the harpies of a deathly civilization.

Hudson's book of natural history essays, *The Naturalist in La Plata* (1892), opens with a sombre meditation on the colonization of the pampas as but one field of a 'systematic war of extermination' waged by civilization against all wild things. 'Nature's masterpieces', more precious than any human artwork, are the remnants of an archaic glory:

Like immortal flowers they have drifted down to us on the ocean of time, and their strangeness and beauty bring to our imaginations a dream and a picture of that unknown world, immeasurably far removed, where man was not . . . Nor does their loss affect us and our times only. The species now being exterminated, not only in South America but everywhere on the globe are, so far as we know, untouched by decadence. They are links in a chain, and branches on the tree of life, with their roots in a past inconceivably remote; and but for our action they would continue to flourish, reaching outward to an equally distant future, blossoming into higher and more beautiful forms, and gladdening innumerable generations of our descendants.[5]

Here Hudson speaks with the prophetic voice of the late twentieth-century ecological movement, although the pattern of an original purity, present degeneration, and future perfection woven into the language of evolutionism (Darwin's 'tree of life') is of his own age.

---

[4] W. H. Hudson, *Far Away and Long Ago* (London, 1985), 230.
[5] Id., *The Naturalist in La Plata* (London, 1892), 29–30.

The nineteenth-century imagination was already familiar with the cultural myth that articulated together the poignant facts of Hudson's experience: union in childhood with a since-vanished natural splendour, and the actual degradation of nature under an imperial, industrial political economy. These were the fables of modernity, not necessarily untrue for being fables, devised by literary Romanticism. In the passage from *Far Away and Long Ago* quoted above, Hudson echoes Wordsworth's great ode, 'Intimations of Immortality from Recollections of Early Childhood', with its complaint: 'The things which I have seen I now can see no more,' 'there hath past away a glory from the earth.' Wordsworth understood the experience of loss to be a subjective phenomenon, the decay of the imagination, although not less universal for that. Between Wordsworth and Hudson, in a series of essays beginning in the 1860s and culminating in the melancholy apocalypticism of 'The Storm Cloud of the Nineteenth Century' (1884), John Ruskin brooded over a second fall of nature that had happened in his lifetime. 'I have seen strange evil brought upon every scene that I best loved, or tried to make beloved by others,' he lamented; 'The light, the air, the waters, all defiled!'[6] What broke the prophet's heart was the objective certainty of the defilement, its status as a world-historical event: if only the ruin were contained in the human mind!

Hudson's sense of his own life and of the fate of nature meshed fluently with these imaginings. More thoroughly than any other writer he infused the tropes of Romantic elegy into the contemporaneous tradition of natural history memoir, devoted to the rapt and scrupulous observation of wildlife in the field. The first masterpiece in this tradition, Gilbert White's *The Natural History of Selborne* (1789), had delighted Hudson when he read it at the age of 16, even as (he later claimed) it failed to touch his 'animism'. When Hudson got to London it was to find the discourse of natural history dominated by the professional sciences, a consequence of the Darwinian revolution. While Hudson accepted Darwin's general argument, and had even once claimed the great man's notice in a dispute over the habits of pampas woodpeckers, he remained temperamentally remote from the new discipline and its institutional style; closer to Ruskin and

[6] *The Literary Criticism of John Ruskin*, ed. Harold Bloom (Gloucester, Mass., 1969), 224–5. For this tradition see Jonathan Bate, *Romantic Ecology: Wordsworth and the Environmental Tradition* (London, 1991).

his 'aesthetic relation of the species', although with fewer of Ruskin's Gothicisms. Darwin himself in his major works, *On the Origin of Species* and *The Descent of Man*, resorted to a language of aesthetic value as a key strategy in justifying his new vision of nature to the Victorian reader. The beauty of complex form, Darwin claimed, survives the absence of a designer (or, indeed, of design). But for Hudson the aesthetic sense is an end in itself rather than a vehicle of rationalization. Nature exists in the shimmer of its apprehension—in the vivid encounter of life with life. Hudson's Romantic Naturalism belongs to an anti-industrial, anti-modernist counter-tradition in British intellectual life, evident in a spate of neo-pastoral writings at the end of the century, many of which celebrated the peculiarly English values of eccentricity, nomadism, and the open road. Hudson's major precursors in the vein are Richard Jefferies and (less obviously but no less crucially) George Borrow, both of whom inform such works as *A Shepherd's Life* (while Hudson's first novel, *The Purple Land*, sketches a kind of *Lavengro* of the pampas). It was Darwin, however, who defined what we shall see to be Hudson's most troubling theme, the final objective correlative for all intimations of loss in nature: extinction.

Green Mansions, with its intensely personal woe for a paradise lost, can certainly be read as a spiritual autobiography in the Romantic manner—the 'closed and clasped volume' of its author's life as well as of its narrator's. In the novel's prologue Hudson gives his protagonist, Mr Abel, certain characteristics that his acquaintances observed in himself: reserve, mysteriousness, an indefinable charm, a fondness for animals and children. No doubt it took the Great War, that holocaust of old kingdoms, ideologies, and a generation of European youth, to bring Hudson's fable into focus for a wider reading public. *Green Mansions* may not be its author's best work of fiction—my own preference is for the wild gaucho tales of *El Ombú* and *The Purple Land*—but it gave definitive expression, for at least half a century, to the modern romantic myth of the loss of nature. Rima, the sacrificial nymph at the heart of the story, found plenty of readers ready to share Hudson's narrator's devotion to her. W. H. Auden once commented on the phenomenon whereby certain works of fiction, not always of the first rank, generate figures who step outside their literary matrix and take on a life of their own—the life of myth—in the cultural imagination: Don Quixote, Faust, Dracula, Sherlock Holmes.[7] For a while Rima, 'the bird-girl' (Hudson does not quite call her that), was such a figure, eclipsing her ground in *Green Mansions* much as *Green Mansions* tended to eclipse the œuvre of W. H. Hudson. Unfortunately, Rima is the aspect of the romance that today's readers will most likely find to have worn least well, since the feminine ideal that does duty for her humanity—a childlike innocence and natural grace—has lost much of its credibility.

Hers is an artificial innocence, despite the narrator's identification of her with her natural setting. *Genius loci* of the unmolested tropical forests, the vegetarian friend of every little creature, Rima does not go about naked, like the Indians, but weaves an opalescent garment for herself from spiders' webs: or is this marvellous gossamer, contrary to what Abel understands, a secretion of her own unfallen body? We learn that she leads a double life—by day the wild wood nymph, by night the demure child of the mission in frock and braids, catering to a shifty guardian. Exiled from her people and her mother-tongue, Rima has already lost the paradise that the new stranger, Abel, so intensely desires her to represent. Abel himself, in the classic pattern of pastoral, has fled from the political turbulence of cities to the green world, via a series of delusive quests (for literary fame, for gold). He makes Rima the idol of his mystic-erotic yearning, only to lose her when she departs to weave her wedding-dress. Themes of violation and extinction cloud the history of this exquisite being. In the account of Rima's origins we hear towards the end of the novel, Nuflo's gang goes after her mother in order to rape her. Shortly afterwards, in the romance's bitter turn, Rima herself is hunted down by Indians and burnt to ashes. Her loss carries a larger desolation: she is the last of her race.

Rima was not the first figure of her kind in Hudson's writing. 'All his life Hudson was haunted by the idea of a mysterious bird-woman, benign or malevolent,' notes Ruth Tomalin.[8] Hudson's first published work of fiction, the magic-realist tale 'Pelino Viera's Confession' (1883), tells of a man who spies on his wife, suspecting her of witchcraft:

Rosaura rose and threw off her night-dress, then, taking ointment from the pot and rubbing it on the palms of her hands, she passed it rapidly over her

---

[7] W. H. Auden, *The Dyer's Hand and Other Essays* (New York, 1948), 407–8.
[8] Tomalin, *W. H. Hudson*, 120.

whole body, arms, and legs, only leaving her face untouched. Instantly she became covered with a plumage of a slaty-blue colour, only on her face there were no feathers. At the same time from her shoulders sprang wings which were incessantly agitated. She hurried forth, closing the door after her; once more the walls trembled or seemed to tremble; a sound of rushing wings was heard, and, mingling with it, shrill peals of laughter; then all was still.[9]

The luckless voyeur applies the ointment to himself, is likewise transformed, and follows his wife across the night sky to an ancient ruined city where the coven holds its sabbath. In a panic he runs her through with a sword, is discovered next morning over her bleeding body, and condemned to death by the authorities. The story's phobic sexual symbolism (naked bride bristling with a nightmarish pubic growth, etc.) scarcely requires exegesis. Metamorphic shape-shiftings between birds and women are a staple of poetic figuration, whether they mark pitiful prey (Philomela, Procne) or frightful raptors (the harpies). Hudson works out a more overtly Ovidian scenario, deftly transposed into South American native culture, in the later tale 'Marta Riquelme'. Here the narrator, a priest making little headway in a heathen backwater, struggles to repress his love for the eponymous Marta, who suffers a ghastly series of tribulations, including abduction by Indians, the loss of all her children, and rejection by her ne'er-do-well husband. When she hides away in the forest the priest seeks her out, only to find that grief has turned her into something inhuman—the mournful kakué-bird of local folklore:

I raised my eyes only to discover that Marta was no longer before me. For even in that moment, when those terrible cries were ringing through my heart, waking the echoes of the mountain solitudes, the awful change had come, and she had looked her last with human eyes on earth and on man! In another form—that strange form of the Kakué—she had fled out of our sight for ever to hide in those gloomy woods which were henceforth to be her dwelling place.[10]

The horrifying transformation of woman into bird completes a violation, a traumatic loss of innocence, as though sexuality itself were a kind of black magic.

But perhaps the most suggestive of Hudson's writings upon this

[9] Hudson, *Tales of the Pampas* (New York, 1916), 119–20.
[10] Ibid. 210.

topic are to be found in his journalism rather than in his fiction. 'Feathered Women' was the title of a letter Hudson wrote to *The Times*, 17 October 1893, reprinted as a pamphlet by the Society for the Protection of Birds (and reproduced as an appendix in Tomalin's biography). Here the theme of an individual violation expands (but also, from a human point of view, dissipates) into the universal disaster of species extinction: innocent birds are slaughtered to create the monstrous hybrid of the feathered woman. No man who loves nature can look upon a woman so adorned 'without a feeling of repugnance for the wearer, however beautiful or charming she may be'. Hudson alludes to Herbert Spencer's notion that women 'intellectually, especially on the side of their aesthetic faculties, occupy a position about mid-way between the civilized man of our era and the pure savage'. Nevertheless, he hopes that the sex may yet be educated to a level 'above wearing the savage ornaments with which the female savage of Venezuela decorates herself, or the necklaces of human ears (captured from the enemy) which a Mexican lady is said to have exhibited in a ballroom'.[11] The rhetorical slippage here between the extinction of birds and the massacre of human beings, across the emblematic figure of the bird-woman, together with the unstable triangulation of civilized man, woman, and savage, takes us close to the thematic core of *Green Mansions*.

Rima herself—innocent, radiant, doomed—is a thoroughly literary figure, with an impeccable pedigree out of romance tradition. Scholars have located sources for her in a range of nineteenth-century novels and poems.[12] She has grander forebears: Milton's Eve, though still unfallen, Echo and her sister nymphs, woodland votaries

---

[11] Tomalin, *W. H. Hudson*, 245. Tomalin also reproduces a *Punch* cartoon from 1892, 'The Rapaciousness of Fashion', depicting a Victorian lady transformed into a harpy with pinions and talons, terrorizing a kingfisher. Hudson returned to the theme in a series of letters and pamphlets over the next few years.

[12] See Carlos H. Baker, 'The Source-book for Hudson's Green Mansions', *PMLA* 61 (1946), 252–7 (citing Sydney Owenson, *The Missionary*, 1811, and Charles Roberts, *The Heart of the Ancient Wood*, 1900); Hoxie N. Fairchild, 'Rima's Mother', *PMLA* 68 (1953), 357–70 (citing Arthur O'Shaughnessy, 'Colibri', in *Songs of a Worker*, 1881); and James V. Fletcher, 'The Creator of Rima, W. H. Hudson: A Belated Romantic', *Sewanee Review*, 41 (1933), 24–40 (citing Wordsworth's Lucy poems, Shelley's Cythna, Meredith's *Love in the Valley*). John T. Frederick, *William Henry Hudson* (New York, 1972), 57, points out that Hudson worked up his descriptions of the tropical rain forest, which he had never visited, from literary sources such as H. W. Bates's *A Naturalist on the River Amazons* (1863), E. F. im Thurn's *Among the Indians of Guiana* (1883), and Alfred Simson's *Travels in the Wilds of Ecuador* (1886).

of Diana like Spenser's Belphebe, aerial maidens like Fenella in Scott's *Peveril of the Peak*, and all the anima-figures that Jay MacPherson has described in her book *The Spirit of Solitude*.[13] Rima is also close kin to the child-women of Victorian fiction: a Little Nell of the jungle, complete with sordid grandfather. How apt that Abel should entertain her with recitals from what Northrop Frye calls 'naïve romance': 'the more ancient romances and ballads, the sweet old verse that, whether glad or sorrowful, seems always natural and spontaneous as the song of a bird, and so simple that even a child can understand it.'

The most likely source for the symbolic scheme that frames Rima is Ruskin's remarkable mythographic treatise, *The Queen of the Air* (1869). Arguing that the most enduring myths arise from natural phenomena, Ruskin denominates the goddess Athena 'the Spirit of Life in material organism'. In a chapter ('Athena in the Earth') from which Hudson would quote extensively in his late work *The Book of a Naturalist*, Ruskin explicates the allegorical meanings of two types of creature: 'the serpent, in which the breath, or spirit, is less than in any other creature, and the earth-power greatest: [and] the bird, in which the breath, or spirit, is more full than in any other creature, and the earth-power least.' These are, in fact, the totem animals of *Green Mansions*, marking opposite poles of the tale's natural order. (Spiders, it seems, can represent either element: the floating gossamer-spider of Abel's delight, the heavy and venomous hermit-spider of his agony.) 'Athena is the air conveying vibration of sound', writes Ruskin, and 'the voice and throat of the bird . . . is the air incarnate': spirit as speech and music. (It turns out that Hudson may have derived Rima's name from a structure in the bird's throat that enables it to sing; see the Explanatory Notes to this edition.) But the serpent 'is a divine hieroglyph of the demoniac power of the earth—of the entire earthly nature': a pre-human writing that inscribes 'the grasp and sting of death'.[14] Unfallen Rima seems immune to this polarity—she weightlessly traverses vertical space, and consorts with the serpent as well as the bird. A lethal coral snake clings to her like an erotic accessory, 'a gaily coloured silken garter just dropped from her leg'.

[13] Jay MacPherson, *The Spirit of Solitude: Conventions and Continuities in Late Romance* (New Haven, Conn., and London, 1982).

[14] Quotations from 'The Queen of the Air' are taken from *The Literary Criticism of John Ruskin*, 281, 266–8, 283. David Miller, *W. H. Hudson and the Elusive Paradise* (New York, 1990), cites Ruskin in a detailed discussion of the symbolism of *Green Mansions*, 139–47.

This is as sexy as she gets; no wonder Abel is promptly bitten, and subjected to a painful discipline of 'threshold symbols'.[15] In a bizarre typological conflation towards the end of the book, Abel, now Cain, goes one better than Eve, and eats the serpent. By that time Rima has fallen from the air and been transformed to a clay urn full of ashes, inscribed with the motto of his loss.

Through Rima, Hudson represents nature as the aesthetic apprehension of a dispersed or sublimated organic form. *Green Mansions* provides a rich illustration of the aesthetic, as distinct from ethical or scientific, categories that have sustained much naturalist and ecological writing. Rima's forests, never felled, belong more to the air than to the earth:

Here Nature is unapproachable with her green, airy canopy, a sun-impregnated cloud—cloud above cloud; and though the highest may be unreached by the eye, the beams yet filter through, illuming the wide spaces beneath—chamber succeeded by chamber, each with its own special lights and shadows. . . . Nature produces her effects at random, and seems only to increase the beautiful illusion by that infinite variety of decoration in which she revels, binding tree to tree in a tangle of anaconda-like lianas, and dwindling down from these huge cables to airy webs and hair-like fibres that vibrate to the wind of the passing insect's wing.

Rima herself appears as the distillation—just barely anthropomorphic—of this vision of a life-form, itself unbodied, that includes all forms and bodies, including the serpentine. 'All the separate and fragmentary beauty and melody and graceful motion scattered throughout nature were concentrated and harmoniously combined in her.'

Before Rima emerges from her green shade, she haunts the woods as a 'voice without a body'—a melodic intonation more like birdsong than human speech. Hudson takes up ancient ideas about linguistic origins that were revived in the Enlightenment, with the blind Scottish poet Thomas Blacklock being perhaps the most literal-minded proponent of the theory that language first emerged from the human mimicry of birdsong. As Jason Wilson has noted, the very name 'Rima' designates the oral art of rhyme or verse—the form of language closest to song—in Spanish, the language that for Hudson en-

---

[15] MacPherson, *Spirit of Solitude*, who lists (in addition to snakebite) 'storm, vanishing phantom-maiden, leap over precipice, and unconsciousness' (p. 242)—not to mention getting lost in a dark forest.

shrined his exiled state.[16] Spanish is the site of a linguistic problem in the novel. Abel never does learn Rima's virginal mother-tongue, and nor of course do we, in what is perhaps the riskiest strategy of Hudson's representation. Rima and Abel converse in Spanish; we read their dialogue in English translation, which accounts for some of its stoniness (this is truly *rima petrosa*). Nevertheless, it is unfortunate that what ought to be the most vibrant passages in the story lie dead on the page. Like Milton before him, Hudson faces the dilemma of having to represent the unfallen in a fallen medium. Perhaps we are meant to be always conscious that we are reading a translation, and that Rima's voice remains inaccessible, save through those early impressionistic notations. (Ornithologists thought highly of Hudson's descriptions of birdsong.) We learn that, just as Rima's name is not really Rima (nor even 'Riolama', so regrettably reminiscent of Hollywood Latin-Americana), so Abel is not her true name for him, that language always remains a barrier between them, and that even when Rima prays to her mother it is in the language of alienation imposed on her—like the plaits and cotton dress she wears indoors—by the Catholic missionary. Hudson is more at ease with the all-too-fallen Indians, whose speech he renders in conventional styles of Ossianic and mock-heroic.

Nature, traditionally if not immemorially, is a woman, and never more so than when Rima communes with her dead mother in the tongue they shared (in contrast to the outburst of Spanish prayer). Yet women, including those fashionable feathered women Hudson denounced, are also, by the same tradition, beings set outside the order of nature, conspicuously unnatural, creatures of artifice. It seems necessary that Rima be both a woman and not one. As nature-sprite she shares, though etherealized, qualities long attributed to Woman: *varium et mutabile semper femina, la donna è mobile*. Rima is nothing if not mercurial, full of 'swift changes of colour and expression', but savingly true to a 'perfect balance of the parts and harmony of the whole'. As Abel falls in love with her, he finds himself remembering other women he has known—specifically, the woman he loved before his flight to the forest:

A daughter of civilisation and of that artificial life, she could never experience such feelings as these and return to nature as I was doing. For women,

[16] Jason Wilson, *W. H. Hudson: The Colonial's Revenge* (London, 1981).

though within narrow limits more plastic than men, are yet without that larger adaptiveness which can take us back to the sources of life, which they have left eternally behind.

While women can never be the subjects of a return to the sources of life, they can, however, be reinvented as its objects. A number of female doubles are conjured up around Rima as the story unfolds, of which Abel's first love is just one transitory, if philosophically convenient, example—this is the first and last we hear of her, in that crucial central chapter (X) on love and female nature.

Another and a more consequential Anti-Rima stalks out of the woods at the height of Abel's pantheistic rapture. This is the 'grotesque human figure' of the old Indian woman, Cla-cla, who is named, we are told, 'probably in imitation of the cry of some bird'. Like Rima's, it is not her true, secret name, although its mimicry of a hollow clucking would seem to stand as a parody of Rima's melodious warbling charged with an unintelligible significance. In contrast to arboreal Rima, Cla-cla maintains a primitive domesticity— she is the 'self-regulating machine' of the savage household. She adores the vulgar music Abel strums on his guitar, and herself administers narratives (presumably devoid of meaningful content or aesthetic value) as an anodyne to her tribe. The other parody-Rima Abel encounters among the savages is the 'copper-coloured drab of the wilderness' offered to him as a bride, Oalava, 'whose physical charms needed no description since they had never been concealed'. These women are the dirt that keeps the nympholept's idol pure.

Everything that Rima is not, the Indian women clarify a relationship of binary opposition that defines the Indians as a category in Hudson's text. Historically the real wild folk of the woods, they appear here in the retrogressive guise of treacherous and bloodthirsty 'savages', Rima's moral and symbolic negatives as well as her deadly foes. At the opening of *Green Mansions* Abel promises to tell his auditor about his 'travels and adventures among the savages', as though this will be the book's main concern. Instead, the savages compose a carnal frame for the ideal figure in the allegorical mirror; Rima reflects, in antithesis, the novel's deep preoccupation. Her fate determines the fate of the Indians who kill her.

Hudson makes much of Rima's racial distinction from the Indians. She is the last survivor of a prelapsarian race of whom we hear only

of female specimens, no doubt those Amazons anticipated in vain by
the early European invaders. Her skin colour is purer than white—it
is a diaphanous ultra-white, a prismatic albino:

Beneath the trees, at a distance, it had seemed a somewhat dim white or pale
grey; near in the strong sunshine it was not white, but alabastrian, semi-
pellucid, showing an underlying rose-colour; and at any point where the
rays fell direct this colour was bright and luminous, as we see in our fingers
when held before a strong firelight. But that part of her skin that remained
in shadow appeared of a dimmer white, and the underlying colour varied
from dim, rosy purple to dim blue.

The unfallen body is translucent to the life it bears. Abel's entranced
description shifts to her eyes:

At first, when lit with anger, they had appeared flame-like; now the iris was of
a peculiar soft or dim and tender red, a shade sometimes seen in flowers.
But only when looked at closely could this delicate hue be discerned . . .
Think not, then, of the red flower, exposed to the light and sun in conjunction with the vivid green of the foliage; think only of such a hue in the half-
hidden iris, brilliant and moist with the eye's moisture, deep with the eye's
depth, glorified by the outward look of a bright, beautiful soul.

The whole passage can be glossed with the striking treatise on eye-
colour—a showpiece of Hudson's poetic naturalism—that occupies
an entire chapter of *Idle Days in Patagonia* (1893). There Hudson explains that human eye-colour is determined by the presence of 'yellow or brown pigment on the outer surface of the iris', which filters
'the dark purple pigment—the *uvea*—on the inner surface'.[17] Rima's
inner pigment shines through, presumably, unsullied by yellow or
brown—the hue of a lower nature, since brown eyes 'express animal
passions rather than intellect and the higher moral feelings', while
'in the inferior creatures the black eye is always keen and cunning or
else soft and mild'.[18]

Hudson's rhapsody on eye-colour modulates into a luxuriant fan-
tasia on human racial difference, which is worth quoting at length:

When going about the world one cannot help thinking that the various races
and tribes of men, differing in the colour of their skins and in the climates
and conditions they live in, ought to have differently-coloured eyes. In
Brazil, I was greatly struck with the magnificent appearance of many of the

---

[17] W. H. Hudson, *Idle Days in Patagonia* (London, 1893), 191.
[18] Ibid. 195.

negro women I saw there; well-formed, tall, majestic creatures, often appropriately clothed in loose white gowns and white turban-like head-dresses; while on their round polished blue-black arms they wore silver armlets. It seemed to me that pale golden irides, as in the intensely black tyrant-bird Lichenops perspicillata, would have given a finishing glory to these sable beauties, completing their strange unique loveliness. Again in that exquisite type of female beauty which we see in the white girl with a slight infusion of negro blood, giving the graceful frizzle to the hair, the purple-red hue to the lips, and the delicate dusky terra-cotta tinge to the skin, an eye more suitable than the dark dull brown would have been the intense orange-brown seen in some lemur's eyes. For many very dark-skinned tribes nothing more beautiful than the ruby-red iris could be imagined; while sea-green eyes would have best suited dusky-pale Polynesians.[19]

This brilliant flight of imaginary genetic engineering (or anthropo-logical pigeon-fancying) elaborates, to adapt Ruskin's phrase, an 'aes-thetic relation of the races'. A similar language of racial character as *colour* occurs very early in *Green Mansions*, in the novel's prologue, where it promises exactly the aesthetic scheme of harmony and bal-ance that we will later find Rima embodying. The British editor re-counts the origin of his intimacy with Abel in an agreement of literary taste: 'This feeling brought us together, and made us two— the nervous olive-skinned Hispano-American of the tropics and the phlegmatic blue-eyed Saxon of the cold north—one in spirit and more than brothers.' As they sit together, and Abel begins his tale, the editor observes 'the two white-clad servants that waited upon us—the brown-faced subtle-eyed old Hindoo butler and an al-most blue-black young Guiana negro'. The decorous composition expresses a pan-colonial colour scheme of mastery and servitude, in which the tint of dominance falls somewhere between 'olive-skinned' and 'brown'.

But the Amerindian savages sink as far below this imperial spec-trum as Rima rises above it. Their colour is (opposite to Rima's) a lustreless non-colour, a drabness variegated only by being dipped in blood. The novel draws a moral continuum between the 'cannibalis-tic' devouring of animal-flesh and the Indians' internecine warfare, and shows the hunting of Rima to be a communal enterprise—the whole village assists in the bonfire, so that women and children as well as warriors are guilty of her death. With this event Abel under-

[19] *Idle Days in Patagonia*, 189.

stands that 'a new nature, black and implacable, [has] taken the place of the old'. Finding out the truth of old Nuflo's description of the Indians as 'devils in human shape', he resolves to be 'a worse devil than themselves', and arranges for their massacre by a rival tribe. Earlier, Abel has conjectured that Rima's people—the original tenants of the green mansions—were wiped out by invading Indians. Rima's death by air and fire thus completes a genocide which provides Abel with the evil logic for his revenge. The massacre of Runi's clan will be merely the next stage in a long historical process of extermination—long enough, and fateful enough, to be rationalized as a process of natural history. He is shaken out of his 'moral insanity' at last by the sight of old Cla-cla, 'lying where she had been struck down, the fire of the blazing house lighting her wide-open glassy eyes and white hair dabbled in blood'. Abel never sees Rima after her death; ashes and some bits of bone are all her remains. Instead, the Indian woman's is the sacrificial body we gaze upon—as though this is what the romance has been after, all along.

The fruit of these catastrophes is wholly bitter. Abel roams the forests like a wild beast, harried by 'serpent fancies', clutching the cinerary urn of his beloved. Guilt for the murders he has instigated pollutes his grief, and both guilt and grief exceed individual measure: while Rima's death represents a mythic disaster, the destruction of nature, a network of allusions (explained in the notes to this edition) suggests that Abel's crime bears the historical burden of European perfidy and violence in the Americas. Internalization, the compensatory mechanism of romantic loss, yields a 'Rima of the mind' who eventually sanctions the bleak self-reliance of a man 'self-forgiven and self-absolved'. Hudson's romance finds its depth in the astringent pathos of these last chapters.

In the opening pages of *The Naturalist in La Plata*, Hudson had looked back from his English horizon of exile to 'the last occasion on which I saw the pampa grass in its full beauty', before he left South America in 1874. Riding out one evening, he and a friend encounter a party of five mounted Indians. Paying no attention to them, the Indians stand up on the backs of their horses to look around for strays. For a few minutes they become monuments of an evanescent natural splendour, as they bear the scene's effects of light and colour:

We continued watching them for some time, as they stood gazing away over the plain in different directions, motionless and silent, like bronze men on strange horse-shaped pedestals of dark stone; so dark in their copper skins and long black hair, against the far-off ethereal sky, flushed with amber light; and at their feet, and all around, the cloud of white and faintly-blushing plumes. That farewell scene was printed very vividly on my memory, but it cannot be shown to another, nor could it be even if a Ruskin's pen or a Turner's pencil were mine; for the flight of the sea-mew is not more impossible to us than the power to picture forth the image of Nature in our souls, when she reveals herself in one of those 'special moments' which have 'special grace' in situations where her wild beauty has never been spoiled by man.[20]

The reader has already been informed that five years after that farewell scene, in 1879, 'the Argentine government determined to rid the country of the aborigines' in a final campaign of pacification. Hudson invests the Indians with an epiphany of the vanishing wilderness and his own loss; their fate can represent the general extinction he mourns.

But the hero of *Green Mansions* cannot see the Indians as part of nature, unless it is that 'new nature, black and implacable', that has taken over the sacred wood. Rima personifies an anguished attempt to tell the difference between the loss of wilderness and what Abel refers to (early in the story) as 'the last act in the great American tragedy'— the destruction of aboriginal peoples who, the fable goes on to suggest, are not aboriginal after all but cruel alien invaders like ourselves. Imperial civilization's desecrations and murders repeat, on an industrial scale, the violence that the savage has already inflicted on the natural world. The idea points back to *The Descent of Man*, where it has formed a notorious crux: the savage occupies a paradoxical, reprobate boundary in Darwin's evolutionary scheme, between animal ancestors who enjoy a pastoral innocence, secured by the natural grace of instinct, and civilized man, who labours to improve himself through culture.[21] Fallen out of nature, not yet having acquired the moral techniques of culture, the savage lurks in a bloody darkness. Hudson's tale also points forward to the political quandary of contemporary ecological movements, as they strive to adjudicate between the protection of natural ecosystems and the claims of indigenous (now 'developing') peoples who inhabit or encroach on them—an opposition sustained by the logic of modern political economies, it

[20] Hudson, *The Naturalist in La Plata*, 7–8.
[21] See my essay, 'Darwin and the Savages', *Yale Journal of Criticism*, 4 (1991), 13–46.

needs to be said, rather than by nature itself. *Green Mansions*, meanwhile, dramatizes the volatile mixture of civilization's lament for wild nature and its blood-guilt for the people of the woods, with an unmatched poignancy.

NOTE ON THE TEXT

Green Mansions was first published in February 1904 by Duckworth & Co., London. In 1912 John Galsworthy introduced Hudson's work to the young Alfred A. Knopf, who went on to launch his own publishing firm with the first American copyright edition of *Green Mansions* in 1916. The present edition of *Green Mansions* reprints the 1916 Knopf edition, with the following corrections: 'far-off wind' for 'far off-wind' (p. 15), 'solemnly' for 'solmenly' (p. 46), 'flourishes' for 'flourished' (p. 83), 'voice be to our' for 'voice be our' (p. 88), 'hurried out' for 'hurried, out' (p. 143), and *sin dios* for *siu dios* (p. 191).

SELECT BIBLIOGRAPHY

Bibliography, Biography, Letters

Curle, Richard (ed.), *W. H. Hudson's Letters to R. B. Cunninghame-Graham* (London: Golden Cockerel Press, 1941).

Garnett, Edward (ed.), *Letters from W. H. Hudson, 1901–22* (New York: Dutton, 1923).

Payne, John R., *W. H. Hudson: A Bibliography* (Folkestone: Dawson, 1977).

Roberts, Morley, *W. H. Hudson: A Portrait* (New York: Dutton, 1924).

Tomalin, Ruth, *W. H. Hudson: A Biography* (London: Faber and Faber, 1982).

Criticism

Alcorn, John, *The Nature Novel from Hardy to Lawrence* (London: Macmillan, 1977).

Baker, Carlos H., 'The Source-book for Hudson's Green Mansions', *PMLA* 61 (1946), 252–7.

Fairchild, Hoxie N., 'Rima's Mother', *PMLA* 68 (1953), 357–70.

Fletcher, James V., 'The Creator of Rima, W. H. Hudson: A Belated Romantic', *Sewanee Review*, 41 (1933), 24–40.

Frederick, John T., *William Henry Hudson* (New York: Twayne, 1972).

Haymaker, Richard E., *From Pampas to Hedgerows and Downs: A Study of W. H. Hudson* (New York: Bookman Associates, 1954).

Landry, Rudolph J., 'The Source of the Name "Rima" in "Green Mansions"', *Notes & Queries*, 201 (1956), 545–6.

MacPherson, Jay, *The Spirit of Solitude: Conventions and Continuities in Late Romance* (New Haven, Conn., and London: Yale University Press, 1982).

Miller, David, *W. H. Hudson and the Elusive Paradise* (New York: St Martin's, 1990).

Ronner, Amy D., *W. H. Hudson: The Man, The Novelist, The Naturalist* (New York: AMS Press, 1986).

Shrubsall, Dennis, *W. H. Hudson: Writer and Naturalist* (Tisbury, Wilts.: Compton Press, 1978).

Wilson, Jason, *W. H. Hudson: The Colonial's Revenge* (London: University of London Institute of Latin American Studies, 1981).

A CHRONOLOGY OF W. H. HUDSON

1841 Born on a ranch, 'The Twenty-Five Ombú Trees', at Quilmes near Buenos Aires, Argentina, 4 August; fourth child of Daniel Hudson and Caroline Augusta Kimble, emigrants from New England.

1846 Family moves to a larger ranch 40 miles away, 'The Acacias'. The children receive a desultory education at home.

1856 WHH falls ill with typhus following a visit to Buenos Aires. Convalescent, embarks on a course of reading.

1857 Reads Gilbert White's *The Natural History of Selborne*. Father loses 'The Acacias'; family returns to 'The Twenty-Five Ombú Trees'.

1858 Near-fatal attack of rheumatic fever weakens WHH's heart, permanently impairing his health.

1859 Death of mother, 4 October. Reads Darwin, *Origin of Species*.

1861 Begins travels throughout Argentina and neighbouring countries.

1865 Sends ornithological specimens to the Director of the Buenos Aires Natural History Museum.

1866 Offers services as ornithological collector to the Smithsonian Institution, Washington, DC; sends letters and specimens over the next three years. Serves in Argentine National Guard during war with Paraguay.

1868 Death of father, 14 January. WHH's ornithological specimens examined by the London Zoological Society, which invites him to become a correspondent.

1870–1 Letters on Argentine ornithology published in *Proceedings of the Zoological Society of London*. Travels in Patagonia.

1874 Sails for England, 1 April, arrives at Southampton, 5 May. Goes on a walking tour of the English countryside. WHH spends the next eighteen years in poverty and obscurity in London.

1876 Resident at Tower House, Westbourne Park. Marries the landlady, Emily Wingrave, who is also a singer and music teacher, 18 May.

1880 Meets the writer Morley Roberts, who becomes a lifelong friend.

1883 Publication of first story, 'Pelino Viera's Confession', in the *Cornhill Magazine*.

1884 Emily's boarding house fails.

1885 Publication of first novel, *The Purple Land that England Lost*; a critical and commercial failure.

1886 Emily Hudson inherits Tower House, henceforth the Hudson's permanent London home. It is heavily mortgaged and they take in boarders.

1887 *A Crystal Age*, Utopian romance.

1888 *Argentine Ornithology*, in collaboration with P. L. Sclater, WHH's correspondent at the London Zoological Society.

1890 Meets R. B. Cunninghame Graham, an admirer of his journalism.

1891 WHH's campaigns on behalf of nature conservation help found the Society for the Protection of Birds (later the RSPB).

1892 Publication of *The Naturalist in La Plata*, natural history essays; praised by reviewers, marking the beginning of WHH's literary reputation. *Fan, The Story of a Young Girl's Life*, an unsuccessful 3-volume slum novel, published under an alias (Henry Harford).

1893 *Idle Days in Patagonia*, a natural history memoir. *Birds in a Village*. WHH befriended by Sir Edward and Lady Grey.

1895 *British Birds*.

1898 *Birds in London*.

1900 *Nature in Downland*. Naturalized as a British citizen.

1901 *Birds and Man*. Awarded Civil List pension of £150 in recognition of natural history writings, on the recommendation of Sir Edward Grey. WHH begins a secret love affair with Linda Gardiner, secretary at the RSPB, which lasts for the remainder of his life. Meets Edward Garnett, who becomes a powerful advocate of his work.

1902 *El Ombú*, South American gaucho and supernatural tales.

1903 *Hampshire Days*.

1904 *Green Mansions*. Successful reissue of *The Purple Land*. WHH meets Margaret Brooke, the Ranee of Sarawak, who becomes a close friend.

1905 *A Little Boy Lost*, children's story.

1908 *The Land's End*.

1909 *Afoot in England*.

1910 *A Shepherd's Life*, based on WHH's conversations with James Lawes ('Caleb Bawcombe'), a retired shepherd he had met in 1901.

1911 Emily Hudson becomes an invalid.

1913 *Adventures Among Birds*.

1914 Emily bedridden; settled at a guesthouse in Worthing with a companion. WHH also unwell.

1916 WHH ill in Cornwall, where from now on he spends his winters. Convalescent, he begins writing down recollections of his childhood in Argentina. New edition of *Green Mansions* published in the

USA, bringing WHH financial comfort for the remainder of his life.

1918   Publication of the childhood memoir, *Far Away and Long Ago*; acclaimed as his masterpiece.

1919   *Birds in Town and Village. The Book of a Naturalist.* WHH's prestige as a naturalist at its height.

1920   *Birds of La Plata*, a new, illustrated edition of WHH's contributions to *Argentine Ornithology. Dead Man's Plack and An Old Thorn*, historical fiction. WHH resigns Civil List pension.

1921   Death of Emily Hudson, 19 March. WHH too ill to travel to her deathbed. *A Traveller in Little Things*.

1922   Dies, 18 August. His estate bequeathed to the RSPB. *A Hind in Richmond Park* published posthumously.

GREEN MANSIONS

A Romance of the
Tropical Forest

PROLOGUE

IT is a cause of very great regret to me that this task has taken so much longer a time than I had expected for its completion. It is now many months—over a year, in fact—since I wrote to Georgetown announcing my intention of publishing, *in a very few months*, the whole truth about Mr Abel. Hardly less could have been looked for from his nearest friend, and I had hoped that the discussion in the newspapers would have ceased, at all events, until the appearance of the promised book. It has not been so; and at this distance from Guiana I was not aware of how much conjectural matter was being printed week by week in the local press, some of which must have been painful reading to Mr Abel's friends. A darkened chamber, the existence of which had never been suspected in that familiar house in Main Street, furnished only with an ebony stand on which stood a cinerary urn, its surface ornamented with flower and leaf and thorn, and winding through it all the figure of a serpent; an inscription, too, of seven short words which no one could understand or rightly interpret; and finally, the disposal of the mysterious ashes—that was all there was relating to an untold chapter in a man's life for imagination to work on. Let us hope that now, at last, the romance-weaving will come to an end. It was, however, but natural that the keenest curiosity should have been excited; not only because of that peculiar and indescribable charm of the man, which all recognised and which won all hearts, but also because of that hidden chapter—that sojourn in the desert, about which he preserved silence. It was felt in a vague way by his intimates that he had met with unusual experiences which had profoundly affected him and changed the course of his life. To me alone was the truth known, and I must now tell, briefly as possible, how my great friendship and close intimacy with him came about.

When, in 1887, I arrived in Georgetown to take up an appointment in a public office, I found Mr Abel an old resident there, a man of means and a favourite in society. Yet he was an alien, a Venezuelan, one of that turbulent people on our border whom the colonists have always looked on as their natural enemies.* The story told to me was that about twelve years before that time he had arrived at Georgetown from some remote district in the interior; that he had journeyed alone on foot across half the continent to the coast, and had first appeared among them, a young stranger, penniless, in rags, wasted almost to a skeleton by fever and misery of all kinds, his face blackened by long exposure to sun and wind. Friendless, with but little English, it was a hard struggle for him to live; but he managed somehow, and eventually letters from Caracas informed him that a considerable property of which he had been deprived was once more his own, and he was also invited to return to his country to take his part in the government of the republic. But Mr Abel, though young, had already outlived political passions and aspirations, and, apparently, even the love of his country; at all events, he elected to stay where he was—his enemies, he would say smilingly, were his best friends—and one of the first uses he made of his fortune was to buy that house in Main Street which was afterwards like a home to me.

I must state here that my friend's full name was Abel Guevez de Argensola, but in his early days in Georgetown he was called by his christian name only, and later he wished to be known simply as 'Mr Abel.'

I had no sooner made his acquaintance than I ceased to wonder at the esteem and even affection with which he, a Venezuelan, was regarded in this British colony. All knew and liked him, and the reason of it was the personal charm of the man, his kindly disposition, his manner with women, which pleased them and excited no man's jealousy—not even the old hot-tempered planter's, with a very young and pretty and light-headed wife—his love of little children, of all wild creatures, of nature, and of whatsoever was furthest removed from the common material interests and concerns of a purely commercial community. The things which excited other men—politics, sport, and the price of crystals—were outside of his thoughts; and when men had done with them for a season, when like the tempest they had 'blown their fill' in office and club-room and house and wanted a change, it was a relief to turn to Mr Abel and get him to discourse of *his* world—the world of nature and of the spirit.*

It was, all felt, a good thing to have a Mr Abel in Georgetown. That it was indeed good for me I quickly discovered. I had certainly not expected to meet in such a place with any person to share my tastes—that love of poetry which has been the chief passion and delight of my life; but such an one I had found in Mr Abel. It surprised me that he, suckled on the literature of Spain, and a reader of only ten or twelve years of English literature, possessed a knowledge of our modern poetry as intimate as my own, and a love of it equally great. This feeling brought us together, and made us two—the nervous olive-skinned Hispano-American of the tropics and the phlegmatic blue-eyed Saxon of the cold north—one in spirit and more than brothers. Many were the daylight hours we spent together and 'tired the sun with talking';* many, past counting, the precious evenings in that restful house of his where I was an almost daily guest. I had not looked for such happiness; nor, he often said, had he. A result of this intimacy was that the vague idea concerning his hidden past, that some unusual experience had profoundly affected him and perhaps changed the whole course of his life, did not diminish, but, on the contrary, became accentuated, and was often in my mind. The change in him was almost painful to witness whenever our wandering talk touched on the subject of the aborigines, and of the knowledge he had acquired of their character and languages when living or travelling among them; all that made his conversation most engaging— the lively, curious mind, the wit, the gaiety of spirit tinged with a tender melancholy—appeared to fade out of it; even the expression of his face would change, becoming hard and set, and he would deal you out facts in a dry mechanical way as if reading them in a book. It grieved me to note this, but I dropped no hint of such a feeling, and would never have spoken about it but for a quarrel which came at last to make the one brief solitary break in that close friendship of years. I got into a bad state of health, and Abel was not only much concerned about it, but annoyed, as if I had not treated him well by being ill, and he would even say that I could get well if I wished to. I did not take this seriously, but one morning, when calling to see me at the office, he attacked me in a way that made me downright angry with him. He told me that indolence and the use of stimulants was the cause of my bad health. He spoke in a mocking way, with a pretence of not quite meaning it, but the feeling could not be wholly disguised. Stung by his reproaches, I blurted out that he had no right to talk to me, even in fun, in such a way. Yes, he said, getting serious, he had the best right—that of our friendship. He would be no true friend if he kept his peace about such a matter. Then, in my haste, I retorted that to me the friendship between us did not seem so perfect and complete as it did to him. One condition of friendship is that the partners in it should be known to each other. He had had my whole life and mind open to him, to read it as in a book. *His* life was a closed and clasped volume to me.

His face darkened, and after a few moments' silent reflection he got up and left me with a cold good-bye, and without that hand-grasp which had been customary between us.

After his departure I had the feeling that a great loss, a great calamity, had befallen me, but I was still smarting at his too candid criticism, all the more because in my heart I acknowledged its truth. And that night, lying awake, I repented of the cruel retort I had made, and resolved to ask his forgiveness and leave it to him to determine the question of our future relations. But he was beforehand with me, and with the morning came a letter begging my forgiveness and asking me to go that evening to dine with him.

We were alone, and during dinner and afterwards, when we sat smoking and sipping black coffee in the verandah, we were unusually quiet, even to gravity, which caused the two white-clad servants that waited on us—the brown-faced subtle-eyed old Hindoo butler and an almost blue-black young Guiana negro—to direct many furtive glances at their master's face. They were accustomed to see him in a more genial mood when he had a friend to dine. To me the change in his manner was not surprising: from the moment of seeing him I had divined that he had determined to open the shut and clasped volume of which I had spoken—that the time had now come for him to speak.

CHAPTER I

NOW that we are cool, he said, and regret that we hurt each other, I am not sorry that it happened. I deserved your reproach: a hundred times I have wished to tell you the whole story of my travels and adventures among the savages, and one of the reasons which prevented me was the fear that it would have an unfortunate effect on our friendship. That was precious, and I desired above everything to keep it. But I must think no more about that now. I must think only of how I am to tell you my story. I will begin at a time when I was twenty-three. It was early in life to be in the thick of politics, and in trouble to the extent of having to fly my country to save my liberty, perhaps my life.

Every nation, someone remarks, has the government it deserves, and Venezuela certainly has the one it deserves and that suits it best. We call it a republic, not only because it is not one, but also because a thing must have a name; and to have a good name, or a fine name, is very convenient—especially when you want to borrow money. If the Venezuelans, thinly distributed over an area of half a million square miles, mostly illiterate peasants, half-breeds, and indigenes, were educated, intelligent men, zealous only for the public weal, it would be possible for them to have a real republic. They have instead a government by cliques, tempered by revolution;* and a very good government it is, in harmony with the physical conditions of the country and the national temperament. Now it happens that the educated men, representing your higher classes, are so few that there are not many persons unconnected by ties of blood or marriage with prominent members of the political groups to which they belong. By this you will see how easy and almost inevitable it is that we should become accustomed to look on conspiracy and revolt against the regnant party—the men of another clique—as only in the natural order of things. In the event of failure such outbreaks are punished, but they are not regarded as immoral. On the contrary, men of the highest intelligence and virtue among us are seen taking a leading part in these adventures. Whether such a condition of things is intrinsically wrong or not, or would be wrong in some circumstances and is not wrong, because inevitable, in others, I cannot pretend to decide;

and all this tiresome prolusion is only to enable you to understand how I—a young man of unblemished character, not a soldier by profession, not ambitious of political distinction, wealthy for that country, popular in society, a lover of social pleasures, of books, of nature—actuated, as I believed, by the highest motives, allowed myself to be drawn very readily by friends and relations into a conspiracy to overthrow the government of the moment, with the object of replacing it by more worthy men—ourselves, to wit.

Our adventure failed because the authorities got wind of the affair and matters were precipitated.* Our leaders at the moment happened to be scattered over the country—some were abroad; and a few hot-headed men of the party, who were in Caracas just then, and probably feared arrest, struck a rash blow: the President was attacked in the street and wounded. But the attackers were seized, and some of them shot on the following day. When the news reached me I was at a distance from the capital, staying with a friend on an estate he owned on the River Quebrada Honda, in the State of Guarico, some fifteen to twenty miles from the town of Zaraza. My friend, an officer in the army, was a leader in the conspiracy; and as I was the only son of a man who had been greatly hated by the Minister of War, it became necessary for us both to fly for our lives. In the circumstances we could not look to be pardoned, even on the score of youth.

Our first decision was to escape to the sea-coast; but as the risk of a journey to La Guayra, or any other port of embarkation on the north side of the country, seemed too great, we made our way in a contrary direction to the Orinoco, and downstream to Angostura. Now, when we had reached this comparatively safe breathing-place—safe, at all events, for the moment—I changed my mind about leaving or attempting to leave the country. Since boyhood I had taken a very peculiar interest in that vast and almost unexplored territory we possess south of the Orinoco, with its countless unmapped rivers and trackless forests; and in its savage inhabitants, with their ancient customs and character, unadulterated by contact with Europeans. To visit this primitive wilderness had been a cherished dream; and I had to some extent even prepared myself for such an adventure by mastering more than one of the Indian dialects of the northern states of Venezuela. And now, finding myself on the south side of our great river, with unlimited time at my disposal, I determined to gratify this wish. My companion took his departure towards the coast, while I set about making preparations and hunting up information from those who had travelled in the interior to trade with the savages. I decided eventually to go back upstream, and penetrate to the interior in the western part of Guayana,* and the Amazonian territory bordering on Colombia and Brazil, and to return to Angostura in about six months' time. I had no fear of being arrested in the semi-independent, and in most part savage region, as the Guayana authorities concerned themselves little enough about the political upheavals at Caracas.

The first five or six months I spent in Guayana, after leaving the city of refuge, were eventful enough to satisfy a moderately adventurous spirit. A complaisant Government employé at Angostura had provided me with a passport, in which it was set down (for few to read) that my object in visiting the interior was to collect information concerning the native tribes, the vegetable products of the country, and other knowledge which would be of advantage to the Republic; and the authorities were requested to afford me protection and assist me in my pursuits.

I ascended the Orinoco, making occasional expeditions to the small Christian settlements in the neighbourhood of the right bank, also to the Indian villages; and travelling in this way, seeing and learning much, in about three months I reached the River Meta. During this period I amused myself by keeping a journal, a record of personal adventures, impressions of the country and people, both semi-civilised and savage; and as my journal grew, I began to think that on my return at some future time to Caracas, it might prove useful and interesting to the public, and also procure me fame; which thought proved pleasurable and a great incentive, so that I began to observe things more narrowly and to study expression. But the book was not to be.

From the mouth of the Meta I journeyed on, intending to visit the settlement of Atahapo,* where the great River Guaviare, with other rivers, empty themselves into the Orinoco. But I was not destined to reach it, for at the small settlement of Manapuri* I fell ill of a low fever; and here ended the first half-year of my wanderings, about which no more need be told.

A more miserable place than Manapuri for a man to be ill of a low fever in could not well be imagined. The settlement, composed of mean hovels, with a few large structures of mud, or plastered wattle, thatched with palm leaves, was surrounded by water, marsh, and forest, the breeding-place of myriads of croaking frogs and of clouds of mosquitoes; even to one in perfect health existence in such a place would have been a burden. The inhabitants mustered about eighty or ninety, mostly Indians of that degenerate class frequently to be met with in small trading outposts. The savages of Guayana are great drinkers, but not drunkards in our sense, since their fermented liquors contain so little alcohol that inordinate quantities must be swallowed to produce intoxication; in the settlements they prefer the white man's more potent poisons, with the result that in a small place like Manapuri one can see enacted, as on a stage, the last act in the great American tragedy. To be succeeded, doubtless, by other and possibly greater tragedies. My thoughts at that period of suffering were pessimistic in the extreme. Sometimes, when the almost continuous rain held up for half a day, I would manage to creep out a short distance; but I was almost past making any exertion, scarcely caring to live, and taking absolutely no interest in the news from Caracas, which reached me at long intervals. At the end of two months, feeling a slight improvement in my health, and with it a returning interest in life and its affairs, it occurred to me to get out my diary and write a brief account of my sojourn at Manapuri. I had placed it for safety in a small deal box, lent to me for the purpose by a Venezuelan trader, an old resident at the settlement, by name Pantaleon—called by all Don Panta—one who openly kept half a dozen Indian wives in his house, and was noted for his dishonesty and greed, but who had proved himself a good friend to me. The box was in a corner of the wretched palm-thatched hovel I inhabited; but on taking it out I discovered that for several weeks the rain had been dripping on it, and that the manuscript was reduced to a sodden pulp. I flung it upon the floor with a curse, and threw myself back on my bed with a groan.

In that desponding state I was found by my friend Panta, who was constant in his visits at all hours; and, when in answer to his anxious inquiries I pointed to the pulpy mass on the mud floor, he turned it over with his foot, and then, bursting into a loud laugh, kicked it out, remarking that he had mistaken the object for some unknown reptile that had crawled in out of the rain. He affected to be astonished that I should regret its loss. It was all a true narrative, he exclaimed; if I wished to write a book for the stay-at-homes to read, I could easily invent a thousand lies far more entertaining than any real experiences. He had come to me, he said, to propose something. He had lived twenty years at that place, and had got accustomed to the climate, but it would not do for me to remain any longer if I wished to live. I must go away at once to a different country—to the mountains, where it was open and dry. 'And if you want quinine when you are there,' he concluded, 'smell the wind when it blows from the south-west, and you will inhale it into your system, fresh from the forest.'* When I remarked despondingly that in my condition it would be impossible to quit Manapuri, he went on to say that a small party of Indians was now in the settlement; that they had come, not only to trade, but to visit one of their own tribe, who was his wife, purchased some years ago from her father. 'And the money she cost me I have never regretted to this day,' said he, 'for she is a good wife—not jealous,' he added, with a curse on all the others. These Indians came all the way from the Queneveta mountains, and were of the Maquiritari tribe.* He, Panta, and, better still, his good wife, would interest them on my behalf, and for a suitable reward they would take me by slow, easy stages to their own country, where I would be treated well and recover my health.

This proposal, after I had considered it well, produced so good an effect on me, that I not only gave a glad consent, but, on the following day, I was able to get about and begin the preparations for my journey with some spirit.

In about eight days I bade good-bye to my generous friend Panta, whom I regarded, after having seen much of him, as a kind of savage beast that had sprung on me, not to rend, but to rescue from death; for we know that even cruel savage brutes and evil men have at times sweet, beneficent impulses, during which they act in a way contrary to their natures, like passive agents of some higher power.* It was a continual pain to travel in my weak condition, and the patience of my Indians was severely taxed; but they did not forsake me; and, at last, the entire distance, which I conjectured to be about sixty-five leagues, was accomplished; and at the end I was actually stronger and better in every way than at the start. From this time my progress towards complete recovery was rapid. The air, with or without any medicinal virtue blown from the cinchona trees in the far-off Andean forest, was tonic; and when I took my walks on the hillside above the Indian village, or later, when able to climb to the summits, the world as seen from those wild Queneveta mountains had a largeness and varied glory of scenery peculiarly refreshing and delightful to the soul.

With the Maquiritari tribe I passed some weeks, and the sweet sensations of returning health made me happy for a time; but such sensations seldom outlast convalescence. I was no sooner well again than I began to feel a restless spirit stirring in me. The monotony of savage life in this place became intolerable. After my long listless period the reaction had come, and I wished only for action, adventure—no matter how dangerous; and for new scenes, new faces, new dialects. In the end I conceived the idea of going on to the Casiquiare river, where I would find a few small settlements, and perhaps obtain help from the authorities there which would enable me to reach the Rio Negro.* For it was now in my mind to follow that river to the Amazons, and so down to Para and the Atlantic coast.

Leaving the Queneveta range, I started with two of the Indians as guides and travelling companions; but their journey ended only half-way to the river I wished to reach; and they left me with some friendly savages living on the Chunapay, a tributary of the Cunucu-mana,* which flows to the Orinoco. Here I had no choice but to wait until an opportunity of attaching myself to some party of travelling Indians, going south-west, should arrive; for by this time I had ex-pended the whole of my small capital in ornaments and calico brought from Manapuri, so that I could no longer purchase any man's service. And perhaps it will be as well to state at this point just what I possessed. For some time I had worn nothing but sandals to protect my feet; my garments consisted of a single suit, and one flan-nel shirt, which I washed frequently, going shirtless while it was dry-ing. Fortunately I had an excellent blue cloth cloak, durable and handsome, given to me by a friend at Angostura, whose prophecy on presenting it, that it would outlast *me*, very nearly came true. It served as a covering by night, and to keep a man warm and comfort-able when travelling in cold and wet weather no better garment was ever made. I had a revolver and metal cartridge-box in my broad leather belt, also a good hunting-knife with strong buckhorn handle and a heavy blade about nine inches long. In the pocket of my cloak I had a pretty silver tinder-box, and a match-box—to be mentioned again in this narrative—and one or two other trifling objects: these I was determined to keep until they could be kept no longer.

During the tedious interval of waiting on the Chunapay I was told a flattering tale by the village Indians, which eventually caused me to abandon the proposed journey to the Rio Negro. These Indians wore necklets, like nearly all the Guayana savages; but one, I observed, possessed a necklet unlike that of the others, which greatly aroused my curiosity. It was made of thirteen gold plates, irregular in form, about as broad as a man's thumb-nail, and linked together with fibres. I was allowed to examine it, and had no doubt that the pieces were of pure gold, beaten flat by the savages. When questioned about it they said it was originally obtained from the Indians of Parahuari, and Parahuari, they further said, was a mountainous country west of the Orinoco. Every man and woman in that place, they assured me, had such a necklet. This report inflamed my mind to such a degree that I could not rest by night or day for dreaming golden dreams,* and considering how to get to that rich district, unknown to civilised men. The Indians gravely shook their heads when I tried to persuade them to take me. They were far enough from the Orinoco, and Parahuari was ten, perhaps fifteen, days' journey further on—a country unknown to them, where they had no relations.

In spite of difficulties and delays, however, and not without pain and some perilous adventures, I succeeded at last in reaching the upper Orinoco, and, eventually, in crossing to the other side. With my life in my hand I struggled on westward through an unknown difficult country,* from Indian village to village, where at any moment I might have been murdered with impunity for the sake of my few belongings. It is hard for me to speak a good word for the Guayana savages; but I must now say that of them, that they not only did me no harm when I was at their mercy during this long journey, but they gave me shelter in their villages, and fed me when I was hungry, and helped me on my way when I could make no return. You must not, however, run away with the idea that there is any sweetness in their disposition, any humane or benevolent instincts such as are found among the civilised nations: far from it. I regard them now, and, fortunately for me, I regarded them then, when, as I have said, I was at their mercy, as beasts of prey, plus a cunning or low kind of intelligence vastly greater than that of the brute; and, for only morality, that respect for the rights of other members of the same family, or tribe, without which even the rudest communities cannot hold together. How, then, could I do this thing, and dwell and travel freely, without receiving harm, among tribes that have no peace with and no kindly feelings towards the stranger, in a district where the white man is rarely or never seen? Because I knew them so well. Without that knowledge, always available, and an extreme facility in acquiring new dialects, which had increased by practice until it was almost like intuition, I should have fared badly after leaving the Maquiritari tribe. As it was, I had two or three very narrow escapes.

To return from this digression. I looked at last on the famous Parahuari mountains, which, I was greatly surprised to find, were after all nothing but hills, and not very high ones. This, however, did not impress me. The very fact that Parahuari possessed no imposing feature in its scenery seemed rather to prove that it must be rich in gold: how else could its name and the fame of its treasures be familiar to people dwelling so far away as the Cunucumana?

But there was no gold. I searched through the whole range, which was about seven leagues long, and visited the villages, where I talked much with the Indians, interrogating them, and they had no necklets of gold, nor gold in any form; nor had they ever heard of its presence in Parahuari, nor in any other place known to them.

The very last village where I spoke on the subject of my quest, albeit now without hope, was about a league from the western extremity of the range, in the midst of a high broken country of forest and savannah and many swift streams; near one of these, called the Curicay, the village stood, among low scattered trees—a large building, in which all the people, numbering eighteen, passed most of their time when not hunting, with two smaller buildings attached to it. The head, or chief, Runi* by name, was about fifty years old, a taciturn, finely formed, and somewhat dignified savage, who was either of a sullen disposition or not well pleased at the intrusion of a white man. And for a time I made no attempt to conciliate him. What profit was there in it at all? Even that light mask, which I had worn so long and with such good effect, incommoded me now: I would cast it aside and be myself—silent and sullen as my barbarous host. If any malignant purpose was taking form in his mind, let it, and let him do his worst; for when failure first stares a man in the face it has so dark and repellent a look that not anything that can be added can make him more miserable; nor has he any apprehension. For weeks I had been searching with eager, feverish eyes in every village, in every rocky crevice, in every noisy mountain streamlet, for the glittering yellow dust I had travelled so far to find. And now all my beautiful dreams—all the pleasure and power to be—had vanished like a mere mirage on the savannah at noon.

It was a day of despair which I spent in this place, sitting all day indoors, for it was raining hard, immersed in my own gloomy thoughts, pretending to doze in my seat, and out of the narrow slits of my half-closed eyes seeing the others, also sitting or moving about, like shadows or people in a dream; and I cared nothing about them, and wished not to seem friendly, even for the sake of the food they might offer me by-and-by.

Towards evening the rain ceased; and rising up I went out a short distance to the neighbouring stream, where I sat on a stone, and casting off my sandals, laved my bruised feet in the cool running water. The western half of the sky was blue again with that tender lucid blue seen after rain, but the leaves still glittered with water, and the wet trunks looked almost black under the green foliage. The rare loveliness of the scene touched and lightened my heart. Away back in the east the hills of Parahuari, with the level sun full on them, loomed with a strange glory against the grey rainy clouds drawing off on that side, and their new mystic beauty almost made me forget how these same hills had wearied, and hurt, and mocked me. On that side, also to the north and south, there was open forest, but to the west a different prospect met the eye. Beyond the stream and the strip of verdure that fringed it, and the few scattered dwarf trees growing near its banks, spread a brown savannah sloping upwards to a long, low, rocky ridge, beyond which rose a great solitary hill, or rather mountain, conical in form, and clothed in forest almost to the summit. This was the mountain Ytaioa, the chief landmark in that district. As the sun went down over the ridge, beyond the savannah, the whole western sky changed to a delicate rose-colour that had the appearance of rose-coloured smoke blown there by some far-off wind, and left suspended—a thin, brilliant veil showing through it the distant sky beyond, blue and ethereal. Flocks of birds, a kind of troupial,* were flying past me overhead, flock succeeding flock, on their way to their roosting-place, uttering as they flew a clear, bell-like chirp; and there was something ethereal too in those drops of melodious sound, which fell into my heart like raindrops falling into a pool to mix their fresh heavenly water with the water of earth.

Doubtless into the turbid tarn of my heart some sacred drops had fallen—from the passing birds, from that crimson disc which had now dropped below the horizon, the darkening hills, the rose and blue of infinite heaven, from the whole visible circle; and I felt purified and had a strange sense and apprehension of a secret innocence and spirituality in nature—a prescience of some bourn, incalculably distant perhaps, to which we are all moving; of a time when the heavenly rain shall have washed us clean from all spot and blemish.* This unexpected peace which I had found now seemed to me of infinitely greater value than that yellow metal I had missed finding, with all its possibilities. My wish now was to rest for a season at this spot, so remote and lovely and peaceful, where I had experienced such unusual feelings, and such a blessed disillusionment.

This was the end of my second period in Guayana; the first had been filled with that dream of a book to win me fame in my country, perhaps even in Europe: the second, from the time of leaving the Queneveta mountains, with the dream of boundless wealth—the old dream of gold in this region that has drawn so many minds since the days of Alonzo Pizarro.* But to remain I must propitiate Runi, sitting silent with gloomy brows over there indoors; and he did not appear to me like one that might be won with words, however flattering. It was clear to me that the time had come to part with my one remaining valuable trinket—the tinder-box of chased silver.

I returned to the house, and going in seated myself on a log by the fire, just opposite to my grim host, who was smoking and appeared not to have moved since I left him. I made myself a cigarette, then drew out the tinder-box, with its flint and steel attached to it by means of two small silver chains. His eyes brightened a little as they curiously watched my movements, and he pointed without speaking to the glowing coals of fire at my feet. I shook my head, and striking the steel, sent out a brilliant spray of sparks, then blew on the tinder and lit my cigarette. This done, instead of returning the box to my pocket I passed the chain through the button-hole of my cloak and let it dangle on my breast as an ornament. When the cigarette was smoked I cleared my throat in the orthodox manner, and fixed my eyes on Runi, who, on his part, made a slight movement to indicate that he was ready to listen to what I had to say.

My speech was long, lasting at least half an hour, delivered in a profound silence; it was chiefly occupied with an account of my wanderings in Guayana; and being little more than a catalogue of names of all the places I had visited, and the tribes and chief or head men with whom I had come in contact, I was able to speak continuously, and so to hide my ignorance of a dialect which was still new to me. The Guayana savage judges a man for his staying powers. To stand as motionless as a bronze statue for one or two hours watching for a bird; to sit or lie still for half a day; to endure pain, not seldom self-inflicted, without wincing; and when delivering a speech to pour it out in a copious stream, without pausing to take breath or hesitating over a word—to be able to do all this is to prove yourself a man, an equal, one to be respected and even made a friend of. What I really wished to say to him was put in a few words at the conclusion of my well-nigh meaningless oration. Everywhere, I said, I had been the Indian's friend, and I wished to be his friend, to live with him at Parahuari, even as I had lived with other chiefs and heads of villages and families; to be looked on by him, as these others had looked on me, not as a stranger or a white man, but as a friend, a brother, an Indian.

I ceased speaking, and there was a slight murmurous sound in the room, as of wind long pent up in many lungs suddenly exhaled; while Runi, still unmoved, emitted a low grunt. Then I rose, and detaching the silver ornament from my cloak presented it to him. He accepted it; not very graciously, as a stranger to these people might have imagined; but I was satisfied, feeling sure that I had made a favourable impression. After a little he handed the box to the person sitting next to him, who examined it and passed it on to a third, and in this way it went round and came back once more to Runi. Then he called for a drink. There happened to be a store of casserie* in the house; probably the women had been busy for some days past in making it, little thinking that it was destined to be prematurely consumed. A large jarful was produced; Runi politely quaffed the first cup; I followed; then the others; and the women drank also, a woman taking about one cupful to a man's three. Runi and I, however, drank the most, for we had our positions as the two principal personages there to maintain. Tongues were loosened now; for the alcohol, small as the quantity contained in this mild liquor is, had begun to tell on our brains. I had not their pottle-shaped stomach, made to hold unlimited quantities of meat and drink; but I was determined on this most important occasion not to deserve my host's contempt—to be compared, perhaps, to the small bird that delicately picks up six drops of water in its bill and is satisfied. I would measure my strength against his, and if necessary drink myself into a state of insensibility. At last I was scarcely able to stand on my legs. But even the seasoned old savage was affected by this time. *In vino veritas*, said the ancients; and the principle holds good where there is no vinum, but only mild casserie. Runi now informed me that he had once known a white man, that he was a bad man, which had caused him to say that all white men were bad; even as David, still more sweepingly, had proclaimed that all men were liars.* Now he found that it was not so, that I was a good man. His friendliness increased with intoxication. He presented me with a curious little tinder-box, made from the conical tail of an armadillo, hollowed out, and provided with a wooden stopper;—this to be used in place of the box I had deprived myself of. He also furnished me with a grass hammock, and had it hung up there and then, so that I could lie down when inclined. There was nothing he would not do for me. And at last, when many more cups had been emptied, and a third or fourth jar brought out, he began to unburthen his heart of its dark and dangerous secrets. He shed tears—for the 'man without a tear' dwells not in the woods of Guayana: tears for those who had been treacherously slain long years ago; for his father, who had been killed by Tripica, the father of Managa, who was still above ground. But let him and all his people beware of Runi. He had spilt their blood before, he had fed the fox and vulture with their flesh, and would never rest while Managa lived with his people at Uritay—the five hills of Uritay, which were two days' journey from Parahuari. While thus talking of his old enemy he lashed himself into a kind of frenzy, smiting his chest and gnashing his teeth; and finally seizing a spear, he buried its point deep into the clay floor, only to wrench it out and strike it into the earth again and again, to show how he would serve Managa, and any one of Managa's people he might meet with—man, woman, or child. Then he staggered out from the door to flourish his spear; and looking to the north-west, he shouted aloud to Managa to come and slay his people and burn down his house, as he had so often threatened to do.

'Let him come! Let Managa come!' I cried, staggering out after him. 'I am your friend, your brother; I have no spear and no arrows, but I have this—this!' And here I drew out and flourished my revolver. 'Where is Managa?' I continued. 'Where are the hills of Uritay?' He pointed to a star low down in the south-west. 'Then,' I shouted, 'let this bullet find Managa, sitting by the fire among his people, and let him fall and pour out his blood on the ground!' And with that I discharged my pistol in the direction he had pointed to. A scream of terror burst out from the women and children, while Runi at my side, in an access of fierce delight and admiration, turned and embraced me. It was the first and last embrace I ever suffered from a naked male savage, and although this did not seem a time for fastidious feelings, to be hugged to his sweltering body was an unpleasant experience.

More cups of casserie followed this outburst; and at last, unable to keep it up any longer, I staggered to my hammock; but being unable to get into it, Runi, overflowing with kindness, came to my assistance, whereupon we fell and rolled together on the floor. Finally, I was raised by the others and tumbled into my swinging bed, and fell at once into a deep, dreamless sleep, from which I did not awake until after sunrise on the following morning.

CHAPTER II

IT is fortunate that casserie is manufactured by an extremely slow, laborious process, since the women, who are the drink-makers, in the first place have to reduce the material (cassava bread) to a pulp by means of their own molars, after which it is watered down and put away in troughs to ferment. Great is the diligence of these willing slaves; but, work how they will, they can only satisfy their lords' love of a big drink at long intervals. Such a function as that at which I had assisted is therefore the result of much patient mastication and silent fermentation—the delicate flower of a plant that has been a long time growing.

Having now established myself as one of the family, at the cost of some disagreeable sensations and a pang or two of self-disgust, I resolved to let nothing further trouble me at Parahuari, but to live the easy, careless life of the idle man, joining in hunting and fishing expeditions when in the mood; at other times enjoying existence in my own way, apart from my fellows, conversing with wild nature in that solitary place.

Besides Runi, there were, in our little community, two oldish men, his cousins I believe, who had wives and grown-up children. Another family consisted of Piaké, Runi's nephew, his brother Kua-kó—about whom there will be much to say—and a sister Oalava. Piaké had a wife and two children; Kua-kó was unmarried and about nineteen or twenty years old; Oalava was the youngest of the three. Last of all, who should perhaps have been first, was Runi's mother, called Cla-cla, probably in imitation of the cry of some bird, for in these latitudes a person is rarely, perhaps never, called by his or her real name, which is a secret jealously preserved, even from near relations.* I believe that Cla-cla herself was the only living being who knew the name her parents had bestowed on her at birth. She was a very old woman, spare in figure, brown as old sun-baked leather, her face written over with innumerable wrinkles, and her long coarse hair perfectly white; yet she was exceedingly active, and seemed to do more work than any other woman in the community; more than that, when the day's toil was over and nothing remained for the others to do, then Cla-cla's night work would begin; and this was to talk all the others, or at all events all the men, to sleep. She was like a self-regulating machine, and punctually every evening, when the door was closed, and the night-fire made up, and every man in his hammock, she would set herself going, telling the most interminable stories, until the last listener was fast asleep: later in the night, if any man woke with a snort or grunt, off she would go again, taking up the thread of the tale where she had dropped it.

Old Cla-cla amused me very much, by night and day, and I seldom tired of watching her owlish countenance as she sat by the fire, never allowing it to sink low for want of fuel; always studying the pot when it was on to simmer, and at the same time attending to the movements of the others about her, ready at a moment's notice to give assistance or to dart out on a stray chicken or refractory child.

So much did she amuse me, although without intending it, that I thought it would be only fair, in my turn, to do something for her entertainment. I was engaged one day in shaping a wooden foil with my knife, whistling and singing snatches of old melodies at my work, when all at once I caught sight of the ancient dame looking greatly delighted, chuckling internally, nodding her head, and keeping time with her hands. Evidently she was able to appreciate a style of music superior to that of the aboriginals, and forthwith I abandoned my foils for the time and set about the manufacture of a guitar, which cost me much labour, and brought out more ingenuity than I had ever thought myself capable of. To reduce the wood to the right thinness, then to bend and fasten it with wooden pegs and with gums, to add the arm, frets, keys, and finally the catgut strings—those of another kind being out of the question—kept me busy for some days. When completed it was a rude instrument, scarcely tunable; nevertheless when I smote the strings, playing lively music, or accompanied myself in singing, I found that it was a great success, and so was as much pleased with my own performance as if I had had the most perfect guitar ever made in old Spain. I also skipped about the floor, strum-strumming at the same time, instructing them in the most lively dances of the whites, in which the feet must be as nimble as the player's fingers. It is true that these exhibitions were always witnessed by the adults with a profound gravity, which would have disheartened a stranger to their ways. They were a set of hollow bronze statues that looked at me, but I knew that the living animals inside of them were tickled at my singing, strumming, and pirouetting. Cla-cla was, however, an exception, and encouraged me not infrequently by emitting a sound, half cackle and half screech, by way of laughter; for she had come to her second childhood, or, at all events, had dropped the stolid mask which the young Guayana savage, in imitation of his elders, adjusts to his face at about the age of twelve, to wear it thereafter all his life long, or only to drop it occasionally when very drunk. The youngsters also openly manifested their pleasure, although, as a rule, they try to restrain their feelings in the presence of grown-up people, and with them I became a great favourite.

By-and-by I returned to my foil-making, and gave them fencing lessons, and sometimes invited two or three of the biggest boys to attack me simultaneously, just to show how easily I could disarm and kill them. This practice excited some interest in Kua-kó, who had a little more of curiosity and geniality and less of the put-on dignity of the others, and with him I became most intimate. Fencing with Kua-kó was highly amusing: no sooner was he in position, foil in hand, than all my instructions were thrown to the winds, and he would charge and attack me in his own barbarous manner, with the result that I would send his foil spinning a dozen yards away, while he, struck motionless, would gaze after it in open-mouthed astonishment.

Three weeks had passed by not unpleasantly when, one morning, I took it into my head to walk by myself across that somewhat sterile savannah west of the village and stream, which ended, as I have said, in a long, low, stony ridge. From the village there was nothing to attract the eye in that direction; but I wished to get a better view of that great solitary hill or mountain of Ytaioa, and of the cloud-like summits beyond it in the distance. From the stream the ground rose in a gradual slope, and the highest part of the ridge for which I made was about two miles from the starting-point—a parched brown plain, with nothing growing on it but scattered tussocks of sere hair-like grass.

When I reached the top and could see the country beyond, I was agreeably disappointed at the discovery that the sterile ground extended only about a mile and a quarter on the further side, and was succeeded by a forest—a very inviting patch of woodland covering five or six square miles, occupying a kind of oblong basin, extending from the foot of Ytaioa on the north to a low range of rocky hills on the south. From the wooded basin long narrow strips of forest ran out in various directions like the arms of an octopus, one pair embracing the slopes of Ytaioa, another much broader belt extending along a valley which cut through the ridge of hills on the south side at right angles, and was lost to sight beyond; far away in the west and south and north distant mountains appeared, not in regular ranges, but in groups or singly, or looking like blue banked-up clouds on the horizon.

Glad at having discovered the existence of this forest so near home, and wondering why my Indian friends had never taken me to it, or ever went out on that side, I set forth with a light heart to explore it for myself, regretting only that I was without a proper weapon for procuring game. The walk from the ridge over the savannah was easy, as the barren, stony ground sloped downward the whole way. The outer part of the wood on my side was very open, composed in most part of dwarf trees that grow on stony soil, and scattered thorny bushes bearing a yellow pea-shaped blossom. Presently I came to thicker wood, where the trees were much taller and in greater variety; and after this came another sterile strip, like that on the edge of the wood, where stone cropped out from the ground and nothing grew except the yellow-flowered thorn bushes. Passing this sterile ribbon, which seemed to extend to a considerable distance north and south, and was fifty to a hundred yards wide, the forest again became dense and the trees large, with much undergrowth in places obstructing the view and making progress difficult.

I spent several hours in this wild paradise, which was so much more delightful than the extensive gloomier forests I had so often penetrated in Guayana: for here, if the trees did not attain to such majestic proportions, the variety of vegetable forms was even greater; as far as I went it was nowhere dark under the trees, and the number of lovely parasites everywhere illustrated the kindly influence of light and air. Even where the trees were largest the sunshine penetrated, subdued by the foliage to exquisite greenish-golden tints, filling the wide lower spaces with tender half-lights, and faint blue-and-grey shadows. Lying on my back and gazing up, I felt reluctant to rise and renew my ramble. For what a roof was that above my head! Roof I call it, just as the poets in their poverty sometimes describe the infinite ethereal sky by that word; but it was no more roof-like and hindering to the soaring spirit than the higher clouds that float in changing forms and tints, and like the foliage chasten the intolerable noonday beams. How far above me seemed that leafy cloudland into which I gazed! Nature, we know, first taught the architect to produce by long colonnades the illusion of distance; but the light-excluding roof prevents him from getting the same effect above. Here Nature is unapproachable with her green, airy canopy, a sun-impregnated cloud—cloud above cloud; and though the highest may be unreached by the eye, the beams yet filter through, illuming the wide spaces beneath—chamber succeeded by chamber, each with its own special lights and shadows. Far above me, but not nearly so far as it seemed, the tender gloom of one such chamber or space is traversed now by a golden shaft of light falling through some break in the upper foliage, giving a strange glory to everything it touches—projecting leaves, and beard-like tuft of moss, and snaky bush-rope. And in the most open part of that most open space, suspended on nothing to the eye, the shaft reveals a tangle of shining silver threads—the web of some large tree-spider. These seemingly distant, yet distinctly visible threads, serve to remind me that the human artist is only able to get his horizontal distance by a monotonous reduplication of pillar and arch, placed at regular intervals, and that the least departure from this order would destroy the effect. But Nature produces her effects at random, and seems only to increase the beautiful illusion by that infinite variety of decoration in which she revels, binding tree to tree in a tangle of anaconda-like lianas, and dwindling down from these huge cables to airy webs and hair-like fibres that vibrate to the wind of the passing insect's wing.

Thus in idleness, with such thoughts for company, I spent my time, glad that no human being, savage or civilised, was with me. It was better to be alone to listen to the monkeys that chattered without offending; to watch them occupied with the unserious business of their lives. With that luxuriant tropical nature, its green clouds and illusive aerial spaces, full of mystery, they harmonised well in language, appearance and motions;—mountebank angels, living their fantastic lives far above earth in a half-way heaven of their own.

I saw more monkeys on that morning than I usually saw in the course of a week's rambling. And other animals were seen; I particularly remember two accouries* I startled, that after rushing away a few yards stopped and stood peering back at me as if not knowing whether to regard me as friend or enemy. Birds, too, were strangely abundant; and altogether this struck me as being the richest hunting-ground I had seen, and it astonished me to think that the Indians of the village did not appear to visit it.

On my return in the afternoon I gave an enthusiastic account of my day's ramble, speaking not of the things that had moved my soul, but only to those which move the Guayana Indian's soul—the animal food he craves, and which, one would imagine, Nature would prefer him to do without, so hard he finds it to wrest a sufficiency from her. To my surprise they shook their heads and looked troubled at what I said; and finally, my host informed me that the wood I had been in was a dangerous place; that if they went there to hunt a great injury would be done to them; and he finished by advising me not to visit it again.

I began to understand from their looks and the old man's vague words that their fear of the wood was superstitious. If dangerous creatures had existed there—tigers, or camoodis,* or solitary murderous savages—they would have said so; but when I pressed them with questions they could only repeat that 'something bad' existed in the place, that animals were abundant there because no Indian who valued his life dared venture into it. I replied that unless they gave me some more definite information I should certainly go again, and put myself in the way of the danger they feared.

My reckless courage, as they considered it, surprised them; but they had already begun to find out that their superstitions had no effect on me, that I listened to them as to stories invented to amuse a child, and for the moment they made no further attempt to dissuade me.

Next day I returned to the forest of evil report, which had now a new and even greater charm—the fascination of the unknown and the mysterious; still, the warning I had received made me distrustful and cautious at first, for I could not help thinking about it. When we consider how much of their life is passed in the woods, which become as familiar to them as the streets of our native town to us, it seems almost incredible that these savages have a superstitious fear of all forests, fearing them as much, even in the bright light of day, as a nervous child with memory filled with ghost-stories fears a dark room. But, like the child in the dark room, they fear the forest only when alone in it, and for this reason always hunt in couples or parties. What, then, prevented them from visiting this particular wood, which offered so tempting a harvest? The question troubled me not a little; at the same time I was ashamed of the feeling, and fought against it; and in the end I made my way to the same sequestered spot where I had rested so long on my previous visit.

In this place I witnessed a new thing, and had a strange experience. Sitting on the ground in the shade of a large tree, I began to hear a confused noise as of a coming tempest of wind mixed with shrill calls and cries. Nearer and nearer it came, and at last a multitude of birds of many kinds, but mostly small, appeared in sight swarming through the trees, some running on the trunks and larger branches, others flitting through the foliage, and many keeping on the wing, now hovering and now darting this way or that. They were all busily searching for and pursuing the insects, moving on at the same time, and in a very few minutes they had finished examining the trees near me, and were gone; but not satisfied with what I had witnessed, I jumped up and rushed after the flock to keep it in sight. All my caution and all recollection of what the Indians had said was now forgot, so great was my interest in this bird-army; but as they moved on without pause they quickly left me behind, and presently my career was stopped by an impenetrable tangle of bushes, vines, and roots of large trees extending like huge cables along the ground. In the midst of this leafy labyrinth I sat down on a projecting root to cool my blood before attempting to make my way back to my former position. After that tempest of motion and confused noises the silence of the forest seemed very profound; but before I had been resting many moments it was broken by a low strain of exquisite bird-melody, wonderfully pure and expressive, unlike any musical sound I had ever heard before. It seemed to issue from a thick cluster of broad leaves of a creeper only a few yards from where I sat. With my eyes fixed on this green hiding-place I waited with suspended breath for its repetition, wondering whether any civilised being had ever listened to such a strain before. Surely not, I thought, else the fame of so divine a melody would long ago have been noised abroad. I thought of the rialejo, the celebrated organ-bird or flute-bird, and of the various ways in which hearers are affected by it. To some its warbling is like the sound of a beautiful mysterious instrument, while to others it seems like the singing of a blithe-hearted child with a highly melodious voice.*
I had often heard and listened with delight to the singing of the rialejo in the Guayana forests, but this song, or musical phrase, was utterly unlike it in character. It was pure, more expressive,

softer—so low that at a distance of forty yards I could hardly have heard it. But its greatest charm was its resemblance to the human voice—a voice purified and brightened to something almost angelic. Imagine, then, my impatience as I sat there straining my sense, my deep disappointment when it was not repeated! I rose at length very reluctantly and slowly began making my way back; but when I had progressed about thirty yards, again the sweet voice sounded just behind me, and turning quickly I stood still and waited. The same voice, but not the same song—not the same phrase; the notes were different, more varied and rapidly enunciated, as if the singer had been more excited. The blood rushed to my heart as I listened; my nerves tingled with a strange new delight, the rapture produced by such music heightened by a sense of mystery. Before many moments I heard it again, not rapid now, but a soft warbling, lower than at first, infinitely sweet and tender, sinking to lisping sounds that soon ceased to be audible; the whole having lasted as long as it would take me to repeat a sentence of a dozen words. This seemed the singer's farewell to me, for I waited and listened in vain to hear it repeated; and after getting back to the starting-point I sat for upwards of an hour, still hoping to hear it once more!

The westering sun at length compelled me to quit the wood, but not before I had resolved to return the next morning and seek for the spot where I had met with so enchanting an experience. After crossing the sterile belt I have mentioned within the wood, and just before I came to the open outer edge where the stunted trees and bushes die away on the border of the savannah, what was my delight and astonishment at hearing the mysterious melody once more! It seemed to issue from a clump of bushes close by; but by this time I had come to the conclusion that there was a ventriloquism in this woodland voice which made it impossible for me to determine its exact direction. Of one thing I was, however, now quite convinced, and that was that the singer had been following me all the time. Again and again as I stood there listening it sounded, now so faint and apparently far off as to be scarcely audible; then all at once it would ring out bright and clear within a few yards of me, as if the shy little thing had suddenly grown bold; but, far or near, the vocalist remained invisible, and at length the tantalising melody ceased altogether.

CHAPTER III

I was not disappointed on my next visit to the forest, nor on several succeeding visits; and this seemed to show that if I was right in believing that these strange, melodious utterances proceeded from one individual, then the bird or being, although still refusing to show itself, was always on the watch for my appearance, and followed me wherever I went. This thought only served to increase my curiosity; I was constantly pondering over the subject, and at last concluded that it would be best to induce one of the Indians to go with me to the wood on the chance of his being able to explain the mystery.

One of the treasures I had managed to preserve in my sojourn with these children of nature, who were always anxious to become possessors of my belongings, was a small prettily fashioned metal match-box, opening with a spring. Remembering that Kua-kó, among others, had looked at this trifle with covetous eyes—the covetous way in which they all looked at it had given it a fictitious value in my own—I tried to bribe him with the offer of it to accompany me to my favourite haunt. The brave young hunter refused again and again; but on each occasion he offered to perform some other service or to give me something in exchange for the box. At last I told him that I would give it to the first person who should accompany me, and fearing that someone would be found valiant enough to win the prize, he at length plucked up a spirit, and on the next day, seeing me going out for a walk, he all at once offered to go with me. He cunningly tried to get the box before starting—his cunning, poor youth! was not very deep. I told him that the forest we were about to visit abounded with plants and birds unlike any I had seen elsewhere, that I wished to learn their names, and everything about them, and that when I had got the required information the box would be his—not sooner. Finally we started, he, as usual, armed with his zabatana,* with which, I imagined, he would procure more game than usually fell to his little poisoned arrows. When we reached the wood I could see that he was ill at ease: nothing would persuade him to go into the deeper parts; and even where it was very open and light he was constantly gazing into bushes and shadowy places, as if expecting to see some frightful creature lying in wait for him.

This behaviour might have had a disquieting effect on me had I not been thoroughly convinced that his fears were purely superstitious, and that there could be no dangerous animal in a spot I was accustomed to walk in every day. My plan was to ramble about with an unconcerned air, occasionally pointing out an uncommon tree or shrub or vine, or calling his attention to a distant bird cry and asking the bird's name, in the hope that the mysterious voice would make itself heard, and that he would be able to give me some explanation of it. But for upwards of two hours we moved about, hearing nothing except the usual bird-voices, and during all that time he never stirred a yard from my side nor made an attempt to capture anything. At length we sat down under a tree, in an open spot close to the border of the wood. He sat down very reluctantly, and seemed more troubled in his mind than ever, keeping his eyes continually roving about, while he listened intently to every sound. The sounds were not few, owing to the abundance of animal and especially of bird life in this favoured spot. I began to question my companion as to some of the cries we heard. There were notes and cries familiar to me as the crowing of the cock—parrot screams and yelping of toucans, the distant wailing calls of maam and duraquara; and shrill laughter-like notes of the large tree-climber as it passed from tree to tree; the quick whistle of cotingas; and strange throbbing and thrilling sounds, as of pigmies beating on metallic drums, of the skulking pitta-thrushes; and with these mingled other notes less well known.* One came from the treetops, where it was perpetually wandering amid the foliage— a low note, repeated at intervals of a few seconds, so thin and mournful and full of mystery, that I half expected to hear that it proceeded from the restless ghost of some dead bird. But no; he only said it was uttered by a 'little bird'—too little presumably to have a name. From the foliage of a neighbouring tree came a few tinkling chirps, as of a small mandolin, two or three strings of which had been carelessly struck by the player. He said that it came from a small green frog that lived in trees; and in this way my rude Indian—vexed perhaps at being asked such trivial questions—brushed away the pretty fantasies my mind had woven in the woodland solitude. For I often listened to this tinkling music, and it had suggested the idea that the place was frequented by a tribe of fairy-like troubadour monkeys, and that if I could only be quick-sighted enough I might one day be able to detect the minstrel sitting, in a green tunic perhaps, cross-legged on some high, swaying bough, carelessly touching his mandolin suspended from his neck by a yellow ribbon.

By-and-by a bird came with low, swift flight, its great tail spread open fan-wise, and perched itself on an exposed bough not thirty yards from us. It was all of a chestnut-red colour, long-bodied, in size like a big pigeon:* its actions showed that its curiosity had been greatly excited, for it jerked from side to side, eyeing us first with one eye, then the other, while its long tail rose and fell in a measured way.

'Look, Kua-kó,' I said in a whisper, 'there is a bird for you to kill.'

But he only shook his head, still watchful.

'Give me the blow-pipe, then,' I said, with a laugh, putting out my hand to take it. But he refused to let me take it, knowing that it would only be an arrow wasted if I attempted to shoot anything.

As I persisted in telling him to kill the bird, he at last bent his lips near me and said in a half-whisper, as if fearful of being overheard, 'I can kill nothing here. If I shot at the bird the daughter of the Didi would catch the dart in her hand and throw it back and hit me here,' touching his breast just over his heart.

I laughed again, saying to myself, with some amusement, that Kua-kó was not such a bad companion after all—that he was not without imagination. But in spite of my laughter his words roused my interest, and suggested the idea that the voice I was curious about had been heard by the Indians, and was as great a mystery to them as to me; since not being like that of any creature known to them, it would be attributed by their superstitious minds to one of the numerous demons or semi-human monsters inhabiting every forest, stream, and mountain; and fear of it would drive them from the wood. In this case, judging from my companion's words, they had varied the form of the superstition somewhat, inventing a daughter of a water-spirit* to be afraid of. My thought was that if their keen, practised eyes had never been able to see this flitting woodland creature with a musical soul, it was not likely that I would succeed in my quest.

I began to question him, but he now appeared less inclined to talk and more frightened than ever, and each time I attempted to speak he imposed silence, with a quick gesture of alarm, while he continued to stare about him with dilated eyes. All at once he sprang to his feet as if overcome with terror, and started running at full speed. His fear infected me, and, springing up, I followed as fast as I could, but he was far ahead of me, running for dear life; and before I had gone forty yards my feet were caught in a creeper trailing along the surface, and I measured my length on the ground. The sudden, violent shock almost took away my senses for a moment, but when I jumped up and stared round to see no unspeakable monster—Curupitá* or other— rushing on to slay and devour me there and then, I began to feel ashamed of my cowardice; and in the end I turned and walked back to the spot I had just quitted and sat down once more. I even tried to hum a tune, just to prove to myself that I had completely recovered from the panic caught from the miserable Indian; but it is never possible in such cases to get back one's serenity immediately, and a vague suspicion continued to trouble me for a time. After sitting there for half an hour or so, listening to distant bird sounds, I began to recover my old confidence, and even to feel inclined to penetrate further into the wood. All at once, making me almost jump, so sudden it was, so much nearer and louder than I had ever heard it before, the mysterious melody began. Unmistakably it was uttered by the same being heard on former occasions; but to-day it was different in character. The utterance was far more rapid, with fewer silent intervals, and it had none of the usual tenderness in it, nor ever once sunk to that low, whisper-like talking, which had seemed to me as if the spirit of the wind had breathed its low sighs in syllables and speech. Now it was not only loud, rapid, and continuous, but, while still musical, there was an incisiveness in it, a sharp ring as of resentment, which made it strike painfully on the sense.

The impression of an intelligent unhuman being addressing me in anger took so firm a hold on my mind that the old fear returned, and, rising, I began to walk rapidly away, intending to escape from the wood. The voice continued violently rating me, as it seemed to my mind, moving with me, which caused me to accelerate my steps; and very soon I would have broken into a run, when its character began to change again. There were pauses now, intervals of silence, long or short, and after each one the voice came to my ear with a more subdued and dulcet sound—more of that melting, flute-like quality it had possessed at other times; and this softness of tone, coupled with the talking-like form of utterance, gave me the idea of a being no longer incensed, addressing me now in a peaceable spirit, reasoning away my unworthy tremors, and imploring me to remain with it in the wood. Strange as this voice without a body was, and always productive of a slightly uncomfortable feeling on account of its mystery, it seemed impossible to doubt that it came to me now in a spirit of pure friendliness; and when I had recovered my composure I found a new delight in listening to it—all the greater because of the fear so lately experienced, and of its seeming intelligence. For the third time I re-seated myself on the same spot, and at intervals the voice talked to me there for some time, and to my fancy expressed satisfaction and pleasure at my presence. But later, without losing its friendly tone, it changed again. It seemed to move away and to be thrown back from a considerable distance; and, at long intervals, it would approach me again with a new sound, which I began to interpret as of command, or entreaty. Was it, I asked myself, inviting me to follow? And if I obeyed, to what delightful discoveries or frightful dangers might it lead? My curiosity, together with the belief that the being—I called it being, not bird, now—was friendly to me, overcame all timidity, and I rose and walked at random towards the interior of the wood. Very soon I had no doubt left that the being had desired me to follow; for there was now a new note of gladness in its voice, and it continued near me as I walked, at intervals approaching me so closely as to set me staring into the surrounding shadowy places like poor scared Kua-kó.

On this occasion, too, I began to have a new fancy, for fancy or illusion I was determined to regard it, that some swift-footed being was treading the ground near me; that I occasionally caught the faint rustle of a light footstep, and detected a motion in leaves and fronds and thread-like stems of creepers hanging near the surface, as if some passing body had touched and made them tremble; and once or twice that I even had a glimpse of a grey, misty object moving at no great distance in the deeper shadows.

Led by this wandering tricksy being, I came to a spot where the trees were very large and the damp dark ground almost free from undergrowth; and here the voice ceased to be heard. After patiently waiting and listening for some time I began to look about me with a slight feeling of apprehension. It was still about two hours before sunset; only in this place the shade of the vast trees made a perpetual twilight: moreover, it was strangely silent here, the few bird cries that reached me coming from a long distance. I had flattered myself that the voice had become to some extent intelligible to me; its outburst of anger caused no doubt by my cowardly flight after the Indian; then its recovered friendliness which had induced me to return; and, finally, its desire to be followed. Now that it had led me to this place of shadow and profound silence, and had ceased to speak and to lead, I could not help thinking that this was my goal, that I had been brought to this spot with a purpose, that in this wild and solitary retreat some tremendous adventure was about to befall me.

As the silence continued unbroken there was time to dwell on this thought. I gazed before me and listened intently, scarcely breathing, until the suspense became painful—too painful at last, and I turned and took a step with the idea of going back to the border of the wood, when close by, clear as a silver bell, sounded the voice once more, but only for a moment—two or three syllables in response to my movement, then it was silent again.

Once more I was standing still, as if in obedience to a command, in the same state of suspense; and whether the change was real or only imagined I know not, but the silence every minute grew more profound and the gloom deeper. Imaginary terrors began to assail me. Ancient fables of men allured by beautiful forms and melodious voices to destruction all at once acquired a fearful significance. I recalled some of the Indian beliefs, especially that of the misshapen, man-devouring monster who is said to beguile his victims into the dark forest by mimicking the human voice—the voice sometimes of a woman in distress—or by singing some strange and beautiful melody. I grew almost afraid to look round lest I should catch sight of him stealing towards me on his huge feet with toes pointing backwards, his mouth snarling horribly to display his great green fangs.* It was distressing to have such fancies in this wild, solitary spot— hateful to feel their power over me when I knew that they were nothing but fancies and creations of the savage mind. But if these supernatural beings had no existence, there were other monsters, only too real, in these woods which it would be dreadful to encounter alone and unarmed, since against such adversaries a revolver would be as ineffectual as a popgun. Some huge camoodi, able to crush my bones like brittle twigs in its constricting coils, might lurk in these shadows, and approach me stealthily, unseen in its dark colour on the dark ground. Or some jaguar or black tiger* might steal towards me, masked by a bush or tree-trunk, to spring upon me unawares. Or worse still, this way might suddenly come a pack of those swift-footed, unspeakably terrible hunting-leopards,* from which every living thing in the forest flies with shrieks of consternation or else

Green Mansions

falls paralysed in their path to be instantly torn to pieces and devoured.

A slight rustling sound in the foliage above me made me start and cast up my eyes. High up, where a pale gleam of tempered sunlight fell through the leaves, a grotesque human-like face, black as ebony and adorned with a great red beard, appeared staring down upon me. In another moment it was gone. It was only a large araguato, or howling monkey, but I was so unnerved that I could not get rid of the idea that it was something more than a monkey. Once more I moved, and again, the instant I moved my foot, clear, and keen, and imperative, sounded the voice! It was no longer possible to doubt its meaning. It commanded me to stand still—to wait—to watch—to listen! Had it cried 'Listen! Do not move!' I could not have understood it better. Trying as the suspense was, I now felt powerless to escape. Something very terrible, I felt convinced, was about to happen, either to destroy or to release me from the spell that held me.

And while I stood thus rooted to the ground, the sweat standing in large drops on my forehead, all at once close to me sounded a cry, fine and clear at first, and rising at the end to a shriek so loud, piercing, and unearthly in character that the blood seemed to freeze in my veins, and a despairing cry to heaven escaped my lips; then, before that long shriek expired, a mighty chorus of thunderous voices burst forth around me; and in this awful tempest of sound I trembled like a leaf; and the leaves on the trees were agitated as if by a high wind, and the earth itself seemed to shake beneath my feet. Indescribably horrible were my sensations at that moment; I was deafened, and would possibly have been maddened had I not, as by a miracle, chanced to see a large araguato on a branch overhead, roaring with open mouth and inflated throat and chest.

It was simply a concert of howling monkeys which had so terrified me! But my extreme fear was not strange in the circumstances; since everything that had led up to the display, the gloom and silence, the period of suspense and my heated imagination, had raised my mind to the highest degree of excitement and expectancy. I had rightly conjectured, no doubt, that my unseen guide had led me to that spot for a purpose; and the purpose had been to set me in the midst of a congregation of araguatos to enable me for the first time fully to appreciate their unparalleled vocal powers. I had always heard them at a distance: here they were gathered in scores, possibly hundreds—

the whole araguato population of the forest, I should think—close to me; and it may give some faint conception of the tremendous power and awful character of the sound thus produced by their combined voices when I say that this animal—miscalled 'howler' in English— would out-roar the mightiest lion that ever woke the echoes of an African wilderness.

This roaring concert, which lasted three or four minutes, having ended, I lingered a few minutes longer on the spot, and not hearing the voice again, went back to the edge of the wood, and then started on my way back to the village.

CHAPTER IV

PERHAPS I was not capable of thinking quite coherently on what had just happened until I was once more fairly outside of the forest shadows—out in that clear open daylight, where things seem what they are, and imagination, like a juggler detected and laughed at, hastily takes itself out of the way. As I walked homewards I paused midway on the barren ridge to gaze back on the scene I had left, and then the recent adventure began to take a semi-ludicrous aspect in my mind. All that circumstance of preparation, that mysterious prelude to something unheard of, unimaginable, surpassing all fables ancient and modern, and all tragedies—to end at last in a concert of howling monkeys! Certainly the concert was very grand, indeed one of the most astounding in nature, but still—I sat down on a stone and laughed freely.

The sun was sinking behind the forest, its broad red disc still showing through the topmost leaves, and the higher part of the foliage was of a luminous green, like green flame, throwing off flakes of quivering, fiery light, but lower down the trees were in profound shadow.

I felt very light-hearted while I gazed on this scene! for how pleasant it was just now to think of the strange experience I had passed through—to think that I had come safely out of it, that no human eye had witnessed my weakness, and that the mystery existed still to fascinate me! For, ludicrous as the dénouement now looked, the cause of all, the voice itself, was a thing to marvel at more than ever. That it proceeded from an intelligent being I was firmly convinced; and although too materialistic in my way of thinking to admit for a moment that it was a supernatural being, I still felt that there was something more than I had at first imagined in Kua-kó's speech about a daughter of the Didi. That the Indians knew a great deal about the mysterious voice, and had held it in great fear, seemed evident. But they were savages, with ways that were not mine; and however friendly they might be towards one of a superior race, there was always in their relations with him a low cunning, prompted partly by suspicion, underlying their words and actions. For the white man to put himself mentally on their level is not more impossible than for these aborigines to be perfectly open, as children are, towards the white. Whatever subject the stranger within their gates exhibits an interest in, that they will be reticent about; and their reticence, which conceals itself under easily invented lies or an affected stupidity, invariably increases with his desire for information. It was plain to them that some very unusual interest took me to the wood, consequently I could not expect that they would tell me anything they might know to enlighten me about the matter; and I concluded that Kua-kó's words about the daughter of the Didi, and what she would do if he blew an arrow at a bird, had accidentally escaped him in a moment of excitement. Nothing, therefore, was to be gained by questioning them, or, at all events, by telling them how much the subject attracted me. And I had nothing to fear; my independent investigations had made this much clear to me; the voice might proceed from a very frolicsome and tricksy* creature, full of wild fantastic humours, but nothing worse. It was friendly to me, I felt sure; at the same time it might not be friendly towards the Indians; for, on that day, it had made itself heard only after my companion had taken flight; and it had then seemed incensed against me, possibly because the savage had been in my company.

That was the result of my reflections on the day's events, when I returned to my entertainer's roof, and sat down among my friends to refresh myself with stewed fowl and fish from the household pot, into which a hospitable woman invited me with a gesture to dip my fingers.

Kua-kó was lying in his hammock, smoking, I think—certainly not reading. When I entered he lifted his head and stared at me, probably surprised to see me alive, unharmed, and in a placid temper. I laughed at the look, and somewhat disconcerted, he dropped his head down again. After a minute or two I took the metal match-box and tossed it on to his breast. He clutched it, and starting up, stared at me in the utmost astonishment. He could scarcely believe his good fortune; for he had failed to carry out his part of the compact and had resigned himself to the loss of the coveted prize. Jumping down to the floor, he held up the box triumphantly, his joy overcoming the habitual stolid look; while all the others gathered about him, each trying to get the box into his own hands to admire it again, notwithstanding that they had all seen it a dozen times before. But it was Kua-kó's now and not the stranger's, and therefore more nearly their own than formerly, and must look different, more beautiful, with a brighter polish on the metal. And that wonderful enamelled cock on the lid—figured in Paris probably, but just like a cock in Guayana, the pet bird which they no more think of killing and eating than we do our purring pussies and lemon-coloured canaries—must now look more strikingly valiant and cock-like than ever, with its crimson comb and wattles, burnished red hackles, and dark green arching tail-plumes. But Kua-kó, while willing enough to have it admired and praised, would not let it out of his hands, and told them pompously that it was not theirs for them to handle, but his—Kua-kó's—for all time; that he had won it by accompanying me—valorous man that he was!—to that evil wood into which they—timid, inferior creatures that they were!—would never have ventured to set foot. I am not translating his words, but that was what he gave them to understand pretty plainly, to my great amusement.

After the excitement was over, Runi, who had maintained a dignified calm, made some roundabout remarks, apparently with the object of eliciting an account of what I had seen and heard in the forest of evil fame. I replied carelessly that I had seen a great many birds and monkeys—monkeys so tame that I might have procured one if I had had a blow-pipe, in spite of my never having practised shooting with that weapon.

It interested them to hear about the abundance and tameness of the monkeys, although it was scarcely news: but how tame they must have been when I, the stranger not to the manner born—not naked, brown-skinned, lynx-eyed, and noiseless as an owl in his movements—had yet been able to look closely at them! Runi only remarked, apropos of what I had told him, that they could not go there to hunt; then he asked me if I feared nothing.

'Nothing,' I replied carelessly. 'The things you fear hurt not the white man, and are no more than this to me,' saying which I took up a little white wood-ash in my hand and blew it away with my breath. 'And against other enemies I have this,' I added, touching my revolver. A brave speech, just after that araguato episode; but I did not make it without blushing—mentally.

He shook his head, and said it was a poor weapon against some enemies; also—truly enough—that it would procure no birds and monkeys for the stew-pot.

Next morning my friend Kua-kó, taking his zabatana, invited me to go out with him, and I consented with some misgivings, thinking he had overcome his superstitious fears, and, inflamed by my account of the abundance of game in the forest, intended going there with me. The previous day's experience had made me think that it would be better in the future to go there alone. But I was giving the poor youth more credit than he deserved: it was far from his intention to face the terrible unknown again. We went in a different direction, and tramped for hours through woods where birds were scarce and only of the smaller kinds. Then my guide surprised me a second time by offering to teach me to use the zabatana. This, then, was to be my reward for giving him the box! I readily consented, and with the long weapon, awkward to carry, in my hand, and imitating the noiseless movements and cautious, watchful manner of my companion, I tried to imagine myself a simple Guayana savage, with no knowledge of that artificial social state to which I had been born, dependent on my skill and little roll of poison-darts for a livelihood. By an effort of the will I emptied myself of my life experience and knowledge—or as much of it as possible—and thought only of the generations of my dead imaginary progenitors, who had ranged these woods back to the dim forgotten years before Columbus; and if the pleasure I had in the fancy was childish, it made the day pass quickly enough. Kua-kó was constantly at my elbow to assist and give advice; and many an arrow I blew from the long tube, and hit no bird. Heaven knows what I hit, for the arrows flew away on their wide and wild career to be seen no more, except a few which my keen-eyed comrade marked to their destination and managed to recover. The result of our day's hunting was a couple of birds, which Kua-kó, not I, shot, and a small opossum his sharp eyes detected high up a tree lying coiled up on an old nest, over the side of which the animal had incautiously allowed his snaky tail to dangle. The number of darts I wasted must have been a rather serious loss to him, but he did not seem troubled at it, and made no remark.

Next day, to my surprise, he volunteered to give me a second lesson, and we went out again. On this occasion he had provided himself with a large bundle of darts, but—wise man!—they were not poisoned, and it therefore mattered little whether they were wasted or not. I believe that on this day I made some little progress; at all events, my teacher remarked that before long I would be able to hit a bird. This made me smile and answer that if he could place me within twenty yards of a bird not smaller than a small man I might manage to touch it with an arrow.

This speech had a very unexpected and remarkable effect. He stopped short in his walk, stared at me wildly, then grinned, and finally burst into a roar of laughter, which was no bad imitation of the howling monkey's performance, and smote his naked thighs with tremendous energy. At length recovering himself, he asked whether a small woman was not the same as a small man, and being answered in the affirmative, went off into a second extravagant roar of laughter.

Thinking it was easy to tickle him while he continued in this mood, I began making any number of feeble jokes—feeble, but quite as good as the one which had provoked such outrageous merriment—for it amused me to see him acting in this unusual way. But they all failed of their effect—there was no hitting the bull's-eye a second time; he would only stare vacantly at me, then grunt like a peccary—not appreciatively—and walk on. Still, at intervals he would go back to what I said about hitting a very big bird, and roar again, as if this wonderful joke was not easily exhausted.

Again on the third day we were out together practising at the birds—frightening, if not killing them; but before noon, finding that it was his intention to go to a distant spot where he expected to meet with larger game, I left him and returned to the village. The blowpipe practice had lost its novelty, and I did not care to go on all day and every day with it; more than that, I was anxious after so long an interval to pay a visit to *my* wood, as I began to call it, in the hope of hearing that mysterious melody, which I had grown to love and to miss when even a single day passed without it.

CHAPTER V

AFTER making a hasty meal at the house, I started, full of pleasing anticipations, for the wood; for how pleasant a place it was to be in! What a wild beauty and fragrance and melodiousness it possessed above all forests, because of that mystery that drew me to it! And it was mine, truly and absolutely—as much mine as any portion of earth's surface could belong to any man—mine with all its products; the precious woods and fruits and fragrant gums that would never be trafficked away; its wild animals that man would never persecute; nor would any jealous savage dispute my ownership or pretend that it was part of his hunting-ground. As I crossed the savannah I played with this fancy; but when I reached the ridgy eminence, to look down once more on my new domain, the fancy changed to a feeling so keen that it pierced to my heart, and was like pain in its intensity, causing tears to rush to my eyes. And caring not in that solitude to disguise my feelings from myself, and from the wide heaven that looked down and saw me—for this is the sweetest thing that solitude has for us, that we are free in it, and no convention holds us—I dropped on my knees and kissed the stony ground, then casting up my eyes, thanked the Author of my being for the gift of that wild forest, those green mansions where I had found so great a happiness!

Elated with this strain of feeling, I reached the wood not long after noon; but no melodious voice gave me familiar and expected welcome; nor did my invisible companion make itself heard at all on that day, or, at all events, not in its usual bird-like warbling language. But on this day I met with a curious little adventure, and heard something very extraordinary, very mysterious, which I could not avoid connecting in my mind with the unseen warbler that so often followed me in my rambles.

It was an exceedingly bright day, without cloud, but windy, and finding myself in a rather open part of the wood, near its border, where the breeze could be felt, I sat down to rest on the lower part of a large branch, which was half broken, but still remained attached to the trunk of the tree, while resting its terminal twigs on the ground. Just before me, where I sat, grew a low, wide-spreading plant, covered with broad, round, polished leaves; and the roundness, stiffness, and perfectly horizontal position of the upper leaves made them look like a collection of small platforms or round table-tops placed nearly on a level. Through the leaves, to the height of a foot or more above them, a slender dead stem protruded, and from a twig at its summit depended a broken spider's web. A minute dead leaf had become attached to one of the loose threads, and threw its small but distinct shadow on the platform leaves below: and as it trembled and swayed in the current of air the black spot trembled with it or flew swiftly over the bright green surfaces, and was seldom at rest. Now, as I sat looking down on the leaves and the small dancing shadow, scarcely thinking of what I was looking at, I noticed a small spider, with a flat body and short legs, creep cautiously out on to the upper surface of a leaf. Its pale red colour barred with velvet black first drew my attention to it, for it was beautiful to the eye; and presently I discovered that this was no web-spinning, sedentary spider, but a wandering hunter, that captured its prey, like a cat, by stealing on it concealed and making a rush or spring at the last. The moving shadow had attracted it, and, as the sequel showed, was mistaken for a fly running about over the leaves, and flitting from leaf to leaf. Now began a series of wonderful manœuvres on the spider's part, with the object of circumventing the imaginary fly, which seemed specially designed to meet this special case; for certainly no insect had ever before behaved in quite so erratic a manner. Each time the shadow flew past, the spider ran swiftly in the same direction, hiding itself under the leaves, always trying to get near without alarming its prey; and then the shadow would go round and round in a small circle, and some new strategic move on the part of the hunter would be called forth. I became deeply interested in this curious scene;* I began to wish that the shadow would remain quiet for a moment or two, so as to give the hunter a chance. And at last I had my wish: the shadow was almost motionless, and the spider moving towards it, yet seeming not to move, and as it crept closer I fancied that I could almost see the little striped body quivering with excitement. Then came the final scene: swift and straight as an arrow the hunter shot himself on to the fly-like shadow, then wiggled round and round, evidently trying to take hold of his prey with fangs and claws; and finding nothing under him, he raised the fore part of his body vertically, as if to stare about him in search of the delusive fly; but the action may have simply expressed astonishment. At this moment I was just on the point of giving free and loud vent to the laughter which I had been holding in, when, just behind me, as if from some person who had been watching the scene over my shoulder and was as much amused as myself at its termination, sounded a clear trill of merry laughter. I started up and looked hastily around, but no living creature was there. The mass of loose foliage I stared into was agitated, as if from a body having just pushed through it. In a moment the leaves and fronds were motionless again; still, I could not be sure that a slight gust of wind had not shaken them. But I was so convinced that I had heard close to me a real human laugh, or sound of some living creature that exactly simulated a laugh, that I carefully searched the ground about me, expecting to find a being of some kind. But I found nothing, and going back to my seat on the hanging branch, I remained seated for a considerable time, at first only listening, then pondering on the mystery of that sweet trill of laughter; and finally I began to wonder whether I, like the spider that chased the shadow, had been deluded, and had seemed to hear a sound that was not a sound.

On the following day I was in the wood again, and after a two or three hours' ramble, during which I heard nothing, thinking it useless to haunt the known spots any longer, I turned southwards and penetrated into a denser part of the forest, where the undergrowth made progress difficult. I was not afraid of losing myself; the sun above and my sense of direction, which was always good, would enable me to return to the starting-point.

In this direction I had been pushing resolutely on for over half an hour, finding it no easy matter to make my way without constantly deviating to this side or that from the course I wished to keep, when I came to a much more open spot. The trees were smaller and scantier here, owing to the rocky nature of the ground, which sloped rather rapidly down; but it was moist and overgrown with mosses, ferns, creepers, and low shrubs, all of the liveliest green. I could not see many yards ahead owing to the bushes and tall fern fronds; but presently I began to hear a low, continuous sound, which, when I had advanced twenty or thirty yards further, I made out to be the gurgling of running water; and at the same moment I made the discovery that my throat was parched and my palms tingling with heat. I hurried on, promising myself a cool draught, when all at once, above the soft dashing and gurgling of the water, I caught yet another sound—a low, warbling note, or succession of notes, which might have been emitted by a bird. But it startled me nevertheless—bird-like warbling sounds had come to mean so much to me—and pausing, I listened intently. It was not repeated, and finally, treading with the utmost caution so as not to alarm the mysterious vocalist, I crept on until, coming to a greenheart with a quantity of feathery foliage of a shrub growing about its roots, I saw that just beyond the tree the ground was more open still, letting in the sunlight from above, and that the channel of the stream I sought was in this open space, about twenty yards from me, although the water was still hidden from sight. Something else was there, which I did see; instantly my cautious advance was arrested. I stood gazing with concentrated vision, scarcely daring to breathe lest I should scare it away.

It was a human being—a girl form, reclining on the moss among the ferns and herbage, near the roots of a small tree. One arm was doubled behind her neck for her head to rest upon, while the other arm was held extended before her, the hand raised towards a small brown bird perched on a pendulous twig just beyond its reach. She appeared to be playing with the bird, possibly amusing herself by trying to entice it on to her hand; and the hand appeared to tempt it greatly, for it persistently hopped up and down, turning rapidly about this way and that, flirting its wings and tail, and always appearing just on the point of dropping on to her finger. From my position it was impossible to see her distinctly, yet I dared not move. I could make out that she was small, not above four feet six or seven inches in height, in figure slim, with delicately shaped little hands and feet. Her feet were bare, and her only garment was a slight chemise-shaped dress reaching below her knees, of a whitish-grey colour, with a faint lustre as of a silky material. Her hair was very wonderful; it was loose and abundant, and seemed wavy or curly, falling in a cloud on her shoulders and arms. Dark it appeared, but the precise tint was indeterminable, as was that of her skin, which looked neither brown nor white. Altogether, near to me as she actually was, there was a kind of mistiness in the figure which made it appear somewhat vague and distant, and a greenish grey seemed the prevailing colour. This tint I presently attributed to the effect of the sunlight falling on her through the green foliage; for once, for a moment, she raised herself to reach her finger nearer to the bird, and then a gleam of unsubdued sunlight fell on her hair and arm, and the arm at that moment appeared of a pearly whiteness, and the hair, just where the light touched it, had a strange lustre and play of iridescent colour.

I had not been watching her more than three seconds before the bird, with a sharp, creaking little chirp, flew up and away in sudden alarm; at the same moment she turned and saw me through the light leafy screen. But although catching sight of me thus suddenly, she did not exhibit alarm like the bird; only her eyes, wide open, with a surprised look in them, remained immovably fixed on my face. And then slowly, imperceptibly—for I did not notice the actual movement, so gradual and smooth it was, like the motion of a cloud of mist which changes its form and place, yet to the eye seems not to have moved—she rose to her knees, to her feet, retired, and with face still towards me, and eyes fixed on mine, finally disappeared, going as if she had melted away into the verdure. The leafage was there occupying the precise spot where she had been a moment before—the feathery foliage of an acacia shrub, and stems and broad, arrow-shaped leaves of an aquatic plant, and slim, drooping fern fronds, and they were motionless, and seemed not to have been touched by something passing through them. She had gone, yet I continued still, bent almost double, gazing fixedly at the spot where I had last seen her, my mind in a strange condition, possessed by sensations which were keenly felt and yet contradictory. So vivid was the image left on my brain that she still seemed to be actually before my eyes; and she was not there, nor had been, for it was a dream, an illusion, and no such being existed, or could exist, in this gross world: and at the same time I knew that she had been there—that imagination was powerless to conjure up a form so exquisite.

With the mental image I had to be satisfied, for although I remained for some hours at that spot I saw her no more, nor did I hear any familiar melodious sound. For I was now convinced that in this wild solitary girl I had at length discovered the mysterious warbler that so often followed me in the wood. At length, seeing that it was growing late, I took a drink from the stream and slowly and reluctantly made my way out of the forest, and went home.

Early next day I was back in the wood full of delightful anticipations, and had no sooner got well among the trees than a soft, warbling sound reached my ears; it was like that heard on the previous day just before catching sight of the girl among the ferns. So soon! thought I, elated, and with cautious steps I proceeded to explore the ground, hoping again to catch her unawares. But I saw nothing; and only after beginning to doubt that I had heard anything unusual, and had sat down to rest on a rock, the sound was repeated, soft and low as before, very near and distinct. Nothing more was heard at this spot, but an hour later, in another place, the same mysterious note sounded near me. During my remaining time in the forest I was served many times in the same way, and still nothing was seen, nor was there any change in the voice.

Only when the day was near its end did I give up my quest, feeling very keenly disappointed. It then struck me that the cause of the elusive creature's behaviour was that she had been piqued at my discovery of her in one of her most secret hiding-places in the heart of the wood, and that it had pleased her to pay me out in this manner.

On the next day there was no change; she was there again, evidently following me, but always invisible, and varied not from that one mocking note of yesterday, which seemed to challenge me to find her a second time. In the end I was vexed, and resolved to be even with her by not visiting the wood for some time. A display of indifference on my part would, I hoped, result in making her less coy in the future.

Next day, firm in my new resolution, I accompanied Kua-kó and two others to a distant spot where they expected that the ripening fruit on a cashew tree would attract a large number of birds. The fruit, however, proved still green, so that we gathered none and killed few birds. Returning together, Kua-kó kept at my side, and by-and-by, falling behind our companions, he complimented me on my good shooting, although, as usual, I had only wasted the arrows I had blown.

'Soon you will be able to hit,' he said; 'hit a bird as big as a small woman'; and he laughed once more immoderately at the old joke. At last, growing confidential, he said that I would soon possess a zabatana of my own, with arrows in plenty. He was going to make the arrows himself, and his uncle Otawinki, who had a straight eye, would make the tube. I treated it all as a joke, but he solemnly assured me that he meant it.

Next morning he asked me if I was going to the forest of evil fame, and when I replied in the negative seemed surprised and, very much to *my* surprise, evidently disappointed. He even tried to persuade me to go, where before I had been earnestly recommended not to go, until, finding that I would not, he took me with him to hunt in the woods. By-and-by he returned to the same subject: he could not understand why I would not go to that wood, and asked me if I had begun to grow afraid.

'No, not afraid,' I replied; 'but I know the place well, and am getting tired of it.' I had seen everything in it—birds and beasts—and had heard all its strange noises.

'Yes, heard,' he said, nodding his head knowingly; 'but you have *seen* nothing strange; your eyes are not good enough yet.'

I laughed contemptuously, and answered that I had seen everything strange the wood contained, including a strange young girl; and I went on to describe her appearance, and finished by asking if he thought a white man was frightened at the sight of a young girl.

What I said astonished him; then he seemed greatly pleased, and, growing still more confidential and generous than on the previous day, he said that I would soon be a most important personage among them, and greatly distinguish myself. He did not like it when I laughed at all this, and went on with great seriousness to speak of the unmade blow-pipe that would be mine—speaking of it as if it had been something very great, equal to the gift of a large tract of land, or the governorship of a province, north of the Orinoco. And by-and-by he spoke of something else more wonderful even than the promise of a blow-pipe, with arrows galore, and this was that young sister of his, whose name was Oalava, a maid of about sixteen, shy and silent and mild-eyed, rather lean and dirty; not ugly, nor yet prepossessing. And this copper-coloured little drab of the wilderness he proposed to bestow in marriage on me! Anxious to pump him, I managed to control my muscles, and asked him what authority he—a young nobody, who had not yet risen to the dignity of buying a wife for himself—could have to dispose of a sister in this offhand way? He replied that there would be no difficulty: that Runi would give his consent, as would also Otawinki, Piaké, and other relations; and last, and *least*, according to the matrimonial customs of these latitudes, Oalava herself would be ready to bestow her person—queyou, worn figleaf-wise, necklace of accouri teeth, and all*—on so worthy a suitor as myself. Finally, to make the prospect still more inviting, he added that it would not be necessary for me to subject myself to any voluntary tortures to prove myself a man and fitted to enter into the purgatorial state of matrimony. He was a great deal too considerate, I said, and, with all the gravity I could command, asked him what kind of torture he would recommend. For me—so valorous a person—'no torture,' he answered magnanimously. But he—Kua-kó—had made up his mind as to the form of torture he meant to inflict some day on his own person. He would prepare a large sack and into it put fire-ants—'As many as that!' he exclaimed triumphantly, stooping and filling his two hands with loose sand. He would put them in the sack, and then get into it himself naked, and tie it tightly round his neck, so as to show to all spectators that the hellish pain of innumerable venomous stings in his flesh could be endured without a groan, and with an unmoved countenance. The poor youth had not an original mind, since this was one of the commonest forms of self-torture among the Guayana tribes.* But the sudden wonderful animation with which he spoke of it, the fiendish joy that illumined his usually stolid countenance, sent a sudden disgust and horror through me. But what a strange inverted kind of fiendishness is this, which delights at the anticipation of torture inflicted on oneself and not on an enemy! And towards others these savages are mild and peaceable! No, I could not believe in their mildness; that was only on the surface, when nothing occurred to rouse their savage, cruel instincts. I could have laughed at the whole matter, but the exulting look on my companion's face had made me sick of the subject, and I wished not to talk any more about it.

But he would talk still—this fellow whose words, as a rule, I had to take out of his mouth with a fork, as we say; and still on the same subject, he said that not one person in the village would expect to see me torture myself; that after what I would do for them all—after delivering them from a great evil—nothing further would be expected of me.

I asked him to explain his meaning; for it now began to appear plain that in everything he had said he had been leading up to some very important matter. It would, of course, have been a great mistake to suppose that my savage was offering me a blow-pipe and a marketable virgin sister from purely disinterested motives.

In reply he went back to that still unforgotten joke about my being able eventually to hit a bird as big as a small woman with an arrow. Out of it all came, when he went on to ask me if that mysterious girl I had seen in the wood was not of a size to suit me as a target when I had got my hand in with a little more practice. That was the great work

I was asked to do for them—that shy, mysterious girl with the melodious wild-bird voice was the evil being I was asked to slay with poisoned arrows! This was why he now wished me to go often to the wood, to become more and more familiar with her haunts and habits, to overcome all shyness and suspicion in her; and at the proper moment, when it would be impossible to miss my mark, to plant the fatal arrow! The disgust he had inspired in me before, when gloating over anticipated tortures, was a weak and transient feeling to what I now experienced. I turned on him in a sudden transport of rage, and in a moment would have shattered the blow-pipe I was carrying in my hand on his head, but his astonished look as he turned to face me made me pause, and prevented me from committing so fatal an indiscretion. I could only grind my teeth and struggle to overcome an almost overpowering hatred and wrath. Finally, I flung the tube down and bade him take it, telling him that I would not touch it again if he offered me all the sisters of all the savages in Guayana for wives.

He continued gazing at me mute with astonishment, and prudence suggested that it would be best to conceal as far as possible the violent animosity I had conceived against him. I asked him somewhat scorn-fully if he believed that I should ever be able to hit anything—bird or human being—with an arrow. 'No,' I almost shouted, so as to give vent to my feelings in some way, and drawing my revolver, 'this is the white man's weapon; but he kills men with it—men who attempt to kill or injure him—but neither with this nor any other weapon does he murder innocent young girls treacherously.'

After that we went on in silence for some time; at length he said that the being I had seen in the wood and was not afraid of was no innocent young girl, but a daughter of the Didi, an evil being; and that so long as she continued to inhabit the wood they could not go there to hunt, and even in other woods they constantly went in fear of meeting her. Too much disgusted to talk with him, I went on in silence; and when we reached the stream near the village I threw off my clothes and plunged into the water to cool my anger before going in to the others.

CHAPTER VI

THINKING about the forest girl while lying awake that night, I came to the conclusion that I had made it sufficiently plain to her how little her capricious behaviour had been relished, and had therefore no need to punish myself more by keeping any longer out of my beloved green mansions. Accordingly, next day, after the heavy rain that fell during the morning hours had ceased, I set forth about noon to visit the wood. Overhead the sky was clear again; but there was no motion in the heavy sultry atmosphere, while dark blue masses of banked-up clouds on the western horizon threatened a fresh downpour later in the day. My mind was, however, now too greatly excited at the prospect of a possible encounter with the forest nymph to allow me to pay any heed to these ominous signs.

I had passed through the first strip of wood, and was in the succeeding stony sterile space, when a gleam of brilliant colour close by on the ground caught my sight. It was a snake lying on the bare earth; had I kept on without noticing it, I should most probably have trodden upon or dangerously near it. Viewing it closely, I found that it was a coral snake, famed as much for its beauty and singularity as for its deadly character.* It was about three feet long, and very slim; its ground colour a brilliant vermilion, with broad jet-black rings at equal distances round its body, each black ring or band divided by a narrow yellow strip in the middle. The symmetrical pattern and vividly contrasted colours would have given it the appearance of an artificial snake made by some fanciful artist, but for the gleam of life in its bright coils. Its fixed eyes, too, were living gems, and from the point of its dangerous arrowy head the glistening tongue flickered ceaselessly as I stood a few yards away regarding it.

'I admire you greatly, Sir Serpent,' I said, or thought, 'but it is dangerous, say the military authorities, to leave an enemy or possible enemy in the rear; the person who does such a thing must be either a bad strategist or a genius, and I am neither.'

Retreating a few paces, I found and picked up a stone about as big as a man's hand, and hurled it at the dangerous-looking head with the intention of crushing it; but the stone hit upon the rocky ground a little on one side of the mark, and being soft flew into a hundred small fragments. This roused the creature's anger, and in a moment with raised head he was gliding swiftly towards me. Again I retreated, not so slowly on this occasion: and finding another stone, I raised and was about to launch it when a sharp, ringing cry issued from the bushes growing near, and, quickly following the sound, forth stepped the forest girl; no longer elusive and shy, vaguely seen in the shadowy wood, but boldly challenging attention, exposed to the full power of the meridian sun, which made her appear luminous and rich in colour beyond example. Seeing her thus, all those emotions of fear and abhorrence invariably excited in us by the sight of an active venomous serpent in our path vanished instantly from my mind: I could now only feel astonishment and admiration at the brilliant being as she advanced with swift, easy, undulating motion towards me; or rather towards the serpent, which was now between us, moving more and more slowly as she came nearer. The cause of this sudden wonderful boldness, so unlike her former habit, was unmistakable. She had been watching my approach from some hiding-place among the bushes, ready no doubt to lead me a dance through the wood with her mocking voice, as on previous occasions, when my attack on the serpent caused that outburst of wrath. The torrent of ringing and to me inarticulate sounds in that unknown tongue, her rapid gestures, and above all her wide-open sparkling eyes and face aflame with colour, made it impossible to mistake the nature of her feeling.

In casting about for some term or figure of speech in which to describe the impression produced on me at that moment, I think of *waspish*, and, better still, *avispada*—literally the same word in Spanish, not having precisely the same meaning nor ever applied contemptuously—only to reject both after a moment's reflection. Yet I go back to the image of an irritated wasp as perhaps offering the best illustration; of some large tropical wasp advancing angrily towards me, as I have witnessed a hundred times, not exactly flying, but moving rapidly, half running and half flying, over the ground, with loud and angry buzz, the glistening wings open and agitated; beautiful beyond most animated creatures in its sharp but graceful lines, polished surface, and varied brilliant colouring, and that wrathfulness that fits it so well and seems to give it additional lustre.

Wonder-struck at the sight of her strange beauty and passion, I forgot the advancing snake until she came to a stop at about five yards from me; then to my horror I saw that it was beside her naked feet. Although no longer advancing, the head was still raised high as if to strike; but presently the spirit of anger appeared to die out of it; the lifted head, oscillating a little from side to side, sunk down lower and lower to rest finally on the girl's bare instep; and lying there motionless, the deadly thing had the appearance of a gaily coloured silken garter just dropped from her leg. It was plain to see that she had no fear of it, that she was one of those exceptional persons to be found, it is said, in all countries, who possess some magnetic quality which has a soothing effect on even the most venomous and irritable reptiles.

Following the direction of my eyes, she too glanced down, but did not move her foot; then she made her voice heard again, still loud and sharp, but the anger was not now so pronounced.

'Do not fear, I shall not harm it,' I said in the Indian tongue.

She took no notice of my speech, and continued speaking with increasing resentment.

I shook my head, replying that her language was unknown to me. Then by means of signs I tried to make her understand that the creature was safe from further molestation. She pointed indignantly at the stone in my hand, which I had forgotten all about. At once I threw it from me, and instantly there was a change; the resentment had vanished, and a tender radiance lit her face like a smile.

I advanced a little nearer, addressing her once more in the Indian tongue; but my speech was evidently unintelligible to her, as she stood now glancing at the snake lying at her feet, now at me. Again I had recourse to signs and gestures; pointing to the snake, then to the stone I had cast away, I endeavoured to convey to her that in the future I would for her sake be a friend to all venomous reptiles, and that I wished her to have the same kindly feelings towards me as towards these creatures. Whether or not she understood me, she showed no disposition to go into hiding again, and continued silently regarding me with a look that seemed to express pleasure at finding herself at last thus suddenly brought face to face with me. Flattered at this, I gradually drew nearer until at the last I was standing at her side, gazing down with the utmost delight into that face which so greatly surpassed in loveliness all human faces I had ever seen or imagined.

And yet to you, my friend, it probably will not seem that she was so beautiful, since I have, alas! only the words we all use to paint commoner, coarser things, and no means to represent all the exquisite details, all the delicate lights, and shades, and swift changes of colour and expression. Moreover, is it not a fact that the strange or unheard of can never appear beautiful in a mere description, because that which is most novel in it attracts too much attention and is given undue prominence in the picture, and we miss that which would have taken away the effect of strangeness—the perfect balance of the parts and harmony of the whole? For instance, the blue eyes of the northerner would, when first described to the black-eyed inhabitants of warm regions, seem unbeautiful and a monstrosity, because they would vividly see with the mental vision that unheard-of blueness, but not in the same vivid way the accompanying flesh and hair tints with which it harmonises.

Think, then, less of the picture as I have to paint it in words than of the feeling its original inspired in me, when looking closely for the first time on that rare loveliness, trembling with delight I mentally cried: 'Oh, why has Nature, maker of so many types and of innumerable individuals of each, given to the world but one being like this?'

Scarcely had the thought formed itself in my mind before I dismissed it as utterly incredible. No, this exquisite being was without doubt one of a distinct race which had existed in this little-known corner of the continent for thousands of generations, albeit now perhaps reduced to a small and dwindling remnant.

Her figure and features were singularly delicate, but it was her colour that struck me most, which indeed made her differ from all other human beings. The colour of the skin would be almost impossible to describe, so greatly did it vary with every change of mood—and the moods were many and transient—and with the angle on which the sunlight touched it, and the degree of light.

Beneath the trees, at a distance, it had seemed a somewhat dim white or pale grey; near in the strong sunshine it was not white, but alabastrian, semi-pellucid, showing an underlying rose-colour; and at any point where the rays fell direct this colour was bright and luminous, as we see in our fingers when held before a strong firelight. But that part of her skin that remained in shadow appeared of a dimmer white, and the underlying colour varied from dim, rosy purple to dim blue. With the skin the colour of the eyes harmonised perfectly. At first, when lit with anger, they had appeared flame-like;

now the iris was of a peculiar soft or dim and tender red, a shade sometimes seen in flowers. But only when looked closely at could this delicate hue be discerned, the pupils being large, as in some grey eyes, and the long, dark, shading lashes at a short distance made the whole eye appear dark. Think not, then, of the red flower, exposed to the light and sun in conjunction with the vivid green of the foliage; think only of such a hue in the half-hidden iris, brilliant and moist with the eye's moisture, deep with the eye's depth, glorified by the outward look of a bright, beautiful soul. Most variable of all in colour was the hair, this being due to its extreme fineness and glossiness, and to its elasticity, which made it lie fleecy and loose on head, shoulders, and back; a cloud with a brightness on its surface made by the freer outer hairs, a fit setting and crown for a countenance of such rare, changeful loveliness. In the shade, viewed closely, the general colour appeared a slate, deepening in places to purple; but even in the shade the nimbus of free flossy hairs half veiled the darker tints with a downy pallor; and at a distance of a few yards it gave the whole hair a vague, misty appearance. In the sunlight the colour varied more, looking now dark, sometimes intensely black, now of a light uncertain hue, with a play of iridescent colour on the loose surface, as we see on the glossed plumage of some birds; and at a short distance, with the sun shining full on her head, it sometimes looked white as a noonday cloud. So changeful was it and ethereal in appearance with its cloud colours, that all other human hair, even of the most beautiful golden shades, pale or red, seemed heavy and dull and dead-looking by comparison.

But more than form and colour and that enchanting variability was the look of intelligence, which at the same time seemed complementary to and one with the all-seeing, all-hearing alertness appearing in her face; the alertness one remarks in a wild creature, even when in repose and fearing nothing; but seldom in man, never perhaps in intellectual or studious man. She was a wild, solitary girl of the woods, and did not understand the language of the country in which I had addressed her. What inner or mind life could such a one have more than that of any wild animal existing in the same conditions? Yet looking at her face it was not possible to doubt its intelligence. This union in her of two opposite qualities, which, with us, cannot or do not exist together, although so novel, yet struck me as the girl's principal charm. Why had Nature not done this before—

why in all others does the brightness of the mind dim that beautiful physical brightness which the wild animals have? But enough for me that that which no man had ever looked for or hoped to find existed here; that through that unfamiliar lustre of the wild life shone the spiritualising light of mind that made us kin.

These thoughts passed swiftly through my brain as I stood feasting my sight on her bright, piquant face; while she on her part gazed back into my eyes, not only with fearless curiosity, but with a look of recognition and pleasure at the encounter so unmistakably friendly that, encouraged by it, I took her arm in my hand, moving at the same time a little nearer to her. At that moment a swift, startled expression came into her eyes; she glanced down and up again into my face; her lips trembled and slightly parted as she murmured some sorrowful sounds in a tone so low as to be only just audible.

Thinking she had become alarmed and was on the point of escaping out of my hands, and fearing, above all things, to lose sight of her again so soon, I slipped my arm around her slender body to detain her, moving one foot at the same time to balance myself; and at that moment I felt a slight blow and a sharp burning sensation shoot into my leg, so sudden and intense that I dropped my arm, at the same time uttering a cry of pain, and recoiled one or two paces from her. But she stirred not when I released her; her eyes followed my movements; then she glanced down at her feet. I followed her look, and figure to yourself my horror when I saw there the serpent I had so completely forgotten, and which even that sting of sharp pain had not brought back to remembrance! There it lay, a coil of its own thrown round one of her ankles, and its head, raised nearly a foot high, swaying slowly from side to side, while the swift forked tongue flickered continuously. Then—only then—I knew what had happened, and at the same time I understood the reason of that sudden look of alarm in her face, the murmuring sounds she had uttered, and the downward startled glance. Her fears had been solely for my safety, and she had warned me! Too late! too late! In moving I had trodden on or touched the serpent with my foot, and it had bitten me just above the ankle. In a few moments I began to realise the horror of my position. 'Must I die! must I die! Oh, my God, is there nothing that can save me?' I cried in my heart.

She was still standing motionless in the same place: her eyes wandered back from me to the snake; gradually its swaying head was lowered again, and the coil unwound from her ankle; then it began to move away, slowly at first, and with the head a little raised, then faster, and in the end it glided out of sight. Gone!—but it had left its venom in my blood—O cursed reptile!

Back from watching its retreat, my eyes returned to her face, now strangely clouded with trouble; her eyes dropped before mine, while the palms of her hands were pressed together, and the fingers clasped and unclasped alternately. How different she seemed now; the brilliant face grown so pallid and vague-looking! But not only because this tragic end to our meeting had pierced her with pain: that cloud in the west had grown up and now covered half the sky with vast lurid masses of vapour, blotting out the sun, and a great gloom had fallen on the earth.

That sudden twilight and a long roll of approaching thunder, reverberating from the hills, increased my anguish and desperation. Death at that moment looked unutterably terrible. The remembrance of all that made life dear pierced me to the core—all that nature was to me, all the pleasures of sense and intellect, the hopes I had cherished—all was revealed to me as by a flash of lightning. Bitterest of all was the thought that I must now bid everlasting farewell to this beautiful being I had found in the solitude—this lustrous daughter of the Didi—just when I had won her from her shyness—that I must go away into the cursed blackness of death, and never know the mystery of her life! It was that which utterly unnerved me, and made my legs tremble under me, and brought great drops of sweat to my forehead, until I thought that the venom was already doing its swift, fatal work in my veins.

With uncertain steps I moved to a stone a yard or two away and sat down upon it. As I did so the hope came to me that this girl, so intimate with nature, might know of some antidote to save me. Touching my leg, and using other signs, I addressed her again in the Indian language.

'The snake has bitten me,' I said. 'What shall I do? Is there no leaf, no root you know that would save me from death? Help me! help me!' I cried in despair.

My signs she probably understood if not my words, but she made no reply; and still she remained standing motionless, twisting and untwisting her fingers, and regarding me with a look of ineffable grief and compassion.

Alas! It was vain to appeal to her: she knew what had happened, and what the result would most likely be, and pitied, but was powerless to help me. Then it occurred to me that if I could reach the Indian village before the venom overpowered me something might be done to save me. Oh, why had I tarried so long, losing so many precious minutes! Large drops of rain were falling now, and the gloom was deeper, and the thunder almost continuous. With a cry of anguish I started to my feet, and was about to rush away towards the village when a dazzling flash of lightning made me pause for a moment. When it vanished I turned a last look on the girl, and her face was deathly pale, and her hair looked blacker than night; and as she looked she stretched out her arms towards me and uttered a low, wailing cry. 'Good-bye for ever!' I murmured, and turning once more from her, rushed away like one crazed into the wood. But in my confusion I had probably taken the wrong direction, for instead of coming out in a few minutes into the open border of the forest, and on to the savannah, I found myself every moment getting deeper among the trees. I stood still, perplexed, but could not shake off the conviction that I had started in the right direction. Eventually I resolved to keep on for a hundred yards or so, and then, if no opening appeared, to turn back and retrace my steps. But this was no easy matter. I soon became entangled in a dense undergrowth, which so confused me that at last I confessed despairingly to myself that for the first time in this wood I was hopelessly lost. And in what terrible circumstances! At intervals a flash of lightning would throw a vivid blue glare down into the interior of the wood and only serve to show that I had lost myself in a place where even at noon in cloudless weather progress would be most difficult; and now the light would only last a moment, to be followed by thick gloom; and I could only tear blindly on, bruising and lacerating my flesh at every step, falling again and again only to struggle up and on again, now high above the surface climbing over prostrate trees and branches, now plunged to my middle in a pool or torrent of water.

Hopeless—utterly hopeless seemed all my mad efforts; and at each pause, when I would stand exhausted, gasping for breath, my throbbing heart almost suffocating me, a dull, continuous, teasing pain in my bitten leg served to remind me that I had but a little time left to exist—that by delaying at first I had allowed my only chance of salvation to slip by.

How long a time I spent fighting my way through this dense black wood I know not; perhaps two or three hours, only to me the hours seemed like years of prolonged agony. At last, all at once, I found that I was free of the close undergrowth, and walking on level ground: but it was darker here—darker than the darkest night; and at length, when the lightning came and flared down through the dense roof of foliage overhead, I discovered that I was in a spot that had a strange look, where the trees were very large and grew wide apart, and with no undergrowth to impede progress beneath them. Here, recovering breath, I began to run, and after a while found that I had left the large trees behind me, and was now in a more open place, with small trees and bushes: and this made me hope for a while that I had at last reached the border of the forest. But the hope proved vain; once more I had to force my way through dense undergrowth, and finally emerged on to a slope where it was open, and I could once more see for some distance around me by such light as came through the thick pall of clouds. Trudging on to the summit of the slope, I saw that there was open savannah country beyond, and for a moment rejoiced that I had got free from the forest. A few steps more, and I was standing on the very edge of a bank, a precipice not less than fifty feet deep. I had never seen that bank before, and therefore knew that I could not be on the right side of the forest. But now my only hope was to get completely away from the trees and then to look for the village, and I began following the bank in search of a descent. No break occurred, and presently I was stopped by a dense thicket of bushes. I was about to retrace my steps when I noticed that a tall slender tree growing at the foot of the precipice, its green top not more than a couple of yards below my feet, seemed to offer a means of escape. Nerving myself with the thought that if I got crushed by the fall I should probably escape a lingering and far more painful death, I dropped into the cloud of foliage beneath me and clutched desperately at the twigs as I fell. For a moment I felt myself sustained; but branch after branch gave way beneath my weight, and then I only remember, very dimly, a swift flight through the air before losing consciousness.

CHAPTER VII

WITH the return of consciousness, I at first had a vague impression that I was lying somewhere, injured, and incapable of motion; that it was night, and necessary for me to keep my eyes fast shut to prevent them from being blinded by almost continuous vivid flashes of lightning. Injured, and sore all over, but warm and dry—surely dry: nor was it lightning that dazzled, but firelight. I began to notice things little by little. The fire was burning on a clay floor a few feet from where I was lying. Before it, on a log of wood, sat or crouched a human figure. An old man, with chin on breast and hands clasped before his drawn-up knees; only a small portion of his forehead and nose visible to me. An Indian I took him to be, from his coarse, lank, grey hair and dark brown skin. I was in a large hut, falling at the sides to within two feet of the floor: but there were no hammocks in it, nor bows and spears, and no skins, not even under me, for I was lying on straw mats. I could hear the storm still raging outside; the rush and splash of rain, and, at intervals, the distant growl of thunder. There was wind, too; I listened to it sobbing in the trees, and occasionally a puff found its way in, and blew up the white ashes at the old man's feet, and shook the yellow flames like a flag. I remembered now how the storm began, the wild girl, the snake-bite, my violent efforts to find a way out of the woods, and, finally, that leap from the bank where recollection ended. That I had not been killed by the venomous tooth, nor the subsequent fearful fall, seemed like a miracle to me. And in that wild, solitary place, lying insensible, in that awful storm and darkness, I had been found by a fellow-creature—a savage, doubtless, but a good Samaritan all the same—who had rescued me from death! I was bruised all over and did not attempt to move, fearing the pain it would give me; and I had a racking headache; but these seemed trifling discomforts after such adventures and such perils. I felt that I had recovered or was recovering from that venomous bite; that I would live and not die—live to return to my country; and the thought filled my heart to overflowing, and tears of gratitude and happiness rose to my eyes.

At such times a man experiences benevolent feelings, and would willingly bestow some of that over-plus of happiness on his fellows to lighten other hearts; and this old man before me, who was probably the instrument of my salvation, began greatly to excite my interest and compassion. For he seemed so poor in his old age and rags, so solitary and dejected as he sat there with knees drawn up, his great, brown, bare feet looking almost black by contrast with the white wood-ashes about them! What could I do for him? What could I say to cheer his spirits in that Indian language, which has few or no words to express kindly feelings? Unable to think of anything better to say, I at length suddenly cried aloud, 'Smoke, old man! Why do you not smoke? It is good to smoke.'

He gave a mighty start, and, turning, fixed his eyes on me. Then I saw that he was not a pure Indian, for although as brown as old leather, he wore a beard and moustache. A curious face had this old man, which looked as if youth and age had made it a battling ground. His forehead was smooth, except for two parallel lines in the middle running its entire length, dividing it in zones; his arched eyebrows were black as ink, and his small black eyes were bright and cunning, like the eyes of some wild carnivorous animal. In this part of his face youth had held its own, especially in the eyes, which looked young and lively. But lower down age had conquered, scribbling his skin all over with wrinkles, while moustache and beard were white as thistledown.

'Aha, the dead man is alive again!' he exclaimed, with a chuckling laugh. This in the Indian tongue; then in Spanish he added, 'But speak to me in the language you know best, señor; for if you are not a Venezuelan call me an owl.'

'And you, old man?' said I.

'Ah, I was right! Why, sir, what I am is plainly written on my face. Surely you do not take me for a pagan! I might be a black man from Africa, or an Englishman, but an Indian—that, no! But a minute ago you had the goodness to invite me to smoke. How, sir, can a poor man smoke who is without tobacco?'

'Without tobacco—in Guayana!'

'Can you believe it? But, sir, do not blame me; if the beast that came one night and destroyed my plants when ripe for cutting had taken pumpkins and sweet potatoes instead, it would have been better for him, if curses have any effect. And the plant grows slowly, sir—it is not an evil weed to come to maturity in a single day. And as for other leaves in the forest, I smoke them, yes; but there is no comfort to the lungs in such smoke.'

'My tobacco-pouch was full,' I said. 'You will find it in my coat, if I did not lose it.'

'The saints forbid!' he exclaimed. 'Grandchild—Rima, have you got a tobacco-pouch with the other things? Give it to me.'

Then I first noticed that another person was in the hut, a slim young girl, who had been seated against the wall on the other side of the fire, partially hid by the shadows. She had my leather belt, with the revolver in its case, and my hunting-knife attached, and the few articles I had had in my pockets, on her lap. Taking up the pouch, she handed it to him, and he clutched it with a strange eagerness.

'I will give it back presently, Rima,' he said. 'Let me first smoke a cigarette—and then another.'

It seemed probable from this that the good old man had already been casting covetous eyes on my property, and that his granddaughter had taken care of it for me. But how the silent, demure girl had kept it from him was a puzzle, so intensely did he seem now to enjoy it, drawing the smoke vigorously into his lungs, and after keeping it ten or fifteen seconds there, letting it fly out again from mouth and nose in blue jets and clouds. His face softened visibly, he became more and more genial and loquacious, and asked me how I came to be in that solitary place. I told him that I was staying with the Indian Runi, his neighbour.

'But, señor,' he said, 'if it is not an impertinence, how is it that a young man of so distinguished an appearance as yourself, a Venezuelan, should be residing with these children of the devil?'

'You love not your neighbours, then?'

'I know them, sir—how should I love them?' He was rolling up his second or third cigarette by this time, and I could not help noticing that he took a great deal more tobacco than he required in his fingers, and that the surplus on each occasion was conveyed to some secret receptacle among his rags. 'Love them, sir! They are infidels, and therefore the good Christian must only hate them. They are thieves—they will steal from you before your very face, so devoid are they of all shame. And also murderers; gladly would they burn this poor thatch above my head, and kill me and my poor grandchild, who shares this solitary life with me, if they had the courage.

But they are all arrant cowards, and fear to approach me—fear even to come into this wood. You would laugh to hear what they are afraid of—a child would laugh to hear it!'

'What do they fear?' I said, for his words had excited my interest in a great degree.

'Why, sir, would you believe it? They fear this child—my grand-daughter, seated there before you. A poor innocent girl of seventeen summers, a Christian who knows her Catechism, and would not harm the smallest thing that God has made—no, not a fly, which is not regarded on account of its smallness. Why, sir, it is due to her tender heart that you are safely sheltered here, instead of being left out of doors in this tempestuous night.'

'To her—to this girl?' I returned in astonishment. 'Explain, old man, for I do not know how I was saved.'

'To-day, señor, through your own heedlessness you were bitten by a venomous snake.'

'Yes, that is true, although I do not know how it came to your know-ledge. But why am I not a dead man, then—have you done something to save me from the effects of the poison?'

'Nothing. What could I do so long after you were bitten? When a man is bitten by a snake in a solitary place he is in God's hands. He will live or die as God wills. There is nothing to be done. But surely, sir, you remember that my poor grandchild was with you in the wood when the snake bit you?'

'A girl was there—a strange girl I have seen and heard before when I have walked in the forest. But not this girl—surely not this girl!'

'No other,' said he, carefully rolling up another cigarette.

'It is not possible!' I returned.

'Ill would you have fared, sir, had she not been there. For after being bitten, you rushed away into the thickest part of the wood, and went about in a circle like a demented person for Heaven knows how long. But she never left you; she was always close to you—you might have touched her with your hand. And at last some good angel who was watching you, in order to stop your career, made you mad altogether and caused you to jump over a precipice and lose your senses. And you were no sooner on the ground than she was with you—ask me not how *she* got down! And when she had propped you up against the bank she came for me. Fortunately the spot where you had fallen is near—not five hundred yards from the door. And I, on my part, was willing to assist her in saving you; for I knew it was no Indian that had fallen, since she loves not that breed, and they come not here. It was not an easy task, for you weigh, señor; but between us we brought you in.'

While he spoke the girl continued sitting in the same listless attitude as when I first observed her, with eyes cast down and hands folded in her lap. Recalling that brilliant being in the wood that had protected the serpent from me, and calmed its rage, I found it hard to believe his words, and still felt a little incredulous.

'Rima—that is your name, is it not?'* I said. 'Will you come here and stand before me, and let me look closely at you?'

'Si, señor,' she meekly answered; and removing the things from her lap she stood up; then, passing behind the old man, came and stood before me, her eyes still bent on the ground—a picture of humility.

She had the figure of the forest girl, but wore now a scanty faded cotton garment, while the loose cloud of hair was confined in two plaits and hung down her back. The face also showed the same delicate lines, but of the brilliant animation and variable colour and expression there appeared no trace. Gazing at her countenance, as she stood there silent, shy, and spiritless before me, the image of her brighter self came vividly to my mind, and I could not recover from the astonishment I felt at such a contrast.

Have you ever observed a humming-bird moving about in an aërial dance among the flowers—a living prismatic gem that changes its colour with every change of position—how in turning it catches the sunshine on its burnished neck and gorget plumes—green and gold and flame-coloured, the beams changing to visible flakes as they fall, dissolving into nothing, to be succeeded by others and yet others? In its exquisite form, its changeful splendour, its swift motions and intervals of aërial suspension, it is a creature of such fairy-like loveliness as to mock all description. And have you seen this same fairy-like creature suddenly perch itself on a twig, in the shade, its misty wings and fanlike tail folded, the iridescent glory vanished, looking like some common dull-plumaged little bird sitting listless in a cage?* Just so great was the difference in the girl, as I had seen her in the forest and as she now appeared under the smoky roof in the firelight.

After watching her for some moments I spoke: 'Rima, there must be a good deal of strength in that frame of yours, which looks so delicate; will you raise me up a little?'

She went down on one knee, and placing her arms round me assisted me to a sitting posture.

'Thank you, Rima—O misery!' I groaned. 'Is there a bone left unbroken in my poor body?'

'Nothing broken,' cried the old man, clouds of smoke flying out
with his words. 'I have examined you well—legs, arms, ribs. For this
is how it was, señor. A thorny bush into which you fell saved you from
being flattened on the stony ground. But you are bruised, sir, black
with bruises; and there are more scratches of thorns on your skin
than letters on a written page.'

'A long thorn might have entered my brain,' I said, 'from the way
it pains. Feel my forehead, Rima; is it very hot and dry?'

She did as I asked, touching me lightly with her little cool hand.
'No, señor, not hot, but warm and moist,' she said.

'Thank Heaven for that!' I said. 'Poor girl! And you followed me
through the wood in all that terrible storm! Ah, if I could lift my
bruised arm I would take your hand to kiss it in gratitude for so great
a service. I owe you my life, sweet Rima—what shall I do to repay so
great a debt?'

The old man chuckled as if amused, but the girl lifted not her eyes
nor spoke.

'Tell me, sweet child,' I said, 'for I cannot realize it yet; was it really
you that saved the serpent's life when I would have killed it—did you
stand by me in the wood with the serpent lying at your feet?'

'Yes, señor,' came her gentle answer.

'And it was you I saw in the wood one day, lying on the ground playing with a small bird?'

'Yes, señor.'

'And it was you that followed me so often among the trees, calling
to me, yet always hiding so that I could never see you?'

'Yes, señor.'

'Oh, this is wonderful!' I exclaimed; whereat the old man chuckled
again.

'But tell me this, my sweet girl,' I continued. 'You never addressed me
in Spanish; what strange musical language was it you spoke to me in?'

She shot a timid glance at my face and looked troubled at the question, but made no reply.

'Señor,' said the old man, 'that is a question which you must excuse
my child from answering. Not, sir, from want of will, for she is docile

and obedient, though I say it, but there is no answer beyond what I can tell you. And this is, sir, that all creatures, whether man or bird, have the voice that God has given them; and in some the voice is musical and in others not so.'

'Very well, old man,' said I to myself; 'there let the matter rest for the present. But, if I am destined to live and not die, I shall not long remain satisfied with your too simple explanation.'

'Rima,' I said, 'you must be fatigued; it is thoughtless of me to keep you standing here so long.'

Her face brightened a little, and bending down she replied in a low voice, 'I am not fatigued, sir. Let me get you something to eat now.'

She moved quickly away to the fire, and presently returned with an earthenware dish of roasted pumpkin and sweet potatoes, and kneeling at my side fed me deftly with a small wooden spoon. I did not feel grieved at the absence of meat and the stinging condiments the Indians love, nor did I even remark that there was no salt in the vegetables, so much was I taken up with watching her beautiful delicate face while she ministered to me. The exquisite fragrance of her breath was more to me than the most delicious viands could have been; and it was a delight each time she raised the spoon to my mouth to catch a momentary glimpse of her eyes, which now looked dark as wine when we lift the glass to see the ruby gleam of light within the purple. But she never for a moment laid aside the silent, meek, constrained manner; and when I remembered her bursting out in her brilliant wrath on me, pouring forth that torrent of stinging invective in her mysterious language, I was lost in wonder and admiration at the change in her, and at her double personality. Having satisfied my wants she moved quietly away, and raising a straw mat disappeared behind it into her own sleeping-apartment, which was divided off by a partition from the room I was in.

The old man's sleeping-place was a wooden cot or stand on the opposite side of the room, but he was in no hurry to sleep, and after Rima had left us put a fresh log on the blaze, and lit another cigarette. Heaven knows how many he had smoked by this time. He became very talkative and called to his side his two dogs, which I had not noticed in the room before, for me to see. It amused me to hear their names—Susio and Goloso: Dirty and Greedy. They were surly-looking brutes, with rough yellow hair, and did not win my heart, but according to his account they possessed all the usual canine virtues; and he was still holding forth on the subject when I fell asleep.

CHAPTER VIII

WHEN morning came I was too stiff and sore to move, and not until the following day was I able to creep out to sit in the shade of the trees. My old host, whose name was Nuflo, went off with his dogs, leaving the girl to attend to my wants. Two or three times during the day she appeared to serve me with food and drink, but she continued silent and constrained in manner as on the first evening of seeing her in the hut.

Late in the afternoon old Nuflo returned, but did not say where he had been; and shortly afterwards Rima reappeared, demure as usual, in her faded cotton dress, her cloud of hair confined in two long plaits. My curiosity was more excited than ever, and I resolved to get to the bottom of the mystery of her life. The girl had not shown herself responsive, but now that Nuflo was back I was treated to as much talk as I cared to hear. He talked of many things, only omitting those which I desired to hear about; but his pet subject appeared to be the divine government of the world—'God's politics'—and its manifest imperfections, or in other words, the manifold abuses which from time to time had been allowed to creep into it. The old man was pious, but like many of his class in my country, he permitted himself to indulge in very free criticisms of the powers above, from the King of Heaven down to the smallest saint whose name figures in the calendar.

'These things, señor,' he said, 'are not properly managed. Consider my position. Here am I compelled for my sins to inhabit this wilderness with my poor granddaughter——'

'She is not your granddaughter!' I suddenly interrupted, thinking to surprise him into an admission.

But he took his time to answer. 'Señor, we are never sure of anything in this world. Not absolutely sure. Thus, it may come to pass that you will one day marry, and that your wife will in due time present you with a son—one that will inherit your fortune and transmit your name to posterity. And yet, sir, in this world, you will never know to a certainty that he is your son.'

'Proceed with what you were saying,' I returned, with some dignity.

'Here we are,' he continued, 'compelled to inhabit this land and do not meet with proper protection from the infidel. Now, sir, this is a crying evil, and it is only becoming in one who has the true faith, and is a loyal subject of the All-Powerful, to point out with due humility that He is growing very remiss in His affairs, and is losing a good deal of His prestige. And what, señor, is at the bottom of it? Favoritism. We know that the Supreme cannot Himself be everywhere, attending to each little trike-traka that arises in the world—matters altogether beneath His notice; and that He must, like the President of Venezuela or the Emperor of Brazil, appoint men—angels if you like—to conduct His affairs and watch over each district. And it is manifest that for this country of Guayana the proper person has not been appointed. Every evil is done and there is no remedy, and the Christian has no more consideration shown him than the infidel. Now, señor, in a town near the Orinoco I once saw on a church the archangel Michael, made of stone, and twice as tall as a man, with one foot on a monster shaped like a cayman, but with bat's wings, and a head and neck like a serpent. Into this monster he was thrusting his spear. That is the kind of person that should be sent to rule these latitudes—a person of firmness and resolution, with strength in his wrist. And yet it is probable that this very man—this St Michael—is hanging about the palace, twirling his thumbs, waiting for an appointment, while other weaker men, and—Heaven forgive me for saying it, not above a bribe, perhaps—are sent out to rule over this province.'

On this string he would harp by the hour; it was a lofty subject on which he had pondered much in his solitary life, and he was glad of an opportunity of ventilating his grievance and expounding his views. At first it was a pure pleasure to hear Spanish again, and the old man, albeit ignorant of letters, spoke well; but this, I may say, is a common thing in our country, where the peasant's quickness of intelligence and poetic feeling often compensate for want of instruction. His views also amused me, although they were not novel. But after a while I grew tired of listening, yet I listened still, agreeing with him, and leading him on to let him have his fill of talk, always hoping that he would come at last to speak of personal matters and give me an account of his history and of Rima's origin. But the hope proved vain; not a word to enlighten me would he drop, however cunningly I tempted him.

'So be it,' thought I; 'but if you are cunning, old man, I shall be cunning too—and patient; for all things come to him who waits.'

He was in no hurry to get rid of me. On the contrary, he more than hinted that I would be safer under his roof than with the Indians, at the same time apologising for not giving me meat to eat.

'But why do you not have meat? Never have I seen animals so abundant and tame as in this wood.'

Before he could reply Rima, with a jug of water from the spring in her hand, came in; glancing at me he lifted his finger to signify that such a subject must not be discussed in her presence; but as soon as she quitted the room he returned to it.

'Señor,' he said, 'have you forgotten your adventure with the snake? Know, then, that my grandchild would not live with me for one day longer if I were to lift my hand against any living creature. For us, señor, every day is fast-day—only without the fish. We have maize, pumpkin, cassava, potatoes, and these suffice. And even of these cultivated fruits of the earth she eats but little in the house, preferring certain wild berries and gums, which are more to her taste, and which she picks here and there in her rambles in the wood. And I, sir, loving her as I do, whatever my inclination may be, shed no blood and eat no flesh.'

I looked at him with an incredulous smile.

'And your dogs, old man?'

'My dogs? Sir, they would not pause or turn aside if a coatimundi* crossed their path—an animal with a strong odour. As a man is, so is his dog. Have you not seen dogs eating grass, sir, even in Venezuela, where these sentiments do not prevail? And when there is no meat—when meat is forbidden—these sagacious animals accustom themselves to a vegetable diet.'

I could not very well tell the old man that he was lying to me—that would have been bad policy—and so I passed it off. 'I have no doubt that you are right,' I said. 'I have heard that there are dogs in China that eat no meat, but are themselves eaten by their owners after being fattened on rice. I should not care to dine on one of your animals, old man.'

He looked at them critically and replied, 'Certainly they are lean.'

'I was thinking less of their leanness than of their smell,' I returned. 'Their odour when they approach me is not flowery, but resembles that of other dogs which feed on flesh, and have offended my too sensitive nostrils even in the drawing-rooms of Caracas. It is not like the fragrance of cattle when they return from the pasture.'

'Every animal,' he replied, 'gives out that odour which is peculiar to its kind'; an incontrovertible fact which left me nothing to say.

When I had sufficiently recovered the suppleness of my limbs to walk with ease I went for a ramble in the wood, in the hope that Rima would accompany me, and that out among the trees she would cast aside that artificial constraint and shyness which was her manner in the house.

It fell out just as I had expected; she accompanied me in the sense of being always near me, or within earshot, and her manner was now free and unconstrained as I could wish; but little or nothing was gained by the change. She was once more the tantalising, elusive, mysterious creature I had first known through her wandering, melo-dious voice. The only difference was that the musical, inarticulate sounds were now less often heard, and that she was no longer afraid to show herself to me. This for a short time was enough to make me happy, since no lovelier being was ever looked upon, nor one whose loveliness was less likely to lose its charm through being often seen.

But to keep her near me or always in sight was, I found, impossible: she would be free as the wind, free as the butterfly, going and coming at her wayward will, and losing herself from sight a dozen times every hour. To induce her to walk soberly at my side or sit down and enter into conversation with me seemed about as impracticable as to tame the fiery-hearted little humming-bird that flashes into sight, remains suspended motionless for a few seconds before your face, then, quick as lightning, vanishes again.

At length, feeling convinced that she was most happy when she had me out following her in the wood, that in spite of her bird-like wild-ness she had a tender, human heart, which was easily moved, I deter-mined to try to draw her closer by means of a little innocent stratagem. Going out in the morning, after calling her several times to no purpose, I began to assume a downcast manner, as if suffering pain or depressed with grief; and at last, finding a convenient ex-posed root under a tree, on a spot where the ground was dry and strewn with loose yellow sand, I sat down and refused to go any further. For she always wanted to lead me on and on, and whenever I paused she would return to show herself, or to chide or encourage me in her mysterious language. All her pretty little arts were now practised in vain: with cheek resting on my hand I still sat, my eyes fixed on that patch of yellow sand at my feet, watching how the small

particles glinted like diamond dust when the sunlight touched them.
A full hour passed in this way, during which I encouraged myself by
saying mentally: 'This is a contest between us, and the most patient
and the strongest of will, which should be the man, must conquer.
And if I win on this occasion it will be easier for me in the future—
easier to discover those things which I am resolved to know, and the
girl must reveal to me, since the old man has proved impracticable.'

Meanwhile she came and went and came again; and at last, finding
that I was not to be moved, she approached and stood near me. Her
face, when I glanced at it, had a somewhat troubled look—both
troubled and curious.

'Come here, Rima,' I said, 'and stay with me for a little while—I
cannot follow you now.'

She took one or two hesitating steps, then stood still again; and at
length, slowly and reluctantly, advanced to within a yard of me. Then
I rose from my seat on the root, so as to catch her face better, and
placed my hand against the rough bark of the tree.

'Rima,' I said, speaking in a low, caressing tone, 'will you stay with
me here a little while and talk to me, not in your language, but in
mine, so that I may understand? Will you listen when I speak to you,
and answer me?'

Her lips moved, but made no sound. She seemed strangely dis-
quieted, and shook back her loose hair, and with her small toes
moved the sparkling sand at her feet, and once or twice her eyes
glanced shyly at my face.

'Rima, you have not answered me,' I persisted. 'Will you not say
"yes"?'

'Yes.'

'Where does your grandfather spend his day when he goes out with
his dogs?'

She shook her head slightly, but would not speak.

'Have you no mother, Rima? Do you remember your mother?'

'My mother! My mother!' she exclaimed in a low voice, but with a
sudden, wonderful animation. Bending a little nearer she continued: 'Oh, she is dead! Her body is in the earth and turned to dust.
Like that,' and she moved the loose sand with her foot. 'Her soul is
up there, where the stars and the angels are, grandfather says. But
what is that to me? I am here—am I not? I talk to her just the same.
Everything I see I point out, and tell her everything. In the day-

time—in the woods, when we are together. And at night when I lie down I cross my arms on my breast—so, and say, "Mother, mother, now you are in my arms; let us go to sleep together." Sometimes I say, "Oh, why will you never answer me when I speak and speak?" Mother—mother—mother!'

At the end her voice suddenly rose to a mournful cry, then sunk, and at the last repetition of the word died to a low whisper.

'Ah, poor Rima! she is dead and cannot speak to you—cannot hear you! Talk to me, Rima; I am living and can answer.'

But now the cloud, which had suddenly lifted from her heart, letting me see for a moment into its mysterious depths—its fancies so childlike and feelings so intense—had fallen again; and my words brought no response, except a return of that troubled look to her face.

'Silent still?' I said. 'Talk to me, then, of your mother, Rima. Do you know that you will see her again some day?'

'Yes, when I die. That is what the priest said.'

'The priest?'

'Yes, at Voa—do you know? Mother died there when I was small— it is so far away! And there are thirteen houses by the side of the river—just here; and on this side—trees, trees.'

This was important, I thought, and would lead to the very knowledge I wished for; so I pressed her to tell me more about the settlement she had named, and of which I had never heard.

'Everything have I told you,' she returned, surprised that I did not know that she had exhausted the subject in those half-dozen words she had spoken.

Obliged to shift my ground, I said at a venture: 'Tell me, what do you ask of the Virgin Mother when you kneel before her picture? Your grandfather told me that you had a picture in your little room.'

'You know!' flashed out her answer, with something like resentment. 'It is all there—in there,' waving her hand towards the hut. 'Out here in the wood it is all gone—like this,' and stooping quickly she raised a little yellow sand on her palm, then let it run away through her fingers.

Thus she illustrated how all the matters she had been taught slipped from her mind when she was out-of-doors, out of sight of the picture. After an interval she added, 'Only mother is here— always with me.'

'Ah, poor Rima!' I said; 'alone without a mother, and only your old grandfather! He is old—what will you do when he dies and flies away to the starry country where your mother is?'

She looked inquiringly at me, then made answer in a low voice, 'You are here.'

'But when I go away?'

She was silent; and not wishing to dwell on a subject that seemed to pain her, I continued: 'Yes, I am here now, but you will not stay with me and talk freely! Will it always be the same if I remain with you? Why are you always so silent in the house, so cold with your old grandfather? So different—so full of life, like a bird, when you are alone in the woods? Rima, speak to me! Am I no more to you than your old grandfather? Do you not like me to talk to you?'

She appeared strangely disturbed at my words. 'Oh, you are not like him,' she suddenly replied. 'Sitting all day on a log by the fire— all day, all day; Goloso and Susio lying beside him—sleep, sleep. Oh, when I saw you in the wood I followed you, and talked and talked; still no answer. Why will you not come when I call? To me!' Then, mocking my voice, 'Rima, Rima! Come here! Do this! Say that! Rima! Rima! It is nothing, nothing—it is not you,' pointing to my mouth; and then, as if fearing that her meaning had not been made clear, suddenly touching my lips with her finger. 'Why do you not answer me?—speak to me—speak to me, like this!' And turning a little more towards me, and glancing at me with eyes that had all at once changed, losing their clouded expression for one of exquisite tenderness, from her lips came a succession of those mysterious sounds which had first attracted me to her, swift and low and bird-like, yet with something so much higher and more soul-penetrating than any bird music. Ah, what feeling and fancies, what quaint turns of expression, unfamiliar to my mind, were contained in those sweet, wasted symbols! I could never know—never come to her when she called, or respond to her spirit. To me they would always be inarticulate sounds, affecting me like a tender spiritual music—a language without words, suggesting more than words to the soul.

The mysterious speech died down to a lisping sound, like the faint note of some small bird falling from a cloud of foliage on the topmost bough of a tree; and at the same time that new light passed from her eyes, and she half averted her face in a disappointed way.

'Rima,' I said at length, a new thought coming to my aid, 'it is true that I am not here,' touching my lips as she had done, 'and that my words are nothing. But look into my eyes, and you will see me there—all, all that is in my heart.'

'Oh, I know what I should see there!' she returned quickly.

'What would you see—tell me?'

'There is a little black ball in the middle of your eye; I should see myself in it no bigger than that,' and she marked off about an eighth of her little fingernail. 'There is a pool in the wood, and I look down and see myself there. That is better. Just as large as I am—not small and black like a small, small fly.' And after saying this a little disdainfully she moved away from my side and out into the sunshine; and then, half turning towards me, and glancing first at my face and then upwards, she raised her hand to call my attention to something there.

Far up, high as the tops of the tallest trees, a great blue-winged butterfly was passing across the open space with loitering flight. In a few moments it was gone over the trees; then she turned once more to me with a little rippling sound of laughter—the first I had heard from her, and called, 'Come, come!'

I was glad enough to go with her then; and for the next two hours we rambled together in the wood; that is, together in her way, for though always near she contrived to keep out of my sight most of the time. She was evidently now in a gay, frolicsome temper; again and again, when I looked closely into some wide-spreading bush, or peered behind a tree, when her calling voice had sounded, her rippling laughter would come to me from some other spot. At length, somewhere about the centre of the wood, she led me to an immense mora tree,* growing almost isolated, covering with its shade a large space of ground entirely free from undergrowth. At this spot she all at once vanished from my side; and after listening and watching some time in vain I sat down beside the giant trunk to wait for her. Very soon I heard a low, warbling sound which seemed quite near.

'Rima! Rima!' I called, and instantly my call was repeated like an echo. Again and again I called, and still the words flew back to me, and I could not decide whether it was an echo or not. Then I gave up calling; and presently the low, warbling sound was repeated, and I knew that Rima was somewhere near me.

'Rima, where are you?' I called.

'Rima, where are you?' came the answer.

'You are behind the tree.'

'You are behind the tree.'

'I shall catch you, Rima.' And this time, instead of repeating my words, she answered, 'Oh no.'

I jumped up and ran round the tree, feeling sure that I should find her. It was about thirty-five or forty feet in circumference; and after going round two or three times I turned and ran the other way, but failing to catch a glimpse of her I at last sat down again.

'Rima, Rima!' sounded the mocking voice as soon as I had sat down. 'Where are you, Rima? I shall catch you, Rima! Have you caught Rima?'

'No, I have not caught her. There is no Rima now. She has faded away like a rainbow—like a drop of dew in the sun. I have lost her; I shall go to sleep.' And stretching myself out at full length under the tree, I remained quiet for two or three minutes. Then a slight rustling sound was heard, and I looked eagerly round for her. But the sound was overhead and caused by a great avalanche of leaves which began to descend on to me from that vast leafy canopy above.

'Ah, little spider-monkey—little green tree-snake—you are there!' But there was no seeing her in that immense aerial palace hung with dim drapery of green and copper-coloured leaves. But how had she got there? Up the stupendous trunk even a monkey could not have climbed, and there were no lianas dropping to earth from the wide horizontal branches that I could see; but by-and-by, looking further away, I perceived that on one side the longest lower branches reached and mingled with the shorter boughs of the neighbouring trees. While gazing up I heard her low, rippling laugh, and then caught sight of her as she ran along an exposed horizontal branch, erect on her feet; and my heart stood still with terror, for she was fifty to sixty feet above the ground.* In another moment she vanished from sight in a cloud of foliage, and I saw no more of her for about ten minutes, when all at once she appeared at my side once more, having come round the trunk of the mora. Her face had a bright, pleased expression, and showed no trace of fatigue or agitation.

I caught her hand in mine. It was a delicate, shapely little hand, soft as velvet, and warm—a real human hand: only now when I held it did she seem altogether like a human being, and not a mocking spirit of the wood, a daughter of the Didi.

'Do you like me to hold your hand, Rima?'

'Yes,' she replied, with indifference.

'Is it I?'

'Yes.' This time as if it was small satisfaction to make acquaintance with this purely physical part of me.

Having her so close gave me an opportunity of examining that light sheeny garment she wore always in the woods. It felt soft and satiny to the touch, and there was no seam nor hem in it that I could see, but it was all in one piece, like the cocoon of the caterpillar. While I was feeling it on her shoulder and looking narrowly at it, she glanced at me with a mocking laugh in her eyes.

'Is it silk?' I asked. Then, as she remained silent, I continued, 'Where did you get this dress, Rima? Did you make it yourself? Tell me.'

She answered not in words, but in response to my question a new look came into her face; no longer restless and full of change in her expression, she was now as immovable as an alabaster statue; not a silken hair on her head trembled; her eyes were wide open, gazing fixedly before her; and when I looked into them they seemed to see and yet not to see me. They were like the clear, brilliant eyes of a bird, which reflect as in a miraculous mirror all the visible world but do not return our look, and seem to see us merely as one of the thousand small details that make up the whole picture. Suddenly she darted out her hand like a flash, making me start at the un-expected motion, and quickly withdrawing it, held up a finger before me. From its tip a minute gossamer spider, about twice the bigness of a pin's head, appeared suspended from a fine, scarcely visible line three or four inches long.

'Look!' she exclaimed, with a bright glance at my face.

The small spider she had captured, anxious to be free, was falling, falling earthward, but could not reach the surface. Leaning her shoulder a little forward, she placed the finger-tip against it, but lightly, scarcely touching, and moving continuously, with a motion rapid as that of a fluttering moth's wing; while the spider, still paying out his line, remained suspended, rising and falling slightly at nearly the same distance from the ground. After a few moments she cried, 'Drop down, little spider.' Her finger's motion ceased, and the minute captive fell, to lose itself on the shaded ground.

'Do you not see?' she said to me, pointing to her shoulder. Just where the finger-tip had touched the garment a round shining spot appeared, looking like a silver coin on the cloth; but on touching it with my finger it seemed part of the original fabric, only whiter and more shiny on the grey ground, on account of the freshness of the web of which it had just been made.

And so all this curious and pretty performance, which seemed instinctive in its spontaneous quickness and dexterity, was merely intended to show me how she made her garments out of the fine floating lines of small gossamer spiders!*

Before I could express my surprise and admiration she cried again, with startling suddenness, 'Look!'

A minute shadowy form darted by, appearing like a dim line traced across the deep glossy mora foliage, then on the lighter green foliage further away. She waved her hand in imitation of its swift, curving flight, then dropping it exclaimed, 'Gone—oh, little thing!'

'What was it?' I asked, for it might have been a bird, a bird-like moth, or a bee.

'Did you not see? And you asked me to look into your eyes!'

'Ah, little squirrel Sakawinki,* you remind me of that!' I said, passing my arm round her waist and drawing her a little closer. 'Look into my eyes now and see if I am blind, and if there is nothing in them except an image of Rima like a small, small fly.'

She shook her head and laughed a little mockingly, but made no effort to escape from my arm.

'Would you like me always to do what you wish, Rima—to follow you in the woods when you say "Come"—to chase you round the tree to catch you, and lie down for you to throw leaves on me, and to be glad when you are glad?'

'Oh yes.'

'Then let us make a compact. I shall do everything to please you, and you must promise to do everything to please me.'

'Tell me.'

'Little things, Rima—none so hard as chasing you round a tree. Only to have you stand or sit by me and talk will make me happy. And to begin you must call me by my name—Abel.'

'Is that your name? Oh, not your real name! Abel, Abel—what is that? It says nothing. I have called you by so many names—twenty, thirty—and no answer.'

'Have you? But, dearest girl, every person has a name—one name he is called by. Your name, for instance, is Rima, is it not?'

'Rima! only Rima—to you? In the morning, in the evening . . . now in this place and in a little while where know I? . . . in the night when you wake and it is dark, dark, and you see me all the same. Only Rima—oh, how strange!'

'What else, sweet girl? Your grandfather Nuflo calls you Rima.'

'Nuflo?' She spoke as if putting a question to herself. 'Is that an old man with two dogs that lives somewhere in the wood?' And then, with sudden petulance, 'And you ask me to talk to you!'

'Oh, Rima, what can I say to you? Listen——'

'No, no,' she exclaimed, quickly turning and putting her fingers on my mouth to stop my speech, while a sudden merry look shone in her eyes. 'You shall listen when I speak, and do all I say. And tell me what to do to please you with your eyes—let me look in your eyes that are not blind.'

She turned her face more towards me, and with head a little thrown back and inclined to one side, gazing now full into my eyes as I had wished her to do. After a few moments she glanced away to the distant trees. But I could see into those divine orbs, and knew that she was not looking at any particular object. All the ever-varying expressions—inquisitive, petulant, troubled, shy, frolicsome—had now vanished from the still face, and the look was inward and full of a strange, exquisite light, as if some new happiness or hope had touched her spirit.

Sinking my voice to a whisper I said, 'Tell me what you have seen in my eyes, Rima?'

She murmured in reply something melodious and inarticulate, then glanced at my face in a questioning way; but only for a moment, then her sweet eyes were again veiled under those drooping lashes.

'Listen, Rima,' I said. 'Was that a humming-bird we saw a little while ago? You are like that, now dark, a shadow in the shadow, seen for an instant, and then—gone, oh, little thing! And now in the sunshine standing still, how beautiful!—a thousand times more beautiful than the humming-bird. Listen, Rima, you are like all beautiful things in the wood—flower, and bird, and butterfly, and green leaf, and frond, and little silky-haired monkey high up in the trees. When I look at you I see them all—all and more, a thousand times, for I see Rima herself. And when I listen to Rima's voice, talking in a language I cannot understand, I hear the wind whispering in the leaves, the gurgling running water, the bee among the flowers, the organ-bird singing far, far away in the shadows of the trees. I hear them all, and more, for I hear Rima. Do you understand me now? Is it I speaking to you—have I answered you—have I come to you?'

She glanced at me again, her lips trembling, her eyes now clouded with some secret trouble. 'Yes,' she replied in a whisper, and then, 'No, it is not you,' and after a moment, doubtfully, 'Is it you?'

But she did not wait to be answered: in a moment she was gone round the mora; nor would she return again for all my calling.

CHAPTER IX

THAT afternoon with Rima in the forest under the mora tree had proved so delightful that I was eager for more rambles and talks with her, but the variable little witch had a great surprise in store for me. All her wild natural gaiety had unaccountably gone out of her: when I walked in the shade she was there, but no longer as the blithe, fantastic being, bright as an angel, innocent and affectionate as a child, tricksy as a monkey, that had played at hide-and-seek with me. She was now my shy, silent attendant, only occasionally visible, and appearing then like the mysterious maid I had found reclining among the ferns who had melted away mist-like from sight as I gazed. When I called she would not now answer as formerly, but in response would appear in sight as if to assure me that I had not been forsaken; and after a few moments her grey shadowy form would once more vanish among the trees. The hope that as her confidence increased and she grew accustomed to talk with me she would be brought to reveal the story of her life had to be abandoned, at all events for the present. I must, after all, get my information from Nuflo, or rest in ignorance. The old man was out for the greater part of each day with his dogs, and from these expeditions he brought back nothing that I could see but a few nuts and fruits, some thin bark for his cigarettes, and an occasional handful of haima gum to perfume the hut of an evening. After I had wasted three days in vainly trying to overcome the girl's now inexplicable shyness, I resolved to give for a while my undivided attention to her grandfather to discover, if possible, where he went and how he spent his time.

My new game of hide-and-seek with Nuflo instead of with Rima began on the following morning. He was cunning: so was I. Going out and concealing myself among the bushes, I began to watch the hut. That I could elude Rima's keener eyes I doubted; but that did not trouble me. She was not in harmony with the old man, and would do nothing to defeat my plan. I had not been long in my hiding-place before he came out, followed by his two dogs, and going to some distance from the door he sat down on a log. For some minutes he smoked, then rose, and after looking cautiously round slipped away among the trees. I saw that he was going off in the direction of the low range of rocky hills south of the forest. I knew that the forest did not extend far in that direction, and thinking that I should be able to catch a sight of him on its borders, I left the bushes and ran through the trees as fast as I could to get ahead of him. Coming to where the wood was very open, I found that a barren plain beyond it, a quarter of a mile wide, separated it from the range of hills; thinking that the old man might cross this open space I climbed into a tree to watch. After some time he appeared, walking rapidly among the trees, the dogs at his heels, but not going towards the open plain; he had, it seemed, after arriving at the edge of the wood, changed his direction, and was going west, still keeping in the shelter of the trees. When he had been gone about five minutes I dropped to the ground and started in pursuit; once more I caught sight of him through the trees, and I kept him in sight for about twenty minutes longer; then he came to a broad strip of dense wood which extended into and through the range of hills, and here I quickly lost him. Hoping still to overtake him, I pushed on, but after struggling through the underwood for some distance, and finding the forest growing more difficult as I progressed, I at last gave him up. Turning eastward I got out of the wood to find myself at the foot of a steep rough hill, one of the range which the wooded valley cut through at right angles. It struck me that it would be a good plan to climb the hill to get a view of the forest belt in which I had lost the old man; and after walking a short distance I found a spot which allowed of an ascent. The summit of the hill was about three hundred feet above the surrounding level, and did not take me long to reach; it commanded a fair view, and I now saw that the belt of wood beneath me extended right through the range, and on the south side opened out into an extensive forest. 'If that is your destination,' thought I, 'old fox, your secrets are safe from me.'

It was still early in the day, and a slight breeze tempered the air and made it cool and pleasant on the hilltop after my exertions. My scramble through the wood had fatigued me somewhat, and resolving to spend some hours on that spot, I looked round for a comfortable resting-place. I soon found a shady spot on the west side of an upright block of stone where I could recline at ease on a bed of lichen. Here, with shoulders resting against the rock, I sat thinking of Rima, alone in her wood to-day, with just a tinge of bitterness in my thoughts which made me hope that she would miss me as much as I missed her; and in the end I fell asleep.

When I woke it was past noon, and the sun was shining directly on me. Standing up to gaze once more on the prospect, I noticed a small wreath of white smoke issuing from a spot about the middle of the forest belt beneath me, and I instantly divined that Nuflo had made a fire at that place, and I resolved to surprise him in his retreat. When I got down to the base of the hill the smoke could no longer be seen, but I had studied the spot well from above, and had singled out a large clump of trees on the edge of the belt as a starting-point; and after a search of half an hour I succeeded in finding the old man's hiding-place. First I saw smoke again through an opening in the trees, then a small rude hut of sticks and palm-leaves. Approaching cautiously, I peered through a crack and discovered old Nuflo engaged in smoking some meat over a fire, and at the same time grilling some bones on the coals. He had captured a coatimundi, an animal somewhat larger than a tame tom cat, with a long snout and long ringed tail: one of the dogs was gnawing at the animal's head, and the tail and the feet were also lying on the floor, among the old bones and rubbish that littered it. Stealing round I suddenly presented myself at the opening to his den, when the dogs rose up with a growl and Nuflo instantly leaped to his feet, knife in hand.

'Aha, old man,' I cried, with a laugh, 'I have found you at one of your vegetarian repasts; and your grass-eating dogs as well!'

He was disconcerted and suspicious, but when I explained that I had seen a smoke while on the hills, where I had gone to search for a curious blue flower which grew in such places, and had made my way to it to discover the cause, he recovered confidence and invited me to join him at his dinner of roast meat.

I was hungry by this time and not sorry to get animal food once more; nevertheless, I ate this meat with some disgust, as it had a rank taste and smell, and it was also unpleasant to have those evil-looking dogs savagely gnawing at the animal's head and feet at the same time.

'You see,' said the old hypocrite, wiping the grease from his moustache, 'this is what I am compelled to do in order to avoid giving offence. My granddaughter is a strange being, sir, as you have perhaps observed——'

'That reminds me,' I interrupted, 'that I wish you to relate her history to me. She is, as you say, strange, and has speech and faculties unlike ours, which shows that she comes of a different race.'

'No, no, her faculties are not different from ours. They are sharper, that is all. It pleases the All-Powerful to give more to some than to others. Not all the fingers on the hand are alike. You will find a man who will take up a guitar and make it speak, while I——'

'All that I understand,' I broke in again. 'But her origin, her history—that is what I wish to hear.'

'And that, sir, is precisely what I am about to relate. Poor child, she was left on my hands by her sainted mother—my daughter, sir—who perished young. Now her birthplace, where she was taught letters and the Catechism by the priest, was in an unhealthy situation. It was hot and wet—always wet—a place suited to frogs rather than to human beings. At length, thinking that it would suit the child better—for she was pale and weakly—to live in a drier atmosphere among mountains, I brought her to this district. For this, señor, and for all I have done for her, I look for no reward here, but to that place where my daughter has got her foot; not, sir, on the threshold, as you might think, but well inside. For, after all, it is to the authorities above, in spite of some blots which we see in their administration, that we must look for justice. Frankly, sir, this is the whole story of my granddaughter's origin.'

'Ah, yes,' I returned, 'your story explains why she can call a wild bird to her hand, and touch a venomous serpent with her bare foot and receive no harm.'

'Doubtless you are right,' said the old dissembler. 'Living alone in the wood she had only God's creatures to play and make friends with; and wild animals, I have heard it said, know those who are friendly towards them.'

'You treat her friends badly,' said I, kicking the long tail of the coatimundi away with my foot, and regretting that I had joined in his repast.

'Señor, you must consider that we are only what Heaven made us. When all this was formed,' he continued, opening his arms wide to indicate the entire creation, 'the Person who concerned himself with this matter gave seeds and fruitlets and nectar of flowers for the sustentation of His small birds. But we have not their delicate appetites. The more robust stomach which he gave to man cries out for meat. Do you understand? But of all this, friend, not one word to Rima!'

I laughed scornfully. 'Do you think me such a child, old man, as to believe that Rima, that little sprite, does not know that you are an eater of flesh? Rima, who is everywhere in the wood, seeing all things, even if I lift my hand against a serpent, she herself unseen.'

'But, sir, if you will pardon my presumption, you are saying too much. She does not come here, and therefore cannot see that I eat meat. In all that wood where she flourishes and sings, where she is in her house and garden, and mistress of the creatures, even of the small butterfly with painted wings, there, sir, I hunt no animal. Nor will my dogs chase any animal there. That is what I meant when I said that if an animal should stumble against their legs, they would lift up their noses and pass on without seeing it. For in that wood there is one law, the law that Rima imposes, and outside of it a different law.'

'I am glad that you have told me this,' I replied. 'The thought that Rima might be near, and, unseen herself, look in upon us feeding with the dogs and, like dogs, on flesh, was one which greatly troubled my mind.'

He glanced at me in his usual quick, cunning way.

'Ah, señor, you have that feeling too—after so short a time with us! Consider, then, what it must be for me, unable to nourish myself on gums and fruitlets, and that little sweetness made by wasps out of flowers, when I am compelled to go far away and eat secretly to avoid giving offence.'

It was hard, no doubt, but I did not pity him; secretly I could only feel anger against him for refusing to enlighten me, while making such a pretence of openness; and I also felt disgusted with myself for having joined him in his rank repast. But dissimulation was necessary, and so, after conversing a little more on indifferent topics, and thanking him for his hospitality, I left him alone to go on with his smoky task.

On my way back to the lodge, fearing that some taint of Nuflo's evil-smelling den and dinner might still cling to me, I turned aside to where a streamlet in the wood widened and formed a deep pool, to take a plunge in the water. After drying myself in the air, and thoroughly ventilating my garments by shaking and beating them, I found an open, shady spot in the wood and threw myself on the grass to wait for evening before returning to the house. By that time the sweet, warm air would have purified me. Besides, I did not consider that I had sufficiently punished Rima for her treatment of me. She would be anxious for my safety, perhaps even looking for me everywhere in the wood. It was not much to make her suffer one day after she had made me miserable for three; and perhaps when she discovered that I could exist without her society she would begin to treat me less capriciously.

So ran my thoughts as I rested on the warm ground, gazing up into the foliage, green as young grass in the lower, shady parts, and above luminous with the bright sunlight, and full of the murmuring sounds of insect life. My every action, word, thought, had my feeling for Rima as a motive. Why, I began to ask myself, was Rima so much to me? It was easy to answer that question: Because nothing so exquisite had ever been created. All the separate and fragmentary beauty and melody and graceful motion found scattered throughout nature were concentrated and harmoniously combined in her. How various, how luminous, how divine she was! A being for the mind to marvel at, to admire continually, finding some new grace and charm every hour, every moment, to add to the old. And there was, besides, the fascinating mystery surrounding her origin to arouse and keep my interest in her continually active.

That was the easy answer I returned to the question I had asked myself. But I knew that there was another answer—a reason more powerful than the first. And I could no longer thrust it back, or hide its shining face with the dull, leaden mask of mere intellectual curiosity. *Because I loved her;* loved her as I had never loved before, never could love any other being, with a passion which had caught something of her own brilliance and intensity, making a former passion look dim and commonplace in comparison—a feeling known to everyone, something old and worn out, a weariness even to think of.

From these reflections I was roused by the plaintive three-syllable call of an evening bird—a nightjar common in these woods; and was surprised to find that the sun had set, and the woods already shadowed with the twilight. I started up and began hurriedly walking homewards, thinking of Rima, and was consumed with impatience to see her; and as I drew near to the house, walking along a narrow path which I knew, I suddenly met her face to face. Doubtless she had heard my approach, and instead of shrinking out of the path and allowing me to pass on without seeing her, as she would have done on the previous day, she had sprung forward to meet me. I was struck with wonder at the change in her as she came with a swift, easy motion, like a flying bird, her hands outstretched as if to clasp mine, her lips parted in a radiant, welcoming smile, her eyes sparkling with joy.

I started forward to meet her, but had no sooner touched her hands than her countenance changed, and she shrunk back trembling, as if the touch had chilled her warm blood; and moving some feet away, she stood with downcast eyes, pale and sorrowful as she had seemed yesterday. In vain I implored her to tell me the cause of this change and of the trouble she evidently felt; her lips trembled as if with speech, but she made no reply, and only shrunk further away when I attempted to approach her; and at length, moving aside from the path, she was lost to sight in the dusky leafage.

I went on alone, and sat outside for some time, until old Nuflo returned from his hunting; and only after he had gone in and had made the fire burn up did Rima make her appearance, silent and constrained as ever.

CHAPTER X

ON the following day Rima continued in the same inexplicable humour; and feeling my defeat keenly, I determined once more to try the effect of absence on her, and to remain away on this occasion for a longer period. Like old Nuflo, I was secret in going forth next morning, waiting until the girl was out of the way, then slipping off among the bushes into the deeper wood; and finally quitting its shelter I set out across the savannah towards my old quarters. Great was my surprise on arriving at the village to find no person there. At first I imagined that my disappearance in the forest of evil fame had caused them to abandon their home in a panic; but on looking round I concluded that my friends had only gone on one of their periodical visits to some neighbouring village. For when these Indians visit their neighbours they do it in a very thorough manner; they all go, taking with them their entire stock of provisions, their cooking utensils, weapons, hammocks, and even their pet animals. Fortunately in this case they had not taken quite everything; my hammock was there, also one small pot, some cassava bread, purple potatoes, and a few ears of maize. I concluded that these had been left for me in the event of my return; also that they had not been gone very many hours, since a log of wood buried under the ashes of the hearth was still alight. Now as their absences from home usually last many days, it was plain that I would have the big naked barn-like house to myself for as long as I thought proper to remain, with little food to eat; but the prospect did not disturb me, and I resolved to amuse myself with music. In vain I hunted for my guitar; the Indians had taken it to delight their friends by twanging its strings. At odd moments during the last day or two I had been composing a simple melody in my brain, fitting it to ancient words;* and now, without an instrument to assist me, I began softly singing to myself:—

> *Muy mas clara que la luna*
> *Sola una*
> *en el mundo vos nacistes.*

After music I made up the fire and parched an ear of maize for my dinner, and while laboriously crunching the dry hard grain I thanked Heaven for having bestowed on me such good molars. Finally, I slung my hammock in its old corner, and placing myself in it in my favourite oblique position, my hands clasped behind my head, one knee cocked up, the other leg dangling down, I resigned myself to idle thought. I felt very happy. How strange, thought I, with a little self-flattery, that I, accustomed to the agreeable society of intelligent men and charming women, and of books, should find such perfect contentment here! But I congratulated myself too soon. The profound silence began at length to oppress me. It was not like the forest, where one has wild birds for company, where their cries, albeit inarticulate, have a meaning and give a charm to solitude. Even the sight and whispered sounds of green leaves and rushes trembling in the wind have for us something of intelligence and sympathy; but I could not commune with mud walls and an earthen pot. Feeling my loneliness too acutely, I began to regret that I had left Rima, then to feel remorse at the secrecy I had practised. Even now, while I inclined idly in my hammock, she would be roaming the forest in search of me, listening for my footsteps, fearing perhaps that I had met with some accident where there was no person to succour me. It was painful to think of her in this way, of the pain I had doubtless given her by stealing off without a word of warning. Springing to the floor, I flung out of the house and went down to the stream. It was better there, for now the greatest heat of the day was over, and the westering sun began to look large, and red, and rayless through the afternoon haze.

I seated myself on a stone within a yard or two of the limpid water: and now the sight of nature and the warm, vital air and sunshine infected my spirit, and made it possible for me to face the position calmly, even hopefully. The position was this: for some days the idea had been present in my mind, and was now fixed there, that this desert was to be my permanent home. The thought of going back to Caracas, that little Paris in America, with its old-world vices, its idle political passions, its empty round of gaieties, was unendurable. I was changed, and this change—so great, so complete—was proof that the old artificial life had not been and could not be the real one, in harmony with my deeper and truer nature. I deceived myself, you will say, as I have often myself said. I had and I had not. It is too long a question to discuss here; but just then I felt that I had quitted the hot, tainted atmosphere of the ballroom, that the morning air of heaven refreshed and elevated me, and was sweet to breathe. Friends and relations I had who were dear to me; but I could forget them, even as I could forget the splendid dreams which had been mine. And the woman I had loved, and who perhaps loved me in return—I could forget her too. A daughter of civilisation and of that artificial life, she could never experience such feelings as these and return to nature as I was doing. For women, though within narrow limits more plastic than men, are yet without that larger adaptiveness which can take us back to the sources of life, which they have left eternally behind. Better, far better for both of us that she should wait through the long, slow months, growing sick at heart with hope deferred;* that, seeing me no more, she should weep my loss, and be healed at last by time, and find love and happiness again in the old way, in the old place.

And while I thus sat thinking, sadly enough, but not despondingly, of past and present and future, all at once on the warm, still air came the resonant, far-reaching *kling-klang* of the campanero* from some leafy summit half a league away. *Kling-klang* fell the sound again, and often again, at intervals, affecting me strangely at that moment, so bell-like, so like the great wide-travelling sounds associated in our minds with Christian worship. And yet so unlike. A bell, yet not made of gross metal dug out of earth, but of an ethereal, sublimer material that floats impalpable and invisible in space—a vital bell suspended on nothing, giving out sounds in harmony with the vastness of blue heaven, the unsullied purity of nature, the glory of the sun, and conveying a mystic, a higher message to the soul than the sounds that surge from tower and belfry.

O mystic bell-bird of the heavenly race of the swallow and dove, the quetzal and the nightingale! When the brutish savage and the brutish white man that slay thee, one for food, the other for the benefit of science, shall have passed away, live still, live to tell thy message to the blameless spiritualised race that shall come after us to possess the earth, not for a thousand years, but for ever; for how much shall thy voice be to our clarified successors when even to my dull, unpurged soul, thou canst speak such high things, and bring it a sense of an impersonal, all-compromising One who is in me and I in him, flesh of his flesh and soul of his soul.

The sounds ceased, but I was still in that exalted mood, and, like a person in a trance, staring fixedly before me into the open wood of scattered dwarf trees on the other side of the stream, when suddenly on the field of vision appeared a grotesque human figure moving towards me. I started violently, astonished and a little alarmed, but in a very few moments I recognised the ancient Cla-cla, coming home with a large bundle of dry sticks on her shoulders, bent almost double under the burden, and still ignorant of my presence. Slowly she came down to the stream, then cautiously made her way over the line of stepping-stones by which it was crossed; and only when within ten yards did the old creature catch sight of me sitting silent and motionless in her path. With a sharp cry of amazement and terror she straightened herself up, the bundle of sticks dropping to the ground, and turned to run from me. That, at all events, seemed her intention, for her body was thrown forward, and her head and arms working like those of a person going at full speed, but her legs seemed paralysed and her feet remained planted on the same spot. I burst out laughing; whereat she twisted her neck until her wrinkled, brown old face appeared over her shoulder staring at me. This made me laugh again, whereupon she straightened herself up once more and turned round to have a good look at me.

'Come, Cla-cla,' I cried; 'can you not see that I am a living man and no spirit? I thought no one had remained behind to keep me company and give me food. Why are you not with the others?'

'Ah, why!' she returned tragically. And then deliberately turning from me and assuming a most unladylike attitude, she slapped herself vigorously on the small of the back, exclaiming, 'Because of my pain here!'

As she continued in that position with her back towards me for some time, I laughed once more and begged her to explain.

Slowly she turned round and advanced cautiously towards me, staring at me all the time. Finally, still eyeing me suspiciously, she related that the others had all gone on a visit to a distant village, she starting with them: that after going some distance a pain had attacked her in her hind quarters, so sudden and acute that it had instantly brought her to a full stop; and to illustrate how full the stop was she allowed herself to go down, very unnecessarily, with a flop to the ground. But she no sooner touched the ground than up she started to her feet again, with an alarmed look on her owlish face, as if she had sat down on a stinging-nettle.

'We thought you were dead,' she remarked, still thinking that I might be a ghost after all.

'No, still alive,' I said. 'And so because you came to the ground with your pain they left you behind! Well, never mind, Cla-cla, we are two now and must try to be happy together.'

By this time she had recovered from her fear and began to feel highly pleased at my return, only lamenting that she had no meat to give me. She was anxious to hear my adventures, and the reason of my long absence. I had no wish to gratify her curiosity, with the truth at all events, knowing very well that with regard to the daughter of the Didi her feelings were as purely savage and malignant as those of Kua-kó. But it was necessary to say something, and, fortifying myself with the good old Spanish notion that lies told to the heathen are not recorded,* I related that a venomous serpent had bitten me; after which a terrible thunderstorm had surprised me in the forest, and night coming on prevented my escape from it; then, next day, remembering that he who is bitten by a serpent dies, and not wishing to distress my friends with the sight of my dissolution, I elected to remain, sitting there in the wood, amusing myself by singing songs and smoking cigarettes; and after several days and nights had gone by, finding that I was not going to die after all, and beginning to feel hungry, I got up and came back.

Old Cla-cla looked very serious, shaking and nodding her head a great deal, muttering to herself; finally, she gave it as her opinion that nothing ever would or could kill me; but whether my story had been believed or not she only knew.

I spent an amusing evening with my old savage hostess. She had thrown off her ailments, and pleased at having a companion in her dreary solitude, she was good-tempered and talkative, and much more inclined to laugh than when the others were present, when she was on her dignity.

We sat by the fire, cooking such food as we had, and talked and smoked; then I sang her songs in Spanish with that melody of my own—

Muy mas clara que la luna;

and she rewarded me by emitting a barbarous chant in a shrill, screechy voice; and, finally, starting up, I danced for her benefit polka, mazurka, and valse, whistling and singing to my motions.

More than once during the evening she tried to introduce serious subjects, telling me that I must always live with them, learn to shoot the birds and catch the fishes, and have a wife; and then she would speak of her granddaughter Oalava, whose virtues it was proper to mention, but whose physical charms needed no description since they had never been concealed. Each time she got on this topic I cut her short, vowing that if I ever married she only should be my wife. She informed me that she was old and past her fruitful period; that not much longer would she make cassava-bread, and blow the fire to a flame with her wheezy old bellows, and talk the men to sleep at night. But I stuck to it that she was young and beautiful, that our descendants would be more numerous than the birds in the forest. I went out to some bushes close by, where I had noticed a passion plant in bloom, and gathering a few splendid scarlet blossoms with their stems and leaves, I brought them in and wove them into a garland for the old dame's head; then I pulled her up, in spite of screams and struggles, and waltzed her wildly to the other end of the room and back again to her seat beside the fire. And as she sat there, panting and grinning with laughter, I knelt before her, and with suitable passionate gestures, declaimed again the old delicate lines sung by Mena* before Columbus sailed the seas:—

> Muy mas clara que la luna
> Sola una
> en el mundo vos nacistes
> tan gentil, que no vecistes
> ni tuvistes
> competedora ninguna
> Desdi niñez en la cuna
> cobrastes fama, beldad,
> con tanta graciosidad,
> que vos dotó la fortuna.

Thinking of another all the time! O poor old Cla-cla, knowing not what the jingle meant nor the secret of my wild happiness, now when I recall you sitting there, your old grey owlish head crowned with scarlet passion flowers, flushed with firelight, against the background of smoke-blackened walls and rafters, how the old undying sorrow comes back to me!

Thus our evening was spent, merrily enough; then we made up the fire with hard wood that would last all night, and went to our hammocks, but wakeful still. The old dame, glad and proud to be on duty once more, religiously went to work to talk me to sleep; but although I called out at intervals to encourage her to go on, I did not attempt

to follow the ancient tales she told, which she had imbibed in childhood from other white-headed grandmothers long, long turned to
dust. My own brain was busy thinking, thinking, thinking now of the
woman I had once loved, far away in Venezuela, waiting and weeping
and sick with hope deferred; now of Rima, wakeful and listening to
the mysterious night-sounds of the forest—listening, listening for
my returning footsteps.

Next morning I began to waver in my resolution to remain absent
from Rima for some days: and before evening my passion, which I
had now ceased to struggle against, coupled with the thought that I
had acted unkindly in leaving her, that she would be a prey to anxiety, overcame me, and I was ready to return. The old woman, who
had been suspiciously watching my movements, rushed out after me
as I left the house, crying out that a storm was brewing, that it was
too late to go far, and night would be full of danger. I waved my hand
in good-bye, laughingly reminding her that I was proof against all
perils. Little she cared what evil might befall me, I thought; but she
loved not to be alone; even for her, low down as she was intellectually, the solitary earthen pot had no 'mind stuff' in it, and could
not be sent to sleep at night with the legends of long ago.

By the time I reached the ridge I had discovered that she had prophesied truly, for now an ominous change had come over nature. A
dull grey vapour had overspread the entire western half of the hea-
vens; down, beyond the forest, the sky looked black as ink, and behind
this blackness the sun had vanished. It was too late to go back now; I
had been too long absent from Rima, and could only hope to reach
Nuflo's lodge, wet or dry, before night closed round me in the forest.

For some moments I stood still on the ridge, struck by the somewhat weird aspect of the shadowed scene before me—the long strip
of dull uniform green, with here and there a slender palm lifting its
feathery crown above the other trees, standing motionless, in strange
relief against the advancing blackness. Then I set out once more at a
run, taking advantage of the downward slope to get well on my way
before the tempest should burst. As I approached the wood there
came a flash of lightning, pale, but covering the whole visible sky,
followed after a long interval by a distant roll of thunder, which lasted
several seconds, and ended with a succession of deep throbs. It was
as if Nature herself, in supreme anguish and abandonment, had cast

herself prone on the earth, and her great heart had throbbed audibly, shaking the world with its beats. No more thunder followed, but the rain was coming down heavily now in huge drops that fell straight through the gloomy, windless air. In half a minute I was drenched to the skin; but for a short time the rain seemed an advantage, as the brightness of the falling water lessened the gloom, turning the air from dark to lighter grey. This subdued rain-light did not last long: I had not been twenty minutes in the wood before a second and greater darkness fell on the earth, accompanied by an even more copious downpour of water. The sun had evidently gone down, and the whole sky was now covered with one thick cloud. Becoming more nervous as the gloom increased, I bent my steps more to the south, so as to keep near the border and more open part of the wood. Probably I had already grown confused before deviating and turned the wrong way, for instead of finding the forest easier, it grew closer and more difficult as I advanced. Before many minutes the darkness so increased that I could no longer distinguish objects more than five feet from my eyes. Groping blindly along, I became entangled in a dense under-growth, and after struggling and stumbling along for some distance in vain endeavours to get through it, I came to a stand at last in sheer despair. All sense of direction was now lost: I was entombed in thick blackness—blackness of night and cloud and rain and of dripping fo-liage and network of branches bound with bush-ropes and creepers in a wild tangle. I had struggled into a hollow, or hole, as it were, in the midst of that mass of vegetation, where I could stand upright and turn round and round without touching anything; but when I put out my hands they came into contact with vines and bushes. To move from that spot seemed folly; yet how dreadful to remain there standing on the sodden earth, chilled with rain, in that awful black-ness in which the only luminous thing one could look to see would be the eyes, shining with their own internal light, of some savage beast of prey. Yet the danger, the intense physical discomfort, and the anguish of looking forward to a whole night spent in that situ-ation, stung my heart less than the thought of Rima's anxiety and of the pain I had carelessly given by secretly leaving her.

It was then, with that pang in my heart, that I was startled by hear-ing, close by, one of her own low, warbled expressions. There could be no mistake; if the forest had been full of the sounds of animal life and songs of melodious birds, her voice would have been instantly distinguished from all others. How mysterious, how infinitely tender it sounded in that awful blackness!—so musical and exquisitely modulated, so sorrowful, yet piercing my heart with a sudden, unutterable joy.

'Rima! Rima!' I cried. 'Speak again. Is it you? Come to me here.'

Again that low, warbling sound, or series of sounds, seemingly from a distance of a few yards. I was not disturbed at her not replying in Spanish: she had always spoken it somewhat reluctantly, and only when at my side; but when calling to me from some distance she would return instinctively to her own mysterious language, and call to me as bird calls to bird. I knew that she was inviting me to follow her, but I refused to move.

'Rima,' I cried again, 'come to me here, for I know not where to step, and cannot move until you are at my side, and I can feel your hand.'

There came no response, and after some moments, becoming alarmed, I called to her again.

Then close by me, in a low, trembling voice, she returned, 'I am here.'

I put out my hand and touched something soft and wet; it was her breast, and moving my hand higher up, I felt her hair, hanging now and streaming with water. She was trembling, and I thought the rain had chilled her.

'Rima—poor child! How wet you are! How strange to meet you in such a place! Tell me, dear Rima, how did you find me?'

'I was waiting—watching—all day. I saw you coming across the savannah, and followed at a distance through the wood.'

'And I had treated you so unkindly! Ah, my guardian angel, my light in the darkness, how I hate myself for giving you pain! Tell me, sweet, did you wish me to come back and live with you again?'

She made no reply. Then, running my fingers down her arm, I took her hand in mine. It was hot, like the hand of one in a fever. I raised it to my lips, and then attempted to draw her to me, but she slipped down and out of my arms to my feet. I felt her there, on her knees, with head bowed low. Stooping and putting my arm round her body, I drew her up and held her against my breast, and felt her heart throbbing wildly. With many endearing words I begged her to speak to me; but her only reply was, 'Come—come,' as she slipped again out of my arms, and holding my hand in hers, guided me through the bushes.

Before long we came to an open path or glade, where the darkness was not profound; and releasing my hand she began walking rapidly before me, always keeping at such a distance as just enabled me to distinguish her grey, shadowy figure, and with frequent doublings to follow the natural paths and openings which she knew so well. In this way we kept on nearly to the end, without exchanging a word, and hearing no sound except the continuous rush of rain, which to our accustomed ears had ceased to have the effect of sound, and the various gurgling noises of innumerable runnels. All at once, as we came to a more open place, a strip of bright firelight appeared before us, shining from the half-open door of Nuflo's lodge. She turned round as much as to say, 'Now you know where you are, ' then hurried on, leaving me to follow as best I could.

CHAPTER XI

THERE was a welcome change in the weather when I rose early next morning; the sky was without cloud, and had that purity in its colour and look of infinite distance seen only when the atmosphere is free from vapour. The sun had not yet risen, but old Nuflo was already among the ashes, on his hands and knees, blowing the embers he had uncovered to a flame. Then Rima appeared only to pass through the room with quick light tread to go out of the door without a word or even a glance at my face. The old man, after watching at the door for a few minutes, turned and began eagerly questioning me about my adventures on the previous evening. In reply I related to him how the girl had found me in the forest lost and unable to extricate myself from the tangled undergrowth.

He rubbed his hands on his knees and chuckled. 'Happy for you, señor,' he said, 'that my granddaughter regards you with such friendly eyes, otherwise you might have perished before morning. Once she was at your side, no light, whether of sun or moon or lantern, was needed, nor that small instrument which is said to guide a man aright in the desert, even in the darkest night—let him that can believe such a thing!'

'Yes, happy for me,' I returned. 'I am filled with remorse that it was all through my fault that the poor child was exposed to such weather.'

'O señor,' he cried airily, 'let not that distress you! Rain and wind and hot suns, from which we seek shelter, do not harm her. She takes no cold, and no fever, with or without ague.'

After some further conversation I left him to steal away unobserved on his own account, and set out for a ramble in the hope of encountering Rima and winning her to talk to me.

My quest did not succeed: not a glimpse of her delicate shadowy form did I catch among the trees; and not one note from her melodious lips came to gladden me. At noon I returned to the house, where I found food placed ready for me, and knew that she had come there during my absence and had not been forgetful of my wants. 'Shall I thank you for this?' I said. 'I ask you for heavenly nectar for the sustentation of the higher winged nature in me, and you give me a boiled sweet potato, toasted strips of sun-dried pumpkins, and a handful of parched maize! Rima! Rima! my woodland fairy, my sweet saviour, why do you yet fear me? Is it that love struggles in you with repugnance? Can you discern with clear spiritual eyes the grosser elements in me, and hate them; or has some false imagination made me appear all dark and evil, but too late for your peace, after the sweet sickness of love has infected you?'

But she was not there to answer me, and so after a time I went forth again and seated myself listlessly on the root of an old tree not far from the house. I had sat there a full hour, when all at once Rima appeared at my side. Bending forward she touched my hand, but without glancing at my face; 'Come with me,' she said, and turning, moved swiftly towards the northern extremity of the forest. She seemed to take it for granted that I would follow, never casting a look behind, nor pausing in her rapid walk; but I was only too glad to obey, and starting up, was quickly after her. She led me by easy ways, familiar to her, with many doublings to escape the undergrowth, never speaking or pausing until we came out from the thick forest, and I found myself for the first time at the foot of the great hill or mountain Ytaioa. Glancing back for a few moments, she waved a hand towards the summit, and then at once began the ascent. Here too it seemed all familiar ground to her. From below the sides had presented an exceedingly rugged appearance—a wild confusion of huge jagged rocks, mixed with a tangled vegetation of trees, bushes, and vines; but following her in all her doublings it became easy enough, although it fatigued me greatly owing to our rapid pace. The hill was conical, but I found that it had a flat top; an oblong or pear-shaped area, almost level, of a soft, crumbly sandstone, with a few blocks and boulders of a harder stone scattered about; and no vegetation, except the grey mountain lichen and a few sere-looking dwarf shrubs.

Here Rima, at a distance of a few yards from me, remained standing still for some minutes, as if to give me time to recover my breath; and I was right glad to sit down on a stone to rest. Finally she walked slowly to the centre of the level area, which was about two acres in extent; rising I followed her, and climbing on to a huge block of stone, began gazing at the wide prospect spread out before me. The day was windless and bright, with only a few white clouds floating at a great height above and casting travelling shadows over that wild, broken country, where forest, marsh, and savannah were only distinguishable by their different colours, like the greys and greens and yellows on a map. At a great distance the circle of the horizon was broken here and there by mountains, but the hills in our neighbourhood were all beneath our feet.

After gazing all round for some minutes, I jumped down from my stand, and leaning against the stone, stood watching the girl, waiting for her to speak. I felt convinced that she had something of the very highest importance (to herself) to communicate, and that only the pressing need of a confidant, not Nuflo, had overcome her shyness of me; and I determined to let her take her own time to say it in her own way. For a while she continued silent, her face averted, but her little movements and the way she clasped and unclasped her fingers showed that she was anxious and her mind working. Suddenly, half turning to me, she began speaking eagerly and rapidly.

'Do you see,' she said, waving her hand to indicate the whole circuit of earth, 'how large it is? Look!' pointing now to mountains in the west. 'Those are the Vahanas—one, two, three—the highest—I can tell you their names—Vahana-Chara, Chumi, Aranoa. Do you see that water? It is a river, called Guaypero. From the hills it comes down, Inaruna is their name, and you can see them there in the south—far, far.' And in this way she went on pointing out and naming all the mountains and rivers within sight. Then she suddenly dropped her hands to her sides, and continued, 'That is all. Because we can see no further. But the world is larger than that! Other mountains, other rivers. Have I not told you of Voa, on the River Voa,* where I was born, where mother died, where the priest taught me, years, years ago? All that you cannot see, it is so far away—so far.'

I did not laugh at her simplicity, nor did I smile or feel any inclination to smile. On the contrary, I only experienced a sympathy so keen that it was like pain, while watching her clouded face, so changeful in its expression, yet in all changes so wistful. I could not yet form any idea as to what she wished to communicate or to discover, but seeing that she paused for a reply I answered, 'The world is so large, Rima, that we can only see a very small portion of it from any one spot. Look at this,' and with a stick I had used to aid me in my ascent I traced a circle six or seven inches in circumference on the soft stone and in its centre placed a small pebble. 'This represents the mountain we are standing on,' I continued, touching the pebble; 'and this line encircling it encloses all of the earth we can see from the mountain-top. Do you understand?—the line I have traced is the blue line of the horizon beyond which we cannot see. And outside of this little circle is all the flat top of Ytaioa representing the world. Consider, then, how small a portion of the world we can see from this spot!'

'And do you know it all?' she returned excitedly. 'All the world?' waving her hand to indicate the little stone plain. 'All the mountains, and rivers, and forests—all the people in the world?'

'That would be impossible, Rima; consider how large it is.'

'That does not matter. Come, let us go together—we two and grandfather, and see all the world; all the mountains and forests, and know all the people.'

'You do not know what you are saying, Rima. You might as well say, "Come, let us go to the sun and find out everything in it."'

'It is you who do not know what you are saying,' she retorted, with brightening eyes which for a moment glanced full into mine. 'We have no wings like birds to fly to the sun. Am I not able to walk on the earth, and run? Can I not swim? Can I not climb every mountain?'

'No, you cannot. You imagine that all the earth is like this little portion you see. But it is not all the same. There are great rivers which you cannot cross by swimming; mountains you cannot climb; forests you cannot penetrate—dark, and inhabited by dangerous beasts, and so vast that all this space your eyes look on is a mere speck of earth in comparison.'

She listened excitedly. 'Oh, do you know all that?' she cried, with a strangely brightening look; and then half turning from me, she added, with sudden petulance, 'Yet only a minute ago you knew nothing of the world—because it is so large! Is anything to be gained by speaking to one who says such contrary things?'

I explained that I had not contradicted myself, that she had not rightly interpreted my words. I knew, I said, something about the principal features of the different countries of the world, as, for instance, the largest mountain ranges, and rivers, and the cities. Also something, but very little, about the tribes of savage men. She heard me with impatience, which made me speak rapidly, in very general terms; and to simplify the matter I made the world stand for the continent we were in. It seemed idle to go beyond that, and her eagerness would not have allowed it.

'Tell me all you know,' she said the moment I ceased speaking. 'What is there—and there—and there?' pointing in various directions. 'Rivers and forests—they are nothing to me. The villages, the tribes, the people everywhere; tell me, for I must know it all.'

'It would take long to tell, Rima.'

'Because you are so slow. Look how high the sun is! Speak, speak! What is there?' pointing to the north.

'All that country,' I said, waving my hands from east to west, 'Is Guayana; and so large is it that you could go in this direction, or in this, travelling for months, without seeing the end of Guayana. Still it would be Guayana; rivers, rivers, rivers, with forests between, and other forests and rivers beyond. And savage people, nations and tribes—Guahibo, Aguaricoto, Ayano, Maco, Piaroa, Quiriquiripo, Tuparito*—shall I name a hundred more? It would be useless, Rima; they are all savages, and live widely scattered in the forests, hunting with bow and arrow and the zabatana. Consider, then, how large Guayana is!'

'Guayana—Guayana! Do I not know all this is Guayana? But beyond, and beyond, and beyond? Is there no end to Guayana?'

'Yes; there northwards it ends at the Orinoco, a mighty river, coming from mighty mountains, compared with which Ytaioa is like a stone on the ground on which we have sat down to rest. You must know that Guayana is only a portion, a half, of our country, Venezuela. Look,' I continued, putting my hand round my shoulder to touch the middle of my back, 'there is a groove running down my spine dividing my body into equal parts. Thus does the great Orinoco divide Venezuela, and on one side of it is all Guayana; and on the other side the countries or provinces of Cumana, Maturin, Barcelona, Bolivar, Guarico, Apure, and many others.' I then gave a rapid description of the northern half of the country, with its vast llanos covered with herds in one part, its plantations of coffee, rice, and sugar-cane in another, and its chief towns; last of all Caracas, the gay and opulent little Paris in America.

This seemed to weary her; but the moment I ceased speaking, and before I could well moisten my dry lips, she demanded to know what came after Caracas—after all Venezuela.

'The ocean—water, water, water,' I replied.

'There are no people there—in the water; only fishes,' she remarked; then suddenly continued, 'Why are you silent—is Venezuela, then, all the world?'

The task I had set myself to perform seemed only at its commencement yet. Thinking how to proceed with it my eyes roved over the level area we were standing on, and it struck me that this little irregular plain, broad at one end, and almost pointed at the other, roughly resembled the South American continent in its form.

'Look, Rima,' I began, 'here we are on this small pebble—Ytaioa; and this line round it shuts us in—we cannot see beyond. Now let us imagine that we can see beyond—that we can see the whole flat mountain-top; and that, you know, is the whole world. Now listen while I tell you of all the countries, and principal mountains, and rivers, and cities of the world.'

The plan I had now fixed on involved a great deal of walking about and some hard work in moving and setting up stones and tracing boundary and other lines; but it gave me pleasure, for Rima was close by all the time, following me from place to place, listening to all I said in silence but with keen interest. At the broad end of the level summit I marked out Venezuela, showing by means of a long line how the Orinoco divided it, and also marking several of the greater streams flowing into it. I also marked the sites of Caracas and other large towns with stones; and rejoiced that we are not like the Europeans, great city builders, for the stones proved heavy to lift. Then followed Colombia and Ecuador on the west; and, successively, Bolivia, Peru, Chile, ending at last in the south with Patagonia, a cold arid land, bleak and desolate. I marked the littoral cities as we progressed on that side, where earth ends and the Pacific Ocean begins, and infinitude.

Then, in a sudden burst of inspiration, I described the Cordilleras to her—that world-long, stupendous chain; its sea of Titicaca, and wintry, desolate Paramo, where lie the ruins of Tiahuanaco, older than Thebes.* I mentioned its principal cities—those small inflamed or festering pimples that attract much attention from appearing on such a body. Quito, called—not in irony, but by its own people—the Splendid and the Magnificent; so high above the earth as to appear but a little way removed from heaven—'de Quito al cielo,' as the saying is. But of its sublime history, its kings and conquerors, Haymar Capac the Mighty, and Huascar, and Atahualpa the Unhappy,* not one word. Many words—how inadequate!—of the summits, white with everlasting snows, above it—above this navel of the world, above the earth, the ocean, the darkening tempest, the condor's flight. Flame-breathing Cotopaxi, whose wrathful mutterings are audible two hundred leagues away, and Chimborazo, Antisana, Sarata, Illimani, Aconcagua*—names of mountains that affect us like the names of gods, implacable Pachacamac and Viracocha,* whose everlasting granite thrones they are. At the last I showed her Cuzco, the city of the sun,* and the highest dwelling-place of men on earth.

I was carried away by so sublime a theme; and remembering that I had no critical hearer, I gave free reins to fancy, forgetting for the moment that some undiscovered thought or feeling had prompted her questions. And while I spoke of the mountains she hung on my words, following me closely in my walk, her countenance brilliant, her frame quivering with excitement.

There yet remained to be described all that unimaginable space east of the Andes; the rivers—what rivers!—the green plains that are like the sea—the illimitable waste of water where there is no land—and the forest region. The very thought of the Amazonian forest made my spirit droop. If I could have snatched her up and placed her on the dome of Chimborazo* she would have looked on an area of ten thousand square miles of earth, so vast is the horizon at that elevation. And possibly her imagination would have been able to clothe it all with an unbroken forest. Yet how small a portion this would be of the stupendous whole—of a forest region equal in extent to the whole of Europe! All loveliness, all grace, all majesty are there; but we cannot see, cannot conceive—come away! From this vast stage, to be occupied in the distant future by millions and myriads of beings, like us of upright form, the nations that will be born when all the existing dominant races on the globe and the civilisations they represent have perished as utterly as those who sculptured the stones of old Tiahuanaco—from this theatre of palms prepared for a drama unlike any which the Immortals have yet witnessed*—I hurried away; and then slowly conducted her along the Atlantic coast, listening to the thunder of its great waves, and pausing at intervals to survey some maritime city.

Never probably since old Father Noah divided the earth among his sons* had so grand a geographical discourse been delivered; and having finished, I sat down, exhausted with my efforts, and mopped my brow, but glad that my huge task was over, and satisfied that I had convinced her of the futility of her wish to see the world for herself.

Her excitement had passed away by now. She was standing a little apart from me, her eyes cast down and thoughtful. At length she approached me and said, waving her hand all round, 'What is beyond the mountains over there, beyond the cities on that side—beyond the world?'

'Water, only water. Did I not tell you?' I returned stoutly; for I had, of course, sunk the Isthmus of Panama beneath the sea.

'Water! All round?' she persisted.

'Yes.'

'Water, and no beyond? Only water—always water?'

I could no longer adhere to so gross a lie. She was too intelligent, and I loved her too much. Standing up, I pointed to distant mountains and isolated peaks.

'Look at those peaks,' I said. 'It is like that with the world—this world we are standing on. Beyond that great water that flows all round the world, but far away, so far that it would take months in a big boat to reach them, there are islands, some small, others as large as this world. But, Rima, they are so far away, so impossible to reach, that it is useless to speak or to think of them. They are to us like the sun and moon and stars, to which we cannot fly. And now sit down and rest by my side, for you know everything.'

She glanced at me with troubled eyes.

'Nothing do I know—nothing have you told me. Did I not say that mountains and rivers and forests are nothing? Tell me about all the people in the world. Look! there is Cuzco over there, a city like no other in the world—did you not tell me so? Of the people nothing. Are they also different from all others in the world?'

'I will tell you that if you will first answer me one question, Rima.'

She drew a little nearer, curious to hear, but was silent.

'Promise that you will answer me,' I persisted, and as she continued silent I added, 'Shall I not ask you, then?'

'Say,' she murmured.

'Why do you wish to know about the people of Cuzco?'

She flashed a look at me, then averted her face. For some moments she stood hesitating, then coming closer, touched me on the shoulder, and said softly, 'Turn away, do not look at me.'

I obeyed, and bending so close that I felt her warm breath on my neck, she whispered, 'Are the people in Cuzco like me? Would they understand me—the things you cannot understand? Do you know?'

Her tremulous voice betrayed her agitation, and her words, I imagined, revealed the motive of her action in bringing me to the summit of Ytaioa, and of her desire to visit and know all the various peoples inhabiting the world. She had begun to realise, after knowing me, her isolation and unlikeness to others, and at the same time to dream that all human beings might not be unlike her and unable to understand her mysterious speech and to enter into her thoughts and feelings.

'I can answer that question, Rima,' I said. 'Ah, no, poor child, there are none there like you—not one, not one. Of all there—priests, soldiers, merchants, workmen, white, black, red, and mixed; men and women, old and young, rich and poor, ugly and beautiful—not one would understand the sweet language you speak.'

She said nothing, and glancing round, I discovered that she was walking away, her fingers clasped before her, her eyes cast down, and looking profoundly dejected. Jumping up, I hurried after her. 'Listen!' I said, coming to her side. 'Do you know that there are others in the world like you who would understand your speech?'

'Oh, do I not! Yes—mother told me. I was young when you died, but, O mother, why did you not tell me more?'

'But where?'

'Oh, do you not think that I would go to them if I knew—that I would ask?'

'Does Nuflo know?'

She shook her head, walking dejectedly along.

'But have you asked him?' I persisted.

'Have I not! Not once—not a hundred times.'

Suddenly she paused. 'Look,' she said, 'now we are standing in Guayana again. And over there in Brazil, and up there towards the Cordilleras it is unknown. And there are people there. Come, let us go and seek for my mother's people in that place. With grandfather, but not the dogs; they would frighten the animals and betray us by barking to cruel men who would slay us with poisoned arrows.'

'O Rima, can you not understand? It is too far. And your grandfather, poor old man, would die of weariness and hunger and old age in some strange forest.'

'Would he die—old grandfather? Then we could cover him up with palm leaves in the forest and leave him. It would not be grandfather; only his body that must turn to dust. He would be away—away where the stars are. *We* should not die, but go on, and on, and on.'

To continue the discussion seemed hopeless. I was silent, thinking of what I had heard—that there were others like her somewhere in that vast green world, so much of it imperfectly known, so many districts never yet explored by white men. True, it was strange that no report of such a race had reached the ears of any traveller; yet here was Rima herself at my side, a living proof that such a race did exist. Nuflo probably knew more than he would say; I had failed, as we have seen, to win the secret from him by fair means, and could not have recourse to foul—the rack and thumbscrew—to wring it from him. To the Indians she was only an object of superstitious fear—a daughter of the Didi—and to them nothing of her origin was known. And she, poor girl, had only a vague remembrance of a few words heard in childhood from her mother, and probably not rightly understood.

While these thoughts had been passing through my mind Rima had been standing silent by, waiting, perhaps, for an answer to her last words. Then stooping, she picked up a small pebble and tossed it three or four yards away.

'Do you see where it fell?' she cried, turning towards me. 'That is on the border of Guayana—is it not? Let us go there first.'

'Rima, how you distress me! We cannot go there. It is all a savage wilderness, almost unknown to men—a blank on the map——'

'The map?—speak no word that I do not understand.'

In a very few words I explained my meaning; even fewer would have sufficed, so quick was her apprehension.

'If it is a blank,' she returned quickly, 'then you know of nothing to stop us—no river we cannot swim, and no great mountains like those where Quito is.'

'But I happen to know, Rima, for it has been related to me by old Indians, that of all places that is the most difficult of access. There is a river there, and although it is not on the map, it would prove more impassable to us than the mighty Orinoco and Amazon. It has vast malarious swamps on its borders, overgrown with dense forest, teeming with savage and venomous animals, so that even the Indians dare not venture near it. And even before the river is reached there is a range of precipitous mountains called by the same name—just there where your pebble fell—the mountains of Riolama——'

Hardly had the name fallen from my lips before a change swift as lightning came over her countenance; all doubt, anxiety, petulance, hope, and despondence, and these in ever-varying degrees, chasing

each other like shadows, had vanished, and she was instinct and burning with some new powerful emotion which had flashed into her soul.

'Riolama! Riolama!' she repeated so rapidly and in a tone so sharp
that it tingled in the brain. 'That is the place I am seeking! There
was my mother found—there are her people and mine! Therefore
was I called Riolama—that is my name!'

'Rima!' I returned, astonished at her words.

'No, no, no—Riolama. When I was a child, and the priest baptised
me, he named me Riolama—the place where my mother was found.
But it was long to say, and they called me Rima.'

Suddenly she became still, and then cried in a ringing voice—

'And he knew it all along—that old man—he knew that Riolama
was near—only there where the pebble fell—that we could go there!'

While speaking she turned towards her home, pointing with raised
hand. Her whole appearance now reminded me of that first meeting
with her when the serpent bit me; the soft red of her irides shone like
fire, her delicate skin seemed to glow with an intense rose-colour,
and her frame trembled with her agitation, so that her loose cloud of
hair was in motion as if blown through by the wind.

'Traitor! Traitor!' she cried, still looking homewards and using
quick, passionate gestures. 'It was all known to you, and you deceived
me all these years; even to me, Rima, you lied with your lips! Oh,
horrible! Was there ever such a scandal known in Guayana? Come,
follow me, let us go at once to Riolama.' And without so much as
casting a glance behind to see whether I followed or no, she hurried
away, and in a couple of minutes disappeared from sight over the edge
of the flat summit.

'Rima! Rima! Come back and listen to me! Oh, you are mad! Come
back! Come back!'

But she would not return or pause and listen; and looking after her
I saw her bounding down the rocky slope like some wild, agile creature possessed of padded hoofs and an infallible instinct; and before
many minutes she vanished from sight among crags and trees lower
down.

'Nuflo, old man,' said I, looking out towards his lodge, 'are there no
shooting pains in those old bones of yours to warn you in time of the
tempest about to burst on your head?'

Then I sat down to think.

CHAPTER XII

To follow impetuous, bird-like Rima in her descent of the hill would have been impossible, nor had I any desire to be a witness of old Nuflo's discomfiture at the finish. It was better to leave them to settle their quarrel themselves, while I occupied myself in turning over these fresh facts in my mind to find out how they fitted into the speculative structure I had been building during the last two or three weeks. But it soon struck me that it was getting late, that the sun would be gone in a couple of hours; and at once I began the descent. It was not accomplished without some bruises and a good many scratches. After a cold draught, obtained by putting my lips to a black rock from which the water was trickling, I set out on my walk home, keeping near the western border of the forest for fear of losing myself. I had covered about half the distance from the foot of the hill to Nuflo's lodge when the sun went down. Away on my left the evening uproar of the howling monkeys burst out, and after three or four minutes ceased; the after silence was pierced at intervals by screams of birds going to roost among the trees in the distance, and by many minor sounds close at hand, of small bird, frog, and insect. The western sky was now like amber-coloured flame, and against that immeasurably distant luminous background the near branches and clustered foliage looked black; but on my left hand the vegetation still appeared of a uniform dusky green. In a little while night would drown all colour, and there would be no light but that of the wandering lantern-fly, always unwelcome to the belated walker in a lonely place, since, like the ignis fatuus, it is confusing to the sight and sense of direction.

With increasing anxiety I hastened on, when all at once a low growl issuing from the bushes some yards ahead of me brought me to a stop. In a moment the dogs, Susio and Goloso, rushed out from some hiding-place furiously barking; but they quickly recognised me and slunk back again. Relieved from fear, I walked on for a short distance; then it struck me that the old man must be about somewhere, as the dogs scarcely ever stirred from his side. Turning back I went to the spot where they had appeared to me; and there, after a while, I caught sight of a dim, yellow form, as one of the brutes rose up to look at me. He had been lying on the ground by the side of a wide-spreading bush, dead and dry, but overgrown by a creeping plant which had completely covered its broad, flat top like a piece of tapestry thrown over a table, its slender terminal stems and leaves hanging over the edge like a deep fringe. But the fringe did not reach to the ground, and under the bush, in its dark interior, I caught sight of the other dog; and after gazing in for some time I also discovered a black, recumbent form, which I took to be Nuflo.

'What are you doing there, old man?' I cried. 'Where is Rima— have you not seen her? Come out.'

Then he stirred himself, slowly creeping out on all fours; and, finally, getting free of the dead twigs and leaves, he stood up and faced me. He had a strange, wild look, his white beard all disordered, moss and dead leaves clinging to it, his eyes staring like an owl's, while his mouth opened and shut, the teeth striking together audibly, like an angry peccary's. After silently glaring at me in this mad way for some moments he burst out: 'Cursed be the day when I first saw you, man of Caracas! Cursed be the serpent that bit you and had not sufficient power in its venom to kill! Ha! you come from Ytaioa, where you talked with Rima? And you have now returned to the tiger's den to mock that dangerous animal with the loss of its whelp. Fool, if you did not wish the dogs to feed on your flesh it would have been better if you had taken your evening walk in some other direction.'

These raging words did not have the effect of alarming me in the least, nor even of astonishing me very much, albeit up till now the old man had always shown himself suave and respectful. His attack did not seem quite spontaneous. In spite of the wildness of his manner and the violence of his speech, he appeared to be acting a part which he had rehearsed beforehand. I was only angry, and stepping forward I dealt him a very sharp rap with my knuckles on his chest. 'Moderate your language, old man,' I said; 'remember that you are addressing a superior.'

'What do you say to me?' he screamed in a shrill, broken voice, accompanying his words with emphatic gestures. 'Do you think you are on the pavement of Caracas? Here are no police to protect you—here we are alone in the desert where names and titles are nothing, standing man to man.'

'An old man to a young one,' I returned. 'And in virtue of my youth

I am your superior. Do you wish me to take you by the throat and shake your insolence out of you?'

'What, do you threaten me with violence?' he exclaimed, throwing himself into a hostile attitude. 'You, the man I saved, and sheltered, and fed, and treated like a son! Destroyer of my peace, have you not injured me enough? You have stolen my grandchild's heart from me; with a thousand inventions you have driven her mad! My child, my angel, Rima, my saviour! With your lying tongue you have changed her into a demon to persecute me! And you are not satisfied, but must finish your evil work by inflicting blows on my worn body! All, all is lost to me! Take my life if you wish it, for now it is worth nothing, and I desire not to keep it!' And here he threw himself on his knees, and tearing open his old, ragged mantle, presented his naked breast to me. 'Shoot! Shoot!' he screeched. 'And if you have no weapon take my knife and plunge it into this sad heart, and let me die!' And drawing his knife from its sheath, he flung it down at my feet.

All this performance only served to increase my anger and contempt; but before I could make any reply I caught sight of a shadowy object at some distance moving towards us—something grey and formless, gliding swift and noiseless, like some great low-flying owl among the trees. It was Rima, and hardly had I seen her before she was with us, facing old Nuflo, her whole frame quivering with passion, her wide-open eyes appearing luminous in that dim light.

'You are here!' she cried in that quick, ringing tone that was almost painful to the sense. 'You thought to escape me! To hide yourself from my eyes in the wood! Miserable! Do you not know that I have need of you—that I have not finished with you yet? Do you then wish to be scourged to Riolama with thorny twigs—to be dragged thither by the beard?'

He had been staring open-mouthed at her, still on his knees, and holding his mantle open with his skinny hands. 'Rima! Rima! have mercy on me!' he cried out piteously. 'Oh, my child, I cannot go to Riolama, it is so far—so far. And I am old and should meet my death. Oh, Rima, child of the woman I saved from death, have you no compassion? I shall die, I shall die!'

'Shall you die? Not until you have shown me the way to Riolama. And when I have seen Riolama with my eyes then you may die, and I shall be glad at your death; and the children and the grandchildren and cousins and friends of all the animals you have slain and fed on shall know that you are dead and be glad at your death. For you have deceived me with lies all these years—even me—and are not fit to live! Come now to Riolama; rise instantly, I command you!'

Instead of rising he suddenly put out his hand and snatched up the knife from the ground. 'Do you then wish me to die?' he cried. 'Shall you be glad at my death? Behold, then I shall slay myself before your eyes. By my own hand, Rima, I am now about to perish, striking the knife into my heart!'

While speaking he waved the knife in a tragic manner over his head, but I made no movement; I was convinced that he had no intention of taking his own life—that he was still acting. Rima, incapable of understanding such a thing, took it differently.

'Oh, you are going to kill yourself!' she cried. 'Oh, wicked man, wait until you know what will happen to you after death. All shall now be told to my mother. Hear my words, then kill yourself.'

She also now dropped on to her knees, and lifting her clasped hands and fixing her resentful sparkling eyes on the dim blue patch of heaven visible beyond the tree-tops, began to speak rapidly in clear, vibrating tones. She was praying to her mother in heaven; and while Nuflo listened absorbed, his mouth open, his eyes fixed on her, the hand that clutched the knife dropped to his side. I also heard with the greatest wonder and admiration. For she had been shy and reticent with me, and now, as if oblivious of my presence, she was telling aloud the secrets of her inmost heart.

'O mother, mother, listen to me, to Rima, your beloved child!' she began. 'All these years I have been wickedly deceived by grand-father—Nuflo—the old man that found you. Often have I spoken to him of Riolama, where you once were, and your people are, and he denied all knowledge of such a place. Sometimes he said that it was at an immense distance, in a great wilderness full of serpents larger than the trunks of great trees, and of evil spirits and savage men, slayers of all strangers. At other times he affirmed that no such place existed; that it was a tale told by the Indians; such false things did he say to me—to Rima, your child. O mother, can you believe such wickedness?

'Then a stranger, a white man from Venezuela, came into our woods: this is the man that was bitten by a serpent, and his name is Abel: only I do not call him by that name, but by other names which I have told you. But perhaps you did not listen, or did not hear, for I spoke softly and not as now, on my knees, solemnly. For I must tell you, O mother, that after you died the priest at Voa told me repeatedly that when I prayed, whether to you or to any of the saints, or to the Mother of Heaven, I must speak as he had taught me, if I wished to be heard and understood. And that was most strange, since you had taught me differently; but you were living then, at Voa, and now that you are in Heaven perhaps you know better. Therefore listen to me now, O mother, and let nothing I say escape you.

'When this white man had been for some days with us a strange thing happened to me, which made me different, so that I was no longer Rima, although Rima still—so strange was this thing; and I often went to the pool to look at myself and see the change in me, but nothing different could I see. In the first place it came from his eyes passing into mine, and filling me just as the lightning fills a cloud at sunset: afterwards it was no longer from his eyes only, but it came into me whenever I saw him, even at a distance, when I heard his voice, and most of all when he touched me with his hand. When he is out of my sight I cannot rest until I see him again; and when I see him then I am glad, yet in such fear and trouble that I hide myself from him. O mother, it could not be told; for once when he caught me in his arms and compelled me to speak of it he did not understand; yet there was need to tell it; then it came to me that only to our people could it be told, for they would understand, and reply to me, and tell me what to do in such a case.

'And now, O mother, this is what happened next. I went to grandfather and first begged and then commanded him to take me to Riolama; but he would not obey, nor give attention to what I said, but whenever I spoke to him of it he rose up and hurried from me; and when I followed he flung back a confused and angry reply, saying in the same breath that it was so long since he had been to Riolama that he had forgotten where it was, and that no such place existed. And which of his words were true and which false I knew not: so that it would have been better if he had returned no answer at all; and there was no help to be got from him. And having thus failed, and there being no other person to speak to except this stranger, I determined to go to him, and in his company seek through the whole world for my people. This will surprise you, O mother, because of that fear which came on me in his presence, causing me to hide from his sight; but my wish was so great that for a time it overcame my fear;

so that I went to him as he sat alone in the wood, sad because he could not see me, and spoke to him, and led him to the summit of Ytaioa to show me all the countries of the world from the summit. And you must also know that I tremble in his presence, not because I fear him as I fear Indians and cruel men; for he has no evil in him, and is beautiful to look at, and his words are gentle, and his desire is to be always with me, so that he differs from all other men I have seen, just as I differ from all women, except from you only, O sweet mother.

'On the mountain-top he marked out and named all the countries of the world, the great mountains, the rivers, the plains, the forests, the cities; and told me also of the peoples, whites and savages, but of our people nothing. And beyond where the world ends there is water, water, water. And when he spoke of that unknown part on the borders of Guayana, on the side of the Cordilleras, he named the mountains of Riolama, and in that way I first found out where my people are. I then left him on Ytaioa, he refusing to follow me, and ran to grandfather and taxed him with his falsehoods; and he, finding I knew all, escaped from me into the woods, where I have now found him once more, talking with the stranger. And now, O mother, seeing himself caught and unable to escape a second time, he has taken up a knife to kill himself, so as not to take me to Riolama; and he is only waiting until I finish speaking to you, for I wish him to know what will happen to him after death. Therefore, O mother, listen well and do what I tell you. When he has killed himself, and has come into that place where you are, see that he does not escape the punishment he merits. Watch well for his coming, for he is full of cunning and deceit, and will endeavour to hide himself from your eyes. When you have recognised him—an old man, brown as an Indian, with a white beard—point him out to the angels, and say, "This is Nuflo, the bad man that lied to Rima." Let them take him and singe his wings with fire, so that he may not escape by flying; and afterwards thrust him into some dark cavern under a mountain, and place a great stone that a hundred men could not remove over its mouth, and leave him there alone and in the dark for ever!'

Having ended, she rose quickly from her knees, and at the same moment Nuflo, dropping the knife, cast himself prostrate at her feet.

'Rima—my child, my child, not that!' he cried out in a voice that was broken with terror. He tried to take hold of her feet with his hands, but she shrank from him with aversion; still he kept on crawling after her like a disabled lizard, abjectly imploring her to forgive him, reminding her that he had saved from death the woman whose enmity had now been enlisted against him, and declaring that he would do anything she commanded him, and gladly perish in her service.

It was a pitiable sight, and moving quickly to her side I touched her on the shoulder and asked her to forgive him.

The response came quickly enough. Turning to him once more she said: 'I forgive you, grandfather. And now get up and take me to Riolama.'

He rose, but only to his knees. 'But you have not told *her!*' he said, recovering his natural voice, although still anxious, and jerking a thumb over his shoulder. 'Consider, my child, that I am old and shall doubtless perish on the way. What would become of my soul in such a case? For now you have told her everything, and it will not be forgotten.'

She regarded him in silence for a few moments, then moving a little way apart, dropped on to her knees again, and with raised hands and eyes fixed on the blue space above, already sprinkled with stars, prayed again.

'O mother, listen to me, for I have something fresh to say to you. Grandfather has not killed himself, but has asked my forgiveness and has promised to obey me. O mother, I have forgiven him, and he will now take me to Riolama, to our people. Therefore, O mother, if he dies on the way to Riolama let nothing be done against him, but re-member only that I forgave him at the last; and when he comes into that place where you are, let him be well received, for that is the wish of Rima, your child.'

As soon as this second petition was ended she was up again and en-gaged in an animated discussion with him, urging him to take her without further delay to Riolama; while he, now recovered from his fear, urged that so important an undertaking required a great deal of thought and preparation; that the journey would occupy about twenty days, and unless he set out well provided with food he would starve before accomplishing half the distance; and his death would leave her worse off than before: he concluded by affirming that he could not start in less time than seven or eight days.

For a while I listened with keen interest to this dispute, and at length interposed once more on the old man's side. The poor girl in her petition had unwittingly revealed to me the power I possessed, and it was a pleasing experience to exercise it. Touching her shoulder again, I assured her that seven or eight days was only a reasonable time in which to prepare for so long a journey: she instantly yielded, and after one glance at my face she moved swiftly away into the darker shadows, leaving me alone with the old man.

As we returned together through the now profoundly dark wood I explained to him how the subject of Riolama had first come up during my conversation with Rima, and he then apologised for the violent language he had used to me. This personal question disposed of, he spoke of the pilgrimage before him, and informed me in confidence that he intended preparing a quantity of smoke-dried meat and packing it in a bag, with a layer of cassava bread, dried pumpkin slips, and such innocent trifles to conceal it from Rima's keen sight and delicate nostrils. Finally, he made a long rambling statement, which, I vainly imagined, was intended to lead up to an account of Rima's origin, with something about her people at Riolama; but it led to nothing except an expression of opinion that the girl was afflicted with a maggot in the brain, but that as she had interest with the powers above, especially with her mother, who was now a very important person among the celestials, it was good policy to submit to her wishes. Turning to me, doubtless to wink (only I missed the sign owing to the darkness), he added that it was a fine thing to have a friend at court. With a little gratulatory chuckle he went on to say that for others it was necessary to obey all the ordinances of the Church, to contribute to its support, hear mass, confess from time to time, and receive absolution: consequently those who went out into the wilderness, where there were no churches and no priests to absolve them, did so at the risk of losing their souls. But with him it was different: he expected in the end to escape the fires of purgatory, and go directly in all his uncleanness to heaven—a thing, he remarked, which happened to very few; and he, Nuflo, was no saint, and had first become a dweller in the desert, as a very young man, in order to escape the penalty of his misdeeds.

I could not resist the temptation of remarking here that to an unregenerate man the celestial country might turn out a somewhat uncongenial place for a residence. He replied airily that he had considered the point and had no fear about the future; that he was old, and from all he had observed of the methods of government followed by those who ruled over earthly affairs from the sky, he had formed a clear idea of that place, and believed that even among so many glorified beings he would be able to meet with those who would prove companionable enough, and would think no worse of him on account of his little blemishes.

How he had first got this idea into his brain about Rima's ability to make things smooth for him after death I cannot say; probably it was the effect of the girl's powerful personality and vivid faith acting on an ignorant and extremely superstitious mind. While she was making that petition to her mother in heaven it did not seem in the least ridiculous to me: I had felt no inclination to smile, even when hearing all that about the old man's wings being singed to prevent his escape by flying. Her rapt look; the intense conviction that vibrated in her ringing, passionate tones; the brilliant scorn with which she, a hater of bloodshed, one so tender towards all living things, even the meanest, bade him kill himself, and only hear first how her vengeance would pursue his deceitful soul into other worlds; the clearness with which she had related the facts of the case, disclosing the inmost secrets of her heart—all this had had a strange, convincing effect on me. Listening to her I was no longer the enlightened, the creedless man. She herself was so near to the supernatural that it seemed brought near me; indefinable feelings, which had been latent in me, stirred into life, and following the direction of her divine, lustrous eyes, fixed on the blue sky above, I seemed to see there another being like herself, a Rima glorified, leaning her pale, spiritual face to catch the winged words uttered by her child on earth. And even now, while hearing the old man's talk, showing as it did a mind darkened with such gross delusions, I was not yet altogether free from the strange effect of that prayer. Doubtless it was a delusion; her mother was not really there above listening to the girl's voice. Still, in some mysterious way, Rima had become to me, even as to superstitious old Nuflo, a being apart and sacred, and this feeling seemed to mix with my passion, to purify and exalt it and make it infinitely sweet and precious.

After we had been silent for some time I said, 'Old man, the result of the grand discussion you have had with Rima is that you have agreed to take her to Riolama, but about my accompanying you not one word has been spoken by either of you.'

He stopped short to stare at me, and although it was too dark to see his face, I felt his astonishment. 'Señor!' he exclaimed, 'we cannot go without you. Have you not heard my granddaughter's words—that it is only because of you that she is about to undertake this crazy journey? If you are not with us in this thing, then, señor, here we must remain. But what will Rima say to that?'

'Very well, I will go, but only on one condition.'

'What is it?' he asked, with a sudden change of tone, which warned me that he was becoming cautious again.

'That you tell me the whole story of Rima's origin, and how you came to be now living with her in this solitary place, and who these people are she wishes to visit at Riolama.'

'Ah, señor, it is a long story, and sad. But you shall hear it all. You must hear it, señor, since you are now one of us; and when I am no longer here to protect her then she will be yours. And although you will never be able to do more than old Nuflo for her, perhaps she will be better pleased; and you, señor, better able to exist innocently by her side, without eating flesh, since you will always have that rare flower to delight you. But the story would take long to tell. You shall hear it all as we journey to Riolama. What else will there be to talk about when we are walking that long distance, and when we sit at night by the fire?'

'No, no, old man, I am not to be put off in that way. I must hear it before I start.'

But he was determined to reserve the narrative until the journey, and after some further argument I yielded the point.

CHAPTER XIII

THAT evening by the fire old Nuflo, lately so miserable, now happy in his delusions, was more than usually gay and loquacious. He was like a child, who by timely submission has escaped a threatened severe punishment. But his lightness of heart was exceeded by mine; and, with the exception of one other yet to come, that evening now shines in memory as the happiest my life has known. For Rima's sweet secret was known to me; and her very ignorance of the meaning of the feeling she experienced, which caused her to fly from me as from an enemy, only served to make the thought of it more purely delightful.

On this occasion she did not steal away like a timid mouse to her own apartment, as her custom was, but remained to give that one evening a special grace, seated well away from the fire in that same shadowy corner where I had first seen her indoors, when I had marvelled at her altered appearance.

From that corner she could see my face, with the firelight full upon it, she herself in shadow, her eyes veiled by their drooping lashes. Sitting there the vivid consciousness of my happiness was like draughts of strong, delicious wine, and its effect was like wine, imparting such freedom to fancy, such fluency, that again and again old Nuflo applauded, crying out that I was a poet, and begging me to put it all into rhyme. I could not do that to please him, never having acquired the art of improvisation—that idle trick of making words jingle which men of Nuflo's class in my country so greatly admire: yet it seemed to me on that evening that my feelings could be adequately expressed only in that sublimated language used by the finest minds in their inspired moments; and, accordingly, I fell to reciting. But not from any modern, nor from the poets of the last century, nor even from the greater seventeenth century. I kept to the more ancient romances and ballads, the sweet old verse that, whether glad or sorrowful, seems always natural and spontaneous as the song of a bird, and so simple that even a child can understand it.

It was late that night before all the romances I remembered or cared to recite were exhausted, and not until then did Rima come out of her shaded corner and steal silently away to her sleeping-place.

Although I had resolved to go with them, and had set Nuflo's mind at rest on the point, I was bent on getting the request from Rima's own lips; and the next morning the opportunity of seeing her alone presented itself, after old Nuflo had sneaked off with his dogs. From the moment of his departure I kept a close watch on the house, as one watches a bush in which a bird he wishes to see has concealed itself, and out of which it may dart at any moment and escape unseen.

At length she came forth, and seeing me in the way, would have slipped back into hiding; for, in spite of her boldness on the previous day, she now seemed shyer than ever when I spoke to her.

'Rima,' I said, 'do you remember where we first talked together under a tree one morning, when you spoke of your mother, telling me that she was dead?'

'Yes.'

'I am going now to that spot to wait for you. I must speak to you again in that place about this journey to Riolama.' As she kept silent, I added, 'Will you promise to come to me there?'

She shook her head, turning half away.

'Have you forgotten our compact, Rima?'

'No,' she returned; and then, suddenly coming near, spoke in a low tone, 'I will go there to please you, and you must also do as I tell you.'

'What do you wish, Rima?'

She came nearer still. 'Listen! You must not look into my eyes, you must not touch me with your hands.'

'Sweet Rima, I must hold your hand when I speak with you.'

'No, no, no,' she murmured, shrinking from me; and finding that it must be as she wished, I reluctantly agreed.

Before I had waited long she appeared at the trysting-place, and stood before me, as on a former occasion, on that same spot of clean yellow sand, clasping and unclasping her fingers, troubled in mind even then. Only now her trouble was different and greater, making her shyer and more reticent.

'Rima, your grandfather is going to take you to Riolama. Do you wish me to go with you?'

'Oh, do you not know that?' she returned, with a swift glance at my face.

'How should I know?'

Her eyes wandered away restlessly. 'On Ytaioa you told me a hundred things which I did not know,' she replied in a vague way, wishing, perhaps, to imply that with so great a knowledge of geography it was strange I did not know everything, even her most secret thoughts.

'Tell me, why must you go to Riolama?'

'You have heard. To speak to my people.'

'What will you say to them? Tell me.'

'What you do not understand. How tell you.'

'I understand you when you speak in Spanish.'

'Oh, that is not speaking.'

'Last night you spoke to your mother in Spanish. Did you not tell her everything?'

'Oh no—not then. When I tell her everything I speak in another way, in a low voice—not on my knees and praying. At night, and in the woods, and when I am alone I tell her. But perhaps she does not hear me; she is not here, but up there—so far! She never answers, but when I speak to my people they will answer me.'

Then she turned away as if there was nothing more to be said.

'Is this all I am to hear from you, Rima—these few words?' I exclaimed. 'So much did you say to your grandfather, so much to your dead mother, but to me you say so little!'

She turned again, and with eyes cast down replied—

'He deceived me—I had to tell him that, and then to pray to mother. But to you that do not understand, what can I say? Only that you are not like him and all those that I knew at Voa. It is so different—and the same. You are you, and I am I; why is it—do you know?'

'No; yes—I know, but cannot tell you. And if you find your people what will you do—leave me to go to them? Must I go all the way to Riolama only to lose you?'

'Where I am there you must be.'

'Why?'

'Do I not see it there?' she returned, with a quick gesture to indicate that it appeared in my face.

'Your sight is keen, Rima—keen as a bird's. Mine is not so keen. Let me look once more into those beautiful wild eyes, then perhaps I shall see in them as much as you see in mine.'

'Oh no, no, not that!' she murmured in distress, drawing away from me; then with a sudden flash of brilliant colour cried—

'Have you forgotten the compact—the promise you made me?'

Her words made me ashamed, and I could not reply. But the shame was as nothing in strength compared to the impulse I felt to clasp

her beautiful body in my arms and cover her face with kisses. Sick
with desire, I turned away, and sitting on a root of the tree, covered
my face with my hands.

She came nearer: I could see her shadow through my fingers; then
her face and wistful, compassionate eyes.

'Forgive me, dear Rima,' I said, dropping my hands again. 'I have
tried so hard to please you in everything! Touch my face with your
hand—only that, and I will go to Riolama with you, and obey you in
all things.'

For a while she hesitated, then stepped quickly aside so that I could
not see her; but I knew that she had not left me, that she was standing
just behind me. And after waiting a moment longer I felt her fingers
touching my skin, softly, trembling over my cheek as if a soft-winged
moth had fluttered against it; then the slight aerial touch was gone,
and she, too, moth-like, had vanished from my side.

Left alone in the wood I was not happy. That fluttering, flattering
touch of her finger-tips had been to me like spoken language, and
more eloquent than language, yet the sweet assurance it conveyed
had not given perfect satisfaction; and when I asked myself why the
gladness of the previous evening had forsaken me—why I was infected with this new sadness when everything promised well for me,
I found that it was because my passion had greatly increased during
the last few hours; even during sleep it had been growing, and
could no longer be fed by merely dwelling in thought on the
charms, moral and physical, of its object, and by dreams of future
fruition.

I concluded that it would be best for Rima's sake as well as my own
to spend a few of the days before setting out on our journey, with my
Indian friends, who would be troubled at my long absence; and, accordingly, next morning I bade good-bye to the old man, promising
to return in three or four days, and then started without seeing
Rima, who had quitted the house before her usual time. After getting
free of the woods, on casting back my eyes I caught sight of the girl
standing under an isolated tree watching me with that vague, misty,
greenish appearance she so frequently had when seen in the light
shade at a short distance.

'Rima!' I cried, hurrying back to speak to her, but when I reached
the spot she had vanished; and after waiting some time, seeing and

hearing nothing to indicate that she was near me, I resumed my walk, half thinking that my imagination had deceived me.

I found my Indian friends home again, and was not surprised to observe a distinct change in their manner towards me. I had expected as much; and considering that they must have known very well where and in whose company I had been spending my time, it was not strange. Coming across the savannah that morning I had first begun to think seriously of the risk I was running. But this thought only served to prepare me for a new condition of things; for now to go back and appear before Rima, and thus prove myself to be a person not only capable of forgetting a promise occasionally, but also of a weak, vacillating mind, was not to be thought of for a moment.

I was received—not welcomed—quietly enough; not a question, not a word, concerning my long absence fell from anyone; it was as if a stranger had appeared among them, one about whom they knew nothing, and consequently regarded with suspicion, if not actual hostility. I affected not to notice the change, and dipped my hand uninvited in the pot to satisfy my hunger, and smoked and dozed away the sultry hours in my hammock. Then I got my guitar and spent the rest of the day over it, tuning it, touching the strings so softly with my finger-tips that to a person four yards off the sound must have seemed like the murmur or buzz of an insect's wings; and to this scarcely audible accompaniment I murmured in an equally low tone a new song.

In the evening, when all were gathered under the roof and I had eaten again, I took up the instrument once more, furtively watched by all those half-closed animal eyes, and swept the strings loudly, and sang aloud. I sang an old simple Spanish melody, to which I had put words in their own language—a language with no words not in everyday use, in which it is so difficult to express feelings out of and above the common. What I had been constructing and practising all the afternoon *sotto voce* was a kind of ballad, an extremely simple tale of a poor Indian living alone with his young family in a season of dearth: how day after day he ranged the voiceless woods to return each evening with nothing but a few withered sour berries in his hand, to find his lean, large-eyed wife still nursing the fire that cooked nothing, and his children crying for food, showing their bones more plainly through their skins every day; and how, without anything miraculous, anything wonderful, happening, that barrenness passed from earth, and the garden once more yielded them pumpkin and maize, and manioc, the wild fruits ripened, and the birds returned, filling the forest with their cries; and so their long hunger was satisfied, and the children grew sleek, and played and laughed in the sunshine; and the wife, no longer brooding over the empty pot, wove a hammock of silk grass, decorated with blue-and-scarlet feathers of the macaw; and in that new hammock the Indian rested long from his labours, smoking endless cigars.

When I at last concluded with a loud note of joy, a long, involuntary suspiration in the darkening room told me that I had been listened to with profound interest; and, although no word was spoken, though I was still a stranger and under a cloud, it was plain that the experiment had succeeded, and that for the present the danger was averted.

I went to my hammock and slept, but without undressing. Next morning I missed my revolver and found that the holster containing it had been detached from the belt. My knife had not been taken, possibly because it was under me in the hammock while I slept. In answer to my inquiries I was informed that Runi had *borrowed* my weapon to take it with him to the forest, where he had gone to hunt, and that he would return it to me in the evening. I affected to take it in good part, although feeling secretly ill at ease. Later in the day I came to the conclusion that Runi had had it in his mind to murder me, that I had softened him by singing that Indian story, and that by taking possession of the revolver he showed that he now only meant to keep me a prisoner. Subsequent events confirmed me in this suspicion. On his return he explained that he had gone out to seek for game in the woods; and, going without a companion, he had taken my revolver to preserve him from dangers—meaning those of a supernatural kind; and that he had had the misfortune to drop it among the bushes while in pursuit of some animal. I answered hotly that he had not treated me like a friend; that if he had asked me for the weapon it would have been lent to him; that as he had taken it without permission he must pay me for it. After some pondering, he said that when he took it I was sleeping soundly; also, that it would not be lost; he would take me to the place where he had dropped it, when we could search together for it.

He was in appearance more friendly towards me now, even asking me to repeat my last evening's song, and so we had that performance all over again to everybody's satisfaction. But when morning came he was not inclined to go to the woods: there was food enough in the house, and the pistol would not be hurt by lying where it had fallen a day longer. Next day the same excuse; still I disguised my impatience and suspicion of him and waited, singing the ballad for the third time that evening. Then I was conducted to a wood about a league and a half away and we hunted for the lost pistol among the bushes, I with little hope of finding it, while he attended to the bird voices and frequently asked me to stand or lie still when a chance of something offered.

The result of that wasted day was a determination on my part to escape from Runi as soon as possible, although at the risk of making a deadly enemy of him and of being compelled to go on that long journey to Riolama with no better weapon than a hunting-knife. I had noticed, while appearing not to do so, that outside of the house I was followed or watched by one or other of the Indians, so that great circumspection was needed. On the following day I attacked my host once more about the revolver, telling him with well-acted indignation that if not found it must be paid for. I went so far as to give a list of the articles I should require, including a bow and arrows, zabatana, two spears, and other things which I need not specify, to set me up for life as a wild man in the woods of Guayana. I was going to add a wife, but as I had already been offered one it did not appear to be necessary. He seemed a little taken aback at the value I set upon my weapon, and promised to go and look for it again. Then I begged that Kua-kó, in whose sharpness of sight I had great faith, might accompany us. He consented, and named the next day but one for the expedition. Very well, thought I, to-morrow their suspicion will be less, and my opportunity will come; then taking up my rude instrument, I gave them an old Spanish song—

Desde aquel doloroso momento: *

but this kind of music had lost its charm for them, and I was asked to give them the ballad they understood so well, in which their interest seemed to increase with every repetition. In spite of anxiety it amused me to see old Cla-cla regarding me fixedly with owlish eyes and lips moving. My tale had no wonderful things in it, like hers of the olden time, which she told only to send her hearers to sleep. Perhaps she had discovered by now that it was the strange honey of melody which made the coarse, common cassava-bread of everyday life in my story so pleasant to the palate. I was quite prepared to receive a proposal to give her music and singing lessons, and to bequeath a guitar to her in my last will and testament. For, in spite of her hoary hair and million wrinkles, she, more than any other savage I had met with, seemed to have taken a draught from Ponce de Leon's undiscovered fountain of eternal youth.* Poor old witch!

The following day was the sixth of my absence from Rima, and one of intense anxiety to me, a feeling which I endeavored to hide by playing with the children, fighting our old comic stick fights, and by strumming noisily on the guitar. In the afternoon, when it was hottest, and all the men who happened to be indoors were lying in their hammocks, I asked Kua-kó to go with me to the stream to bathe. He refused—I had counted on that—and earnestly advised me not to bathe in the pool I was accustomed to, as some little caribe fishes* had made their appearance there and would be sure to attack me. I laughed at his idle tale, and taking up my cloak swung out of the door, whistling a lively air. He knew that I always threw my cloak over my head and shoulders as a protection from the sun and stinging flies when coming out of the water, and so his suspicion was not aroused, and I was not followed. The pool was about ten minutes' walk from the house; I arrived at it with palpitating heart, and going round to its end, where the stream was shallow, sat down to rest for a few moments and take a few sips of cool water dipped up in my palm. Presently I rose, crossed the stream, and began running, keeping among the low trees near the bank until a dry gully, which extended for some distance across the savannah, was reached. By following its course the distance to be covered would be considerably increased, but the shorter way would have exposed me to sight and made it more dangerous. I had put forth too much speed at first, and in a short time my exertions, and the hot sun, together with my intense excitement, overcame me. I dared not hope that my flight had not been observed; I imagined that the Indians, unencumbered by any heavy weight, were already close behind me, and ready to launch their deadly spears at my back. With a sob of rage and despair I fell prostrate on my face in the dry bed of the stream, and for two or three minutes remained thus exhausted and unmanned, my heart throbbing so violently that my whole frame was shaken. If my enemies had come on me then disposed to kill me, I could not have lifted a hand in defence of my life. But minutes passed, and they came not. I rose and went on, at a fast walk now, and when the sheltering stream-bed ended, I stooped among the sere dwarfed shrubs scattered about here and there on its southern side; and now creeping and now running, with an occasional pause to rest and look back, I at last reached the dividing ridge at its southern extremity. The rest of the way was over comparatively easy ground, inclining downwards; and with that glad green forest now full in sight, and hope growing stronger every minute in my breast, my knees ceased to tremble, and I ran on again, scarcely pausing until I had touched and lost myself in the welcome shadows.

CHAPTER XIV

Ah that return to the forest where Rima dwelt, after so anxious a day, when the declining sun shone hotly still, and the green woodland shadows were so grateful! The coolness, the sense of security, allayed the fever and excitement I had suffered on the open savannah; I walked leisurely, pausing often to listen to some bird voice or to admire some rare insect or parasitic flower shining star-like in the shade. There was a strangely delightful sensation in me. I likened myself to a child that, startled at something it had seen while out playing in the sun, flies to its mother to feel her caressing hand on its cheek and forget its tremors. And describing what I felt in that way, I was a little ashamed and laughed at myself; nevertheless the feeling was very sweet. At that moment Mother and Nature seemed one and the same thing. As I kept to the more open part of the wood, on its south-ernmost border, the red flame of the sinking sun was seen at intervals through the deep humid green of the higher foliage. How every object it touched took from it a new wonderful glory! At one spot, high up where the foliage was scanty, and slender bush ropes and moss de-pended like broken cordage from a dead limb—just there, bathing itself in that glory-giving light, I noticed a fluttering bird, and stood still to watch its antics. Now it would cling, head downwards, to the slender twigs, wings and tail open; then, righting itself, it would flit from waving line to line, dropping lower and lower; and anon soar upwards a distance of twenty feet and alight to recommence the flitting and swaying and dropping towards the earth. It was one of those birds that have a polished plumage, and as it moved this way and that, flirting its feathers, they caught the beams and shone at moments like glass or burnished metal. Suddenly another bird of the same kind dropped down to it as if from the sky, straight and swift as a falling stone; and the first bird sprang up to meet the comer, and after rapidly wheeling round each other for a moment they fled away in company, screaming shrilly through the wood, and were instantly lost to sight, while their jubilant cries came back fainter and fainter at each repetition.

I envied them not their wings: at that moment earth did not seem fixed and solid beneath me, nor I bound by gravity to it. The faint, floating clouds, the blue infinite heaven itself, seemed not more ethereal and free than I, or the ground I walked on. The low, stony hills on my right hand, of which I caught occasional glimpses through the trees, looking now blue and delicate in the level rays, were no more than the billowy projections on the moving cloud of earth: the trees of unnumbered kinds—great mora, cecropia, and greenheart, bush and fern and suspended lianas, and tall palms balancing their feathery foliage on slender stems—all was but a fantastic mist embroidery covering the surface of that floating cloud on which my feet were set, and which floated with me near the sun.

The red evening flame had vanished from the summits of the trees, the sun was setting, the woods in shadow, when I got to the end of my walk. I did not approach the house on the side of the door, yet by some means those within became aware of my presence, for out they came in a great hurry, Rima leading the way, Nuflo behind her, waving her arms and shouting. But as I drew near the girl dropped behind and stood motionless regarding me, her face pallid and showing strong excitement. I could scarcely remove my eyes from her eloquent countenance: I seemed to read in it relief and gladness mingled with surprise and something like vexation. She was piqued perhaps that I had taken her by surprise, that after much watching for me in the wood I had come through it undetected when she was indoors.

'Happy the eyes that see you!' shouted the old man, laughing boisterously.

'Happy are mine that look on Rima again,' I answered. 'I have been long absent.'

'Long—you may say so,' returned Nuflo. 'We had given you up. We said that, alarmed at the thought of the journey to Riolama, you had abandoned us.'

'*We* said!' exclaimed Rima, her pallid face suddenly flushing. 'I spoke differently.'

'Yes, I know—I know!' he said airily, waving his hand. 'You said that he was in danger, that he was kept against his will from coming. He is present now—let him speak.'

'She was right,' I said. 'Ah, Nuflo, old man, you have lived long, and got much experience, but not insight—not that inner vision that sees further than the eyes.'

'No, not that—I know what you mean,' he answered. Then, tossing his hand towards the sky, he added, 'The knowledge you speak of comes from there.'

The girl had been listening with keen interest, glancing from one to the other. 'What!' she spoke suddenly, as if unable to keep silence, 'do you think, grandfather, that *she* tells me—when there is danger—when the rain will cease—when the wind will blow—everything? Do I not ask and listen, lying awake at night? She is always silent, like the stars.'

Then, pointing to me with her finger, she finished—

'*He* knows so many things! Who tells them to *him?*'

'But distinguish, Rima. You do not distinguish the great from the little,' he answered loftily. '*We* know a thousand things, but they are things that any man with a forehead can learn. The knowledge that comes from the blue is not like that—it is more important and miraculous. Is it not so, señor?' he ended, appealing to me.

'Is it, then, left for me to decide?' said I, addressing the girl.

But though her face was towards me she refused to meet my look and was silent. Silent, but not satisfied: she doubted still, and had perhaps caught something in my tone that strengthened her doubt.

Old Nuflo understood the expression. 'Look at me, Rima,' he said, drawing himself up. 'I am old, and he is young—do I not know best? I have spoken and have decided it.'

Still that unconvinced expression, and her face turned expectant to me.

'Am I to decide?' I repeated.

'Who, then?' she said at last, her voice scarcely more than a murmur; yet there was reproach in the tone, as if she had made a long speech and I had tyrannously driven her to it.

'Thus, then, I decide,' said I. 'To each of us, as to every kind of animal, even to small birds and insects, and to every kind of plant, there is given something peculiar—a fragrance, a melody, a special instinct, an art, a knowledge, which no other has. And to Rima has been given this quickness of mind and power to divine distant things; it is hers, just as swiftness and grace and changeful, brilliant colour are the humming-bird's; therefore she need not that anyone dwelling in the blue should instruct her.'

The old man frowned and shook his head; while she, after one swift, shy glance at my face, and with something like a smile flitting over her delicate lips, turned and reëntered the house.

I felt convinced from that parting look that she had understood me, that my words had in some sort given her relief; for, strong as was her faith in the supernatural, she appeared as ready to escape from it, when a way of escape offered, as from the limp cotton gown and constrained manner worn in the house. The religion and cotton dress were evidently remains of her early training at the settlement of Voa.

Old Nuflo, strange to say, had proved better than his word. Instead of inventing new causes for delay, as I had imagined would be the case, he now informed me that his preparations for the journey were all but complete, that he had only waited for my return to set out.

Rima soon left us in her customary way, and then, talking by the fire, I gave an account of my detention by the Indians and of the loss of my revolver, which I thought very serious.

'You seem to think little of it,' I said, observing that he took it very coolly. 'Yet I know not how I shall defend myself in case of an attack.'

'I have no fear of an attack,' he answered. 'It seems to me the same thing whether you have a revolver or many revolvers and carbines and swords, or no revolver—no weapon at all. And for a very simple reason. While Rima is with us, so long as we are on her business, we are protected from above. The angels, señor, will watch over us by day and night. What need of weapons, then, except to procure food?'

'Why should not the angels provide us with food also?' said I.

'No, no, that is a different thing,' he returned. 'That is a small and low thing, a necessity common to all creatures, which all know how to meet. You would not expect an angel to drive away a cloud of mosquitoes, or to remove a bush-tick from your person. No, sir, you may talk of natural gifts, and try to make Rima believe that she is what she is, and knows what she knows, because, like a humming-bird or some plants with a peculiar fragrance, she has been made so. It is wrong, señor, and pardon me for saying it, it ill becomes you to put such fables into her head.'

I answered, with a smile, 'She herself seems to doubt what you believe.'

'But, señor, what can you expect from an ignorant girl like Rima? She knows nothing, or very little, and will not listen to reason. If she would only remain quietly indoors, with her hair braided, and pray and read her Catechism, instead of running about after flowers and birds and butterflies and such unsubstantial things, it would be better for both of us.'

'In what way, old man?'

'Why, it is plain that if she would cultivate the acquaintance of the people that surround her—I mean those that come to her from her sainted mother—and are ready to do her bidding in everything, she could make it more safe for us in this place. For example, there is Runi and his people, why should they remain living so near us as to be a constant danger when a pestilence of small-pox or some other fever might easily be sent to kill them off?'

'And have you ever suggested such a thing to your grandchild?'

He looked surprised and grieved at the question.'Yes, many times, señor,' he said. 'I should have been a poor Christian had I not mentioned it. But when I speak of it she gives me a look and is gone, and I see no more of her all day, and when I see her she refuses even to answer me;—so perverse, so foolish is she in her ignorance; for, as you can see for yourself, she has no more sense or concern about what is most important than some little painted fly that flits about all day long without any object.'

CHAPTER XV

THE next day we were early at work. Nuflo had already gathered, dried, and conveyed to a place of concealment the greater portion of his garden produce. He was determined to leave nothing to be taken by any wandering party of savages that might call at the house during our absence. He had no fear of a visit from his neighbours; they would not know, he said, that he and Rima were out of the wood. A few large earthen pots, filled with shelled maize, beans, and sun-dried strips of pumpkin, still remained to be disposed of. Taking up one of these vessels and asking me to follow with another, he started off through the wood. We went a distance of five or six hundred yards; then made our way down a very steep incline, close to the border of the forest on the western side; arrived at the bottom, we followed the bank a little further, and I then found myself once more at the foot of the precipice over which I had desperately thrown myself on the stormy evening after the snake had bitten me. Nuflo, stealing silently and softly before me through the bushes, had observed a caution and secrecy in approaching this spot resembling that of a wise old hen when she visits her hidden nest to lay an egg. And here was his nest, his most secret treasure-house, which he had probably not revealed even to me without a sharp inward conflict, notwithstanding that our fates were now linked together. The lower portion of the bank was of rock; and in it, about ten or twelve feet above the ground, but easily reached from below, there was a natural cavity large enough to contain all his portable property. Here, besides the food-stuff, he had already stored a quantity of dried tobacco leaf, his rude weapons, cooking utensils, ropes, mats, and other objects. Two or three more journeys were made for the remaining pots, after which we adjusted a slab of sandstone to the opening, which was fortunately narrow, plastered up the crevices with clay, and covered them over with moss to hide all traces of our work.

Towards evening, after we had refreshed ourselves with a long siesta, Nuflo brought out from some other hiding-place two sacks; one weighing about twenty pounds and containing smoke-dried meat, also grease and gum for lighting purposes, and a few other small objects. This was his load; the other sack, which was smaller and contained parched corn and raw beans, was for me to carry.

The old man, cautious in all his movements, always acting as if surrounded by invisible spies, delayed setting out until an hour after dark. Then, skirting the forest on its west side, we left Ytaioa on our right hand, and after travelling over rough, difficult ground, with only the stars to light us, we saw the waning moon rise not long before dawn. Our course had been a north-easterly one at first; now it was due east, with broad, dry savannahs and patches of open forest as far as we could see before us. It was weary walking on that first night, and weary waiting on the first day when we sat in the shade during the long, hot hours, persecuted by small stinging flies; but the days and nights that succeeded were far worse, when the weather became bad with intense heat and frequent heavy falls of rain. The one compensation I had looked for, which would have outweighed all the extreme discomforts we suffered, was denied me. Rima was no more to me or with me now than she had been during those wild days in her native woods, when every bush and bole and tangled creeper or fern-frond had joined in a conspiracy to keep her out of my sight. It is true that at intervals in the daytime she was visible, sometimes within speaking distance, so that I could address a few words to her, but there was no companionship, and we were fellow-travellers only like birds flying independently in the same direction, not so widely separated but that they can occasionally hear and see each other. The pilgrim in the desert is sometimes attended by a bird, and the bird, with its freer motions, will often leave him a league behind and seem lost to him, but only to return and show its form again; for it has never lost sight nor recollection of the traveller toiling slowly over the surface. Rima kept us company in some such wild erratic way as that. A word, a sign from Nuflo was enough for her to know the direction to take; the distant forest or still more distant mountain near which we should have to pass. She would hasten on and be lost to our sight, and when there was a forest in the way she would explore it, resting in the shade and finding her own food; but invariably she was before us at each resting or camping place.

Indian villages were seen during the journey, but only to be avoided: and in like manner, if we caught sight of Indians travelling or camping at a distance, we would alter our course, or conceal ourselves to escape observation. Only on one occasion, two days after setting out, were we compelled to speak with strangers. We were going round a hill, and all at once came face to face with three persons travelling in an opposite direction—two men and a woman, and, by a strange fatality, Rima at that moment happened to be with us. We stood for some time talking to these people, who were evidently surprised at our appearance, and wished to learn who we were; but Nuflo, who spoke their language like one of themselves, was too cunning to give any true answer. They, on their side, told us that they had been to visit a relative at Chani, the name of a river three days ahead of us, and were now returning to their own village at Baila-baila, two days beyond Parahuari. After parting from them Nuflo was much troubled in his mind for the rest of that day. These people, he said, would probably rest at some Parahuari village, where they would be sure to give a description of us, and so it might eventually come to the knowledge of our unneighbourly neighbour Runi that we had left Ytaioa.

Other incidents of our long and wearisome journey need not be related. Sitting under some shady tree during the sultry hours, with Rima only too far out of earshot, or by the nightly fire, the old man told me little by little and with much digression, chiefly on sacred subjects, the strange story of the girl's origin.

About seventeen years back—Nuflo had no sure method to compute time by—when he was already verging on old age, he was one of a company of nine men, living a kind of roving life in the very part of Guayana through which we were now travelling; the others, much younger than himself, were all equally offenders against the laws of Venezuela, and fugitives from justice. Nuflo was the leader of this gang, for it happened that he had passed a great portion of his life outside the pale of civilisation, and could talk the Indian language, and knew this part of Guayana intimately. But according to his own account he was not in harmony with them. They were bold, desperate men, whose evil appetites had so far only been whetted by the crimes they had committed; while he, with passions worn out, recalling his many bad acts, and with a vivid conviction of the truth of all he had been taught in early life—for Nuflo was nothing if not religious—was now grown timid and desirous only of making his peace with Heaven. This difference of disposition made him morose and quarrelsome with his companions; and they would, he said, have murdered him without remorse if he had not been so useful to them. Their favourite plan was to hang about the neighbourhood of some small isolated settlement, keeping a watch on it, and, when most of the male inhabitants were absent, to swoop down on it and work their will. Now shortly after one of these raids it happened that a woman they had carried off, becoming a burden to them, was flung into a river to the alligators; but when being dragged down to the waterside she cast up her eyes, and in a loud voice cried to God to execute vengeance on her murderers. Nuflo affirmed that he took no part in this black deed: nevertheless, the woman's dying appeal to Heaven preyed on his mind; he feared that it might have won a hearing, and the 'person' eventually commissioned to execute vengeance—after the usual days, of course—might act on the principle of the old proverb—*Tell me whom you are with, and I will tell you what you are*—and punish the innocent (himself to wit) along with the guilty. But while thus anxious about his spiritual interests he was not yet prepared to break with his companions. He thought it best to temporise, and succeeded in persuading them that it would be unsafe to attack another Christian settlement for some time to come; that in the interval they might find some pleasure, if no great credit, by turning their attention to the Indians. The infidels, he said, were God's natural enemies and fair game to the Christian. To make a long story short, Nuflo's Christian band, after some successful adventures, met with a reverse which reduced their number from nine to five. Flying from their enemies they sought safety at Riolama, an uninhabited place, where they found it possible to exist for some weeks on game, which was abundant, and wild fruits.

One day at noon, while ascending a mountain at the southern extremity of the Riolama range, in order to get a view of the country beyond the summit, Nuflo and his companions discovered a cave; and finding it dry, without animal occupants, and with a level floor, they at once determined to make it their dwelling-place for a season. Wood for firing and water were to be had close by; they were also well provided with smoked fish of a tapir they had slaughtered a day or two before, so that they could afford to rest for a time in so comfortable a shelter. At a short distance from the cave they made a fire on the rock to toast some slices of meat for their dinner; and while thus engaged all at once one of the men uttered a cry of astonishment, and casting up his eyes Nuflo beheld, standing near and regarding them with surprise and fear in her wide-open eyes, a woman of a most wonderful appearance. The one slight garment she had on was silky and white as the snow on the summit of some great mountain, but of the snow when the sinking sun touches and gives it some delicate changing colour which is like fire. Her dark hair was like a cloud from which her face looked out, and her head was surrounded by an aureole like that of a saint in a picture, only more beautiful. For, said Nuflo, a picture is a picture, and the other was a reality, which is finer. Seeing her he fell on his knees and crossed himself; and all the time her eyes, full of amazement and shining with such a strange splendour that he could not meet them, were fixed on him and not on the others; and he felt that she had come to save his soul, in danger of perdition owing to his companionship with men who were at war with God and wholly bad.

But at this moment his comrades, recovering from their astonishment, sprang to their feet, and the heavenly woman vanished. Just behind where she had stood, and not twelve yards from them, there was a huge chasm in the mountain, its jagged precipitous sides clothed with thorny bushes; the men now cried out that she had made her escape that way, and down after her they rushed, pell-mell.

Nuflo cried out after them that they had seen a saint and that some horrible thing would befall them if they allowed any evil thought to enter their hearts; but they scoffed at his words, and were soon far down out of hearing, while he, trembling with fear, remained praying to the woman that had appeared to them, and had looked with such strange eyes at him, not to punish him for the sins of the others.

Before long the men returned, disappointed and sullen, for they had failed in their search for the woman; and perhaps Nuflo's warning words had made them give up the chase too soon. At all events, they seemed ill at ease, and made up their minds to abandon the cave: in a short time they left the place to camp that night at a considerable distance from the mountain. But they were not satisfied: they had now recovered from their fear, but not from the excitement of an evil passion; and finally, after comparing notes, they came to the conclusion that they had missed a great prize through Nuflo's cowardice; and when he reproved them they blasphemed all the saints in the calendar and even threatened him with violence. Fearing to remain longer in the company of such godless men, he only waited until they slept, then rose up cautiously, helped himself to most of the provisions, and made his escape, devoutly hoping that after losing their guide they would all speedily perish.

Finding himself alone now and master of his own actions, Nuflo was in terrible distress, for while his heart was in the utmost fear, it yet urged him imperiously to go back to the mountain, to seek again for that sacred being who had appeared to him, and had been driven away by his brutal companions. If he obeyed that inner voice, he would be saved; if he resisted it then there would be no hope for him, and along with those who had cast the woman to the alligators he would be lost eternally. Finally, on the following day, he went back, although not without fear and trembling, and sat down on a stone just where he had sat toasting his tapir meat on the previous day. But he waited in vain, and at length that voice within him, which he had so far obeyed, began urging him to descend into the valley-like chasm down which the woman had escaped from his comrades, and to seek for her there. Accordingly he rose and began cautiously and slowly climbing down over the broken jagged rocks and through a dense mass of thorny bushes and creepers. At the bottom of the chasm a clear, swift stream of water rushed with foam and noise along its rocky bed; but before reaching it, and when it was still twenty yards lower down, he was startled by hearing a low moan among the bushes, and looking about for the cause, he found the wonderful woman—his saviour, as he expressed it. She was not now standing nor able to stand, but half reclining among the rough stones, one foot, which she had sprained in that headlong flight down the ragged slope, wedged immovably between the rocks; and in this painful position she had remained a prisoner since noon on the previous day. She now gazed on her visitor in silent consternation; while he, casting himself prostrate on the ground, implored her forgiveness and begged to know her will. But she made no reply; and at length, finding that she was powerless to move, he concluded that, though a saint and one of the beings that men worship, she was also flesh and liable to accidents while sojourning on earth; and perhaps, he thought, that accident which had befallen her had been specially designed by the powers above to prove him. With great labour, and not without causing her much pain, he succeeded in extricating her from her position; and then finding that the injured foot was half crushed and blue and swollen, he took her up in his arms and carried her to the stream. There, making a cup of a broad green leaf, he offered her water, which she drank eagerly; and he also laved her injured foot in the cold stream and bandaged it with fresh aquatic leaves; finally he made her a soft bed of moss and dry grass and placed her on it. That night he spent keeping watch over her, at intervals applying fresh wet leaves to her foot as the old ones became dry and wilted from the heat of the inflammation.

The effect of all he did was that the terror with which she regarded him gradually wore off; and next day, when she seemed to be recovering her strength, he proposed by signs to remove her to the cave higher up, where she would be sheltered in case of rain. She appeared to understand him, and allowed herself to be taken up in his arms, and carried with much labour to the top of the chasm. In the cave he made her a second couch, and tended her assiduously. He made a fire on the floor and kept it burning night and day, and supplied her with water to drink and fresh leaves for her foot. There was little more that he could do. From the choicest and fattest bits of toasted tapir flesh he offered her she turned away with disgust. A little cassava-bread soaked in water she would take, but seemed not to like it. After a time, fearing that she would starve, he took to hunting after wild fruits, edible bulbs and gums, and on these small things she subsisted during the whole time of their sojourn together in the desert.

The woman, although lamed for life, was now so far recovered as to be able to limp about without assistance, and she spent a portion of each day out among the rocks and trees on the mountains. Nuflo at first feared that she would now leave him, but before long he became convinced that she had no such intentions. And yet she was profoundly unhappy. He was accustomed to see her seated on a rock, as if brooding over some secret grief, her head bowed, and great tears falling from half-closed eyes.

From the first he had conceived the idea that she was in the way of becoming a mother at no distant date—an idea which seemed to accord badly with the suppositions as to the nature of this heavenly being he was privileged to minister to and so win salvation; but he was now convinced of its truth, and he imagined that in her condition he had discovered the cause of that sorrow and anxiety which preyed continually on her. By means of that dumb language of signs which enabled them to converse together a little, he made it known to her that at a great distance from the mountains there existed a place where there were beings like herself, women, and mothers of children, who would comfort and tenderly care for her. When she had understood, she seemed pleased and willing to accompany him to that distant place; and so it came to pass that they left their rocky shelter and the mountains of Riolama far behind. But for several days, as they slowly journeyed over the plain, she would pause at intervals in her limping walk to gaze back on those blue summits, shedding abundant tears.

Fortunately the village Voa, on the river of the same name, which was the nearest Christian settlement to Riolama, whither his course was directed, was well known to him; he had lived there in former years, and what was of great advantage, the inhabitants were ignorant of his worst crimes, or, to put it in his own subtle way, of the crimes committed by the men he had acted with. Great was the astonishment and curiosity of the people of Voa when, after many weeks' travelling, Nuflo arrived at last with his companion. But he was not going to tell the truth, nor even the least particle of the truth, to a gaping crowd of inferior persons. For these, ingenious lies: only to the priest he told the whole story, dwelling minutely on all he had done to rescue and protect her; all of which was approved by the holy man, whose first act was to baptise the woman for fear that she was not a Christian. Let it be said to Nuflo's credit that he objected to this ceremony, arguing that she could not be a saint, with an aureole in token of her sainthood, yet stand in need of being baptised by a priest. A priest—he added, with a little chuckle of malicious pleasure—who was often seen drunk, who cheated at cards, and was sometimes suspected of putting poison on his fighting-cock's spur to make sure of the victory! Doubtless the priest had his faults; but he was not without humanity, and for the whole seven years of that unhappy stranger's sojourn at Voa he did everything in his power to make her existence tolerable. Some weeks after arriving she gave birth to a female child, and then the priest insisted on naming it Riolama, in order, he said, to keep in remembrance the strange story of the mother's discovery at that place.

Rima's mother could not be taught to speak either Spanish or Indian; and when she found that the mysterious and melodious sounds that fell from her own lips were understood by none she ceased to utter them, and thereafter preserved an unbroken silence among the people she lived with. But from the presence of others she shrank, as if in disgust or fear, excepting only Nuflo and the priest, whose kindly intentions she appeared to understand and appreciate. So far her life in the village was silent and sorrowful.

With her child it was different; and every day that was not wet, taking the little thing by the hand, she would limp painfully out into the forest, and there, sitting on the ground, the two would commune with each other by the hour in their wonderful language.

At length she began to grow perceptibly paler and feebler week by week, day by day, until she could no longer go out into the wood, but sat or reclined, panting for breath in the dull hot room, waiting for death to release her. At the same time little Rima, who had always appeared frail, as if from sympathy, now began to fade and look more shadowy, so that it was expected she would not long survive her parent. To the mother death came slowly, but at last it seemed so near that Nuflo and the priest were together at her side waiting to see the end. It was then that little Rima, who had learnt from infancy to speak in Spanish, rose from the couch where her mother had been whispering to her, and began with some difficulty to express what was in the dying woman's mind. Her child, she had said, could not continue to live in that hot wet place, but if taken away to a distance where there were mountains and a cooler air she would survive and grow strong again.

Hearing this, old Nuflo declared that the child should not perish; that he himself would take her away to Parahuari, a distant place where there were mountains and dry plains and open woods; that he would watch over her and care for her there as he had cared for her mother at Riolama.

When the substance of this speech had been made known by Rima to the dying woman, she suddenly rose up from her couch, which she had not risen from for many days, and stood erect on the floor, her wasted face shining with joy. Then Nuflo knew that God's angels had come for her, and put out his arms to save her from falling; and even while he held her that sudden glory went out from her face, now of a dead white like burnt-out ashes; and murmuring something soft and melodious, her spirit passed away.

Once more Nuflo became a wanderer, now with the fragile-looking little Rima for companion, the sacred child who had inherited the position of his intercessor from a sacred mother. The priest, who had probably become infected with Nuflo's superstitions, did not allow them to leave Voa empty-handed, but gave the old man as much calico as would serve to buy hospitality and whatsoever he might require from the Indians for many a day to come.

At Parahuari, where they arrived safely at last, they lived for some little time at one of the villages. But the child had an instinctive aversion to all savages, or possibly the feeling was derived from her mother, for it had shown itself early at Voa, where she had refused to learn their language; and this eventually led Nuflo to go away and live apart from them, in the forest by Ytaioa, where he made himself a house and garden. The Indians, however, continued friendly with him and visited him with frequency. But when Rima grew up, developing into that mysterious woodland girl I found her, they became suspicious, and in the end regarded her with dangerously hostile feeling. She, poor child, detested them because they were incessantly at war with the wild animals she loved, her companions; and having no fear of them, for she did not know that they had it in their minds to turn their little poisonous arrows against herself, she was constantly in the woods frustrating them; and the animals, in league with her, seemed to understand her note of warning and hid themselves or took to flight at the approach of danger. At length their hatred and fear grew to such a degree that they determined to make away with her, and one day, having matured a plan, they went to the wood and spread themselves two and two about it. The couples did not keep together, but moved about or remained concealed at a distance of forty or fifty yards apart, lest she should be missed. Two of the savages, armed with blow-pipes, were near the border of the forest on the side nearest to the village, and one of them, observing a motion in the foliage of a tree, ran swiftly and cautiously towards it to try and catch a glimpse of the enemy. And he did see her no doubt, as she was there watching both him and his companions, and blew an arrow at her, but even while in the act of blowing it he was himself struck by a dart that buried itself deep in his flesh just over the heart. He ran some distance with the fatal barbed point in his flesh and met his comrade, who had mistaken him for the girl and shot him. The wounded man threw himself down to die, and dying related that he had fired at the girl sitting up in a tree and that she had caught the arrow in her hand only to hurl it instantly back with such force and precision that it pierced his flesh just over the heart. He had seen it all with his own eyes, and his friend who had accidentally slain him believed his story and repeated it to the others. Rima had seen one Indian shoot the other, and when she told her grandfather he explained to her that it was an accident, but he guessed why the arrow had been fired.

From that day the Indians hunted no more in the wood; and at length one day Nuflo, meeting an Indian who did not know him and with whom he had some talk, heard the strange story of the arrow, and that the mysterious girl who could not be shot was the offspring of an old man and a Didi who had become enamoured of him; that, growing tired of her consort, the Didi had returned to her river, leaving her half-human child to play her malicious pranks in the wood.

This, then, was Nuflo's story, told not in Nuflo's manner, which was infinitely prolix; and think not that it failed to move me—that I failed to bless him for what he had done, in spite of his selfish motives.

CHAPTER XVI

WE were eighteen days travelling to Riolama, on the last two making little progress, on account of continuous rain, which made us miserable beyond description. Fortunately the dogs had found, and Nuflo had succeeded in killing, a great ant-eater, so that we were well supplied with excellent, strength-giving flesh. We were among the Riolama mountains at last, and Rima kept with us, apparently expecting great things. I expected nothing, for reasons to be stated by-and-by. My belief was that the only important thing that could happen to us would be starvation.

The afternoon of the last day was spent in skirting the foot of a very long mountain, crowned at its southern extremity with a huge, rocky mass resembling the head of a stone sphinx above its long, couchant body, and at its highest part about a thousand feet above the surrounding level. It was late in the day, raining fast again, yet the old man still toiled on, contrary to his usual practice, which was to spend the last daylight hours in gathering firewood and in constructing a shelter. At length, when we were nearly under the peak, he began to ascend. The rise in this place was gentle, and the vegetation, chiefly composed of dwarf thorn trees rooted in the clefts of the rock, scarcely impeded our progress; yet Nuflo moved obliquely, as if he found the ascent difficult, pausing frequently to take breath and look round him. Then we came to a deep, ravine-like cleft in the side of the mountain, which became deeper and narrower above us, but below it broad-ened out to a valley; its steep sides as we looked down were clothed with dense, thorny vegetation, and from the bottom rose to our ears the dull sound of a hidden torrent. Along the border of this ravine Nuflo began toiling upwards, and finally brought us out upon a stony plateau on the mountain-side. Here he paused, and turning and regarding us with a look as of satisfied malice in his eyes, remarked that we were at our journey's end, and he trusted the sight of that barren mountainside would compensate us for all the discomforts we had suffered during the last eighteen days.

I heard him with indifference. I had already recognised the place from his own exact description of it, and I now saw all that I had looked to see—a big, barren hill. But Rima, what had she expected that her face wore that blank look of surprise and pain? 'Is this the place where mother appeared to you?' she suddenly cried. 'The very place—this! this!' Then she added, 'The cave where you tended her—where is it?'

'Over there,' he said, pointing across the plateau, which was partially overgrown with dwarf trees and bushes, and ended at a wall of rock, almost vertical and about forty feet high.

Going to this precipice, we saw no cave until Nuflo had cut away two or three tangled bushes, revealing an opening behind, about half as high and twice as wide as the door of an ordinary dwelling-house.

The next thing was to make a torch, and aided by its light we groped our way in and explored the interior. The cave, we found, was about fifty feet long, narrowing to a mere hole at the extremity; but the anterior portion formed an oblong chamber, very lofty, with a dry floor. Leaving our torch burning, we set to work cutting bushes to supply ourselves with wood enough to last us all night. Nuflo, poor old man, loved a big fire dearly; a big fire and fat meat to eat (the ranker its flavour the better he liked it) were to him the greatest blessings that man could wish for: in me also the prospect of a cheerful blaze put a new heart, and I worked with a will in the rain, which increased in the end to a blinding downpour. By the time I dragged my last load in, Nuflo had got his fire well alight, and was heaping on wood in a most lavish way. 'No fear of burning our house down to-night,' he remarked, with a chuckle—the first sound of that description he had emitted for a long time.

After we had satisfied our hunger, and had smoked one or two cigarettes, the unaccustomed warmth, and dryness, and the firelight affected us with drowsiness, and I had probably been nodding for some time; but starting at last and opening my eyes, I missed Rima. The old man appeared to be asleep, although still in a sitting posture close to the fire. I rose and hurried out, drawing my cloak close around me to protect me from the rain; but what was my surprise on emerging from the cave to feel a dry, bracing wind in my face and to see the desert spread out for leagues before me in the brilliant white light of a full moon! The rain had apparently long ceased, and only a few thin white clouds appeared moving swiftly over the wide blue expanse of heaven. It was a welcome change, but the shock of surprise and pleasure was instantly succeeded by the maddening fear that Rima was lost to me. She was nowhere in sight beneath, and running to the end of the little plateau to get free of the thorn trees, I turned my eyes towards the summit, and there, at some distance above me, caught sight of her standing motionless and gazing upwards. I quickly made my way to her side, calling to her as I approached; but she only half turned to cast a look at me and did not reply.

'Rima,' I said, 'why have you come here? Are you actually thinking of climbing the mountain at this hour of the night?'

'Yes—why not?' she returned, moving one or two steps from me.

'Rima—sweet Rima, will you listen to me?'

'Now? Oh, no—why do you ask that? Did I not listen to you in the wood before we started, and you also promised to do what I wished? See, the rain is over and the moon shines brightly. Why should I wait? Perhaps from the summit I shall see my people's country. Are we not near it now?'

'Oh, Rima, what do you expect to see? Listen—you must listen, for I know best. From that summit you would see nothing but a vast dim desert, mountain and forest, mountain and forest, where you might wander for years, or until you perished of hunger, or fever, or were slain by some beast of prey or by savage men; but oh, Rima, never, never, never would you find your people, for they exist not. You have seen the false water of the mirage on the savannah, when the sun shines bright and hot; and if one were to follow it he would at last fall down and perish, with never a cool drop to moisten his parched lips. And your hope, Rima—this hope to find your people which has brought you all the way to Riolama—is a mirage, a delusion, which will lead to destruction if you will not abandon it.'

She turned to face me with flashing eyes. 'You know best!' she exclaimed. 'You know best, and tell me that! Never until this moment have you spoken falsely. Oh, why have you said such things to me—named after this place, Riolama? Am I also like that false water you speak of—no divine Rima, no sweet Rima? My mother, had she no mother, no mother's mother? I remember her, at Voa, before she died, and this hand seems real—like yours; you have asked to hold it. But it is not he that speaks to me—not one that showed me the whole world on Ytaioa. Ah, you have wrapped yourself in a stolen cloak, only you have left your old grey beard behind! Go back to the cave and look for it, and leave me to seek my people alone!'

Once more, as on that day in the forest when she prevented me from killing the serpent, and as on the occasion of her meeting with

Nuflo after we had been together on Ytaioa, she appeared transformed and instinct with intense resentment—a beautiful human wasp, and every word a sting.

'Rima,' I cried, 'you are cruelly unjust to say such words to me. If you know that I have never deceived you before, give me a little credit now. You are no delusion—no mirage, but Rima, like no other being on earth. So perfectly truthful and pure I cannot be, but rather than mislead you with falsehoods I would drop down and die on this rock, and lose you and the sweet light that shines on us for ever.'

As she listened to my words, spoken with passion, she grew pale and clasped her hands: 'What have I said? What have I said?' She spoke in a low voice charged with pain, and all at once she came nearer, and with a low, sobbing cry sank down at my feet, uttering, as on the occasion of finding me lost at night in the forest near her home, tender, sorrowful expressions in her own mysterious language. But before I could take her in my arms she rose again quickly to her feet and moved away a little space from me.

'Oh no, no, it cannot be that you know best!' she began again. 'But I know that you have never sought to deceive me. And now, because I falsely accused you I cannot go there without you'—pointing to the summit —'but must stand still and listen to all you have to say.'

'You know, Rima, that your grandfather has now told me your history—how he found your mother at this place, and took her to Voa, where you were born; but of your mother's people he knows nothing, and therefore he can now take you no further.'

'Ah, you think that! He says that now; but he deceived me all these years, and if he lied to me in the past, can he not still lie, affirming that he knows nothing of my people, even as he affirmed that he knew not Riolama?'

'He tells lies and he tells truth, Rima, and one can be distinguished from the other. He spoke truthfully at last, and brought us to this place, beyond which he cannot lead you.'

'You are right; I must go alone.'

'Not so, Rima, for where you go there we must go; only you will lead and we follow, believing only that our quest will end in disappointment, if not in death.'

'Believe that and yet follow! Oh no! Why did he consent to lead me so far for nothing?'

'Do you forget that you compelled him? You know what he believes; and he is old and looks with fear at death, remembering his evil deeds, and is convinced that only through your intercession and your mother's, he can escape from perdition. Consider, Rima, he could not refuse, to make you more angry and so deprive himself of his only hope.'

My words seemed to trouble her, but very soon she spoke again with renewed animation. 'If my people exist, why must it be disappointment and perhaps death? He does not know; but she came to him here—did she not? The others are not here, but perhaps not far off. Come, let us go to the summit together to see from it the desert beneath us—mountain and forest, mountain and forest. Somewhere there! You said that I had knowledge of distant things. And shall I not know which mountain—which forest?'

'Alas! no, Rima; there is a limit to your far-seeing; and even if that faculty were as great as you imagine it would avail you nothing, for there is no mountain, no forest, in whose shadow your people dwell.'

For a while she was silent, but her eyes and clasping fingers were restless and showed her agitation. She seemed to be searching in the depths of her mind for some argument to oppose to my assertions. Then in a low, almost despondent voice, with something of reproach in it, she said, 'Have we come so far to go back again? You were not Nuflo to need my intercession, yet you came too.'

'Where you are there I must be—you have said it yourself. Besides, when we started I had some hope of finding your people. Now I know better, having heard Nuflo's story. Now I know that your hope is a vain one.'

'Why? Why? Was she not found here—mother? Where, then, are the others?'

'Yes, she was found here, alone. You must remember all the things she spoke to you before she died. Did she ever speak to you of her people—speak of them as if they existed, and would be glad to receive you among them some day?'

'No. Why did she not speak of that? Do you know—can you tell me?'

'I can guess the reason, Rima. It is very sad—so sad that it is hard to tell it. When Nuflo tended her in the cave and was ready to worship her and do everything she wished, and conversed with her by signs, she showed no wish to return to her people. And when he offered her, in a way she understood, to take her to a distant place, where she would be among strange beings, among others like Nuflo, she readily consented, and painfully performed that long journey to Voa. Would you, Rima, have acted thus—would you have gone so far away from your beloved people, never to return, never to hear of them or speak to them again? Oh no, you could not; nor would she, if her people had been in existence. But she knew that she had survived them, that some great calamity had fallen upon and destroyed them. They were few in number, perhaps, and surrounded on every side by hostile tribes, and had no weapons, and made no war. They had been preserved because they inhabited a place apart, some deep valley perhaps, guarded on all sides by lofty mountains and impenetrable forests and marshes; but at last the cruel savages broke into this retreat and hunted them down, destroying all except a few fugitives, who escaped singly like your mother, and fled away to hide in some distant solitude.'

The anxious expression on her face deepened as she listened to one of anguish and despair; and then, almost before I concluded, she suddenly lifted her hands to her head, uttering a low, sobbing cry, and would have fallen on the rock had I not caught her quickly in my arms. Once more in my arms—against my breast, her proper place! But now all that bright life seemed gone out of her; her head fell on my shoulder, and there was no motion in her except at intervals a slight shudder in her frame accompanied by a low, gasping sob. In a little while the sobs ceased, the eyes were closed, the face still and deathly white, and with a terrible anxiety in my heart I carried her down to the cave.

CHAPTER XVII

As I re-entered the cave with my burden Nuflo sat up and stared at me with a frightened look in his eyes. Throwing my cloak down I placed the girl on it and briefly related what had happened.

He drew near to examine her; then placed his hand on her heart. 'Dead!—she is dead!' he exclaimed.

My own anxiety changed to an irrational anger at his words. 'Old fool! She has only fainted,' I returned. 'Get me some water, quick.'

But the water failed to restore her, and my anxiety deepened as I gazed on that white, still face. Oh, why had I told her that sad tragedy I had imagined with so little preparation? Alas! I had succeeded too well in my purpose, killing her vain hope and her at the same moment.

The old man, still bending over her, spoke again. 'No, I will not believe that she is dead yet; but, sir, if not dead, then she is dying.'

I could have struck him down for his words. 'She will die in my arms, then,' I exclaimed, thrusting him roughly aside, and lifting her up with the cloak beneath her.

And while I held her thus, her head resting on my arm, and gazed with unutterable anguish into her strangely white face, insanely praying to Heaven to restore her to me, Nuflo fell on his knees before her, and with bowed head, and hands clasped in supplication, began to speak.

'Rima! Grandchild!' he prayed, his quivering voice betraying his agitation. 'Do not die just yet: you must not die—not wholly die—until you have heard what I have to say to you. I do not ask you to answer in words—you are past that, and I am not unreasonable. Only, when I finish, make some sign—a sigh, a movement of the eyelid, a twitch of the lips, even in the small corners of the mouth; nothing more than that, just to show that you have heard, and I shall be satisfied. Remember all the years that I have been your protector, and this long journey that I have taken on your account; also all that I did for your sainted mother before she died at Voa, to become one of the most important of those who surround the Queen of Heaven, and who, when they wish for any favour, have only to say half a word to get it. And do not cast in oblivion that at the last I obeyed your wish and brought you safely to Riolama. It is true that in some small things I deceived you; but that must not weigh with you, because it is a small matter and not worthy of mention when you consider the claims I have on you. In your hands, Rima, I leave everything, relying on the promise you made me, and on my services. Only one word of caution remains to be added. Do not let the magnificence of the place you are now about to enter, the new sights and colours, and the noise of shouting, and musical instruments and blowing of trumpets, put these things out of your head. Nor must you begin to think meanly of yourself and be abashed when you find yourself surrounded by saints and angels; for you are not less than they, although it may not seem so at first when you see them in their bright clothes, which, they say, shine like the sun. I cannot ask you to tie a string round your finger: I can only trust to your memory, which was always good, even about the smallest things; and when you are asked, as no doubt you will be, to express a wish, remember before everything to speak of your grandfather, and his claims on you, also on your angelic mother, to whom you will present my humble remembrances.'

During this petition, which in other circumstances would have moved me to laughter but now only irritated me, a subtle change seemed to come to the apparently lifeless girl to make me hope. The small hand in mine felt not so icy cold, and though no faintest colour had come to the face, its pallor had lost something of its deathly waxen appearance; and now the compressed lips had relaxed a little and seemed ready to part. I laid my finger-tips on her heart and felt, or imagined that I felt, a faint fluttering; and at last I became convinced that her heart was really beating.

I turned my eyes on the old man, still bending forward, intently watching for the sign he had asked her to make. My anger and disgust at his gross earthy egoism had vanished. 'Let us thank God, old man,' I said, the tears of joy half choking my utterance. 'She lives— she is recovering from her fit.'

He drew back, and on his knees, with bowed head, murmured a prayer of thanks to Heaven.

Together we continued watching her face for half an hour longer, I still holding her in my arms, which could never grow weary of that sweet burden, waiting for other, surer signs of returning life; and she seemed now like one that had fallen into a profound, death-like sleep which must end in death. Yet when I remembered her face as it had looked an hour ago, I was confirmed in the belief that the progress to recovery, so strangely slow, was yet sure. So slow, so gradual was this passing from death to life that we had hardly ceased to fear when we noticed that the lips were parted, or almost parted, that they were no longer white, and that under her pale, transparent skin a faint, bluish-rosy colour was now visible. And at length, seeing that all danger was past and recovery so slow, old Nuflo withdrew once more to the fireside, and stretching himself out on the sandy floor, soon fell into a deep sleep.

If he had not been lying there before me in the strong light of the glowing embers and dancing flames, I could not have felt more alone with Rima—alone amid those remote mountains, in that secret cavern, with lights and shadows dancing on its grey vault. In that profound silence and solitude the mysterious loveliness of the still face I continued to gaze on, its appearance of life without consciousness, produced a strange feeling in me, hard, perhaps impossible, to describe.

Once, when clambering among the rough rocks, overgrown with forest, among the Queneveta mountains, I came on a single white flower which was new to me, which I have never seen since. After I had looked long at it, and passed on, the image of that perfect flower remained so persistently in my mind that on the following day I went again, in the hope of seeing it still untouched by decay. There was no change; and on this occasion I spent a much longer time looking at it, admiring the marvellous beauty of its form, which seemed so greatly to exceed that of all other flowers. It had thick petals, and at first gave me the idea of an artificial flower, cut by a divinely inspired artist from some unknown precious stone, of the size of a large orange and whiter than milk, and yet, in spite of its opacity, with a crystalline lustre on the surface. Next day I went again, scarcely hoping to find it still unwithered; it was fresh as if only just opened; and after that I went often, sometimes at intervals of several days, and still no faintest sign of any change, the clear, exquisite lines still undimmed, the purity and lustre as I had first seen it. Why, I often asked, does not this mystic forest flower fade and perish like others? That first impression of its artificial appearance had soon left me; it was, indeed, a flower, and, like other flowers, had life and growth, only with that transcendent beauty it had a different kind of life. Unconscious, but higher; perhaps immortal. Thus it would continue to bloom when I had looked my last on it; wind and rain and sunlight would never stain, never tinge, its sacred purity; the savage Indian, though he sees little to admire in a flower, yet seeing this one would veil his face and turn back; even the browsing beast crashing his way through the forest, struck with its strange glory, would swerve aside and pass on without harming it. Afterwards I heard from some Indians, to whom I described it, that the flower I had discovered was called Hata; also that they had a superstition concerning it—a strange belief. They said that only one Hata flower existed in the world; that it bloomed in one spot for the space of a moon; that on the disappearance of the moon in the sky the Hata disappeared from its place, only to reappear blooming in some other spot, sometimes in some distant forest.* And they also said that whosoever discovered the Hata flower in the forest would overcome all his enemies and obtain all his desires, and finally outlive other men by many years. But, as I have said, all this I heard afterwards, and my half–superstitious feeling for the flower had grown up independently in my own mind. A feeling like that was in me while I gazed on the face that had no motion, no consciousness in it,* and yet had life, a life of so high a kind as to match with its pure, surpassing loveliness. I could almost believe that, like the forest flower, in this state and aspect it would endure for ever; endure and perhaps give of its own immortality to everything around it—to me, holding her in my arms and gazing fixedly on the pale face framed in its cloud of dark, silken hair; to the leaping flames that threw changing lights on the dim stony wall of rock; to old Nuflo and his two yellow dogs stretched out on the floor in eternal, un-awakening sleep.

This feeling took such firm possession of my mind that it kept me for a time as motionless as the form I held in my arms. I was only re-leased from its power by noting still further changes in the face I watched, a more distinct advance towards conscious life. The faint colour, which had scarcely been more than a suspicion of colour, had deepened perceptibly; the lids were lifted so as to show a gleam of the crystal orbs beneath; the lips, too, were slightly parted.

And, at last, bending lower down to feel her breath, the beauty and sweetness of those lips could no longer be resisted, and I touched them with mine. Having once tasted their sweetness and fragrance, it was impossible to keep from touching them again and again. She was not conscious—how could she be and not shrink from my caress? Yet there was a suspicion in my mind, and drawing back I gazed into her face once more. A strange new radiance had overspread it. Or was this only an illusive colour thrown on her skin by the red firelight? I shaded her face with my open hand, and saw that her pallor had really gone, that the rosy flame on her cheeks was part of her life. Her lustrous eyes, half open, were gazing into mine. Oh, surely consciousness had returned to her! Had she been sensible of those stolen kisses? Would she now shrink from another caress? Trembling I bent down and touched her lips again, lightly, but lingeringly, and then again, and when I drew back and looked at her face the rosy flame was brighter, and the eyes, more open still, were looking into mine. And gazing with those open, conscious eyes, it seemed to me that at last, at last, the shadow that had rested between us had vanished, that we were united in perfect love and confidence, and that speech was superfluous. And when I spoke it was not without doubt and hesitation: our bliss in those silent moments had been so complete, what could speaking do but make it less!

'My love, my life, my sweet Rima, I know that you will understand me now as you did not before, on that dark night—do you remember it, Rima?—when I held you clasped to my breast in the wood. How it pierced my heart with pain to speak plainly to you as I did on the mountain to-night—to kill the hope that had sustained and brought you so far from home! But now that anguish is over; the shadow has gone out of those beautiful eyes that are looking at me. It is because loving me, knowing now what love is, knowing, too, how much I love you, that you no longer need to speak to any other living being of such things? To tell it, to show it, to me is now enough—is it not so, Rima? How strange it seemed, at first, when you shrank in fear from me! But, afterwards, when you prayed aloud to your mother, opening all the secrets of your heart, I understood it. In that lonely, isolated life in the wood you had heard nothing of love, of its power over the heart, its infinite sweetness; when it came to you at last it was a new, inexplicable thing, and filled you with misgivings and tumultuous thoughts, so that you feared it and hid yourself from its cause. Such tremors would be felt if it had always been night, with no light except that of the stars and the pale moon, as we saw it a little while ago on the mountain; and, at last, day dawned, and a strange, unheard-of rose and purple flame kindled in the eastern sky, foretelling the coming sun. It would seem beautiful beyond anything that night had shown to you, yet you would tremble, and your heart beat fast at that strange sight; you would wish to fly to those who might be able to tell you its meaning, and whether the sweet things it prophesied would ever really come. That is why you wished to find your people, and came to Riolama to seek them: and when you knew—when I cruelly told you—that they would never be found, then you imagined that that strange feeling in your heart must remain a secret for ever, and you could not endure the thought of your loneliness. If you had not fainted so quickly, then I should have told you what I must tell you now. They are lost, Rima—your people—but I am with you, and know what you feel, even if you have no words to tell it. But what need of words? It shines in your eyes, it burns like a flame in your face; I can feel it in your hands. Do you not also see it in my face—all that I feel for you, the love that makes me happy? For this is love, Rima, the flower and the melody of life, the sweetest thing, the sweet miracle that makes our two souls one.'

Still resting in my arms, as if glad to rest there, still gazing into my face, it was clear to me that she understood my every word. And then, with no trace of doubt or fear left, I stooped again, until my lips were on hers; and when I drew back once more, hardly knowing which bliss was greatest—kissing her delicate mouth or gazing into her face—she all at once put her arms about my neck and drew herself up until she sat on my knee.

'Abel—shall I call you Abel now—and always?' she spoke, still with her arms round my neck. 'Ah, why did you let me come to Riolama? I would come! I made him come—old grandfather, sleeping there: he does not count, but you—you! After you had heard my story, and knew that it was all for nothing! And all I wished to know was there—in you. Oh, how sweet it is! But a little while ago, what pain! When I stood on the mountain when you talked to me, and I knew that you knew best, and tried and tried not to know. At last I could try no more; they were all dead like mother; I had chased the false water on the savannah. "Oh, let me die too," I said, for I could not bear the pain. And afterwards, here in the cave, I was like one asleep, and when I woke I did not really wake. It was like morning with the light teasing me to open my eyes and look at it. Not yet, dear light; a little while longer, it is so sweet to lie still. But it would not leave me, and stayed teasing me still, like a small shining green fly; until, because it teased me so, I opened my lids just a little. It was not morning, but the firelight, and I was in your arms, not in my little bed. Your eyes looking, looking into mine. But I could see yours better. I remembered everything then, how you once asked me to look into your eyes. I remembered so many things—oh, so many!'

'How many things did you remember, Rima?'

'Listen, Abel, do you ever lie on the dry moss and look straight up into a tree and count a thousand leaves?'

'No, sweetest, that could not be done, it is so many to count. Do you know how many a thousand are?'

'Oh, do I not! When a humming-bird flies close to my face and stops still in the air, humming like a bee, and then is gone, in that short time I can count a hundred small round bright feathers on its throat. That is only a hundred; a thousand are more, ten times. Looking up I count a thousand leaves; then stop counting, because there are thousands more behind the first, and thousands more, crowded together so that I cannot count them. Lying in your arms, looking up into your face, it was like that; I could not count the things I remembered. In the wood, when you were there, and before; and long, long ago at Voa, when I was a child with mother.'

'Tell me some of the things you remembered, Rima.'

'Yes, one—only one now. When I was a child at Voa mother was very lame—you know that. Whenever we went out, away from the houses, into the forest, walking slowly, slowly, she would sit under a tree while I ran about playing. And every time I came back to her I would find her so pale, so sad, crying—crying. That was when I would hide and come softly back so that she would not hear me coming. "Oh, mother, why are you crying? Does your lame foot hurt you?" And one day she took me in her arms and told me truly why she cried.'

She ceased speaking, but looked at me with a strange new light coming into her eyes.

'Why did she cry, my love?'

'Oh, Abel, can you understand—now—at last!' And putting her lips close to my ear, she began to murmur soft, melodious sounds that told me nothing. Then drawing back her head, she looked again at me, her eyes glistening with tears, her lips half parted with a smile, tender and wistful.

Ah, poor child! in spite of all that had been said, all that had happened, she had returned to the old delusion that I must understand her speech. I could only return her look, sorrowfully and in silence.

Her face became clouded with disappointment, then she spoke again with something of pleading in her tone. 'Look, we are not now apart, I hiding in the wood, you seeking, but together, saying the same things. In your language—yours and now mine. But before you came I knew nothing, nothing, for there was only grandfather to talk to. A few words each day, the same words. If yours is mine, mine must be yours. Oh, do you not know that mine is better?'

'Yes, better; but alas! Rima, I can never hope to understand your sweet speech, much less to speak it. The bird that only chirps and twitters can never sing like the organ-bird.'

Crying, she hid her face against my neck, murmuring sadly between her sobs, 'Never—never!'

How strange it seemed, in that moment of joy, such a passion of tears, such despondent words!

For some minutes I preserved a sorrowful silence, realising for the first time, so far as it was possible to realise such a thing, what my inability to understand her secret language meant to her—that finer language in which alone her swift thoughts and vivid emotions could be expressed. Easily and well as she seemed able to declare herself in my tongue, I could well imagine that to her it would seem like the merest stammering. As she had said to me once when I asked her to speak in Spanish, 'That is not speaking.' And so long as she could not commune with me in that better language, which reflected her mind, there would not be that perfect union of soul she so passionately desired.

By-and-by, as she grew calmer, I sought to say something that would be consoling to both of us. 'Sweetest Rima,' I spoke, 'it is so sad that I can never hope to talk with you in your way; but a greater love than this that is ours we could never feel, and love will make us happy, unutterably happy, in spite of that one sadness. And perhaps, after a while, you will be able to say all you wish in my language, which is also yours, as you said some time ago. When we are back again in the beloved wood, and talk once more under that tree where we first talked, and under the old mora, where you hid yourself and threw down leaves on me, and where you caught the little spider to show me how you made yourself a dress, you shall speak to me in your own sweet tongue, and then try to say the same things in mine. . . And in the end, perhaps, you will find that it is not so impossible as you think.'

She looked at me, smiling again through her tears, and shook her head a little.

'Remember what I have heard, that before your mother died you were able to tell Nuflo and the priest what her wish was. Can you not, in the same way, tell me why she cried?'

'I can tell you, but it will not be telling you.'

'I understand. You can tell the bare facts. I can imagine something more, and the rest I must lose. Tell me, Rima.'

Her face became troubled; she glanced away and let her eyes wander round the dim, firelit cavern; then they returned to mine once more.

'Look,' she said, 'grandfather lying asleep by the fire. So far away from us—oh, so far! But if we were to go out from the cave, and on and on to the great mountains where the city of the sun is, and stood there at last in the midst of great crowds of people, all looking at us, talking to us, it would be just the same. They would be like the trees and rocks and animals—so far! Not with us nor we with them. But we are everywhere alone together, apart—we two. It is love; I know it now, but I did not know it before because I had forgotten what she told me. Do you think I can tell you what she said when I asked her why she cried? Oh no! Only this, she and another were like one, always, apart from the others. Then something came—something came! O Abel, was that the something you told me about on the mountain? And the other was lost for ever, and she was alone in the forests and mountains of the world. Oh, why do we cry for what is lost? Why do we not quickly forget it and feel glad again? Now only do I know what you felt, O sweet mother, when you sat still and cried, while I ran about and played and laughed! O poor mother! Oh, what pain!' And hiding her face against my neck, she sobbed once more.

To my eyes also love and sympathy brought the tears; but in a little while the fond, comforting words I spoke and my caresses recalled her from that sad past to the present; then, lying back as at first, her head resting on my folded cloak, her body partly supported by my encircling arm and partly by the rock we were leaning against, her half-closed eyes turned to mine expressed a tender assured happiness—the chastened gladness of sunshine after rain; a soft delicious languor that was partly passionate with the passion etherealised.

'Tell me, Rima,' I said, bending down to her, 'in all those troubled days with me in the woods had you no happy moments? Did not something in your heart tell you that it was sweet to love, even before you knew what love meant?'

'Yes; and once—O Abel, do you remember that night, after returning from Ytaioa, when you sat so late talking by the fire—I in the shadow, never stirring, listening, listening; you by the fire with the light on your face, saying so many strange things? I was happy then—oh, how happy! It was black night and raining, and I a plant growing in the dark, feeling the sweet rain-drops falling, falling on my leaves. Oh, it will be morning by-and-by and the sun will shine on my wet leaves; and that made me glad till I trembled with happiness. Then suddenly the lightning would come, so bright, and I would tremble with fear, and wish that it would be dark again. That was when you looked at me sitting in the shadow, and I could not take my eyes away quickly and could not meet yours, so that I trembled with fear.'

'And now there is no fear—no shadow; now you are perfectly happy?'

'Oh, so happy! If the way back to the wood was longer, ten times, and if the great mountains, white with snow on their tops, were between, and the great dark forest, and rivers wider than Orinoco, still I would go alone without fear, because you would come after me, to join me in the wood, to be with me at last and always.'

'But I should not let you go alone, Rima—your lonely days are over now.'

She opened her eyes wider, and looked earnestly into my face. 'I must go back alone, Abel,' she said. 'Before day comes I must leave you. Rest here, with grandfather, for a few days and nights, then follow me.'

I heard her with astonishment. 'It must not be, Rima,' I cried. 'What, let you leave me—now you are mine—to go all that distance, through all that wild country where you might lose yourself and perish alone? Oh, do not think of it!'

She listened, regarding me with some slight trouble in her eyes, but smiling a little at the same time. Her small hand moved up my arm and caressed my cheek; then she drew my face down to hers until our lips met. But when I looked at her eyes again I saw that she had not consented to my wish. 'Do I not know all the way now,' she spoke, 'all the mountains, rivers, forests—how should I lose myself? And I must return quickly, not step by step, walking—resting, resting—walking, stopping to cook and eat, stopping to gather firewood, to make a shelter—so many things! Oh, I shall be back in half the time; and I have so much to do.'

'What can you have to do, love?—everything can be done when we are in the wood together.'

A bright smile with a touch of mockery in it flitted over her face as she replied, 'Oh, must I tell you that there are things you cannot do? Look, Abel,' and she touched the slight garment she wore, thinner now than at first, and dulled by long exposure to sun and wind and rain.

I could not command her, and seemed powerless to persuade her; but I had not done yet, and proceeded to use every argument I could find to bring her round to my view; and when I finished she put her arms around my neck and drew herself up once more. 'O Abel, how happy I shall be!' she said, taking no notice of all I had said. 'Think of me alone, days and days, in the wood, waiting for you, working all the time; saying, "Come quickly, Abel; come slow, Abel. O Abel, how long you are! Oh, do not come until my work is finished!" And when it is finished and you arrive you shall find me, but not at once. First you will seek for me in the house, then in the wood, calling, "Rima! Rima!" And she will be there, listening, hid in the trees, wishing to be in your arms, wishing for your lips—oh, so glad, yet fearing to show herself. Do you know why? He told you—did he not?—that when he first saw her she was standing before him, all in white—a dress that was like snow on the mountain-tops, when the sun is setting and gives it rose and purple colour. I shall be like that, hidden among the trees, saying, "Am I different—not like Rima? Will he know me—will he love me just the same?" Oh, do I not know that you will be glad, and love me, and call me beautiful? Listen! Listen!' she suddenly exclaimed, lifting her face.

Among the bushes not far from the cave's mouth a small bird had broken out in song, a clear, tender melody soon taken up by other birds further away.

'It will soon be morning,' she said, and then clasped her arms about me once more and held me in a long, passionate embrace; then slipping away from my arms and with one swift glance at the sleeping old man, passed out of the cave.

For a few moments I remained sitting, not yet realising that she had left me, so suddenly and swiftly had she passed from my arms and my sight; then, recovering my faculties, I started up and rushed out in hopes of overtaking her.

It was not yet dawn, but there was still some light from the full moon, now somewhere behind the mountains. Running to the verge of the bush-grown plateau, I explored the rocky slope beneath without seeing her form, and then called, 'Rima! Rima!'

A soft, warbling sound, uttered by no bird, came up from the shadowy bushes far below; and in that direction I ran on; then pausing called again. The sweet sound was repeated once more, but much lower down now, and so faintly that I scarcely heard it. And when I went on further, and called again and again, there was no reply, and I knew that she had indeed gone on that long journey alone.

CHAPTER XVIII

WHEN Nuflo at length opened his eyes he found me sitting alone and despondent by the fire, just returned from my vain chase. I had been caught in a heavy mist on the mountain-side, and was wet through as well as weighed down by fatigue and drowsiness, consequent upon the previous day's laborious march and my night-long vigil; yet I dared not think of rest. *She* had gone from me, and I could not have prevented it; yet the thought that I had allowed her to slip out of my arms, to go away alone on that long, perilous journey, was as intolerable as if I had consented to it.

Nuflo was at first startled to hear of her sudden departure; but he laughed at my fears, affirming that after having once been over the ground she could not lose herself; that she would be in no danger from the Indians, as she would invariably see them at a distance and avoid them, and that wild beasts, serpents, and other evil creatures would do her no harm. The small amount of food she required to sustain life could be found anywhere; furthermore, her journey would not be interrupted by bad weather, since rain and heat had no effect on her. In the end he seemed pleased that she had left us, saying that with Rima in the wood the house and cultivated patch and hidden provisions and implements would be safe, for no Indian would venture to come where she was. His confidence reassured me, and casting myself down on the sandy floor of the cave, I fell into a deep slumber, which lasted until evening; then I only woke to share a meal with the old man, and sleep again until the following day.

Nuflo was not ready to start yet; he was enamoured of the unaccustomed comforts of a dry sleeping-place and a fire blown about by no wind and into which fell no hissing rain-drops. Not for two days more would he consent to set out on the return journey, and if he could have persuaded me our stay at Riolama would have lasted a week.

We had fine weather at starting; but before long it clouded, and then for upwards of a fortnight we had it wet and stormy, which so hindered us that it took us twenty-three days to accomplish the return journey, whereas the journey out had only taken eighteen. The adventures we met with and the pains we suffered during this long march need not be related. The rain made us miserable, but we suffered more from hunger than from any other cause, and on more than one occasion were reduced to the verge of starvation. Twice we were driven to beg for food at Indian villages, and as we had nothing to give in exchange for it, we got very little. It is possible to buy hospitality from the savage without fish-hooks, nails, and calico; but on this oc-casion I found myself without that impalpable medium of exchange, which had been so great a help to me on my first journey to Parahuari. Now I was weak and miserable and without cunning. It is true that we could have exchanged the two dogs for cassava-bread and corn, but we should then have been worse off than ever. And in the end the dogs saved us by an occasional capture—an armadillo surprised in the open and seized before it could bury itself in the soil, or an iguana, opossum, or labba,* traced by means of their keen sense of smell to its hiding-place. Then Nuflo would rejoice and feast, rewarding them with the skin, bones, and entrails. But at length one of the dogs fell lame, and Nuflo, who was very hungry, made its lame-ness an excuse for despatching it, which he did apparently without compunction, notwithstanding that the poor brute had served him well in its way. He cut up and smoke-dried the flesh, and the intoler-able pangs of hunger compelled me to share the loathsome food with him. We were not only indecent, it seemed to me, but cannibals to feed on the faithful servant that had been our butcher. 'But what does it matter?' I argued with myself. 'All flesh, clean and unclean, should be, and is, equally abhorrent to me, and killing animals a kind of mur-der. But now I find myself constrained to do this evil thing that good may come. Only to live I take it now—this hateful strength-giver that will enable me to reach Rima, and the purer, better life that is to be.'

During all that time, when we toiled onwards league after league in silence, or sat silent by the nightly fire, I thought of many things; but the past, with which I had definitely broken, was little in my mind. Rima was still the source and centre of all my thoughts; from her they rose, and to her returned. Thinking, hoping, dreaming, sus-tained me in those dark days and nights of pain and privation. Imagin-ation was the bread that gave me strength, the wine that exhilarated. What sustained old Nuflo's mind I know not. Probably it was like a chrysalis, dormant, independent of sustenance; the bright-winged image to be called at some future time to life by a great shouting of angelic hosts and noises of musical instruments slept secure, coffined in that dull, gross nature.

The old beloved wood once more! Never did his native village in some mountain valley seem more beautiful to the Switzer, returning, war-worn, from long voluntary exile,* than did that blue cloud on the horizon—the forest where Rima dwelt, my bride, my beautiful—and towering over it the dark cone of Ytaioa, now seem to my hungry eyes! How near at last—how near! And yet the two or three intervening leagues to be traversed so slowly, step by step—how vast the distance seemed! Even at far Riolama, when I set out on my return, I scarcely seemed so far from my love. This maddening impatience told on my strength, which was small, and hindered me. I could not run nor even walk fast; old Nuflo, slow, and sober, with no flame consuming his heart, was more than my equal in the end, and to keep up with him was all I could do.

At the finish he became silent and cautious, first entering the belt of trees leading away through the low range of hills at the southern extremity of the wood. For a mile or upwards we trudged on in the shade; then I began to recognise familiar ground, the old trees under which I had walked or sat, and knew that a hundred yards further on there would be a first glimpse of the palm-leaf thatch. Then all weakness forsook me; with a low cry of passionate longing and joy I rushed on ahead; but I strained my eyes in vain for a sight of that sweet shelter; no patch of pale yellow colour appeared amidst the universal verdure of bushes, creepers, and trees—trees beyond trees, trees towering above trees.

For some moments I could not realise it. No, I had surely made a mistake, the house had not stood on that spot; it would appear in sight a little further on. I took a few uncertain steps onwards, and then again stood still, my brain reeling, my heart swelling nigh to bursting with anguish. I was still standing motionless, with hand pressed to my breast, when Nuflo overtook me. 'Where is it—the house?' I stammered, pointing with my hand. All his stolidity seemed gone now; he was trembling too, his lips silently moving. At length he spoke: 'They have come—the children of hell have been here, and have destroyed everything!'

'Rima! What has become of Rima?' I cried; but without replying he walked on, and I followed.

The house, we soon found, had been burnt down. Not a stick remained. Where it had stood a heap of black ashes covered the ground—nothing more. But on looking round we could discover no sign of human beings having recently visited the spot. A rank growth of grass and herbage now covered the once clear space surrounding the site of the dwelling, and the ash heap looked as if it had been lying there for a month at least. As to what had become of Rima the old man could say no word. He sat down on the ground overwhelmed at the calamity: Runi's people had been there, he could not doubt it, and they would come again, and he could only look for death at their hands. The thought that Rima had perished, that she was lost, was unendurable. It could not be! No doubt the Indians had come and destroyed the house during our absence; but she had returned, and they had gone away again to come no more. She would be somewhere in the forest, perhaps not far off, impatiently waiting our return. The old man stared at me while I spoke; he appeared to be in a kind of stupor, and made no reply: and at last, leaving him still sitting on the ground, I went into the wood to look for Rima.

As I walked there, occasionally stopping to peer into some shadowy glade or opening, and to listen, I was tempted again and again to call the name of her I sought aloud; and still the fear that by so doing I might bring some hidden danger on myself, perhaps on her, made me silent. A strange melancholy rested on the forest, a quietude seldom broken by a distant bird's cry. How, I asked myself, should I ever find her in that wide forest while I moved about in that silent, cautious way? My only hope was that she would find me. It occurred to me that the most likely place to seek her would be some of the old haunts known to us both, where we had talked together. I thought first of the mora tree, where she had hidden herself from me, and thither I directed my steps. About this tree, and within its shade, I lingered for upwards of an hour; and, finally, casting my eyes up into the great dim cloud of green and purple leaves, I softly called, 'Rima, Rima, if you have seen me, and have concealed yourself from me in your hiding-place, in mercy answer me—in mercy come down to me now!' But Rima answered not, nor threw down any red glowing leaves to mock me: only the wind, high up, whispered something low and sorrowful in the foliage; and turning I wandered away at random into the deeper shadows.

By-and-by I was startled by the long, piercing cry of a wild fowl, sounding strangely loud in the silence; and no sooner was the air still again than it struck me that no bird had uttered that cry. The Indian is a good mimic of animal voices, but practice had made me able to distinguish the true from the false bird note. For a minute or so I stood still, at a loss what to do, then moved on again with greater caution, scarcely breathing, straining my sight to pierce the shadowy depths. All at once I gave a great start, for directly before me, on the projecting root in the deeper shade of a tree, sat a dark, motionless human form. I stood still, watching it for some time, not yet knowing that it had seen me, when all doubts were put to flight by the form rising and deliberately advancing—a naked Indian with a zabatana in his hand. As he came up out of the deeper shade I recognised Piaké, the surly elder brother of my friend Kua-kó.

It was a great shock to meet him in the wood, but I had no time to reflect just then. I only remembered that I had deeply offended him and his people, that they probably looked on me as an enemy, and would think little of taking my life. It was too late to attempt to escape by flight; I was spent with my long journey and the many privations I had suffered, while he stood there in his full strength with a deadly weapon in his hand.

Nothing was left but to put a bold face on, greet him in a friendly way, and invent some plausible story to account for my action in secretly leaving the village.

He was now standing still, silently regarding me, and glancing round I saw that he was not alone: at a distance of about forty yards on my right hand two other dusky forms appeared watching me from the deep shade.

'Piaké!' I cried, advancing three or four steps.

'You have returned,' he answered, but without moving. 'Where from?'

'Riolama.'

He shook his head, then asked where it was.

'Twenty days towards the setting sun,' I said. As he remained silent I added, 'I heard that I could find gold in the mountains there. An old man told me, and we went to look for gold.'

'What did you find?'

'Nothing.'

'Ah!'

And so our conversation appeared to be at an end. But after a few moments my intense desire to discover whether the savages knew aught of Rima or not made me hazard a question.

'Do you live here in the forest now?' I asked.

He shook his head, and after a while said, 'We come to kill animals.'

'You are like me now,' I returned quickly; 'you fear nothing.'

He looked distrustfully at me, then came a little nearer and said—

'You are very brave. I should not have gone twenty days' journey with no weapons and only an old man for companion. What weapons did you have?'

I saw that he feared me, and wished to make sure that I had it not in my power to do him some injury. 'No weapon except my knife,' I replied, with assumed carelessness. With that I raised my cloak so as to let him see for himself, turning my body round before him. 'Have you found my pistol?' I added.

He shook his head; but he appeared less suspicious now and came close up to me. 'How do you get food? Where are you going?' he asked.

I answered boldly, 'Food! I am nearly starving. I am going to the village to see if the women have got any meat in the pot, and to tell Runi all I have done since I left him.'

He looked at me keenly, a little surprised at my confidence perhaps, then said that he was also going back and would accompany me. One of the other men now advanced, blow-pipe in hand, to join us, and, leaving the wood, we started to walk across the savannah.

It was hateful to have to recross that savannah again, to leave the woodland shadows where I had hoped to find Rima; but I was powerless: I was a prisoner once more, the lost captive recovered and not yet pardoned, probably never to be pardoned. Only by means of my own cunning could I be saved, and Nuflo, poor old man, must take his chance.

Again and again as we tramped over the barren ground, and when we climbed the ridge, I was compelled to stand still to recover breath, explaining to Piaké that I had been travelling day and night, with no meat during the last three days, so that I was exhausted. This was an exaggeration, but it was necessary to account in some way for the faintness I experienced during our walk, caused less by fatigue and want of food than by anguish of mind.

At intervals I talked to him, asking after all the other members of the community by name. At last, thinking only of Rima, I asked him if any other person or persons besides his people came to the wood now or lived there.

He said no.

'Once,' I said, 'there was a daughter of the Didi, a girl you all feared: is she there now?'

He looked at me with suspicion and then shook his head. I dared not press him with more questions; but after an interval he said plainly, 'She is not there now.'

And I was forced to believe him; for had Rima been in the wood *they* would not have been there. She was not there, this much I had discovered. Had she, then, lost her way, or perished on that long journey from Riolama? Or had she returned only to fall into the hands of her cruel enemies? My heart was heavy in me; but if these devils in human shape knew more than they had told me, I must, I said, hide my anxiety and wait patiently to find it out, should they spare my life. And if they spared me and had not spared that other sacred life interwoven with mine, the time would come when they would find, too late, that they had taken to their bosom a worse devil than themselves.

CHAPTER XIX

MY arrival at the village created some excitement; but I was plainly no longer regarded as a friend or one of the family. Runi was absent, and I looked forward to his return with no little apprehension; he would doubtless decide my fate. Kua-kó was also away. The others sat or stood about the great room, staring at me in silence. I took no notice, but merely asked for food, then for my hammock, which I hung up in the old place, and lying down I fell into a doze. Runi made his appearance at dusk. I rose and greeted him, but he spoke no word, and, until he went to his hammock, sat in sullen silence, ignoring my presence.

On the following day the crisis came. We were once more gathered in the room—all but Kua-kó and another of the men, who had not yet returned from some expedition—and for the space of half an hour not a word was spoken by anyone. Something was expected; even the children were strangely still, and whenever one of the pet birds strayed in at the open door, uttering a little plaintive note, it was chased out again, but without a sound. At length Runi straightened himself on his seat and fixed his eyes on me; then cleared his throat and began a long harangue, delivered in the loud, monotonous sing-song which I knew so well and which meant that the occasion was an important one. And as is usual in such efforts, the same thought and expressions were used again and again, and yet again, with dull, angry insistence. The orator of Guayana to be impressive must be long, however little he may have to say. Strange as it may seem, I listened critically to him, not without a feeling of scorn at his lower intelligence. But I was easier in my mind now. From the very fact of his addressing such a speech to me I was convinced that he wished not to take my life, and would not do so if I could clear myself of the suspicion of treachery.

I was a white man, he said, they were Indians; nevertheless they had treated me well. They had fed me and sheltered me. They had done a great deal for me: they had taught me the use of the zabatana, and had promised to make one for me, asking for nothing in return. They had also promised me a wife. How had I treated them? I had deserted them, going away secretly to a distance, leaving them in doubt as to my intentions. How could they tell why I had gone, and where? They had an enemy. Managa was his name; he and his people hated them;

I knew that he wished them evil; I knew where to find him, for they had told me. That was what they thought when I suddenly left them. Now I returned to them, saying that I had been to Riolama. He knew where Riolama was, although he had never been there: it was so far. Why did I go to Riolama? It was a bad place. There were Indians there, a few; but they were not good Indians like those of Parahuari, and would kill a white man. *Had* I gone there? Why had I gone there?

He finished at last, and it was my turn to speak, but he had given me plenty of time, and my reply was ready. 'I have heard you,' I said. 'Your words are good words. They are the words of a friend. I am the white man's friend, you say: is he my friend? He went away secretly, saying no word: why did he go without speaking to his friend who had treated him well? Has he been to my enemy Managa? Perhaps he is a friend of my enemy? Where has he been? I must now answer these things, saying true words to my friend. You are an Indian, I am a white man. You do not know all the white man's thoughts. These are the things I wish to tell you. In the white man's country are two kinds of men. There are the rich men, who have all that a man can desire—houses made of stone, full of fine things, fine clothes, fine weapons, fine ornaments; and they have horses, cattle, sheep, dogs—everything they desire. Because they have gold, for with gold the white man buys everything. The other kind of white men are the poor, who have no gold and cannot buy or have anything: they must work hard for the rich man for the little food he gives them, and a rag to cover their nakedness; and if he gives them shelter they have it; if not they must lie down in the rain out of doors. In my own country, a hundred days from here, I was the son of a great chief, who had much gold, and when he died it was all mine, and I was rich. But I had an enemy, one worse than Managa, for he was rich and had many people. And in a war his people overcame mine, and he took my 0gold, and all I possessed, making me poor. The Indian kills his enemy, but the white man takes his gold, and that is worse than death. Then I said: I have been a rich man and now I am poor, and must work like a dog for some rich man, for the sake of the little food he will throw me at the end of each day. No, I cannot do it! I will go away and live with the Indians, so that those who have seen me a rich man shall never see me working like a dog for a master, and cry out and mock at me. For the Indians are not like white men: they have no gold; they are not rich and poor; all are alike. One roof covers them from the rain and sun. All have weapons which they make; all kill birds in the forest and catch fish in the rivers; and the women cook the meat and all eat from one pot. And with the Indians, I will be an Indian, and hunt in the forest and eat with them and drink with them. Then I left my country and came here, and lived with you, Runi, and was well treated. And now, why did I go away? This I have now to tell you. After I had been here a certain time I went over there to the forest. You wished me not to go, because of an evil thing, a daughter of the Didi, that lived there; but I feared nothing and went. There I met an old man, who talked to me in the white man's language. He had travelled and seen much, and told me one strange thing. On a mountain at Riolama he told me that he had seen a great lump of gold, as much as a man could carry. And when I heard this I said, "With the gold I could return to my country, and buy weapons for myself and all my people and go to war with my enemy and deprive him of all his possessions and serve him as he served me." I asked the old man to take me to Riolama; and when he had consented I went away from here without saying a word, so as not to be prevented. It is far to Riolama, and I had no weapons; but I feared nothing. I said, "If I must fight I must fight, and if I must be killed I must be killed." But when I got to Riolama I found no gold. There was only a yellow stone which the old man had mistaken for gold. It was yellow, like gold, but it would buy nothing. Therefore I came back to Parahuari again, to my friend; and if he is angry with me still because I went away without informing him, let him say, "Go and seek elsewhere for a new friend, for I am your friend no longer."'

I concluded thus boldly, because I did not wish him to know that I had suspected him of harbouring any sinister designs, or that I looked on our quarrel as a very serious one. When I had finished speaking he emitted a sound which expressed neither approval nor disapproval, but only the fact that he had heard me. But I was satisfied. His expression had undergone a favourable change; it was less grim. After a while he remarked, with a peculiar twitching of the mouth which might have developed into a smile, 'The white man will do much to get gold. You walked twenty days to see a yellow stone that would buy nothing.' It was fortunate that he took this view of the case, which was flattering to his Indian nature, and perhaps touched his sense of the ludicrous. At all events, he said nothing to discredit my story, to which they had all listened with profound interest.

From that time it seemed to be tacitly agreed to let bygones be bygones; and I could see that as the dangerous feeling that had threatened my life diminished the old pleasure they had once found in my company returned. But my feelings towards them did not change, nor could they while that black and terrible suspicion concerning Rima was in my heart. I talked again freely with them, as if there had been no break in the old friendly relations. If they watched me furtively whenever I went out of doors I affected not to see it. I set to work to repair my rude guitar, which had been broken in my absence, and studied to show them a cheerful countenance. But when alone, or in my hammock, hidden from their eyes, free to look into my own heart, then I was conscious that something new and strange had come into my life; that a new nature, black and implacable, had taken the place of the old. And sometimes it was hard to conceal this fury that burnt in me; sometimes I felt an impulse to spring like a tiger on one of the Indians, to hold him fast by the throat until the secret I wished to learn was forced from his lips, then to dash his brains out against the stone. But they were many, and there was no choice but to be cautious and patient if I wished to outwit them with a cunning superior to their own.

Three days after my arrival at the village, Kua-kó returned with his companion. I greeted him with affected warmth, but was really pleased that he was back, believing that if the Indians knew anything of Rima he among them all would be most likely to tell it.

Kua-kó appeared to have brought some important news, which he discussed with Runi and the others; and on the following day I noticed that preparations for an expedition were in progress. Spears and bows and arrows were got ready, but not blow-pipes, and I knew by this that the expedition would not be a hunting one. Having discovered so much, also that only four men were going out, I called Kua-kó aside and begged him to let me go with them. He seemed pleased at the proposal, and at once repeated it to Runi, who considered for a little and then consented.

By-and-by he said, touching his bow, 'You cannot fight with our weapons; what will you do if we meet an enemy?'

I smiled and returned that I would not run away. All I wished to show him was that his enemies were my enemies, that I was ready to fight for my friend.

He was pleased at my words, and said no more and gave me no

weapons. Next morning, however, when we set out before daylight, I made the discovery that he was carrying my revolver fastened to his waist. He had concealed it carefully under the one simple garment he wore, but it bulged slightly, and so the secret was betrayed. I had never believed that he had lost it, and I was convinced that he took it now with the object of putting it into my hands at the last moment in case of meeting with an enemy.

From the village we travelled in a north-westerly direction, and before noon camped in a grove of dwarf trees, where we remained until the sun was low, then continued our walk through a rather barren country. At night we camped again beside a small stream, only a few inches deep, and after a meal of smoked meat and parched maize prepared to sleep till dawn on the next day.

Sitting by the fire I resolved to make a first attempt to discover from Kua-kó anything concerning Rima which might be known to him. Instead of lying down when the others did I remained seated, my guardian also sitting—no doubt waiting for me to lie down first. Presently I moved nearer to him and began a conversation in a low voice, anxious not to rouse the attention of the other men.

'Once you said that Oalava would be given to me for a wife,' I began: 'Some day I shall want a wife.'

He nodded approval, and remarked sententiously that the desire to possess a wife was common to all men.

'What has been left to me?' I said despondingly and spreading out my hands. 'My pistol gone, and did I not give Runi the tinder-box, and the little box with a cock painted on it to you? I had no return—not even the blow-pipe. How, then, can I get me a wife?'

He, like the others—dull-witted savage that he was—had come to the belief that I was incapable of the cunning and duplicity they practised. I could not see a green parrot sitting silent and motionless amidst the green foliage as they could; I had not their preternatural keenness of sight; and, in like manner, to deceive with lies and false seeming was their faculty and not mine. He fell readily into the trap. My return to practical subjects pleased him. He bade me hope that Oalava might yet be mine in spite of my poverty. It was not always necessary to have things to get a wife: to be able to maintain her was enough; some day I would be like one of themselves, able to kill animals and catch fish. Besides, did not Runi wish to keep me with them for other reasons? But he could not keep me wifeless. I could do much: I could sing and make music; I was brave and feared nothing; I could teach the children to fight.

He did not say, however, that I could teach anything to one of his years and attainments.

I protested that he gave me too much praise, that they were just as brave. Did they not show a courage equal to mine by going every day to hunt in that wood which was inhabited by the daughter of the Didi?

I came to this subject with fear and trembling, but he took it quietly. He shook his head, and then all at once began to tell me how they first came to go there to hunt. He said that a few days after I had secretly disappeared, two men and a woman, returning home from a distant place where they had been on a visit to a relation, stopped at the village. These travellers related that two days' journey from Ytaioa they had met three persons travelling in an opposite direction: an old man with a white beard, followed by two yellow dogs, a young man in a big cloak, and a strange-looking girl. Thus it came to be known that I had left the wood with the old man and the daughter of the Didi. It was great news to them, for they did not believe that we had any intention of returning, and at once they began to hunt in the wood, and went there every day, killing birds, monkeys, and other animals in numbers.

His words had begun to excite me greatly, but I studied to appear calm, and only slightly interested, so as to draw him on to say more.

'Then we returned,' I said at last. 'But only two of us, and not together. I left the old man on the road, and *she* left us in Riolama. She went away from us into the mountains—who knows whither!'

'But she came back!' he returned, with a gleam of devilish satisfaction in his eyes that made the blood run cold in my veins.

It was hard to dissemble still, to tempt him to say something that would madden me! 'No, no,' I answered, after considering his words. 'She feared to return; she went away to hide herself in the great mountains beyond Riolama. She could not come back.'

'But she came back!' he persisted, with that triumphant gleam in his eyes once more. Under my cloak my hand had clutched my knife-handle, but I strove hard against the fierce, almost maddening impulse to pluck it out and bury it, quick as lightning, in his accursed throat.

He continued: 'Seven days before you returned we saw her in the wood. We were always expecting, watching, always afraid; and when hunting we were three and four together. On that day I and three others saw her. It was in an open place, where the trees are big and wide apart. We started up and chased her when she ran from us, but feared to shoot. And in one moment she climbed up into a small tree, then, like a monkey, passed from its highest branches into a big tree. We could not see her there, but she was there in the big tree, for there was no other tree near—no way of escape. Three of us sat down to watch, and the other went back to the village. He was long gone; we were just going to leave the tree, fearing that she would do us some injury, when he came back, and with him all the others, men, women, and children. They brought axes and knives. Then Runi said, "Let no one shoot an arrow into the tree thinking to hit her, for the arrow would be caught in her hand and thrown back at him. We must burn her in the tree; there is no way to kill her except by fire." Then we went round and round looking up, but could see nothing; and someone said, She has escaped, flying like a bird from the tree; but Runi answered that fire would show. So we cut down the small tree, and lopped the branches off and heaped them round the big trunk. Then, at a distance, we cut down ten more small trees, and afterwards, further away, ten more, and then others, and piled them all round, tree after tree, until the pile reached as far from the trunk as that,' and here he pointed to a bush forty to fifty yards from where we sat.

The feeling with which I had listened to this recital had become intolerable. The sweat ran from me in streams; I shivered like a person in a fit of ague, and clenched my teeth together to prevent them from rattling. 'I must drink,' I said, cutting him short and rising to my feet. He also rose, but did not follow me, when, with uncertain steps, I made my way to the waterside, which was ten or twelve yards away. Lying prostrate on my chest, I took a long draught of clear cold water, and held my face for a few moments in the current. It sent a chill through me, drying my wet skin, and bracing me for the concluding part of the hideous narrative. Slowly I stepped back to the fireside and sat down again, while he resumed his old place at my side.

'You burnt the tree down,' I said. 'Finish telling me now and let me sleep—my eyes are heavy.'

'Yes. While the men cut and brought trees, the women and children gathered dry stuff in the forest and brought it in their arms and piled it round. Then they set fire to it on all sides, laughing and shouting, "Burn, burn, daughter of the Didi!" At length all the lower branches of the big tree were on fire, and the trunk was on fire, but above it was still green, and we could see nothing. But the flames went up higher and higher with a great noise; and at last from the top of the tree, out of the green leaves, came a great cry, like the cry of a bird, "Abel! Abel!" and then looking we saw something fall; through leaves and smoke and flame it fell like a great white bird killed with an arrow and falling to the earth, and fell into the flames beneath. And it was the daughter of the Didi, and she was burnt to ashes like a moth in the flames of a fire, and no one has ever heard or seen her since.'

It was well for me that he spoke rapidly, and finished quickly. Even before he had quite concluded I drew my cloak round my face and stretched myself out. And I suppose that he at once followed my example, but I had grown blind and deaf to outward things just then. My heart no longer throbbed violently; it fluttered and seemed to grow feebler and feebler in its action: I remember that there was a dull, rushing sound in my ears, that I gasped for breath, that my life seemed ebbing away. After these horrible sensations had passed, I remained quiet for about half an hour; and during this time the picture of that last act in the hateful tragedy grew more and more distinct and vivid in my mind, until I seemed to be actually gazing on it, that my ears were filled with the hissing and crackling of the fire, the exultant shouts of the savages, and above all the last piercing cry of 'Abel! Abel!' from the cloud of burning foliage. I could not endure it longer, and rose at last to my feet. I glanced at Kua-kó lying two or three yards away, and he, like the others, was, or appeared to be, in a deep sleep; he was lying on his back, and his dark firelit face looked as still and unconscious as a face of stone. Now was my chance to escape—if to escape was my wish. Yes; for I now possessed the coveted knowledge, and nothing more was to be gained by keeping with my deadly enemies. And now, most fortunately for me, they had brought me far on the road to that place of the five hills where Managa lived—Managa, whose name had been often in my mind since my return to Parahuari. Glancing away from Kua-kó's still stone-like face, I caught sight of that pale solitary star which Runi had pointed out to me low down in the northwestern sky when I had asked him where his enemy lived. In that direction we had been travelling since leaving the village; surely if I walked all night by to-morrow I could reach Managa's hunting-ground, and be safe and think over what I had heard and on what I had to do.

I moved softly away a few steps, then thinking that it would be well to take a spear in my hand, I turned back, and was surprised and startled to notice that Kua-kó had moved in the interval. He had turned over on his side, and his face was now towards me. His eyes appeared closed, but he might be only feigning sleep, and I dared not go back to pick up the spear. After a moment's hesitation I moved on again, and after a second glance back and seeing that he did not stir, I waded cautiously across the stream, walked softly twenty or thirty yards, and then began to run. At intervals I paused to listen for a moment; and presently I heard a pattering sound as of footsteps coming swiftly after me. I instantly concluded that Kua-kó had been awake all the time watching my movements, and that he was now following me. I now put forth my whole speed, and while thus running could distinguish no sound. That he would miss me, for it was very dark, although with a starry sky above, was my only hope; for with no weapon except my knife my chances would be small indeed should he overtake me. Besides, he had no doubt roused the others before starting, and they would be close behind. There were no bushes in that place to hide myself in and let them pass me; and presently, to make matters worse, the character of the soil changed, and I was running over level clayey ground, so white with a salt efflorescence that a dark object moving on it would show conspicuously at a distance. Here I paused to look back and listen, when distinctly came the sound of footsteps, and the next moment I made out the vague form of an Indian advancing at a rapid rate of speed and with his uplifted spear in his hand. In the brief pause I had made he had advanced almost to within hurling distance of me, and turning, I sped on again, throwing off my cloak to ease my flight. The next time I looked back he was still in sight, but not so near; he had stopped to pick up my cloak, which would be his now, and this had given me a slight advantage. I fled on, and had continued running for a distance perhaps of fifty yards when an object rushed past me, tearing through the flesh of my left arm close to the shoulder on its way; and not knowing that I was not badly wounded nor how near my pursuer might be, I turned in desperation to meet him, and saw him not above twenty-five yards away, running towards me with something bright in his hand. It was Kua-kó, and after wounding me with his spear he was about to finish me with his knife. O fortunate young savage, after such a victory, and with that noble blue cloth cloak for trophy and covering, what fame and happiness will be yours! A change swift as lightning had come over me, a sudden exultation. I was wounded, but my right hand was sound and clutched a knife as good as his, and we were on an equality. I waited for him calmly. All weakness, grief, despair had vanished, all feelings except a terrible raging desire to spill his accursed blood; and my brain was clear and my nerves like steel, and I remembered with something like laughter our old amusing encounters with rapiers of wood. Ah, that was only making believe and childish play; this was reality. Could any white man, deprived of his treacherous, far-killing weapon, meet the resolute savage, face to face and foot to foot and equal him with the old primitive weapons? Poor youth, this delusion will cost you dear! It was scarcely an equal contest when he hurled himself against me, with only his savage strength and courage to match my skill; in a few moments he was lying at my feet, pouring out his life blood on that white thirsty plain. From his prostrate form I turned, the wet, red knife in my hand, to meet the others, still thinking that they were on the track and close at hand. Why had he stooped to pick up the cloak if they were not following—if he had not been afraid of losing it? I turned only to receive their spears, to die with my face to them; nor was the thought of death terrible to me; I could die calmly now after killing my first assailant. But had I indeed killed him? I asked, hearing a sound like a groan escape from his lips. Quickly stooping I once more drove my weapon to the hilt in his prostrate form, and when he exhaled a deep sigh, and his frame quivered, and the blood spurted afresh, I experienced a feeling of savage joy. And still no sound of hurrying footsteps came to my listening ears and no vague forms appeared in the darkness. I concluded that he had either left them sleeping or that they had not followed in the right direction. Taking up the cloak, I was about to walk on, when I noticed the spear he had thrown at me lying where it had fallen some yards away, and picking that up also, I went on once more, still keeping the guiding star before me.

CHAPTER XX

THAT good fight had been to me like a draught of wine, and made me for a while oblivious of my loss and of the pain from my wound. But the glow and feeling of exultation did not last: the lacerated flesh smarted; I was weak from loss of blood, and oppressed with sensations of fatigue. If my foes had appeared on the scene they would have made an easy conquest of me; but they came not, and I continued to walk on, slowly and painfully, pausing often to rest.

At last, recovering somewhat from my faint condition, and losing all fear of being overtaken, my sorrow revived in full force, and thought returned to madden me.

Alas! this bright being, like no other in its divine brightness, so long in the making, now no more than a dead leaf, a little dust, lost and forgotten for ever—O pitiless! O cruel!

But I knew it all before—this law of nature and of necessity, against which all revolt is idle: often had the remembrance of it filled me with ineffable melancholy; only now it seemed cruel beyond all cruelty.

Not nature the instrument, not the keen sword that cuts into the bleeding tissues, but the hand that wields it—the unseen unknown something, or person, that manifests itself in the horrible workings of nature.

'Did you know, beloved, at the last, in that intolerable heat, in that moment of supreme anguish, that *he* is unlistening, unhelpful as the stars, that you cried not to him? To me was your cry: but your poor, frail fellow-creature was not there to save, or, failing that, to cast himself into the flames and perish with you, hating God.'

Thus, in my insufferable pain, I spoke aloud; alone in that solitary place, a bleeding fugitive in the dark night, looking up at the stars I cursed the Author of my being* and called on Him to take back the abhorred gift of life.

Yet, according to my philosophy, how vain it was! All my bitterness and hatred and defiance were as empty, as ineffectual, as utterly futile, as are the supplications of the meek worshipper, and no more than the whisper of a leaf, the light whirr of an insect's wing. Whether I loved Him who was over all, as when I thanked Him on my knees for guiding me to where I had heard so sweet and mysterious a melody, or hated and defied Him as now, it all came from Him—love and hate, good and evil.

But I know—I knew then—that in one thing my philosophy was false, that it was not the whole truth; that though my cries did not touch nor come near Him they would yet hurt me; and, just as a prisoner maddened at his unjust fate beats against the stone walls of his cell until he falls back bruised and bleeding to the floor, so did I wilfully bruise my own soul, and knew that those wounds I gave myself would not heal.

Of that night, the beginning of the blackest period of my life, I shall say no more; and over subsequent events I shall pass quickly.

Morning found me at a distance of many miles from the scene of my duel with the Indian, in a broken, hilly country, varied with savannah and open forest. I was well-nigh spent with my long march, and felt that unless food was obtained before many hours my situation would be indeed desperate. With labour I managed to climb to the summit of a hill about three hundred feet high, in order to survey the surrounding country, and found that it was one of a group of five, and conjectured that these were the five hills of Uritay, and that I was in the neighbourhood of Managa's village. Coming down I proceeded to the next hill, which was higher; and before reaching it came to a stream in a narrow valley dividing the hills, and proceeding along its banks in search of a crossing-place, I came full in sight of the settlement sought for. As I approached people were seen moving hurriedly about; and by the time I arrived, walking slowly and painfully, seven or eight men were standing before the village, some with spears in their hands, the women and children behind them, all staring curiously at me. Drawing near I cried out in a somewhat feeble voice that I was seeking for Managa; whereupon a grey-haired man stepped forth, spear in hand, and replied that he was Managa, and demanded to know why I sought him. I told him a part of my story, enough to show that I had a deadly feud with Runi, that I had escaped from him after killing one of his people.

I was taken in and supplied with food; my wound was examined and dressed; and then I was permitted to lie down and sleep, while Managa, with half a dozen of his people, hurriedly started to visit the scene of my fight with Kua-kó, not only to verify my story, but partly with the hope of meeting Runi. I did not see him again until the next morning, when he informed me that he had found the spot where I had been overtaken, that the dead man had been discovered by the others and carried back towards Parahuari. He had followed the trace for some distance, and he was satisfied that Runi had come thus far in the first place only with the intention of spying on him.

My arrival, and the strange tidings I had brought, had thrown the village into a great commotion; it was evident that from that time Managa lived in constant apprehension of a sudden attack from his old enemy. This gave me great satisfaction; it was my study to keep the feeling alive, and, more than that, to drop continual hints of his enemy's secret murderous purpose, until he was wrought up to a kind of frenzy of mingled fear and rage. And being of a suspicious and somewhat truculent temper, he one day all at once turned on me as the immediate cause of his miserable state, suspecting perhaps that I only wished to make an instrument of him. But I was strangely bold and careless of danger then, and only mocked at his rage, telling him proudly that I feared him not; that Runi, his mortal enemy and mine, feared not him but me; that Runi knew perfectly well where I had taken refuge and would not venture to make his meditated attack while I remained in his village, but would wait for my departure. 'Kill me, Managa,' I cried, smiting my chest as I stood facing him. 'Kill me, and the result will be that he will come upon you unawares and murder you all, as he has resolved to do sooner or later.'

After that speech he glared at me in silence, then flung down the spear he had snatched up in his sudden rage and stalked out of the house and into the wood, but before long he was back again seated in his old place, brooding on my words with a face black as night.

It is painful to recall that secret dark chapter of my life—that period of moral insanity. But I wish not to be a hypocrite, conscious or unconscious, to delude myself or another with this plea of insanity. My mind was very clear just then; past and present were clear to me; the future clearest of all: I could measure the extent of my action and speculate on its future effect, and my sense of right or wrong—of individual responsibility—was more vivid than at any other period of my life. Can I even say that I was blinded by passion? Driven, perhaps, but certainly not blinded. For no reaction, or submission, had followed on that furious revolt against the unknown being, personal or not, that is behind nature, in whose existence I believed. I was still in revolt: I would hate Him, and show my hatred by being like Him, as He appears to us reflected in that mirror of Nature. Had He given me good gifts—the sense of right and wrong and sweet humanity? The beautiful sacred flower He had caused to grow in me I would crush ruthlessly; its beauty and fragrance and grace would be dead for ever; there was nothing evil, nothing cruel and contrary to my nature, that I would not be guilty of, glorying in my guilt. This was not the temper of a few days: I remained for close upon two months at Managa's village, never repenting nor desisting in my efforts to induce the Indians to join me in that most barbarous adventure on which my heart was set.

I succeeded in the end: it would have been strange if I had not. The horrible details need not be given. Managa did not wait for his enemy, but fell on him unexpectedly, an hour after nightfall in his own village. If I had really been insane during those two months, if some cloud had been on me, some demoniacal force dragging me on, the cloud and insanity vanished and the constraint was over in one moment, when that hellish enterprise was completed. It was the sight of an old woman, lying where she had been struck down, the fire of the blazing house lighting her wide-open glassy eyes and white hair dabbled in blood, which suddenly, as by a miracle, wrought this change in my brain. For they were all dead at last, old and young, all who had lighted the fire round that great green tree in which Rima had taken refuge, who had danced round the blaze, shouting, 'Burn! burn!'

At the moment my glance fell on that prostrate form, I paused and stood still, trembling like a person struck with a sudden pang in the heart, who thinks that his last moment has come to him unawares. After a while I slunk away out of the great circle of firelight into the thick darkness beyond. Instinctively I turned towards the forests across the savannah—my forest again; and fled away from the noise and the sight of flames, never pausing until I found myself within the black shadow of the trees. Into the deeper blackness of the interior I dared not venture: on the border I paused to ask myself what I did there alone in the night time. Sitting down I covered my face with my hands as if to hide it more effectually than it could be hidden by night and the forest shadows. What horrible thing—what calamity that frightened my soul to think of, had fallen on me? The revulsion of feeling, the unspeakable horror, the remorse, was more than I could bear. I started up with a cry of anguish, and would have slain myself to escape at that moment; but Nature is not always and utterly cruel, and on this occasion she came to my aid. Consciousness forsook me, and I lived not again until the light of early morning was in the east; then found myself lying on the wet herbage—wet with rain that had lately fallen. My physical misery was now so great that it prevented me from dwelling on the scenes witnessed on the previous evening. Nature was again merciful in this. I only remembered that it was necessary to hide myself, in case the Indians should be still in the neighbourhood and pay the wood a visit. Slowly and painfully I crept away into the forest, and there sat for several hours, scarcely thinking at all, in a half-stupefied condition. At noon the sun shone out and dried the wood. I felt no hunger, only a vague sense of bodily misery, and with it the fear that if I left my hiding-place I might meet some human creature face to face. This fear prevented me from stirring until the twilight came, when I crept forth and made my way to the border of the forest, to spend the night there. Whether sleep visited me during the dark hours or not I cannot say: day and night my condition seemed the same; I experienced only a dull sensation of utter misery which seemed in spirit and flesh alike, an inability to think clearly, or for more than a few moments consecutively, about anything. Scenes in which I had been principal actor came and went, as in a dream when the will slumbers: now with devilish ingenuity and persistence I was working on Managa's mind; now standing motionless in the forest listening for that sweet, mysterious melody; now staring aghast at old Cla-cla's wide-open glassy eyes and white hair dabbled in blood; then suddenly, in the cave at Riolama, I was fondly watching the slow return to life and colour to Rima's still face.

When morning came again I felt so weak that a vague fear of sinking down and dying of hunger at last roused me and sent me forth in quest of food. I moved slowly and my eyes were dim to see, but I knew so well where to seek for small morsels—small edible roots and leafstalks, berries, and drops of congealed gum—that it would have been strange in that rich forest if I had not been able to discover something to stay my famine. It was little, but it sufficed for the day. Once more Nature was merciful to me; for that diligent seeking among the concealing leaves left no interval for thought; every chance morsel gave a momentary pleasure, and as I prolonged my search my steps grew firmer, the dimness passed from my eyes. I was more forgetful of self, more eager, and like a wild animal with no thought or feeling beyond its immediate wants. Fatigued at the end, I fell asleep as soon as darkness brought my busy rambles to a close, and did not wake until another morning dawned.

My hunger was extreme now. The wailing notes of a pair of small birds, persistently flitting round me, or perched with gaping bills and wings trembling with agitation, served to remind me that it was now breeding-time; also that Rima had taught me to find a small bird's-nest. She found them only to delight her eyes with the sight; but they would be food for me; the crystal and yellow fluid in the gem-like, white or blue or red-speckled shells would help to keep me alive. All day I hunted, listening to every note and cry, watching the motions of every winged thing, and found, besides gums and fruits, over a score of nests containing eggs, mostly of small birds, and although the labour was great and the scratches many, I was well satisfied with the result.

A few days later I found a supply of Haima gum, and eagerly began picking it from the tree; not that it could be used, but the thought of the brilliant light it gave was so strong in my mind that mechanically I gathered it all. The possession of this gum, when night closed round me again, produced in me an intense longing for artificial light and warmth. The darkness was harder than ever to endure. I envied the fireflies their natural lights, and ran about in the dusk to capture a few and hold them in the hollow of my two hands, for the sake of their cold, fitful flashes. On the following day I wasted two or three hours trying to get fire in the primitive method with dry wood, but failed, and lost much time, and suffered more than ever from hunger in consequence. Yet there was fire in everything; even when I struck at hard wood with my knife sparks were emitted. If I could only arrest those wonderful heat and light-giving sparks! And all at once, as if I had just lighted upon some new, wonderful truth, it occurred to me that with my steel hunting-knife and a piece of flint fire could be obtained. Immediately I set about preparing tinder with dry moss, rotten wood, and wild cotton; and in a short time I had the wished fire, and heaped wood dry and green on it to make it large. I nursed it well, and spent the night beside it; and it also served to roast some huge white grubs which I had found in the rotten wood of a prostrate trunk. The sight of these great grubs had formerly disgusted me; but they tasted good to me now, and stayed my hunger, and that was all I looked for in my wild forest food.

For a long time an undefined feeling prevented me from going near the site of Nuflo's burnt lodge. I went there at last; and the first thing I did was to go all round the fatal spot, cautiously peering into the rank herbage, as if I feared a lurking serpent; and at length, at some distance from the blackened heap, I discovered a human skeleton, and knew it to be Nuflo's. In his day he had been a great armadillo hunter, and these quaint carrion eaters had no doubt revenged themselves by devouring his flesh when they found him dead—killed by the savages.

Having once returned to this spot of many memories, I could not quit it again; while my wild woodland life lasted here must I have my lair, and being here I could not leave that mournful skeleton above ground. With labour I excavated a pit to bury it, careful not to cut or injure a broad-leafed creeper that had begun to spread itself over the spot; and after refilling the hole I drew the long, trailing stems over the mound.

'Sleep well, old man,' said I, when my work was done; and these few words, implying neither censure nor praise, was all the burial service that old Nuflo had from me.

I then visited the spot where the old man, assisted by me, had concealed his provisions before starting for Riolama, and was pleased to find that it had not been discovered by the Indians. Besides the store of tobacco-leaf, maize, pumpkin, potatoes, and cassava-bread, and the cooking utensils, I found among other things a chopper—a great acquisition, since with it I would be able to cut down small palms and bamboos to make myself a hut.

The possession of a supply of food left me time for many things: time in the first place to make my own conditions; doubtless after them there would be further progression on the old lines—luxuries added to necessaries; a healthful, fruitful life of thought and action combined; and at last a peaceful, contemplative old age.

I cleared away ashes and rubbish, and marked out the very spot where Rima's separate bower had been for my habitation, which I intended to make small. In five days it was finished; then after lighting a fire, I stretched myself out in my dry bed of moss and leaves with a feeling that was almost triumphant. Let the rain now fall in torrents, putting out the firefly's lamp; let the wind and thunder roar their loudest, and the lightnings smite the earth with intolerable light, frightening the poor monkeys in their wet, leafy habitations, little would I heed it all on my dry bed, under my dry, palm-leaf thatch, with glorious fire to keep me company and protect me from my ancient enemy, Darkness.

From that first sleep under shelter I woke refreshed, and was not driven by the cruel spur of hunger into the wet forest. The wished time had come of rest from labour, of leisure for thought. Resting here, just where she had rested, night by night clasping a visionary mother in her arms, whispering tenderest words in a visionary ear, I too now clasped her in my arms—a visionary Rima. How different the nights had seemed when I was without shelter, before I had rediscovered fire! How had I endured it? That strange ghostly gloom of the woods at night-time full of innumerable strange shapes; still and dark, yet with something seen at times moving amidst them, dark and vague and strange also—an owl, perhaps, or bat, or great winged moth, or nightjar. Nor had I any choice then but to listen to the night-sounds of the forest; and they were various as the day-sounds, and for every day-sound, from the faintest lisping and softest trill to the deep boomings and piercing cries, there was an analogue; always with something mysterious, unreal in its tone, something proper to the night. They were ghostly sounds, uttered by the ghosts of dead animals; they were a hundred different things by turns, but always with a meaning in them, which I vainly strove to catch—something to be interpreted only by a sleeping faculty in us, lightly sleeping, and now, now on the very point of awaking!

Now the gloom and the mystery was shut out; now I had that which stood in the place of pleasure to me, and was more than pleasure. It was a mournful rapture to lie awake now, wishing not for sleep and oblivion, hating the thought of daylight that would come at last to drown and scare away my vision. To be with Rima again—my lost Rima recovered—mine, mine at last! No longer the old vexing doubt now—'You are you and I am I—why is it?'—the question asked when our souls were near together, like two raindrops side by side, drawing irresistibly nearer, ever nearer: for now they had touched and were not two, but one inseparable drop, crystallised beyond change, not to be disintegrated by time, nor shattered by death's blow, nor resolved by any alchemy.

I had other company besides this unfailing vision, and the bright dancing fire that talked to me in its fantastic fire language. It was my custom to secure the door well on retiring: grief had perhaps chilled my blood, for I suffered less from heat than from cold at this period, and the fire seemed grateful all night long; I was also anxious to exclude all small winged and creeping night-wanderers. But to exclude them entirely proved impossible: through a dozen invisible chinks they would find their way to me; also some entered by day to lie concealed until after nightfall. A monstrous hairy hermit spider found an asylum in a dusky corner of the hut, under the thatch, and day after day he was there, all day long, sitting close and motionless; but at dark he invariably disappeared—who knows on what murderous errand! His hue was a deep dead-leaf yellow, with a black and grey pattern, borrowed from some wild cat; and so large was he that his great outspread hairy legs, radiating from the flat disc of his body, would have covered a man's open hand. It was easy to see him in my small interior; often in the night-time my eyes would stray to his corner, never to encounter that strange hairy figure; but daylight failed not to bring him. He troubled me; but now, for Rima's sake, I could slay no living thing except from motives of hunger. I had it in my mind to injure him—to strike off one of his legs, which would not be missed much, as they were many—so as to make him go away and return no more to so inhospitable a place. But courage failed me. He might come stealthily back at night to plunge his long, crooked falces into my throat, poisoning my blood with fever and delirium and black death.* So I left him alone, and glanced furtively and fearfully at him, hoping that he had not divined any thoughts; thus we lived on unsocially together. More companionable, but still in an uncomfortable way, were the large crawling, running insects—crickets, beetles, and others. They were shapely and black and polished, and ran about here and there on the floor, just like intelligent little horseless carriages; then they would pause with their immovable eyes fixed on me, seeing, or in some mysterious way divining my presence; their pliant horns waving up and down, like delicate instruments used to test the air. Centipedes and millipedes in dozens came too, and were not welcome. I feared not their venom, but it was a weariness to see them; for they seemed no living things, but the vertebræ of snakes and eels and long slim fishes, dead and desiccated, made to move mechanically over walls and floor by means of some jugglery of nature. I grew skilful at picking them up with a pair of pliant green twigs, to thrust them into the outer darkness.

One night a moth fluttered in and alighted on my hand as I sat by the fire, causing me to hold my breath as I gazed on it. Its fore wings were pale grey, with shadings dark and light written all over in finest characters with some twilight mystery or legend; but the round underwings were clear amber-yellow, veined like a leaf with red and purple veins; a thing of such exquisite chaste beauty that the sight of it gave me a sudden shock of pleasure. Very soon it flew up circling about, and finally lighted on the palm-leaf thatch directly over the fire. The heat, I thought, would soon drive it from the spot; and, rising, I opened the door, so that it might find its way out again into its own cool, dark, flowery world. And standing by the open door I turned and addressed it: 'O night-wanderer of the pale, beautiful wings, go forth, and should you by chance meet her somewhere in the shadowy depths, revisiting her old haunts, be my messenger——' Thus much had I spoken, when the frail thing loosened its hold to fall without a flutter, straight and swift, into the white blaze beneath. I sprang forward with a shriek, and stood staring into the fire, my whole frame trembling with a sudden, terrible emotion. Even thus had Rima fallen—fallen from the great height—into the flames that instantly consumed her beautiful flesh and bright spirit! O cruel Nature!

A moth that perished in the flame; an indistinct faint sound; a dream in the night; the semblance of a shadowy form moving mist-like in the twilight gloom of the forest, would suddenly bring back a vivid memory, the old anguish, to break for a while the calm of that period. It was calm then after the storm. Nevertheless, my health deteriorated. I ate little and slept little and grew thin and weak. When I looked down on the dark, glassy forest pool, where Rima would look no more to see herself so much better than in the small mirror of her lover's pupil, it showed me a gaunt, ragged man with a tangled mass of black hair falling over his shoulders, the bones of his face showing through the dead-looking, sun-parched skin, the sunken eyes with a gleam in them that was like insanity.

To see this reflection had a strangely disturbing effect on me. A torturing voice would whisper in my ear: 'Yes, you are evidently going mad. By-and-by you will rush howling through the forest, only to drop down at last and die: and no person will ever find and bury *your* bones. Old Nuflo was more fortunate in that he perished first.'

'A lying voice!' I retorted in sudden anger. 'My faculties were never keener than now. Not a fruit can ripen but I find it. If a small bird darts by with a feather or straw in its bill I mark its flight, and it will be a lucky bird if I do not find its nest in the end. Could a savage born in the forest do more? He would starve where I find food!'

'Ay, yes, there is nothing wonderful in that,' answered the voice. 'The stranger from a cold country suffers less from the heat, when days are hottest, than the Indian who knows no other climate. But mark the result! The stranger dies, while the Indian, sweating and gasping for breath, survives. In like manner the low-minded savage, cut off from all human fellowship, keeps his faculties to the end, while your finer brain proves your ruin.'

I cut from a tree a score of long, blunt thorns, tough and black as whalebone, and drove them through a strip of wood in which I had burnt a row of holes to receive them, and made myself a comb, and combed out my long, tangled hair to improve my appearance.

'It is not the tangled condition of your hair,' persisted the voice, 'but your eyes, so wild and strange in their expression, that show the approach of madness. Make your socks as smooth as you like, and add a garland of those scarlet, star-shaped blossoms hanging from the bush behind you—crown yourself as you crowned old Cla-cla—but the crazed look will remain just the same.'

And being no longer able to reply, rage and desperation drove me to an act which only seemed to prove that the hateful voice had prophesied truly. Taking up a stone I hurled it down on the water to shatter the image I saw there, as if it had been no faithful reflection of myself, but a travesty, cunningly made of enamelled clay or some other material, and put there by some malicious enemy to mock me.

CHAPTER XXI

MANY days had passed since the hut was made—how many may not be known, since I notched no stick and knotted no cord—yet never in my rambles in the wood had I seen that desolate ash-heap where the fire had done its work. Nor had I looked for it. On the contrary, my wish was never to see it, and the fear of coming accidentally upon it made me keep to the old familiar paths. But at length, one night, without thinking of Rima's fearful end, it all at once occurred to me that the hated savage, whose blood I had shed on the white savannah, might have only been practising his natural deceit when he told me that most pitiful story. If that were so—if he had been prepared with a fictitious account of her death to meet my questions—then Rima might still exist: lost, perhaps, wandering in some distant place, exposed to perils day and night, and unable to find her way back, but living still! Living! her heart on fire with the hope of re-union with me, cautiously threading her way through the under-growth of immeasurable forests; spying out the distant villages and hiding herself from the sight of all men, as she knew so well how to hide; studying the outlines of distant mountains, to recognise some familiar landmark at last, and so find her way back to the old wood once more! Even now, while I sat there idly musing, she might be somewhere in the wood—somewhere near me; but after so long an absence full of apprehension, waiting in concealment for what to-morrow's light might show.

I started up and replenished the fire with trembling hands, then set the door open to let the welcoming stream out into the wood. But Rima had done more; going out into the black forest in the pitiless storm, she had found and led me home. Could I do less! I was quickly out in the shadows of the wood. Surely it was more than a mere hope that made my heart beat so wildly! How could a sensation so strangely sudden, so irresistible in its power, possess me unless she were living and near? Can it be, can it be that we shall meet again? To look again into your divine eyes—to hold you again in my arms at last! I so changed—so different! But the old love remains; and of all that has happened in your absence I shall tell you nothing—not one word; all shall be forgotten now—sufferings, madness, crime, remorse! Nothing shall ever vex you again—not Nuflo, who vexed you every day; for he is dead now—murdered, only I shall not say that—and I have decently buried his poor old sinful bones. We alone together in the wood—*our* wood now! The sweet old days again; for I know that you would not have it different, nor would I.

Thus I talked to myself, mad with the thoughts of the joy that would soon be mine; and at intervals I stood still and made the forest echo with my calls. 'Rima! Rima!' I called again and again, and waited for some response; and heard only the familiar night-sounds—voices of insect and bird and tinkling tree-frog, and a low murmur in the topmost foliage, moved by some light breath of wind unfelt below. I was drenched with dew, bruised and bleeding from falls in the dark, and from rocks and thorns and rough branches, but had felt nothing; gradually the excitement burnt itself out; I was hoarse with shouting and ready to drop down with fatigue, and hope was dead: and at length I crept back to my hut, to cast myself on my grass bed and sink into a dull, miserable, desponding stupor.

But on the following morning I was out once more, determined to search the forest well; since, if no evidence of the great fire Kua-kó had described to me existed, it would still be possible to believe that he had lied to me, and that Rima lived. I searched all day and found nothing; but the area was large, and to search it thoroughly would require several days.

On the third day I discovered the fatal spot, and knew that never again would I behold Rima in the flesh, that my last hope had indeed been a vain one. There could be no mistake: just such an open place as the Indian had pictured to me was here, with giant trees standing apart; while one tree stood killed and blackened by fire, surrounded by a huge heap, sixty or seventy yards across, of prostrate charred tree-trunks and ashes. Here and there slender plants had sprung up through the ashes, and the omnipresent small-leaved creepers were beginning to throw their pale green embroidery over the blackened trunks. I looked long at the vast funeral tree that had a buttressed girth of not less than fifty feet, and rose straight as a ship's mast, with its top about a hundred and fifty feet from the earth. What a distance to fall, through burning leaves and smoke, like a white bird shot dead with a poisoned arrow, swift and straight into that sea of flame below! How cruel imagination was to turn that desolate ash-heap, in spite of feathery foliage and embroidery of creepers, into roaring leaping flames again—to bring those dead savages back, men, women, and children—even the little ones I had played with—to set them yelling around me, 'Burn! burn!' Oh, no this damnable spot must not be her last resting-place! If the fire had not utterly consumed her, bones as well as sweet tender flesh, shrivelling her like a frail white-winged moth into the finest white ashes, mixed inseparably with the ashes of stems and leaves innumerable, then whatever remained of her must be conveyed elsewhere to be with me, to mingle with my ashes at last.

Having resolved to sift and examine the entire heap, I at once set about my task. If she had climbed into the central highest branch, and had fallen straight, then she would have dropped into the flames not far from the roots; and so to begin I made a path to the trunk, and when darkness overtook me I had worked all round the tree, in a width of three to four yards, without discovering any remains. At noon on the following day I found the skeleton, or, at all events, the larger bones, rendered so fragile by the fierce heat they had been subjected to, that they fell to pieces when handled. But I was careful—how careful!—to save these last sacred relics, all that was now left of Rima!—kissing each white fragment as I lifted it, and gathering them all in my old frayed cloak, spread out to receive them. And when I had recovered them all, even to the smallest, I took my treasure home.

Another storm had shaken my soul, and had been succeeded by a second calm, which was more complete and promised to be more enduring than the first. But it was no lethargic calm; my brain was more active than ever; and by-and-by it found a work for my hands to do, of such a character as to distinguish me from all other forest hermits, fugitives from their fellows, in that savage land. The calcined bones I had rescued were kept in one of the big, rudely shaped, half-burnt earthen jars, which Nuflo had used for storing grain and other food-stuff. It was of a wood-ash colour; and after I had given up my search for the peculiar fine clay he had used in its manufacture—for it had been in my mind to make a more shapely funeral urn myself—I set to work to ornament its surface. A portion of each day was given to this artistic labour; and when the surface was covered with a pattern of thorny stems, and a trailing creeper with curving leaf and twining tendril, and pendent bud and blossom, I gave it colour. Purples and black only were used, obtained from the juices of some deeply coloured berries; and when a tint, or shade, or line failed to satisfy me I erased it, to do it again; and this so often that I never completed my work. I might, in the proudly modest spirit of the old sculptors, have inscribed on the vase the words, *Abel was doing this*. For was not my ideal beautiful like theirs, and the best that my art could do only an imperfect copy—a rude sketch? A serpent was represented wound round the lower portion of the jar, dull-hued, with a chain of irregular black spots or blotches extending along its body: and if any person had curiously examined these spots he would have discovered that every other one was a rudely shaped letter, and that the letters, by being properly divided, made the following words:—

Sin vos y sin dios y mi.*

Words that to some might seem wild, even insane in their extravagance, sung by some ancient forgotten poet; or possibly the motto of some love-sick knight-errant, whose passion was consumed to ashes long centuries ago. But not wild nor insane to me, dwelling alone on a vast stony plain in everlasting twilight, where there was no motion, nor any sound; but all things, even trees, ferns, and grasses, were stone.* And in that place I had sat for many a thousand years, drawn up and motionless, with stony fingers clasped round my legs, and forehead resting on my knees; and there would I sit, unmoving, immovable, for many a thousand years to come—I, no longer I, in a universe where *she* was not, and God was not.

The days went by, and to others grouped themselves into weeks and months; to me they were only days—not Saturday, Sunday, Monday, but nameless. They were so many and their sum so great, that all my previous life, all the years I had existed before this solitary time, now looked like a small island immeasurably far away, scarcely discernible, in the midst of that endless desolate waste of nameless days.

My stock of provisions had been so long consumed that I had forgotten the flavour of pulse and maize and pumpkins and purple and sweet potatoes. For Nuflo's cultivated patch had been destroyed by the savages—not a stem, not a root had they left: and I, like the sorrowful man that broods on his sorrow and the artist who thinks only of his art, had been improvident, and had consumed the seed without putting a portion into the ground. Only wild food, and too little of that, found with much seeking and got with many hurts. Birds screamed at and scolded me; branches bruised and thorns scratched me; and still worse were the angry clouds of waspish things no bigger than flies. Buzz—buzz! Sting—sting! A serpent's tooth has failed to kill me; little do I care for your small drops of fiery venom so that I get at the spoil—grubs and honey. My white bread and purple wine! Once my soul hungered after knowledge; I took delight in fine thoughts finely expressed; I sought them carefully in printed books: now only this vile bodily hunger, this eager seeking for grubs and honey, and ignoble war with little things!

A bad hunter I proved after larger game. Bird and beast despised my snares, which took me so many waking hours at night to invent, so many daylight hours to make. Once, seeing a troop of monkeys high up in the tall trees, I followed and watched them for a long time, thinking how royally I should feast if by some strange un-heard-of accident one were to fall disabled to the ground and be at my mercy. But nothing impossible happened, and I had no meat. What meat did I ever have except an occasional fledgling, killed in its cradle, or a lizard, or small tree-frog detected, in spite of its green colour, among the foliage? I would roast the little green minstrel on the coals. Why not? Why should he live to tinkle on his mandolin and clash his airy cymbals with no appreciative ear to listen? Once I had a different and strange kind of meat; but the starved stomach is not squeamish. I found a serpent coiled up in my way in a small glade, and arming myself with a long stick, I roused him from his siesta, and slew him without mercy. Rima was not there to pluck the rage from my heart and save his evil life. No coral snake this, with slim, tapering body, ringed like a wasp with brilliant colour; but thick and blunt, with lurid scales, blotched with black; also a broad, flat, murderous head, with stony, ice-like, whity-blue eyes, cold enough to freeze a victim's blood in its veins and make it sit still, like some wide-eyed creature carved in stone, waiting for the sharp, inevitable stroke—so swift, at last, so long in coming. 'O abominable flat head, with icy-cold, human-like, fiend-like eyes, I shall cut you off and throw you away!' And away I flung it, far enough in all conscience; yet I walked home troubled with a fancy that somewhere, somewhere down on the black, wet soil where it had fallen, through all that dense, thorny tangle and millions of screening leaves, the white, lid-less, living eyes were following me still,* and would always be follow-ing me in all my goings and comings and windings about in the forest. And what wonder? For were we not alone together in this dreadful solitude, I and the serpent, eaters of the dust, singled out and cursed above all cattle?* *He* would not have bitten me, and I— faithless cannibal!—had murdered him. That cursed fancy would live on, worming itself into every crevice of my mind; the severed head would grow and grow in the night-time to something monstrous at last, the hellish white lidless eyes increasing to the size of two full moons. 'Murderer! murderer!' they would say; 'first a murderer of your own fellow-creatures—that was a small crime; but God, our enemy, had made them in His image, and he cursed you; and we two were together, alone and apart—you and I, murderer! you and I, murderer!'

I tried to escape the tyrannous fancy of thinking of other things and by making light of it. 'The starved, bloodless brain,' I said, 'has strange thoughts.' I fell to studying the dark, thick, blunt body in my hands; I noticed that the livid, rudely blotched, scaly surface showed in some lights a lovely play of prismatic colours. And growing poetical, I said, 'When the wild west wind broke up the rainbow on the flying grey cloud and scattered it over the earth, a fragment doubtless fell on this reptile to give it that tender celestial tint. For thus it is Nature loves all her children, and gives to each some beauty, little or much; only to me, her hated stepchild, she gives no beauty, no grace. But stay, am I not wronging her? Did not Rima, beautiful above all things, love me well? said she not that I was beautiful?'

'Ah, yes, that was long ago,' spoke the voice that mocked me by the pool when I combed out my tangled hair. 'Long ago, when the soul that looked from your eyes was not the accursed thing it is now. *Now* Rima would start at the sight of them; now she would fly in terror from their insane expression.'

'O spiteful voice, must you spoil even such appetite as I have for this fork-tongued spotty food? You by day and Rima by night—what shall I do—what shall I do?'

For it had now come to this, that the end of each day brought not sleep and dreams, but waking visions. Night by night, from my dry grass bed I beheld Nuflo sitting in his old doubled-up posture, his big brown feet close to the white ashes—sitting silent and miserable. I pitied him; I owed him hospitality; but it seemed intolerable that he should be there. It was better to shut my eyes; for then Rima's arms would be round my neck; the silky mist of her hair

against my face, her flowery breath mixing with my breath. What a luminous face was hers! Even with close-shut eyes I could see it vividly,
the translucent skin showing the radiant rose beneath, the lustrous
eyes, spiritual and passionate, dark as purple wine under their dark
lashes. Then my eyes would open wide. No Rima in my arms! But
over there, a little way back from the fire, just beyond where old Nuflo
had sat brooding a few minutes ago, Rima would be standing, still
and pale and unspeakably sad. Why does she come to me from the
outside darkness to stand there talking to me, yet never once lifting
her mournful eyes to mine? 'Do not believe it, Abel; no, that was only
a phantom of your brain, the What-I-was that you remember so well.
For do you not see that when I come she fades away and is nothing?
Not that—do not ask it. I know that I once refused to look into your
eyes, and afterwards, in the cave at Riolama, I looked long and was
happy—unspeakably happy! But now—oh, you do not know what
you ask; you do not know the sorrow that has come into mine; that
if you once beheld it for very sorrow you would die. And you must
live. But I will wait patiently, and we shall be together in the end, and
see each other without disguise. Nothing shall divide us. Only wish
not for it soon; think not that death will ease your pain, and seek it
not. Austerities? Good works? Prayers? They are not seen; they are
not heard, they are less than nothing, and there is no intercession. I
did not know it then, but you knew it. Your life was your own; you
are not saved nor judged! acquit yourself—undo that which you have
done, which Heaven cannot undo—and Heaven will say no word nor
will I. You cannot, Abel, you cannot. That which you have done is
done, and yours must be the penalty and the sorrow—yours and
mine—yours and mine—yours and mine.'

This, too, was a phantom, a Rima of the mind, one of the shapes
the ever-changing black vapours of remorse and insanity would
take; and all her mournful sentences were woven out of my own
brain. I was not so crazed as not to know it; only a phantom, an illusion, yet more real than reality—real as my crime and vain remorse
and death to come. It was, indeed, Rima returned to tell me that I
that loved her had been more cruel to her than her cruellest enemies; for they had but tortured and destroyed her body with fire, while
I had cast this shadow on her soul—this sorrow transcending all
sorrows, darker than death, immitigable, eternal.

If I could only have faded gradually, painlessly, growing feebler in body and dimmer in my senses each day, to sink at last into sleep! But it could not be. Still the fever in my brain, the mocking voice by day, the phantoms by night; and at last I became convinced that unless I quitted the forest before long, death would come to me in some terrible shape. But in the feeble condition I was now in, and without any provisions, to escape from the neighbourhood of Parahuari was impossible, seeing that it was necessary at starting to avoid the villages where the Indians were of the same tribe as Runi, who would recognise me as the white man who was once his guest and afterwards his implacable enemy. I must wait, and in spite of a weakened body and a mind diseased, struggle still to wrest a scanty subsistence from wild nature.

One day I discovered an old prostrate tree, buried under a thick growth of creeper and fern, the wood of which was nearly or quite rotten, as I proved by thrusting my knife to the haft in it. No doubt it would contain grubs—those huge, white wood-borers which now formed an important item in my diet. On the following day I returned to the spot with a chopper and a bundle of wedges to split the trunk up, but had scarcely commenced operations when an animal, startled at my blows, rushed or rather wriggled from its hiding-place under the dead wood at a distance of a few yards from me. It was a robust, round-headed, short-legged creature, about as big as a good-sized cat, and clothed in a thick, greenish-brown fur. The ground all about was covered with creepers, binding the ferns, bushes, and old dead branches together; and in this confused tangle the animal scrambled and tore with a great show of energy, but really made very little progress; and all at once it flashed into my mind that it was a sloth—a common animal, but rarely seen on the ground*—with no tree near to take refuge in. The shock of joy this discovery produced was great enough to unnerve me, and for some moments I stood trembling, hardly able to breathe; then recovering I hastened after it, and stunned it with a blow from my chopper on its round head.

'Poor sloth!' I said as I stood over it. 'Poor old lazy-bones! Did Rima ever find you fast asleep in a tree, hugging a branch as if you loved it, and with her little hand pat your round, human-like head; and laugh mockingly at the astonishment in your drowsy, waking eyes; and scold you tenderly for wearing your nails so long, and for being so ugly? Lazy-bones, your death is revenged! O to be out of this wood—away from this sacred place—to be anywhere where killing is not murder!'

Then it came into my mind that I was now in possession of the supply of food which would enable me to quit the wood. A noble capture! As much to me as if a stray, migratory mule had rambled into the wood and found me, and I him. Now I would be my own mule, patient, and long-suffering, and far-going, with naked feet hardened to hoofs, and a pack of provender on my back to make me independent of the dry, bitter grass on the sunburnt savannahs.

Part of that night and the next morning was spent in curing the flesh over a smoky fire of green wood and in manufacturing a rough sack to store it in, for I had resolved to set out on my journey. How safely to convey Rima's treasured ashes was a subject of much thought and anxiety. The clay vessel on which I had expended so much loving, sorrowful labour had to be left, being too large and heavy to carry; eventually I put the fragments into a light sack; and in order to avert suspicion from the people I would meet on the way, above the ashes I packed a layer of roots and bulbs. These I would say contained medicinal properties, known to the white doctors, to whom I would sell them on my arrival at a Christian settlement, and with the money buy myself clothes to start life afresh.

On the morrow I would bid a last farewell to that forest of many memories. And my journey would be eastwards, over a wild savage land of mountains, rivers, and forests, where every dozen miles would be like a hundred of Europe; but a land inhabited by tribes not unfriendly to the stranger. And perhaps it would be my good fortune to meet with Indians travelling east who would know the easiest routes; and from time to time some compassionate voyager would let me share his wood-skin, and many leagues would be got over without weariness, until some great river, flowing through British or Dutch Guiana, would be reached; and so on, and on, by slow or swift stages, with little to eat perhaps, with much labour and pain, in hot sun and in storm, to the Atlantic at last, and towns inhabited by Christian men.

In the evening of that day, after completing my preparations, I supped on the remaining portions of the sloth, not suitable for preservation, roasting bits of fat on the coals and boiling the head and bones into a broth; and after swallowing the liquid I crunched the bones and sucked the marrow, feeding like some hungry carnivorous animal.

Glancing at the fragments scattered on the floor, I remembered old Nuflo, and how I had surprised him at his feast of rank coatimundi in his secret retreat. 'Nuflo, old neighbour,' said I, 'how quiet you are under your green coverlet, spangled just now with yellow flowers! It is no sham sleep, old man, I know. If any suspicion of these curious doings, this feast of flesh on a spot once sacred, could flit like a small moth into your mouldy hollow skull, you would soon thrust out your old nose to sniff the savour of roasting fat once more.'

There was in me at that moment an inclination to laughter: it came to nothing, but affected me strangely, like an impulse I had not experienced since boyhood—familiar, yet novel. After the good-night to my neighbour, I tumbled into my straw and slept soundly, animal-like. No fancies and phantoms that night: the lidless, white, implacable eyes of the serpent's severed head were turned to dust at last: no sudden dream-glare lighted up old Cla-cla's wrinkled dead face and white, blood-dabbled locks: old Nuflo stayed beneath his green coverlet; nor did my mournful spirit-bride come to me to make my heart faint at the thought of immortality.

But when morning dawned again it was bitter to rise up and go away for ever from that spot where I had often talked with Rima—the true and the visionary. The sky was cloudless and the forest wet as if rain had fallen; it was only a heavy dew, and it made the foliage look pale and hoary in the early night. And the light grew, and a whis-pering wind sprung as I walked through the wood; and the fast-evaporating moisture was like a bloom on the feathery fronds and grass and rank herbage; but on the higher foliage it was like a faint iridescent mist—a glory above the trees. The everlasting beauty and freshness of nature was over all again, as I had so often seen it with joy and adoration before grief and dreadful passions had dimmed my vision. And now as I walked, murmuring my last farewell, my eyes grew dim again with the tears that gathered to them.

CHAPTER XXII

BEFORE that well-nigh hopeless journey to the coast was half over I became ill—so ill that anyone who had looked on me might well have imagined that I had come to the end of my pilgrimage. That was what I feared. For days I remained sunk in the deepest despondence; then, in a happy moment, I remembered how, after being bitten by the serpent, when death had seemed near and inevitable, I had madly rushed away through the forest in search of help, and wandered lost for hours in the storm and darkness, and in the end escaped death, probably by means of these frantic exertions. The recollection served to inspire me with a new desperate courage. Bidding good-bye to the Indian village where the fever had smitten me, I set out once more on that apparently hopeless adventure. Hopeless, indeed, it seemed to one in my weak condition. My legs trembled under me when I walked, while hot sun and pelting rain were like flame and stinging ice to my morbidly sensitive skin.

For many days my sufferings were excessive, so that I often wished myself back in that milder purgatory of the forest, from which I had been so anxious to escape. When I try to retrace my route on the map there occurs a break here—a space on the chart where names of rivers and mountains call up no image to my mind, although, in a few cases, they were names I seem to have heard in a troubled dream. The impressions of nature received during that sick period are blurred, or else so coloured and exaggerated by perpetual torturing anxiety, mixed with half-delirious night-fancies, that I can only think of that country as an earthly inferno, where I fought against every imaginable obstacle, alternately sweating and freezing, toiling as no man ever toiled before. Hot and cold, cold and hot, and no medium. Crystal waters; green shadows under coverture of broad, moist leaves; and night with dewy fanning winds—these chilled but did not refresh me; a region in which there was no sweet and pleasant thing; where even the Ita palm and mountain glory and airy epiphyte starring the woodland twilight with pendent blossoms had lost all grace and beauty; where all brilliant colours in earth and heaven were like the unmitigated sun that blinded my sight and burnt my brain. Doubtless I met with help from the natives, otherwise I do not see how I could have continued my journey: yet, in my dim mental picture of that period I see myself incessantly dogged by hostile savages. They flit like ghosts through the dark forest; they surround me and cut off all retreat, until I burst through them, escaping out of their very hands, to fly over some wide, naked savannah, hearing their shrill, pursuing yells behind me, and feeling the sting of their poisoned arrows in my flesh.

This I set down to the workings of remorse in a disordered mind and to clouds of venomous insects perpetually shrilling in my ears and stabbing me with their small, fiery needles.

Not only was I pursued by phantom savages and pierced by phantom arrows, but the creations of the Indian imagination had now become as real to me as anything in nature. I was persecuted by that superhuman man-eating monster supposed to be the guardian of the forest. In dark, silent places he is lying in wait for me: hearing my slow, uncertain footsteps he starts up suddenly in my path, out-yelling the bearded aguaratos in the trees; and I stand paralysed, my blood curdled in my veins. His huge, hairy arms are round me; his foul, hot breath is on my skin; he will tear my liver out with his great green teeth to satisfy his raging hunger. Ah, no, he cannot harm me! For every ravening beast, every cold-blooded, venomous thing, and even the frightful Curupitá, half brute and half devil, that shared the forest with her, loved and worshipped Rima, and that mournful burden I carried, her ashes, was a talisman to save me. He has left me, the semi-human monster, uttering such wild, lamentable cries as he hurries away into the deeper, darker woods, that horror changes to grief, and I, too, lament Rima for the first time: a memory of all the mystic, unimaginable grace and loveliness and joy that had vanished smites on my heart with such sudden, intense pain that I cast myself prone on the earth and weep tears that are like drops of blood.

Where, in the rude savage heart of Guiana was this region where the natural obstacles and pain and hunger and thirst and everlasting weariness were terrible enough without the imaginary monsters and legions of phantoms that peopled it, I cannot say. Nor can I conjecture how far I strayed north or south from my course. I only know that marshes that were like Sloughs of Despond,* and barren and wet savannahs, were crossed; and forests that seemed infinite in extent and never to be got through; and scores of rivers that boiled round the sharp rocks, threatening to submerge or dash in pieces the frail bark canoe—black and frightful to look on as rivers in hell; and nameless mountain after mountain to be toiled round or toiled over. I may have seen Roraima* during that mentally clouded period. I vaguely remember a far-extending gigantic wall of stone that seemed to bar all further progress—a rocky precipice rising to a stupendous height, seen by moonlight, with a huge sinuous rope of white mist suspended from its summit; as if the guardian camoodi of the mountain had been a league-long spectral serpent which was now dropping its coils from the mighty stone table to frighten away the rash intruder.

That spectral moonlight camoodi was one of many serpent fancies that troubled me. There was another, surpassing them all, which attended me many days. When the sun grew hot overhead and the way was over open savannah country I would see something moving on the ground at my side and always keeping abreast of me. A small snake, one or two feet long. No, not a small snake, but a sinuous mark in the pattern on a huge serpent's head, five or six yards long, always moving deliberately at my side. If a cloud came over the sun, or a fresh breeze sprang up, gradually the outline of that awful head would fade and the well-defined pattern would resolve itself into the motlings on the earth. But if the sun grew more and more hot and dazzling as the day progressed, then the tremendous ophidian head would become increasingly real to my sight, with glistening scales and symmetrical markings; and I would walk carefully not to stumble against or touch it; and when I cast my eyes behind me I could see no end to its great coils extending across the savannah. Even looking back from the summit of a high hill I could see it stretching leagues and leagues away through forests and rivers, across wide plains, valleys and mountains, to lose itself at last in the infinite blue distance.

How or when this monster left me—washed away by cold rains perhaps—I do not know. Probably it only transformed itself into some new shape, its long coils perhaps changing into those endless processions and multitudes of pale-faced people I seem to remember having encountered. In my devious wanderings I must have reached the shores of the undiscovered great White Lake, and passed through the long shining streets of Manoa, the mysterious city in the wilderness.* I see myself there, the wide thoroughfare filled from end to end with people, gaily dressed as if for some high festival, all drawing aside to let the wretched pilgrim pass, staring at his fever and famine-wasted figure, in its strange rags, with its strange burden.

A new Ahasuerus,* cursed by inexpiable crime, yet sustained by a great purpose.

But Ahasuerus prayed ever for death to come to him and ran to meet it, while I fought against it with all my little strength. Only at intervals, when the shadows seemed to lift and give me relief, would I pray to Death to spare me yet a little longer; but when the shadows darkened again and hope seemed almost quenched in utter gloom, then I would curse it and defy its power.

Through it all I clung to the belief that my will would conquer, that it would enable me to keep off the great enemy from my worn and suffering body until the wished goal was reached; then only would I cease to fight and let death have its way. There would have been comfort in this belief had it not been for that fevered imagination which corrupted everything that touched me and gave it some new hateful character. For soon enough this conviction that the will would triumph grew to something monstrous, a parent of monstrous fancies. Worst of all, when I felt no actual pain, but only unutterable weariness of body and soul, when feet and legs were numb so that I knew not whether I trod on dry hot rock or in slime, was the fancy that I was already dead, so far as the body was concerned—had perhaps been dead for days—that only the unconquerable will survived to compel the dead flesh to do its work.

Whether it really was will—more potent than the bark of barks and wiser than the physicians—or merely the *vis medicatrix** with which nature helps our weakness even when the will is suspended, that saved me I cannot say; but it is certain that I gradually recovered health, physical and mental, and finally reached the coast comparatively well, although my mind was still in a gloomy, desponding state when I first walked the streets of Georgetown, in rags, half-starved and penniless.

But even when well, long after the discovery that my flesh was not only alive, but that it was of an exceedingly tough quality, the idea born during the darkest period of my pilgrimage, that die I must, persisted in my mind. I had lived through that which would have killed most men—lived only to accomplish the one remaining purpose of my life. Now it was accomplished; the sacred ashes brought so far, with such infinite labour, through so many and such great perils, were safe and would mix with mine at last. There was nothing more in life to make me love it or keep me prisoner in its weary chains. This prospect of near death faded in time; love of life returned, and the earth had recovered its everlasting freshness and beauty: only that feeling about Rima's ashes did not fade or change, and is as strong now as it was then. Say that it is morbid—call it superstition if you like; but there it is, the most powerful motive I have known, always in all things to be taken into account—a philosophy of life to be made to fit it. Or take it as a symbol, since that may come to be one with the thing symbolised. In those darkest days in the forest I had her as a visitor—a Rima of the mind, whose words when she spoke reflected my despair. Yet even then I was not entirely without hope. Heaven itself, she said, could not undo that which I had done; and she also said that if I forgave myself Heaven would say no word, nor would she. That is my philosophy still: prayers, austerities, good works—they avail nothing, and there is no intercession, and outside of the soul there is no forgiveness in heaven or earth for sin. Nevertheless there is a way, which every soul can find out for itself—even the most rebellious, the most darkened with crime and tormented by remorse. In that way I have walked; and, self-forgiven and self- absolved, I know that if she were to return once more and appear to me—even here where her ashes are—I know that her divine eyes would no longer refuse to look into mine, since the sorrow which seemed eternal and would have slain me to see would not now be in them.

EXPLANATORY NOTES

3 *natural enemies*: a long-standing boundary dispute between Venezuela and British Guiana came to a crisis in 1887, when Venezuela cut diplomatic ties with Britain; it was resolved in 1899, after US President Grover Cleveland invoked the Monroe Doctrine to ward off British intervention. Georgetown is the capital of the former British colony.

4 *the world of nature and of the spirit*: Abel shares these characteristics (mysterious charm, aloofness, love of nature, and attachment to children) with his author, W. H. Hudson.

5 *'tired the sun with talking'*: from the opening lines of 'Heraclitus' by William Johnson (1823–92):

> They told me, Heraclitus, they told me you were dead,
> They brought me bitter news to hear and bitter tears to shed.
> I wept, as I remembered, how often you and I
> Had tired the sun with talking and sent him down the sky.

7 *a government by cliques, tempered by revolution*: the Republic of Venezuela, formally constituted in 1830, alternated between spasms of civil war and dictatorial rule by *caudillos* (members of the landholding oligarchy). Abel refers to the turbulent period from the Federal Revolution (1858–63) to the autocracy of President Guzmán Blanco (1870).

8 *matters were precipitated*: Guzmán Blanco consolidated his presidency with a repression (1870–2) in which anyone suspected of sedition was liable to be imprisoned and shot without trial. The attempt of Abel and his friends (who were presumably Conservatives) may be based on the unsuccessful rising by Guzmán's former comrade Matías Salazar (1872), although the date might be cutting it a little fine for the romance's chronology: Abel must arrive in Georgetown at the end of his adventures around 1875.

9 *Guayana*: large interior province of Venezuela, south of the Orinoco, now called Amazonas; not to be confused with the adjacent colony of British Guiana, now Guyana.

Atahapo: S. Fernando de Atabapo.

Manapuri: probably S. Jose de Maipures is meant.

11 *fresh from the forest*: quinine, used to treat malaria, is extracted from the bark of the cinchona tree, native to the eastern slope of the Andes.

Queneveta mountains . . . Maquiritari tribe: a map in James Mudie Spence's *The Land of Bolivar; or, War, Peace and Adventure in the Republic of Venezuela* (1878) shows the Queneveta mountains running west from the Ventuari river, a major tributary of the upper Orinoco, and marks them as territory of the Maquiritare (Makiritari) Indians. They do not appear on modern maps.

11 *agents of some higher power*: the name Panta (Pantaleon) amplifies the echo of a well-known tale by Balzac, 'A Passion in the Desert' (*Une passion dans le désert*, 1832), in which a soldier lost in the wilderness is befriended—and saved from quicksand—by a panther (or 'lion of Egypt'). The phrase that concludes the story anticipates the inscription (see below, p. 191) on Abel's cinerary urn: 'C'est Dieu sans les hommes', 'God is there, and man is not'.

12 *Casiquiare river . . . Rio Negro*: the so-called Casiquiare Canal, a natural waterway, flows from the upper Orinoco to the headwaters of the Rio Negro in the Amazon basin. It was explored by the pioneer of naturalist expeditions in South America, Baron Alexander von Humboldt, in 1800.

Cunucumana: the Cunucunuma (*sic*) flows south from the supposed site of the Queneveta mountains to the upper Orinoco.

13 *golden dreams*: the obsessive motive in European narratives of South American invasion. Abel's adventure recalls the primal encounter of Columbus with natives wearing gold ornaments, who assured him the metal came from the interior.

an unknown difficult country: at this point Abel's journey disappears from the map. The Parahuari hills, Runi's village, and Mt. Ytaioa are located somewhere north of the headwaters of the Rio Negro and west of the upper Orinoco, near the present Colombia–Venezuela border.

14 *Runi*: an Indian called Rúmi appears in Alfred Simson, *Travels in the Wilds of Ecuador* (1886), chs. 13–14; the name also recalls the Rupununi, a river in Guyana.

15 *troupial*: a kind of yellow and black oriole, *Icterus icterus*, the Venezuelan national bird.

16 *some bourn . . . clean from all spot and blemish*: echo of *Hamlet*, III. i. 79–80, 'The undiscovered country, from whose bourn | No traveller returns', and 1 Pet. 1: 19, 'without blemish and without spot'.

Alonzo Pizarro: this should be Gonzalo, brother of Francisco Pizarro, the conqueror of Peru. In 1540 he led an expedition into the Ecuadorean interior in search of the fabled city of El Dorado, 'the golden one', a native emperor who was supposed to powder his body with gold-dust.

17 *casserie*: fermented drink derived from cassava root (manioc). Its preparation is described at the beginning of the next chapter.

18 *all men were liars*: Ps. 116: 11, 'I said in my haste, All men are liars.'

20 *even from near relations*: according to Everard F. im Thurn, *Among the Indians of Guiana* (1883; Hudson's principal source of information about the region's ethnology and natural history), Indians are named after 'some plant, bird, or other natural object', but these names are hardly used, 'apparently on the ground that the name is part of the man, and that he who knows the name has part of the owner of that name in his power'; Indians address each other 'only according to the relationship of the caller and the called, as brother, sister, father, mother, and so on . . . An Indian, therefore, when he has to do with a European, asks the latter to give him a name' (p. 220).

24 *accouries*: ground-dwelling rodent, *Dasyprocta agouti*, 'in appearance like a rabbit on long legs, and with coarse, chestnut-coloured hair': Thurn, *Among the Indians of Guiana* (p. 108).

25 *tigers, or camoodis*: jaguars or anacondas.

26 *melodious voice*: Hudson bases his account of *Cyphorinus cantans* (a kind of wren) on descriptions by other naturalists, notably Henry Walter Bates, *The Naturalist on the River Amazons* (1863): 'When its singular notes strike the ear for the first time, the impression cannot be resisted that they are produced by a human voice. Some musical boy must be gathering fruits in the thicket, and is singing a few notes to cheer himself. The tones become more fluty and plaintive; they are now those of a flageolot, and notwithstanding the utter impossibility of the thing, one is for a moment convinced that some one is playing that instrument. No bird is to be seen, however closely the surrounding trees and bushes may be scanned, and yet the voice seems to come from the thicket closest to one's ear' (Penguin edn., 1988, 367). Hudson quotes the passage in his *Idle Days in Patagonia* (1893), 154.

28 *zabatana*: blow-gun. Hudson adapts the Amazon name (properly *zarabatana*) from Bates, *The Naturalist on the River Amazons*, ch. 11.

29 *less well known*: of the birds named here, *maam* is the tinamou, a partridge-like bird (*Tinamus* or *Crypturellus*); *duraquara*, the marbled wood-quail (*Odontophorus guianensis*); *cotingas*, small bright blue and purple birds (*Cotinga cotinga*); *tree-climber*, possibly a treehunter (*Thripadectes*); *pitta-thrush*, an ant-thrush (*Pittidae*), although now classified as an Old World family; perhaps then the Pihas (*Lipaugus*).

30 *like a big pigeon*: perhaps this is a squirrel jay, *Piaya cayana*.

a water-spirit: 'di-dis, beings in shape something between men and monkeys, who live in the forests near river banks': Thurn, *Among the Indians of Guiana* (p. 385).

31 *Curupitá*: wood-demon of the Amazon basin. 'The Curupíra is a mysterious being, whose attributes are uncertain, for they vary according to locality. Sometimes he is described as a kind of orang-otang, being covered with long shaggy hair, and living in trees. At others he is said to have cloven feet and a bright red face': Bates, *The Naturalist on the River Amazons* (p. 34). This episode inspired Geoffrey Household's *Dance of the Dwarfs* (1968), a horror-story variation on *Green Mansions*. In Household's novel the European hero does not fail to have sex with his jungle nymph (fragrant with 'an undefinable blend of young animal and fresh vegetable'); unfortunately, the mysterious spirits haunting the woods turn out to be giant bloodsucking stoats.

33 *great green fangs*: the Curupitá, alluded to earlier. Humboldt mentions legends of a 'hairy man' or '*great devil* of the woods' whose footprints show the toes pointing backwards (*A Personal Narrative of Travels to the Equinoctial Regions of America*, trans. T. Ross, 1907, ii. 270–2).

33 *black tiger*: black jaguar. Thurn says that all species of wild cat in the region
    are called 'tiger' (*Among the Indians of Guiana*, III).

    hunting-leopards: Thurn recounts tales of 'real or mythical animals called
    warracaba tigers', pack-hunters that terrorize the woods, which he con-
    jectures might be based on sightings of families of pumas (*Among the In-
    dians of Guiana*, III–14).

37 *tricksy*: epithet that Prospero bestows upon Ariel in *The Tempest*, v. i. 226.

42 *deeply interested in this curious scene*: Hudson devotes an entire chapter of *The
    Naturalist in La Plata* (1892) to spiders: 'spiders I have always observed and
    admired in a non-scientific spirit . . . I have even learnt to love them'
    (p. 179).

47 *queyou . . . and all*: the *queyou* is a small apron made from bark or brightly
    coloured seeds. Thurn notes that the Indian women, less adorned than the
    men, 'wear no feathers, and scarcely any teeth, except those of the acourie'
    (*Among the Indians of Guiana*, 199).

48 *self-torture among the Guayana tribes*: Thurn describes the ordeals a man
    must undergo before he can choose a bride: 'Without flinching, he suffers
    the infliction of wounds in his flesh; or he allows himself to be sewn up in a
    hammock full of fire-ants; or by some other similar tests he shows his
    courage' (*Among the Indians of Guiana*, 221).

50 *its deadly character*: coral snakes, like cobras, inject a neurotoxic venom,
    which attacks the nervous system. The venom of other New World snakes
    is haemotoxic, destructive of the blood cells: slower-acting but deadlier.

63 *that is your name, is it not?*: Rudolph J. Landry suggests that Hudson de-
    rived the name from an anatomical structure in the larynx of songbirds:
    'the *rima* is the passage in the glottis between the vocal chords and the
    aretenoid cartilages, and it is the upper *rima* which gives utterance to the
    note': 'The Source of the Name "Rima" in "Green Mansions" ', *Notes &
    Queries*, 201 (1956), 545–6. Jason Wilson points out that it is also the
    Spanish word for rhyme or verse: *W. H. Hudson: The Colonial's Revenge*
    (London, 1981).

    listless in a cage: compare *The Naturalist in La Plata*: 'The minute exquisite
    form, when the bird hovers on misty wings . . . forms a picture of airy
    loveliness that baffles description. All this glory disappears when the bird
    is dead, and even when it alights to rest on a bough' (p. 206). Hoxie N.
    Fairchild has suggested that the comparison of Rima with a humming-
    bird derives from Arthur O'Shaughnessy's poem 'Colibri' (1881): 'Rima's
    Mother', *PMLA* 68 (1953), 357–73.

68 *coatimundi*: arboreal relative of the racoon, *Nasua nasua*. It is described in
    the next chapter.

73 *mora tree*: hardwood, *Mora excelsa*, remarkable for its height.

74 *fifty to sixty feet above the ground*: a typical appearance of nymph-like
    heroines of romance. Compare Scott's *Waverley*, ch. 23: 'it was with a sen-
    sation of horror that Waverley beheld Flora and her attendant appear, like

inhabitants of another region, propped, as it were, in mid air, upon this trembling structure.'

76 *gossamer spiders*: Hudson gives a rhapsodic description of them in *The Naturalist in La Plata*: 'most spiritual of living things . . . weaving their gauzy veil over the earth and floating unseen, like an ethereal vital dust, in the atmosphere' (p. 184).

Sakawinki: the 'pretty little bright-coloured' squirrel monkey, *Chrysothrix sciureus* (Thurn, *Among the Indians of Guiana*, 110), rather than the saki (*Pithecia*).

86 *ancient words*: see note to p. 91, below.

88 *sick with hope deferred*: compare Prov. 13: 12,'Hope deferred maketh the heart sick.'

campanero: the bell-bird, named *Chasmarhynchus carunculatus* by Thurn, *Procnias alba* (or *averano*) by modern ornithologists. Apparently its call more resembles the striking of an iron bar than a bell.

90 *lies told to the heathen are not recorded*: the theme of an officially sanctioned Spanish perfidy during the Conquest was established by Bartolome De Las Casas in *A Brief Account of the Destruction of the Indies* (1542), which cites several instances of Spaniards lying to Indians as a matter of policy; see pp. 88 and 109 in the Penguin translation by Nigel Griffin (1992). I am grateful to Roland Greene for this reference.

91 *Mena*: Juan de Mena (1411–56), Spanish court poet and man of letters. The lines that follow make up the opening stanza of one of his *Decires amorosos*: 'Brighter far than the moon, alone in the world you were born, so gracious that you have no rival. Since infancy in the cradle you have acquired fame and beauty, with the charm that Fortune gave you for a dowry.' I thank Julian Weiss for this information.

98 *Voa, on the River Voa*: perhaps the Colombian river 'Oa or Uua' (Uva), a tributary of the Guaviare, on the 1878 map in Spence, *The Land of Bolivar*; a long way to the north-west, if so.

100 *Guahibo . . . Tuparito*: these names of Guayanan tribes appear to have been taken from the map in Spence, *The Land of Bolivar*. Some of them are mentioned in Humboldt's *Personal Narrative*.

101 *older than Thebes*: in *The Naturalist in La Plata* Hudson alludes to 'the belief expressed by the famous American archaeologist, Squiers, that the ruined city of Tiahuanaco, in the vicinity of Lake Titicaca, is as old as Thebes and the Pyramids' (p. 315).

Haymar Capac . . . Huascar, and Atahualpa the Unhappy: Huayna Capac (d. 1525), last of the great Inca emperors, divided his kingdom between his sons, Huascar-Inca and Atahualpa, who fought over it; Atahualpa was treacherously imprisoned and executed by Pizarro at the Conquest (1533).

102 *Cotopaxi . . . Aconcagua*: notable Ecuadorean volcanoes and Andean peaks. Aconcagua, at 6,960 m., is the highest mountain in the western hemisphere.

102 *Pachacamac and Viracocha*: the Incas 'acknowledged a Supreme Being, the Creator and Ruler of the universe, whom they adored under the different names of Pachacamac and Viracocha': William H. Prescott, *History of the Conquest of Peru* (London, 1908), 55.

Cuzco, the city of the sun: once the splendid Inca capital, looted by Pizarro.

Chimborazo: Ecuadorean volcano, 6,310 m. Humboldt, who made a partial ascent in 1802, believed it to be the highest point on earth.

unlike any which the Immortals have yet witnessed: Utopian futurist romances were fashionable in the last few decades of the nineteenth century. Hudson had written an unsuccessful one, *A Crystal Age* (1887).

old Father Noah divided the earth among his sons: Gen. 10 recounts the division of the nations among the sons of Noah after his death.

123 *Desde aquel doloroso momento*: 'Ever since that sorrowful moment'.

124 *fountain of eternal youth*: the quest for which is supposed to have led to the discovery of Florida by Juan Ponce de León (*c*.1460–1521).

caribe fishes: 'cannibal fish', piranhas.

151 *some distant forest*: this legend seems familiar (something like it turns up in the 1941 Universal Studios film *The Wolf Man*), but I have been unable to trace a South American source.

the face that had no motion, no consciousness in it: here, as later (p. 191), Hudson echoes Wordsworth's great lyric of 1800:

> A slumber did my spirit seal,
>   I had no human fears:
> She seem'd a thing that could not feel
>   The touch of earthly years.
>
> No motion has she now, no force
>   She neither hears nor sees
> Roll'd round in earth's diurnal course
>   With rocks and stones and trees.

161 *labba*: ground-dwelling rodent (*Coelogenys paca*): 'an animal like a large guinea-pig, with brown skin spotted with white' (Thurn, *Among the Indians of Guiana*, 108).

162 *exile*: nostalgia was understood to be the particular affliction of the mountain-dwelling Swiss.

177 *I cursed the Author of my being*: compare Job 2: 9, 'curse God, and die'.

185 *black death*: compare Hudson's description of the Mygale (bird-eating) spider in *The Naturalist in La Plata*: 'Their long, shiny black, sickle-shaped falces are dangerous weapons' (pp. 191–2).

191 *Sin vos y sin dios y mi*: 'without you and without God and myself'. Abel glosses at the end of the paragraph: 'I, no longer I, in a universe where *she* was not, and God was not.'

no motion, nor any sound; but all things, even trees, ferns, and grasses, were stone:

another echo of Wordsworth, 'A Slumber did My Spirit Seal' , last stanza—as perhaps is the urn itself ('diurnal'). See above, note to p. 151.

192 *following me still*: Hudson describes the sinister fascination of the pit-viper's countenance, 'in spite of the tenderness I cherish towards the entire ophidian race', in *Idle Days in Patagonia*: 'Looking at a serpent of this kind, and I have looked at many a one, the fancy is born in me that I am regarding what was once a fellow-being, perhaps one of those cruel desperate wretches I have encountered on the outskirts of civilization, who for his crimes has been changed into the serpent form, and cursed with immortality' (p. 28).

193 *cursed above all cattle*: Gen. 3: 14.

195 *rarely seen on the ground*: sloths descend to the ground to defecate, although they are not supposed to travel far from the tree.

199 *Sloughs of Despond*: see John Bunyan, *The Pilgrim's Progress* (1678): 'it is the descent whither the scum and filth that attends conviction for sin doth continually run, and therefore is it called the Slough of Despond' (Penguin edn., 1965, 46).

200 *Roraima*: table-mountain (2,810 m.) in Guyana near the Venezuelan and Brazilian borders. It is supposed to have suggested the setting for Sir Arthur Conan Doyle's South American romance, *The Lost World* (1912).

mysterious city in the wilderness: see Sir Walter Ralegh, *The Discovery of the Empire of Guiana* (1596; repr. 1848): 'Manoa the emperiall Citie of Guiana, which the Spanyardes call El Dorado . . . founded upon a lake of salt water of 200 leagues long like unto Mare Caspium' (p. 13). Manoa and its White Sea occupied various legendary locations, more or less associated with the source of the Orinoco, until debunked by Humboldt at the beginning of the nineteenth century. (Nevertheless rumours persisted well into the twentieth.)

201 *Ahasuerus*: the Wandering Jew, condemned to walk the earth for eternity for having insulted Christ. A figment of medieval anti-Semitism, popularized in the nineteenth century by Eugène Sue's romance *Le Juif errant* (1844).

vis medicatrix: healing force.

The Oxford World's Classics Website

www.worldsclassics.co.uk

- Information about new titles
- Explore the full range of Oxford World's Classics
- Links to other literary sites and the main OUP webpage
- Imaginative competitions, with bookish prizes
- Peruse *Compass*, the Oxford World's Classics magazine
- Articles by editors
- Extracts from Introductions
- A forum for discussion and feedback on the series
- Special information for teachers and lecturers

www.worldsclassics.co.uk

American Literature

British and Irish Literature

Children's Literature

Classics and Ancient Literature

Colonial Literature

Eastern Literature

European Literature

History

Medieval Literature

Oxford English Drama

Poetry

Philosophy

Politics

Religion

The Oxford Shakespeare

A complete list of Oxford Paperbacks, including Oxford World's Classics, OPUS, Past Masters, Oxford Authors, Oxford Shakespeare, Oxford Drama, and Oxford Paperback Reference, is available in the UK from the Academic Division Publicity Department, Oxford University Press, Great Clarendon Street, Oxford OX2 6DP.

In the USA, complete lists are available from the Paperbacks Marketing Manager, Oxford University Press, 198 Madison Avenue, New York, NY 10016.

Oxford Paperbacks are available from all good bookshops. In case of difficulty, customers in the UK can order direct from Oxford University Press Bookshop, Freepost, 116 High Street, Oxford OX1 4BR, enclosing full payment. Please add 10 per cent of published price for postage and packing.